THE SUNDAY GIRLS

During the Great Depression, like many others in Dundee, the Neill family are struggling to make ends meet. Ann would love to stay at school but following the death of her mother she is forced to become a housemaid to support her family. Her employer, Mrs Barrie, couldn't be kinder, but the spiteful housekeeper Miss Hood makes Ann's life a misery. When she meets Maddie, the daughter of a prosperous Dundee solicitor, the only thing they have in common is that they were both born on a Sunday, but they become firm friends, finding fun and laughter in good times and bad.

THE SUNDAY GIRLS

THE SUNDAY GIRLS

by

Maureen Reynolds

Magna Large Print Books
Long Preston, North Yorkshire,
BD23 4ND, England.

British Library Cataloguing in Publication Data.

Reynolds, Maureen
    The Sunday girls.

    A catalogue record of this book is
    available from the British Library

    ISBN   978-0-7505-2846-7

First published in Great Britain in 2007
by Black & White Publishing Ltd.

Published in Large Print 2008 by arrangement with
Black & White Publishing Limited

Magna Large Print is an imprint of Library Magna Books Ltd.

Printed and bound in Great Britain by
T.J. (International) Ltd., Cornwall, PL28 8RW

DEDICATION

To my husband, Ally, and
my family, Alick, George, Steven and Wendy

1

What a day to have a baby – especially at Lily's age.

A small group of concerned neighbours had gathered in a tight group in the dim coolness of the damp staircase, grateful to be shielded from the fierce rays of the sun in the July heatwave – a heatwave that had appeared like a golden oasis after weeks of grey, steel-tipped clouds and heavy rain. Now, each day was hotter and more humid than the previous one. Like a furnace being stoked up daily, the build-up of accumulated heat descended on the grimy courtyards of number 30 Hilltown, a densely populated huddle of tiny-roomed flats that saw neither daylight nor sun through their minuscule windows.

But, as I left the tiny one-roomed flat that was home to Mum, Dad and me, the weather was a million miles away in my thoughts. I heard the soft murmur of the women's voices. Nellie, our next-door neighbour stood with a worried look on her pale, pinched face which was the legacy from living in her dark, cramped house – that and insufficient nourishment. She clutched a small sleeping child in her fragile, stick-like white arms, oblivious to the fact that he had been sick at some point before drowsing off. A milky stain had spread in a sour-smelling wet patch down the front of her cheap cotton frock – a frock which, in its heyday, had been a vivid cornflower blue, had now, because it had been washed and worn for so long, faded to a nondescript grey.

'Ann, is that the baby coming?' she asked. 'We thought it was due in August?'

I paused briefly, the sound of Dad's urgent command to fetch both the midwife and Granny Neill still ringing in my ears. Still I knew that my parents would appreciate the neighbours' concern so I called out as I dashed past them on the narrow, low-walled stairwell, 'Mum's pains have started and I'm away to fetch Mrs Grey, the midwife at Rosebank Road. Then I've to go and fetch Granny Neill from the Overgate to come as well.'

Rita, another neighbour, said, 'Is there anything we can do to help?'

Some of our other neighbours were standing around and they all nodded in agreement.

I stopped, anxious to be on my way but also unsure if Dad wanted any other help. 'Well, Dad's in the house with Mum so, if he needs help, maybe he'll ask for it himself.'

As I turned away, Rita, who must have thought I was out of earshot, turned to her pals with a sad shake of her head. 'We all know that Lily is a bit old to be having another baby – especially after a gap of fifteen years.' She stopped, making sure she had the full attention of her small audience. 'Lily was forty-two on her last birthday and, like the rest of us, she has a man out of work and there's precious little hope of him finding another job.'

Rita shivered in spite of the heat. She was as plump as Nellie was skinny and her fleshy face wobbled like an unstable jelly. 'Heavens it's bad enough going into labour when you're young and fit. Just think what a trial it must be when you're forty-two.'

She rolled her eyes and glanced down at the toddler at her feet. Clad only in a grimy torn vest and a yellow, urine-stained nappy, he was playing quite happily with an empty custard tin, oblivious to the drama unfolding around him.

Nellie glanced around the assembled company before dropping her voice to a hoarse whisper. 'Well, Lily did tell me that she was hoping this might just be the change of life but she was really worried when she knew she was expecting.'

She stopped talking when she noticed the wet stain. Holding the fabric away from her thin body, she said, with a trace of disgust in her voice, 'Would you look at this? That wee devil Jimmy has been sick down the front of my frock. Kids!! Who would have them if they could help it?' Still her sharp words were softened by the maternal look she bestowed on the baby's downy head.

I stood motionless on the stairs. Not only had I witnessed the scene but, because of the arch-shaped construction of the stairs, Rita and Nellie's words had rebounded off the walls in an amplified echo and to say I was worried was an understatement.

After this brief moment of eavesdropping, I turned on my heels and darted out on to the Hilltown. Running up the steep slope as fast as I could, the memory of Mum's sharp cries was still fresh in my ears. The neighbours' words had also put an icy cold fear in my heart and this fear seemed to pump energy into my legs.

I barely felt the heat from the pavement through the thin soles of my well-worn sandals yet, compared to the horde of children who were running around in their bare feet, my worn shoes were a luxury. Their feet slapped noisily against the dry, dusty paving stones and their shrill shrieks of laughter contrasted with my own secret worry and concern.

Mrs Grey the midwife, although now middle-aged, was always busy and in demand. Because of her low charges, she was called out to help deliver most of the births in the neighbourhood. On this particularly hot Sunday afternoon, I found her sitting on a decrepit chair with her knitting in her lap. Tucked in beside the knitting was her cat. A large ball of sludge-coloured wool, the exact shade of the cat, was spiked on to the sharp points of the needles. From a distance, it looked as if the cat had been knitted from the wool like some child's toy.

In an effort to escape the hot rays of the sun, she had placed her chair in a rectangular shaded spot in the long narrow courtyard, a yard that stretched between two tall tenements. In spite of the shade, she had obviously been too tired for any activity and she was asleep.

Like a demented dervish I rushed up to her, alarming her with my rude awakening while trying to keep the fear at bay. 'Mrs Grey, Mrs Grey, will you come with me quickly? Mum needs you.'

Bunty Grey opened her eyes in confusion while the khaki-coloured cat shot off into the distance with a gleam of outrage in his eyes. She looked at me over the top of her spectacles. 'Goodness me, what a fright you gave me.' She squinted at me before recognition dawned in her pale watery eyes. 'You'll be Ann Neill – Johnny and Lily's lassie from the foot of the Hilltown. Well, just let me get my bag and I'll come with you.'

I waited impatiently until she appeared. A few minutes later she came bustling towards me, wearing a crisp-looking cotton dress and carrying a black bag clutched in her soft podgy looking hand, a hand that didn't match up with her wrinkled face.

As we set off down the hill, once more making our way through the scores of noisy, sweating children, I explained my mission. 'I've to take you up to the house then go and get my Granny Neill from the Overgate.'

Thankful when we reached our close, I ran ahead of her up the well-worn stairs and I could hear her laboured breathing behind me.

The women were still standing where I left them. Rita greeted the midwife warmly. 'Another baby in the close, Mrs Grey – we seem to be populating the entire Hilltown in this wee corner.'

The midwife laughed before heading off down the gloomy lobby to our small flat. When she reached the door, she turned. 'Go and fetch your granny, Ann.'

When she opened our door I heard the sharp distressing moans echo down the passageway. These were punctuated by Dad's soft soothing voice, 'Here's Mrs Grey now, Lily.'

Now that the midwife had arrived, the women began to disperse – some back to their dark, dingy houses while others made their way down towards the sunshine. They glanced with sympathy at me as I trooped down with them.

'Now you're not to worry, young Ann – about your mum I mean,' said Rita, placing her plump arm around my shoulders.

'No, that's right,' said Nellie. 'I'll tell you something. I was in a worse state than your mum when wee Jimmy was born and look at me now – as fit as a fiddle.'

This statement was untrue because she had the emaciated look of a starving sparrow. However I was grateful for this reassurance.

My grandparents lived up the close beside Horatio Leslie's fish shop in the Overgate. Fortunately for me their window overlooked the street and Granny was seated on her favourite comfy chair which she had pulled over to the open window. A fat feather cushion was draped over the windowsill and Granny's two plump arms were draped on its surface like two pampered Pekinese pooches.

She didn't see me standing on the pavement because she was listening intently to her neighbour Alice who sat like her twin at the adjoining window. I hated to interrupt her as it was a well-known fact that she enjoyed this social form of relaxation immensely. There was nothing better in life than a good going conversation on a Sunday afternoon – especially if it included some innocuous gossip or maybe a bit of scandal. Today the sunshine was an added bonus.

As for Grandad, I knew he would be at the far end of the kitchen with his Sunday paper and pipe filled with black tarry Bogey Roll, blowing

14

streams of foul-smelling smog into the cramped room. I often thought my grandparents were like the figures in a weather house – one sitting in the fresh air and the other surrounded perpetually by a thick fog.

I shouted up at the half-reclining figure, 'Granny, Dad says can you come to the house? Mum's pains have started.'

Nan Neill turned an anxious face to Alice who also looked concerned. 'That's Lily's baby coming and her not due for another month. Still, some children aye seem to be in a hurry to enter this world.' She withdrew her plump frame from the comfort of her cushion and muttered, 'What a time to have a baby – in the middle of this heat.'

Like the midwife, she appeared in a couple of minutes, bustling through the close with a red perspiring face and a woollen herringbone tweed coat draped over her arm. On seeing the look on my face, she explained the coat, 'Well, it's like this – babies have a bad habit of arriving in the middle of the night and the sun will not be shining then.'

I was shocked. 'Do you mean to say that Mum will have to suffer these terrible pains for hours yet?'

She looked worried. 'Oh, well, maybe it won't be as long as that. I mind fine when you were born. That was on a Sunday as well but it wasn't as hot as this – blowing a real blizzard it was.'

On that slightly cheerier note, we headed quickly for home, Granny hurrying beside me while, for her sake, I tried to walk a bit slower. At this pace, we made our way through the busy

15

streets, both of us thinking our own thoughts about the coming birth.

Thankfully we were soon at our door. On entering the house, I saw Mum lying on the double bed that occupied the entire corner of the kitchen, right beside the fireplace. In spite of the fire being unlit, the temperature inside the room was almost unbearable. The heat was caused by the kettle and two pots of water that were boiling furiously on the gas cooker.

Bunty Grey turned when we entered and I was taken aback by Mum's slim figure on the bed. Streaks of sweat dripped down her face and her dark hair clung in tendrils to her scalp. They looked like strands of wet seaweed. She let out a yelp of pain, like an animal in distress. Her thin body, covered only by a thin sheet, shook fitfully while Dad made a soothing noise. 'Here's Granny as well, Lily. We're all here to help you.' Although he tried to hide it, a note of anguish was in his voice. 'And I'll stay here with you.'

But Bunty had other ideas and as she and Nan bustled around the mother-to-be. She said, 'Johnny, now that Nan's here, will you take Ann outside and we'll let you both know when the baby comes?'

With Dad still protesting, she ushered us both out. 'Honestly, Lily will be fine and there's really no room for everybody in this wee room.' Her sleeves were rolled up, showing strong muscular arms, and she exuded an air of capable confidence.

I looked over at Mum but she didn't appear to see me or hear me. Her pain was obviously so

16

intense that it obliterated her surroundings.

Dad turned back and placed an arm around her shoulders. 'It won't be long now, Lily,' he said, a broad smile lighting up his face which was still handsome in spite of his unshaven, stubbled look.

Outside, the neighbours had disappeared from the stair landing. Now that Lily had the expertise of the two women, they knew that to linger in the dismal lobby was a waste of fresh air and sunshine. As we passed out of the close and into the street, they were sitting on a motley collection of tatty old kitchen chairs placed strategically to catch the maximum amount of sunlight.

Dad went to join a group of men who were lounging around a shop doorway. Like him, they were all jobless. Each face held a mask of weary despair, their shoulders slumped in a downcast manner – postures that were witness to their helpless resignation of years with no work.

Although none of the men were members of the Communist Party, they all supported the National Unemployment Workers Movement and a few of them had even been on the Hunger Marches to London to protest about unemployment and the dire living conditions – conditions that were met with cruel callousness from a government that was blind and deaf to their pleas for help.

'Aye, you'll soon have another mouth to feed, Johnny,' said old Joe who was one of Dad's oldest friends. Although only in his early sixties, he looked much older. His thin face was so wrinkled that the deep furrows resembled tramlines. He had been badly injured in the Great War and had spent a long time in hospital afterwards with shrapnel wounds. The legacy of pain from that time was still etched on his face but, on good days like today, he often said he felt better.

He turned a quizzical eye to his friend. 'How do you think you'll manage now?'

Dad merely shrugged his shoulders and shook his head wordlessly.

Joe turned to the group of men with an angry gesture. 'You know, apart from Will and Jimmy...' He pointed a thin, yellow, nicotine-stained finger in the direction of two skinny youths who regularly hung out with the older men. The two lads had suffered from rickets in their childhood and they had the bow-legged look that was one of the symptoms of this disease caused by the deficiency of vitamin D. 'Apart from them, most of us fought in the war and we remember when half of our comrades were killed at Neuve Chapelle and Loos.'

The men nodded, their eyes clouding over at the memory of that carnage.

'Aye, a lot of my mates died in that battle and a lot more never came home from the other trenches,' said Dad.

Joe was now on his soapbox, an expression his pals used when faced by his outbursts. 'Aye, half of the Black Watch wiped out and what were the survivors promised? We were promised a land fit for heroes and what do we end up with? A land with no work or money to buy bread and margarine, never mind bloody milk and honey.'

He opened a small tin that held a collection of cigarette stubs. Deftly extricating the golden strands of tobacco from a few of the stubs, he placed them on a thin cigarette paper which he then rolled in his gnarled hands. He handed the new cigarette to Dad. 'Here – have a smoke on me. In the Yankee pictures you see at the cinema, cigars are aye handed out when a baby is born but I've no cigars so you'll just have to take this home-made effort – a cross between a Wild Woodbine and a Capstan with a wee touch of Players thrown in.'

I leant against the wall, watching Dad's worried face. Across the road, up a side alley, I saw an iron-railed veranda, its entire length filled with chattering women and whining children. In the midst of all this noisy humanity I felt so alone and forlorn, worried sick about Mum and wishing Danny were here. He was not only my cousin but my best friend.

I gazed in dismay at my brown sun-tanned legs and arms. How I longed to look like Danny with his lovely clear skin, deep blue eyes and auburn hair. I was lumbered with a cap of black hair cut short in an Eton crop, which I hated, and my eyes were dark brown. His mother Hattie was Dad's sister. Although he had inherited his good looks from his maternal side, his colouring was almost identical to that of Pat Ryan, his Irish father, now long dead.

Just the very thought of him filled me with pleasure. Although only a few months older than me, he was already a good three inches taller – a fact that my parents had noticed. 'Aye he's going to be a good-looking six-footer one day,' they had said barely a week ago.

I closed my eyes, letting the warm sun shine over me as the multitude of voices merged in the background like the humming buzz from a swarm of bees.

'Hello, Ann – so I've caught you sleeping,' said a familiar voice rising above the hum.

It was Danny and I watched as he effortlessly ran towards me, the sun shining on his hair, highlighting deep golden streaks that intertwined with the deep red. Looking at him through half opened eyes it seemed as if his hair was on fire. In spite of my worry, I laughed, thinking what a coincidence his appearance was. I had just finished reading a book about Aladdin and his magic lamp and, as he approached, I made a rubbing movement with my hands.

'What are you doing?' He had a puzzled frown on his boyish face.

'I'm rubbing my magic lamp. I made a wish for you to be here and here you are. It must be the genie's work.'

'Who's Jeannie? Is she a pal?' His puzzled frown deepened.

'No, Danny, it's just a story I've been reading. I'll tell you about it sometime.' I moved over to make a space for him. 'You've heard that Mum's baby is coming? Mrs Grey and Granny Neill are with her now so we're just waiting on news,' I said as I pointed over to where Dad was still standing with his clutch of cronies. His apprehensive face never strayed from our close.

Danny gave him a wave. 'Aye, I've heard. Rosie was telling everybody at the Overgate.'

Rosie's mother was Alice, Granny's next-door neighbour and adjoining window confidante. A year or two younger than my parents, Rosie was unmarried and a staunch member of the Salvation Army.

'She was just back from the Citadel when I met her and she gave me the message.'

He extricated a small bag of squashed-up, sticky sweets from his pocket and pushed it under my nose. Choosing one sweet from this gooey mass took all the expertise of a master demolition worker and the one I eventually picked was so large that it made speaking almost impossible.

'It's funny about your mum, Ann...' He stopped when he saw my puzzled look but still chewed noisily on his sweet, wiping dribbles from his chin with a thin hand. 'As I was saying, it's funny about your mum having the baby early. Mrs Pringle – the woman Mum works for in the Perth Road – well, she was taken in to the Forthill nursing home this morning to have her baby and she's early as well. In fact, the new nursery is not finished yet but Mum has been running around trying to put the finishing touches to it today.'

He gave his sweet a final loud crunch and sat back with a sigh. 'What a pity your mum doesn't have a new nursery as well.'

I nodded sadly as I visualised our tiny flat in my mind's eye. My parents had the big double bed in the corner of the room while I had the tiny re-cessed bed in the closet with its flowery cotton curtained screen. No matter how hard I tried, I couldn't imagine where the newcomer could possibly sleep.

'Mrs Pringle has an older daughter – is that right?' I asked, trying to block out the depressing image of our cramped living conditions.

Danny nodded. 'That's right. Her name is Maddie and, although she's the same age as us, she's still at the school. She's a pupil at the Harris Academy – not one of the tuppenny-ha'penny schools like we went to.'

I wondered aloud if Maddie was perhaps sitting in the sun like us, waiting for news of the forth-coming birth.

Danny said no. She was on holiday with her aunt in Tayport. His mention of school brought the problems I'd had since leaving a few months ago to the surface.

'I've been looking for a job for weeks but there's nothing. With Dad not working and now another mouth to feed, things are getting harder. Still maybe something will turn up.' I sounded doubt-ful and I suddenly realised that my hopeless tone matched exactly the desolate conversation of the men.

They were normally hard-working men but now young and old alike had been thrown on to the scrapheap of high unemployment and they were angrily discussing the plans for the forth-coming means test. The test was said to be like an inquisition and even those with very little money were to be subjected to investigation. An obvious lack of money didn't stop officials from poking their noses into people's lives. Those sent round to people's homes to examine their circum-stances often didn't believe them when they claimed to be penniless and would assume they must be hiding a secret source of income – often supposing they were not declaring wages brought into the household by a son or daughter.

'You'll not get any money from the dole office,' said Joe, who seemed to know quite a lot about the coming legislation. 'If you've any money saved up or maybe have a member of your family working or even a lodger, then you'll get sweet Fanny Adams.'

The men laughed bitterly. 'Well, that lets us off the hook then. None of us have any savings.'

'There's no money in our socks or under the bed,' said Dad, 'but I wish we had.'

I turned to Danny. 'What kind of a job would you like?' I made it sound as if jobs were ten a penny.

He hesitated. 'I don't really care as long as I was earning a wage but I would like to see other parts of the world. Still, I suppose I never will. What would you like to do, Ann?'

Being such a lover of books, there was no doubt in my mind. 'A job in the library – now that would be a dream come true but, like you, Danny, I don't suppose it'll ever happen.'

Suddenly Granny appeared, her face flushed deep red with beads of perspiration visible on her upper lip. She quickly wiped her face with a cloth as she walked towards the men.

'You've got another wee lass, Johnny. Lily's fine and she wants to see you.' Her flustered glance swept over Danny and me. 'You can see your mum as well, Ann.' And, with these dramatic words, she waddled back up the close.

Dad threw down the butt of his cigarette and stamped it out with the heel of his tackety boot.

The men slapped him on the back. 'Well, you'll be glad that's it over now and another wee lass as a sister to Ann.' Their faces all turned towards me and although their voices were cheerful, each man had a shadow of sadness in his eyes. Yes and another mouth to feed, they said silently.

Bunty Grey was busy with her bag when I entered. To my immense relief, whatever paraphernalia involved in childbirth was now all out of sight – except for the kettle which was still simmering on the stove.

Mum's face was as white as the sheet but she was propped up against the ugly wooden headboard, two thin pillows at her back and a cup of tea in her thin hands. A mewing sound came from the small bundle that lay in the drawer on the floor – my new sister.

Dad went straight over to the bed and sat gingerly on the bright crocheted cover that was now placed over the sheet. Bunty pulled aside the small blanket to let me see the baby's face. As if she knew she had an audience, the wailing sound stopped and I saw her lovely little face with such a pretty rosebud mouth.

'We're going to call her Lily, after her mum,' said Dad proudly. Moving from the bed to gaze at his new daughter, he added, 'She's just like a wee flower – like her mother.'

Bunty Grey snapped her bag shut. 'She's no' that wee – she's a strapping eight pounds and a Sunday girl.' She bent over the baby and crooned in a soothing, sing-song kind of intonation. 'The baby that's born on the Sabbath day, is blithe and bonny and good and gay.'

Mum smiled weakly but Dad laughed. 'Well, that makes it two Sunday girls because Ann was a Sabbath day baby too.'

Meanwhile, Rita and Nellie had heard the good news and they stood outside on the landing, chatting to Danny who obviously felt ill at ease in this women-orientated world.

As soon as the midwife left they came in. I was sent to make another pot of tea while they gathered around the bed. 'Imagine such a big baby, Lily,' they said in unison as they flitted between the bed and the baby. 'And you almost a month early. Heavens, what size would she have been if you had gone the full term?'

After I'd done my hostess turn with the teapot, Danny and I sat on the stairs as the tiny room was cramped and overflowing with the grown-ups.

Granny's voice wafted out to us as she bustled around the room like a clucking hen. 'Ann can sleep at the Overgate tonight – just to give you two a bit of time to yourselves.'

Danny chuckled. 'Looks like a tight squash because I'm supposed to be staying with Granny tonight as well. Mum wasn't sure when she would get back from the Perth Road. In fact, Granny was saying that she spends more time there than she does in the house but I don't mind.'

Although Hattie had a nice flat in the Westport, it was a well-known fact that she spent so little time in it.

'Anyway,' said Danny, with a grin, 'I've got loads of relations in Lochee. I can aye stay there.'

Danny's father, the late Pat Ryan, had three sisters who were all married and, as well as them, there were Dad and Ma Ryan, his grandparents. They all lived in Atholl Street – an Irish community in Lochee. Nicknamed Tipperary, it housed hundreds of families. The people were descended from the influx of immigrants who had left Ireland at the turn of the century to work in the city's many jute mills. These families were housed in similar conditions to ourselves and a thousand light years away from people like Mr and Mrs Pringle.

By now, Danny and I had moved out into the street. Lengthening shadows, heralding the approach of night, patterned the dusty pavements but it was still hot and golden. Groups of children still played noisily, scampering around in the pursuit of their many games. Muffled voices from people still sitting in the sun washed over us like waves on the shore. Cooking smells wafted down from the multitude of open doors, making us both feel very hungry.

Danny gave an impish grin. 'Stovies for our tea tonight, I think.'

I grinned back at him. Granny Neill's stovies were a legend and the mainstay of her family's nourishment. This dish, made with large slices of potatoes and onions cooked in a large dollop of dripping, was usually served with thick slices of bread.

Suddenly Hattie appeared on the opposite side of the road and all my culinary thoughts disappeared. We watched as she weaved her way through the crowds of noisy children. Never one to hurry or even get harassed, she glided gracefully upwards. She was smartly dressed in her Sunday best outfit – a long-sleeved crêpe-de-Chine frock almost the same grey shade as the string of pearls.

around her neck.

She didn't see us as she glided like a grey wraith into the close but we quickly followed her retreating figure, watching in amusement as she skilfully avoided the grimy children.

It was only because we were hot on her heels that we witnessed her complete surprise at the new arrival. In fact, she was almost speechless when faced with the crying baby in the makeshift bed which was a drawer from the wardrobe. Danny and I coming up behind her also added to her discomfort and she looked nonplussed at the scene.

'When did this happen?' she asked, when she had recovered her voice. She nodded towards the baby. 'I thought you had another month to go, Lily?'

'Well, babies come when they're ready,' snapped her mother. 'We couldn't let you know because you were working as usual.' Nan Neill sometimes mimicked her daughter's posh tones.

Hattie disregarded this sarcasm. 'Well, what a coincidence,' she said, glancing at the assembled company of relatives and neighbours alike. 'Mrs Pringle had a daughter today as well – in the nursing home, of course.' There was a slight peevishness in her tone, almost as if Mum had gone ahead and had Lily early to keep up with Mrs Pringle.

Although I didn't think she meant to be unkind, this comparison wasn't lost on Mum who lay back on her threadbare pillows with a look of exasperation on her tired face.

Dad leapt up from the bed and led Hattie over to the baby. 'Come and meet Lily. She wasn't born in a posh nursing home but we love her very much.'

Hattie stuttered. Dropping her pseudo-posh accent in her confusion. 'Oh, I didn't mean to suggest anything else. She's a right bonny wee baby and I'm glad you're over it, Lily.' She stopped and seemed to recover some of her earlier poise. 'Now, you must get your strength back because you look all washed out.'

She stopped again when Dad glared at her.

'But that's only natural, isn't it? I mean having a baby at your...'

Dad glared once more and Hattie became silent.

She fiddled with her gloves and turned her attention to her son. 'Now, Danny, are you coming home with me or are you staying with Granny?'

'I'll just come with you because Ann is staying with Granny tonight.' He gave me a large grin. He didn't help matters when he added, 'I'll not be coming just now as I haven't been to Lochee yet to see Ma and Dad Ryan.'

A strange expression flitted over Hattie's face but whether it was because of the mention of the Ryan family it was difficult to say. She turned away, her posh manner now back firmly in place.

'Well, I'll be off.'

In the Neill household, everyone knew that Hattie had become a right lady since her move to the Pringle family –'right gentrified', as Granny called it.

Granny now turned with a look of undisguised glee on her face but not before the exit of Danny with his mother. 'Good for you, Lily. You fairly upstaged our Hattie with your unexpected arrival. Did you see her face? Put out of joint it was and her mouth was so wide open that she could have swallowed one of Horatio Leslie's fish fillets whole.'

We all laughed at the memory of her comical face and we were still laughing when she reappeared. Poking her head around the door, her cheeks red from the exertion of climbing the stairs again, she said, 'I forgot to say, because of all this kerfuffle. Mrs Pringle's wee lass is to be called Joy because, after all these years, they had given up hope of ever having another child.' She darted back out.

Because of her quick departure, she didn't hear my parents murmur to each other. 'No, neither did we think we'd have another baby.'

As usual, Granny had the last word. 'That Hattie makes me so mad. Wee Lily's birth is looked on as a kerfuffle while Mrs Pringle's Joy is treated by her as the birth of the blinking century.'

Dad merely smiled tenderly at Mum and held her hand. I thought it was so romantic.

2

I was fast asleep when the knock came to the door but the whispered voices echoing in the lobby wakened me. At first I thought the commotion was some sort of dream – a fantasy of muffled and anxious voices that somehow were distorted and amplified in my head. They weren't loud – more like stage whispers – which I think made the conversation more sinister to my ears. I certainly felt there was something malevolent in the hoarseness of the voice. Something, I'm not sure what, filled me with a dreadful fear. There was a nagging feeling of foreboding even before the words penetrated my brain.

Wiping sleep from my eyes, I slipped out of bed and opened the door of the small bedroom. My rough, flannelette nightgown flapped around my ankles, impeding my progress, and I felt the coolness from the linoleum floor against my feet. I could make out Granny's voice but the other person's whispers sounded strange – probably because they were punctuated with harsh sobs. Because the voice sounded unfamiliar, it came as a great surprise to see Rita, our neighbour, standing at the open door.

Granny was putting on her thick coat. I could see her silhouette outlined by the gas lamp on the stair.

'What's wrong, Granny?' I asked, aware of a cold feeling in my stomach.

The two women stopped whispering and swung around to face me. Rita's hand swept up to her face as if to shield herself from some dreaded thing but I could see she had been crying.

Granny put a hand on my shoulder and tried to lead me back to my tiny bedroom. 'Just go back to bed, Ann. I'll not be long and Grandad is here to look after you.' Although she sounded calm, the look of distress on her face was evident.

'There's something wrong with Mum, isn't there?' I shouted, trying to keep the awful fear at bay – a fear that was threatening to erupt any moment. 'I want to come with you.'

I ran back to my tiny room. Tugging the scratchy nightgown over my head, I searched in the darkness for my frock and sandals. I then darted out beside the two women who immediately exchanged a wary glance. I could well imagine Granny putting a finger to her lips and saying, 'Not a word to Ann, Rita.' But instead she busied herself by taking my tatty old trench coat down from the hook behind the door. 'Here, you'd better take your coat – the night air will be really cold.'

With that she pushed me gently through the door, leaving Grandad behind looking bewildered and dishevelled in his hastily-donned clothes. He also looked extremely sad.

Rita was quiet as we slipped down the dimly lit stairs and into the deserted Overgate. A full moon glowed in the clear sky that already had the hint of dawn at its edges. The tall grey tenements that appeared decrepit under a bright sun now looked magical in the moonlight. From somewhere in the distance, a clock struck three chimes, gentle peals that floated over this shadowy, slumbering landscape.

I turned to Granny. 'What's wrong with Mum? Is she not well?' I spoke in a breathless anxious whisper, frightened of what the answer would be and also frightened to talk too loud in case I disturbed a peacefully sleeping population.

'Well your mum has been taken to the Royal Infirmary. She took bad about an hour ago but we're sure she'll be as right as rain soon. Your dad is with her and we'll have good news soon.' She sounded reassuring.

Rita nodded. 'Aye, just give her a day or two and she'll be as good as new.'

We were passing a row of darkened windows when the sharp whimpering wails of a baby stabbed the quiet air. I suddenly remembered Lily.

Almost as if she read my thoughts, Rita turned with a hoarse whisper, 'Nellie has got her and between us we'll look after her till your mum gets better.'

These words, meant as a comforter, didn't soothe me. I felt a dull grip of fear and also felt quite sick. Still, by the time we reached the house, I was feeling grateful because the cold night air had penetrated my coat's thin fabric and my bare legs were chilled.

The house had strange unlived-in look. The fire was still out and the ashes lay in a grey dead mass in the grate. There was also a feeling of desolation which matched my mood exactly.

To my surprise, I noticed that the bedclothes had been stripped from the big double bed. My own closet bed was untouched but the other one lay with its blue and white-striped mattress exposed.

A large wet patch was visible, as if someone had recently scrubbed the ticking. I couldn't fathom it out. I knew that some small children wet their beds but surely Mum wouldn't have been carted off to hospital for something as simple as that. I had started to hunt for sheets and blankets, a puzzled frown on my face, when Rita appeared.

'Come on out of there,' she said. 'We're all in Nellie's house and she's making a cup of tea.' She bustled ahead of me but then waited to firmly close the door behind me.

'Rita, what's the matter with Mum? I saw the bed...' Before I could finish, she butted in. 'Now just be quiet and behave yourself like a good lassie. After all, you're not supposed to be here, are you?' Her fleshy cheeks wobbled. 'Your mum's in good hands at the DRI and no doubt she'll be on her feet before long.'

Duly chastised, I did as I was told. Nellie's house was almost identical to ours – one small room with no view from the tiny window except the grey brickwork of another tenement. Under this minuscule window, the small black sink and the coal bunker lay together and even the furniture looked the same. In fact, the two rooms could have been interchanged at any point and I doubt if we would have known the difference.

A small fire was burning in the grate and beside it, still lying in her drawer and fast asleep, was the baby. I went over to gaze down at her face. Nellie had swung the arm of the gas lamp over to the opposite direction which meant Lily's face was in shadow. In spite of this, I could still see her rose-bud mouth and smooth downy cheeks. She was the most beautiful baby I had ever seen.

Nellie came over. 'Try and not waken her, Ann,' she said as she buttoned up the faded frock. 'She's just been fed and what a real howling match it was.'

I sat beside the fire with a cup of tea clutched in my cold hands while the three women settled themselves on the edge of the bed, which like ours, was right beside the fireplace.

'The baby was making a real racket and it's just as well that I'm still feeding my wee lad or else we would be in Queer Street,' said Nellie.

'We'll take Lily over to the Overgate later on if the hospital wants to keep her mother in for a few days,' said Granny. 'Ann can get a baby's bottle and some milk when the shops open.' She stopped. 'I've just noticed, Nellie, where's your man?' She nodded at the empty bed where it was obvious that someone had recently been lying.

She laughed. 'He's upstairs with Rita's man – having a smoke and a gossip no doubt.'

Granny uttered a huge sigh that almost rocked her entire body. 'Well, if we don't hear anything by six o'clock, then Ann and I will go up to the hospital to see what the news is.'

I let this conversation wash over me. My fear had now materialised into a cold feeling of numbness. I just had to believe that Mum would get well again and come home – not just for Lily's sake but for us all. Another thing I knew for sure was that the women, despite their outward cheerfulness, were putting on a face for my benefit.

The memory of Rita's harsh sobs in the Overgate lobby was still fresh in my mind. A battered old clock ticked merrily on the mantelpiece – a clock bought from a market stall or maybe the second-hand shop across the street. Nearly everyone bought their household goods from this shop. The items had all seen better days but when money was almost nonexistent, the second-hand dealer's prices were a huge selling point.

The clock suddenly chimed five. Dawn didn't make its glorious appearance at this small window – not like Granny's generously sized window above the fish shop. Her window greeted the day and the sunshine like a welcome friend.

For the second time in twenty-four hours, I wished desperately that Danny was here. Asleep at his house in the Westport, neither Hattie nor he was aware of this terrible drama.

The women had also now lapsed into silence and the only sounds in the room were Granny's slight wheeze and the relentless merry ticking of the clock. An hour later Granny stood up and reached for her coat.

'Right then, we'll head up to the hospital to see what the news is.' Her lined face had a grey pallor so unlike her normal ruddy colouring.

Rita held up her hand, her head cocked towards the door. 'Wait a minute. I think I hear footsteps on the stair, Nan.'

I held my breath, listening to the unmistakable sound of a tack-tipped boot scraping against the worn stone stairs, a sound that matched the slow beat of a drum.

'That's Johnny's step right enough,' said Rita. 'I just hope that Lily is fine.'

There was a sound as he first went towards our house then the steps echoed along the passage as he retraced his progress back to Nellie's door.

As soon as we saw his face we knew the news was bad. In spite of being a handsome man, he now looked terrible. His face was the colour of putty with dark pouches under his eyes and a blue unshaven shadow around his cheeks and jowls. He wore a knitted scarf around the frayed shirt neck, the ends hanging down over the front of the threadbare jacket. He was not wearing any socks.

The women opened their mouths to speak but he held up one hand while the other hand covered his eyes. 'Lily died an hour ago.' His voice was rough with unshed tears. 'The doctors just couldn't stop the bleeding.'

I propelled myself across the room like a rocket, almost knocking him through the still-open door. I buried my head in the woolly muffler and I felt the roughness of his face. It was like sandpaper.

'No, Dad, no,' I cried. Tears were streaming down my face and neck, soaking the collar of my frock. 'No, Dad, it's not true. It's not true.'

Dad rocked back and forth, holding me tightly. 'Shush, Ann,' he crooned. 'Shush.'

I felt his tears on my hair as we stood together in our grief.

Granny came over and put her arms around both our shoulders. 'Come on, Johnny and Ann. Let's get back to the house. We've all had a terrible shock but standing here won't help. Don't worry about the baby, she can stay here.' She turned towards Rita and Nellie and the two women nodded wordlessly, misery written all over their faces. 'Well, that's settled then – we'll come back later and pick her up.'

As usual, she was a tower of strength. Although sorely distressed herself, she was still able to see ahead and deal with the nitty-gritty of life – life that still had to go on in spite of grief or disaster. At that moment, however, Granny would have been the last person to admit her strength.

We allowed ourselves to be gently ushered out but, when we reached the lobby, Dad made a beeline for our house.

Granny stopped him. 'No, son, let it be for now – wait till later.' She turned to me. 'The same goes for you, Ann.'

Like two zombies, we let her help us out into the street where pale sunshine was already casting golden patches on the pavement. Tears still streaked down my cheeks and I suddenly became aware of their salty taste – something I had never noticed before. The strange thing was that, for many years after Mum's sudden and untimely death, anytime I recalled that dreadful morning, it was this trivial fact I remembered – also the memory of Lily sleeping through that dramatic night, unaware of the tragedy. We were all grateful for that small mercy.

When I told Granny later on about remembering the tears and their saltiness, she said that this was common. Soldiers who had experienced the most traumatic times in the trenches often said that the sight of mud on their shoes brought back the horrors. I knew this was true. Although Dad's own trench warfare horrors were now mostly buried in his subconscious, sometimes, if his jacket got soaked, his eyes glazed over as if he was remembering the trenches.

I can't recall the few days that passed between Mum's death and the burial. No doubt like Dad, I've buried them deep in my soul and maybe someday they will erupt like Vesuvius, spilling all the grief and despair of that terrible week into the open – but not now.

The funeral was held on Thursday. After a week of hot sunshine and blue cloudless skies, the weather finally broke. Rain streamed down from a black ominous-looking sky that held the threat of thunder in its darkness. The desolate grey streets matched our desolate emotions, especially Dad's. He had aged visibly and become thinner since Mum's death. Before, he could have passed for a handsome thirty-year-old but now he looked nearer sixty.

Mum was being buried at Balgay cemetery. It was a simple service in view of the fact that we didn't belong to a church. After the carnage of the war, Dad had refused to believe in any God. Because of this, Rosie had arranged for one of her fellow Salvation Army friends to conduct the small graveside service. Major Borland was a tall gangly-looking man in his early thirties. His eager boyish face was topped by a thick thatch of straw-coloured hair.

His eloquence was without fault. 'Dust to dust in the sure and certain...'

I heard the words but they didn't penetrate my brain. I was too painfully aware that, less than a week ago, Mum was alive. If not exactly full of beans, she at least hadn't seemed ill. I couldn't help thinking that, in giving life to Lily, she had forfeited her own life.

I stood beside Danny and Hattie and Rosie, just a few steps behind Dad, Granny and Grandad. It was strange to see Grandad Neill out in the fresh air as he never went any further than the small tobacconist's shop a few steps from his close, the shop where he called once a week for his usual supply of thick black Bogey Roll and a box of matches. Due to the fact he suffered from chronic bronchitis, this pipe smoking was a bad habit that Granny had tried for years to break but she had failed.

His breathing sounded laboured and, every now and then, his hoarse cough almost drowned out the Major's words. Even although the rain had lessened, the cemetery, in spite of its green foliage, still had a forlorn air that lingered like a miasma above the heads of the mourners.

Danny's aunts and uncles from Tipperary in Lochee stood beside a group of Dad's friends from the Hilltown. Rita and her husband were amongst a smattering of neighbours. Nellie, who was acting as a surrogate mother to Lily and had done so since the night of Mum's death, hadn't managed to come.

Standing slightly to Hattie's left was a stranger. A small middle-aged man, he was dapper looking in a smart dark suit which contrasted sharply with the attire of the other men. He was almost bald except for a fringe of grey hair and he carried a soft hat in his pigskin-leather gloved hands.

In the distance, a deep roar of thunder growled and the sky became black again. Large fat rain-drops splashed at our feet but no one moved. Dad hunched his thin shoulders, trying to wrap his misery inside his threadbare overcoat, a thin coat he had owned for as long as I could remember. He looked so pathetic and ill that a surge of emotion rose up in my throat, like a bolt tightening my muscles. This emotion gurgled upwards as if threatening to erupt and I tried so hard not to cry. Dad was upset enough without the added worry of me so I stared resolutely ahead, planting my vision squarely on a grotesquely sculpted angel that guarded, with outstretched wings, an equally ugly tombstone.

Behind this angel were rows of moss-crusted, weatherbeaten gravestones. Some had glass vases filled with wilted and decaying flowers while others had dried-up wreaths, placed there at some time in the recent past in mute remembrance for loved ones. Chipped stone urns stood beside the headstones, some of which were standing while others lay resting on their backs, knocked over by wind or neglect or maybe that old enemy – Time.

Perhaps, I thought, if I gazed long enough at the final resting places of long-dead citizens it would somehow lessen my grief and anguish – that maybe this terrible day would soon be over. But then, what about afterwards? What about all the terrible days that lay ahead? I had no idea what lay in store for us – especially Lily, that poor innocent and motherless infant.

Then, with a few emotional words, the service was over and the Major offered his sympathy to Dad. He then headed over in my direction. 'Hello, Ann,' he said. His handshake had a nice firm quality to it and his voice was soft and cultured but much later, in the quiet of the night, I couldn't recall a word he had said.

Danny, I noticed, had been crying, his blue eyes looking more vivid and bright because of their wetness. My whole body felt numb, even my brain. He took my hand and we stumbled along the uneven path towards the entrance of the cemetery.

The sound of thunder was much nearer now

and a sudden thunderous clap roared almost over our heads. It seemed as if even the elements matched our mood.

Another ordeal lay ahead in the shape of offering some hospitality and refreshments to our friends. It had been decided a few days earlier that these refreshments would be given in Granny's house – not that it was any grander than our own home but it did have the advantage of being slightly larger.

When we reached the Overgate, I was surprised to see the narrow street full of people, noise and bustle. Because our world had come to an end, I somehow thought that this terrible isolation was universal.

I said as much to Danny. 'We're all shattered about Mum but everybody here looks so cheery.' As if to emphasise my words, a loud shriek arose from a small group of children huddled around something that was causing immense amusement.

'Life has to go on, Ann,' he replied sympathetically. 'For all we know, there's maybe a lot of miserable folk here who are just as heartbroken as us.'

He guided me gently past shops almost devoid of customers. In a hard-up life, the middle of the week was the worst time for money and the poverty that lay amongst these streets showed in the scarcity of customers.

I averted my head as we passed the fish shop as I hated the smell. It held an odour of death which seemed to linger even long after the shop was closed. I also disliked the sight of dead fish lying on the marble slab with their mouths gaping wide open and their large glassy and staring eyes.

41

It was hard to believe that, until a few days ago, these fish had been alive in the wild waters of some vast ocean – just as Mum had been alive.

If the tumult of life went on as usual on the street then at least the neighbours in the close were quiet. The men doffed their cloth caps as we passed while the women offered a few words of sympathy. Even the children were subdued – no doubt they'd been warned that a smacking would ensue if they broke the respectful silence.

Granny had provided a small tea of meat paste sandwiches and a couple of plates of biscuits. She was ably assisted by Alice and her daughter Rosie.

Not everyone who had been at the cemetery was here but I was surprised to see the dapper man in the smart suit. However, it now seemed as if his presence was to remain a mystery no more because Hattie approached with him in tow. She had a sad expression – a look that Granny often referred to as her 'coffin face'.

This soon changed to a brittle smile. 'Ann, I want you to meet Mr Pringle. He's a solicitor.'

I looked blankly at her, my mind racing ahead at the mention of a solicitor. I wondered what he wanted with me.

'Mr Pringle,' repeated Hattie brightly before leaning forward and almost hissing in my ear. 'He's the husband of the woman I work for.' She spoke through gritted teeth which couldn't have been easy since she was also trying to keep her introductory smile on her face.

The penny dropped. 'Oh, Mr Pringle, thank you for coming to Mum's funeral.' I was trying to remember my manners. Something that Mum was always strong on. The snag was that I hadn't experienced such a sad and traumatic time before so I was at a loss to know what was expected of me. I quickly remembered his wife and their new daughter. What was she called? Oh, yes, Joy. 'I hope your wife and baby are well, Mr Pringle.'

'Yes they are both fine, Ann. We were all devastated by your mother's death and, if we can help the family in any way, please don't hesitate to ask. Now we mean that,' he said in a solemn, gracious manner.

Meanwhile, Hattie hovered at his elbow, desperate, no doubt, to show him off like a prize specimen.

Granny appeared and whispered angrily to her, 'This is not some social occasion you know, Hattie.'

Hattie's face went red, a mixture of emotions flitting over her refined features, the main one being embarrassment at the thought that Mr Pringle may have heard the rebuke.

Fortunately he had already moved over to speak to Dad and the two men retired to a couple of chairs by the window, with a cup of tea and a sorry-looking, dehydrated meat paste sandwich.

Danny stood beside Kit, Lizzie and Belle, his aunts from Lochee. Their husbands had long since departed back to Lochee for a pint of beer at the Nine Bells bar. With none of the men in work, this pub offered drink on the credit slate, the bill being settled at the end of the week when the dole money was picked up.

I moved over to speak to Danny and, as I approached the group, I was surprised to see

Granny's sister Bella. She was sitting in the comfiest chair. I knew she hadn't been to the cemetery and I also knew that she hadn't entered after us.

She saw my puzzlement. 'I've been sitting here for hours and I just wondered when you were coming over to see me.' She sounded cross. Granny was plump but Bella, on the other hand, was simply fat. She sat like an ill-natured Buddha with her fat little hands folded across her bosom.

'I didn't know you were here, Bella,' I said truthfully. 'Thank you for coming.'

Danny gave me a sympathetic look while his aunts made a comical face at me. Luckily, because they stood behind her, these grimaces went unnoticed by Bella.

'Well, it's my duty, Ann, although I have to say that your father hasn't come over either,' she remarked peevishly.

I turned around to see dad still talking to Mr Pringle – much to Hattie's annoyance.

'Silly old bat, that Bella,' said Kit softly to me. 'Does she not know that she should be coming to you and not the other way around?'

Once again I was thankful that this remark had gone unheard. Bella wasn't deaf but she had what Granny called 'selective hearing'. Her ears seemed to register what she wanted to hear but discarded everything else.

'I didn't see you come in, Bella,' I said, raising my voice against Kit's mumbles.

'Oh, I sat here while Alice and Rosie helped Nan make the sandwiches. I can't make sandwiches with my condition and that's why I didn't go along to Balgay in this awful weather. I'm no' daft.'

I heard Kit mumble again, sotto voce, but Bella continued her spiel. 'I mean, look at your grand-dad – ending up in his bed.' She sounded so superior. As if we had all been daft enough to stand at Mum's grave in a thunderstorm for the sake of pleasure.

'Dear God,' I thought, 'please let this awful, terrible day be over soon.'

Bella was still talking. 'He's been coughing since he came back.'

This was true and, in fact, I was really worried about him. Granny had sent him straight to my little bed in the cupboard with a hot-water bottle. Even now, his hoarse coughing could be heard. Hattie even glanced in that direction a few times. From her expression, I thought she was wishing she could spirit Mr Pringle away from us lower classes.

'No, no,' said Bella, 'I've to watch myself because I don't keep well. I've got lots of things wrong with me.' As if to emphasise her statement, she pointed to various parts of her body while Danny and his aunts almost exploded with laughter, which no doubt they would have done if the occasion hadn't been such a sad one. I heard Kit snort like a pig for a few seconds before she recovered her decorum.

We all knew about Bella's ailments and the fact that she had more than any doctor had heard of. The thing was, like all true hypochondriacs, she possessed a perfect constitution. Still that didn't stop her enjoying her ill health. I felt a bit sorry for her and I often thought her ailments were a result of her loneliness. She had never married and had lived in her childhood house, a one-roomed flat in Cochrane Street, in the over-populated Crescent area.

She took a small bottle from her large message bag and proceeded to take a drink from it. 'I'm just taking my medicine,' she explained. 'I've to take it often or this flares up again.' She tapped a point somewhere between her bosom and her hips.

'Aye a swig of Johnny Walker does wonders for the digestion so share it around,' said Kit.

Bella ignored her. 'No, as I aye say, it's better to be safe than sorry so a wee taste of this medicine calms down all my complaints.'

I was taken aback at Kit's remark. Surely this old woman wasn't swigging whisky from a medicine bottle. No, I thought, Kit was just inventing it but, as Bella leaned towards me, I smelled her breath and I knew it was true.

She glanced over again at the window. 'That chap that's been gossiping to your father is leaving now so go over and tell him I want to see him.'

Mr Pringle was shaking hands with Granny while Hattie hovered again at his shoulder like a guardian angel – much to Kit's amusement – before he left he came over and once again offered his help.

'Goodbye, Ann. Now remember what we spoke about.'

As soon as he went out the door, I passed on Bella's command to Dad. He groaned. 'What does that devil want? No doubt all the ins and outs of your poor mother's death.' He wiped his eyes with his hand. 'What a day it's been.'

I agreed with him. It was a terrible day. Granny came over and I saw lines of tiredness on her face. 'Yon Mr Pringle is a real gent. Still I expect Hattie is making sure that he knows she doesn't live here in the Overgate. Probably telling him about her top-floor flat in the Westport with its great view. Heavens, her window looks over roofs and chimneys but she'll make it sound like some airy-fairy Alpine scene.'

'Johnny, Johnny – over here,' cried a querulous voice from the direction of the comfy chair.

'Aye, he's a right nice man,' said Dad. 'Now for Bella.'

Granny groaned. 'It looks like she's here for the duration.'

'What are your plans for Ann and the baby?' asked Bella. 'You'll have a lot on your plate...' She stopped as Rosie approached. Glaring at her briefly, she turned her back on the younger woman's presence and pointedly ignored her. 'I'm just asking what arrangements have been made for your kids.'

'Are you offering to help out, Bella?' said Dad wearily.

Bella almost collapsed, her complexion turning a pasty white. 'Oh, I would help out if I was able but, with my ill health, I wouldn't have the strength to look after two kids! No, no, with my varicose veins, I've to rest my legs for most of the day and no' to mention my heartburn and my...'

Dad held up his hand as if warding off something contagious. 'I'm just kidding you, Bella. I know what a sick woman you are and we wouldn't throw ourselves on your mercy. Anyway it's been

47

settled for a wee while at least. Ann and Lily will stay here with Granny and Ann will help to look after her, the wee soul.'

He glanced at Rosie and Kit. 'Rosie and Alice plus Danny's aunts from Lochee have all offered to help out – to give Granny a break. Aye they're a great bunch of folk, just like ourselves with not a shilling between them.'

By now the colour had returned to Bella's cheeks and she took the bottle out again. 'Just my medicine,' she said, holding it aloft this time so we could all see the chemist's well-worn label.

I heard Kit murmur something about the bottle looking like it had originated at the turn of the century but Bella was still talking.

'Aye, Johnny, it's one thing to want to help out but another thing to be able.'

Rosie, who had been standing patiently in the background, put her arm around Dad's shoulder. She looked so wholesome, if somewhat old-fashioned, with her straight dark hair tied back in an untidy bun. There was no doubting the sincerity in her well-scrubbed appearance and in her brown eyes behind their steel-rimmed spectacles. 'Mum and I are away back next door, Johnny,' she said, 'but we'll do all we can to help out.'

'Thanks for all your help, Rosie, getting Major Borland to do the service. We really appreciate it.' He turned to Alice who was an older copy of her daughter. 'The sandwiches were lovely and you're both good friends to us.'

It looked as if Rosie might burst into tears but she gave Dad a hug and she hurried through the door, followed by her mother.

Bella, meanwhile, was settling back in her chair. She had no intention of moving by the looks of it. 'I'll just have another cup of tea and a meat paste sandwich before I go.'

Granny groaned again. 'Well, it will just have to be a quick cup because we've to pick Lily up at the Hilltown and then get her settled.'

As it turned out, we didn't have to go because Nellie turned up with her. 'I thought you would have enough to do without having to come for the wee lass.' She suddenly stopped. 'Or maybe you would like me to keep her for a wee while longer.'

'Not at all,' said Granny, taking the tiny bundle from the younger woman's arms. 'No, Nellie, you've been a right gem and we'll never be able to thank you for all you've done.'

Nellie's face flushed a bright red. It was obvious from this look that she was unused to getting compliments or even to be thanked for anything. Her husband, although not an unkind man, was just like lots of other men on the Hilltown – a bit thoughtless and selfish with the idea that life revolved around him.

'It's been no bother, Nan, and you know you only have to ask and I'll look after her at any time for you.'

We all crowded around the baby who lay peacefully asleep.

'What a bonny wee lass she is,' said Kit, as she and her two sisters gazed down at Lily. 'Let's hand her over to Bella for the night – just to give her a treat.'

'Now, Kit...' Granny said reprovingly.

'Well, she's more healthy than you, Nan, and

49

you're so good to everybody, especially in a crisis,' said Kit brusquely.

Lizzie looked thoughtful. 'Well, maybe she really is not well. Even a hypochondriac can sometimes be ill.'

We all looked over to Bella who had settled back in her chair with her cup of tea and it looked as if it would take a crane to remove her.

Once again, I thought this interminable day would never come to an end but, like all things, it did. With the timely arrival of Lily, the mourners departed singly or in groups, all trooping down the stairs. Their sympathy and regretful murmurs lingered behind like a sincere afterthought.

With the departure of Danny, who left in the wake of his aunts, a despondency settled on me like a dark cloud. There was also the added worry of Dad who was planning on going home to the Hilltown, a move that not only upset Granny but me as well. Neither of us had lived there since the night of Mum's death – Dad had been staying with his pal Joe – but he was adamant that the Overgate house couldn't possibly accommodate us all. He was right of course but that didn't soothe Granny.

Dad and I walked through the streets that were still busy with people. It was early evening and the storm had long since passed over, leaving a cool breeze that had dried up the wet puddles on the pavements. It was as if the heatwave was over and we would never again see the sun.

I was dreading going into the house. After a few days' absence, it would feel musty and damp and I couldn't erase my last sight of it from my memory. On entering the door, my first glance told me that my dread was unjustified and it came as a pleasant shock to see a bright fire burning in the grate. The bed was made up with bedclothes smelling as if newly washed, a kettle was simmering on the gas and everything was as neat and tidy as it had been in Mum's time.

Although Dad had said little on the journey home, I knew he was also dreading his return – no doubt feeling the same as me. When he saw the neat cosy room, tears formed in his eyes.

'Would you look at what the neighbours have done for me? I bet this is Rita and Nellie's work. I don't think I'll ever be able to repay them.' He brushed the tears away with the frayed end of his jacket sleeve.

I was also grateful to the women but still unsure of how he would cope on his own. 'I'll stay here for a wee while, Dad. Granny will manage Lily during the night and I'll be there to do all the heavy work during the day.' I removed my coat but he made me put it on again.

He also wouldn't hear of it. 'No, Ann, your granny needs all the help she can get. No, just you go back and I'll be fine – honest.'

I shook my head and was about to argue with him when a gentle tap sounded at the door. A familiar face appeared around it. It was Joe.

'Can I come in? I saw you coming up the close,' he said, hesitating when he saw my face. 'Well, maybe I'll come back later, Johnny. I see you're busy with Ann.'

Dad almost threw himself at the retreating figure like a drowning man grasping a rope. 'No, Joe, come in. It's good to see you and Ann is just leaving.' I knew he didn't mean to be curt but it still sounded like a dismissal.

Joe looked wary and unsure. 'Well, I thought you would maybe like a wee bit of company. The lads and me didn't come back to the house after the service because we felt you had enough folk to feed without us as well.' He glanced kindly at me with such a look of concern that tears stung the back of my eyes.

'It's good of you to come round, Joe. Dad does need some company tonight,' I said before hurrying out through the door. 'But not my company,' I thought bitterly.

As I reluctantly retraced my steps, I had the feeling that Dad was lucky with such good neighbours and friends around him. They wouldn't see him stuck.

Lily was awake when I returned. Granny was testing the water in the basin by dipping her elbow in the water. 'Just seeing if the water's the right temperature and, while I bath the baby, will you heat up her milk in yon pot on the stove?'

I did as I was told, pouring the liquid into the boat-shaped bottle and fastening a rubber teat over the narrow opening. It was a hard job and some of the hot milk spilled over my hands but, after a few futile attempts, I was successful.

'Now hold the bottle under the cold tap till the milk cools down. When you think it's cooled down, shake some on the back of your hand and it should just be warm.'

Granny deftly placed the small pink creature on her ample lap. This tiny body was now shrieking with hunger and indignation, her little fists and legs kicking wildly.

Grandad came through. He looked a lot better now than when he came home from the funeral. The sleep and the hot-water bottle had done a power of good and he now carried his pipe and evening paper in his hands. He stopped dead when faced by Lily howling like a pack of wolves. 'Now, now my wee pet, what's the matter with you?' He took her tiny hand in one of his rough callused ones. 'Now Grandad will give you your bottle and I'll sing some songs to you.'

We were both flabbergasted but he sat down with the now dressed-for-bed baby on his lap and the bottle in his fist, the pipe and paper completely forgotten. 'There now, my wee lassie, here's your supper. Then tomorrow I'll take you for a walk along the Esplanade. Will you like that? Of course you will.'

As we looked on in amazement, Lily settled back and sucked noisily on her bottle. It would seem that she had given the old man a new lease of life. As if guessing this, she opened her eyes in a funny unfocused and squinting way. I then noticed with surprise that they were blue – just like Danny's.

3

Danny had a job. He had been hounding all the shops in the area looking for work. After months of disappointment, Lipton's grocery shop in the Overgate finally had a vacancy for a message boy and Danny happened to be in the right spot at the right time.

I was standing by the window, waiting for Grandad to come home from his daily walk with Lily, when I heard a sharp, piercing whistle followed by someone calling my name.

Danny was standing under the window beside a solidly built black bike. It had a square iron frame at the front that held a wicker basket. A brightly painted panel between the two large wheels extolled the virtues of shopping at Lipton's. Danny looked so pleased with himself that he was in grave danger of exploding with smugness.

'Come on down and see my great bike,' he called up.

I gazed at him with pleasure. 'Oh, you've got a job, Danny!' I cried. I hurtled through the house like a whirlwind and, in my haste, I almost knocked over a couple of elderly ladies who were passing the close at the time. After their initial shock at nearly being flattened, they went on their way muttering, 'Bairns today have no manners. That lassie almost knocked us sideways.'

Danny looked very workmanlike. 'I can't stay long,' he said, taking a rag from his pocket and giving the nameplate a quick wipe. His face was a picture of pride and satisfaction. 'I've got to deliver these messages to the Hawkhill – right to the very top. It will be a long climb but I can always push the bike if it gets too steep.'

Being built on the slopes of the Law Hill, a lot of Dundee's streets were very steep but I knew Danny was just teasing me. A big strong lad like him could tackle any steep braes.

I saw a large collection of brown packages nestling in the big basket. 'You've been really lucky to get this job, Danny.' I tried hard not to sound envious. I didn't want to spoil his pleasure. 'I've been hunting for months now and there's not a glimmer of work – the entire country is in a depression. At least that's what everyone tells me.'

He grinned a large smile that almost sliced his face in half. 'I know I was lucky. The manager at Lipton's said I was spending more time in his shop than some of the assistants so he gave me the first chance of a message boy's job. The other lad became ill and had to give the job up. It's a terrible shame and I hope he gets better soon and manages to get another job.'

'Oh, I hope so too,' I said, 'but it'll not be easy. Every week I go along to the dole office in Gellatly Street and there's aye queues of folk waiting there. The jute mills are laying off more workers and we're all in the same boat – jobless.' I tried not to sound sad but I gave a wistful sigh.

Danny agreed with me. 'Aye, you're right. All the Ryans are on the dole as well. They all worked in Cox's mill until the lay-offs.'

I nodded. 'I saw Kit and Lizzie in the queue but there was no sign of Belle. The Lochee folk are complaining about having to travel all the way into the town. They should have their own dole office in Lochee, they were all saying. It would save them having to walk miles as they never have enough money for the tram.'

Danny's smile vanished. He knew his relations were almost living on the breadline and much worse was to come. 'It's terrible. The last I visited them, they were all worried about this new means test that's coming and they say things will get much harder.'

He gave the bike another polish and I could see it was in danger of being polished right down to the bare iron. 'Still, what do you think of my new job?' He posed beside the bike, tall, slim and beaming.

'I think you look really handsome and all the old women in the big houses will just adore you and give you lots of tips,' I said truthfully.

He looked surprised. 'That's exactly what Maddie said.' On seeing my blank look, he explained. 'Aye, Maddie Pringle – you know, the folk in the Perth Road?'

'Oh, her,' I said snootily, not happy that she seemed to be on such friendly terms with him. 'Well, you're not that handsome, Danny Ryan, so don't get big-headed about it.'

He grinned. 'You're just jealous. But never mind. What about me giving you a ride on the bike after the messages are delivered?'

Although still annoyed by the mention of Maddie Pringle, I couldn't resist his offer. 'Right, then. I'll be here most of the day although I did think of visiting Dad later.'

He hopped on the bike and, as he pedalled away, he shouted, 'Well, that's settled then – I'll pick you up and give you a run to the Hilltown. Mind you, it all depends when I get finished. Sometimes I'm still delivering messages at ten o'clock at night.'

As he disappeared from sight towards the steep incline of the Hawkhill, I spotted Grandad. He was negotiating his way around a group of gossiping women who always seemed to commandeer the entire width of the pavement. So intense were their rapt expressions as they delved into the minutiae of life, they genuinely didn't realise they were blocking the pavement to all the pedestrians.

Grandad had Lily in his arms, his gnarled hands rough looking and weather-beaten against the baby's shawl. Still he looked cheerful, his cheeks pink from the fresh air and the exercise. In the beginning, Granny had been sceptical about these walks, believing they would be a short-lived thing. 'Just mark my words – this is just a two-day wonder. Just wait till the novelty wears off – then he'll be back to his bad old habits.'

But he had proved her wrong. With Lily now almost three months old, he had faithfully taken her out every day. Not only that, he had even gone as far as smoking his pipe in the courtyard, saying, 'I can't let the wee lass breathe in all this thick smoke.'

Granny's face had been a picture and, although amazed by this new man in her life, she was still unsure. 'What a pity you hadn't turned over a new leaf years ago – then maybe my own lungs wouldn't be all choked up with smog.'

There was nothing wrong with her lungs or indeed her health but she always felt better after her little protest and she was secretly pleased by her man's renewed lease of life. Even his terrible cough didn't seem so bad these days.

Grandad spotted me as he deftly skirted around the women. He placed Lily in my arms. 'Take Lily home, Ann. I've got a message to go for and I'll not be long.' He turned smartly on his heels and headed towards Long Wynd.

Granny was nonplussed. Her face was a picture of bewilderment when I told her what he'd said. 'He said he had a message to go for and it wasn't to the tobacconist's shop?' This was obviously something of a novelty for her.

'No, Granny, he didn't go to the tobacconist's. He went in the direction of Long Wynd but he didn't say anything else.'

The puzzle however was soon solved. We heard a heavy thumping sound, as if something metallic was being hauled up the stairs. The door was flung open in triumph and Grandad stood there like a conquering hero but instead of a sword and shield he held the handle of a battered old pram. To say it had seen better days was an understatement and, in a square mile full of ancient, decrepit prams, this one was a clear winner.

'Well,' he said, brandishing an eloquent hand over the monstrosity, 'what do you both think?'

Granny was almost speechless. 'In the name of God, Dad, where did you get that?'

Taking her reaction as a compliment, he beamed. 'I bought it from Jeemy's Emporium. Got a real bargain as well. Just cost me half a crown.'

'Half a crown?' said Granny, spluttering so hard that tiny droplets of spittle erupted into the air.

Grandad's smile grew wider. He obviously hadn't picked up on the angry message that was being directed at him. 'Well, I got it cheap because Jeemy says if he ever needs anything delivered – just wee things,' he hastened to add, 'well, I can deliver them when I'm out with Lily for her walks.'

Granny stood with her hands on her hips. She

looked formidable. 'Do you mean to tell me that you bought that pram from "Jumping Jeemy"?' This was the nickname of the second-hand dealer and it came from the fact that the odd flea or four were sometimes observed jumping around the vast pile of musty clothes that lay in an untidy heap in the minuscule shop. In a hard-up, poverty-stricken community, it was a well-known fact that someone had to be almost destitute before purchasing any garment from him. His only real customers were the Lascars, seamen who regularly arrived at the docks and made a foray into the local shops. To them, one second-hand shop was much like another so they didn't seem to be all that choosy.

Grandad, his manner now well and truly deflated by Granny's stance, muttered, 'Well, the baby is getting really heavy to carry, Nan, so I thought I could give her a wee hurl in the pram every day.' His face grew stubborn looking. 'Anyway, it'll clean up fine after a wee wash.' He sounded unhappy. His wonderful idea wasn't proving such a success after all. He had obviously thought his wife and granddaughter would have been ecstatic and falling over the pram with wild cries of delight and complimentary mutterings.

I smiled. It now looked as if Grandad was also going into the delivery business, just like Danny. 'I think it's a lovely idea, Grandad!' I said it more to cheer him up than anything because he looked so miserable.

It worked and his face lit up immediately. 'There you are, Nan. Ann likes it and I was just thinking of Lily. She'll love her wee hurls in it.'

Granny relented and moved gingerly towards

the contraption as she referred to it. Still, she kept her distance. 'It's in not too bad a condition,' she conceded as she circled it warily. 'At least the wheels are not buckled but it'll still need a damn good scrub.'

Because she wouldn't let it into her kitchen before its decontamination, we had to work in the confines of the outside lobby. Granny brought an enamel pail filled with hot soapy water and a generous dollop of bleach. After an initial wash, she then added a large amount of San Izal disinfectant which turned the water creamy white. The acrid fumes from this concoction almost knocked the three of us out – never mind any lone lingering flea. The pram was reasonably clean which was surprising and apart from its general scruffiness it was basically sound.

Grandad was chuffed. 'I told you – didn't I say that it was in good nick? Jeemy didn't keep it in the shop because there was no room so he parked it in the close beside the shop.'

'Well, thank goodness for small mercies,' said Granny, handing me the bucket. 'It's a shame to waste this good hot water. Put it down the toilet and it'll freshen it up.'

The toilet, a tiny cubicle situated like some afterthought on the communal stair, was shared by ten families. After doing what I was told, I reckoned that anyone foolhardy enough to use it within the next hour could well pass out from the fumes.

Thankfully, the pram was minus any grimy mattress on which anything nasty could still lurk and, after every nook and cranny had well and truly been fumigated, Lily was allowed to be placed in it. The eiderdown was taken from the bed and folded over to make a comfy base for her.

'There's just the one thing, Dad,' Granny warned. 'You're not to carry any of Jeemy's mangy clothes in that pram. If you have to deliver anything, make sure it's well wrapped up and put in a message bag, not beside the baby.'

Grandad, who would have agreed to anything now that the victory was his, nodded.

'I mean it,' she warned him sternly, casting a steely eye at him. 'If I see as much as one flea hopping about that pram, then it's going straight on the midden.'

Much later, I left them sitting at the window with the pram and Lily parked between them. Granny was leaning out and telling Alice all about the new acquisition at home.

Alice was full of praise for Grandad's visionary thinking. 'Oh, it'll be grand for Lily.' Then she dropped her voice to a whisper. 'I see somebody's put San Izal down the lavvy. Charley from next door came out with tears running down his cheeks and everybody is moaning about it.'

Granny sensibly remained silent. It was one thing to be praised for a spotlessly clean pram but having the close up in arms over poisonous fumes was another.

I wandered down the Overgate, hoping to run into Danny. I knew I couldn't wait till his deliveries were finished before going to see Dad. I thought I might see him as he circumnavigated the narrow streets on his trusty black bike. It was almost seven o'clock and, although the street was

61

always thronged with people, tonight it seemed to be much busier than normal. Large groups congregated at each corner of the many streets that led on to the Overgate. Crowds of people going towards the High Street hurried past me. A small group of men, dressed in their ill-fitting clothes and with cloth caps on their heads made a circled detour around me, half skipping in their haste. As they hurried past, I heard some of the breathless conversation. 'Better get a move on or we'll miss the march.' On that note, they quickened their pace to a run.

Lipton's shop was almost empty, with only a mere handful of customers in the process of buying some essentials in the grocery line. The staff, dressed in long white aprons over their white shirts and blouses were not exactly run off their feet but neither were they slouching around. One man was busy slicing bacon, turning the huge cartwheel handle in time to the slithering sound as blade met gammon joint. Meanwhile, his colleague stood beside a huge mound of butter. I watched in fascination as he pushed his wooden pallet into the golden mound. He then deftly patted the unformed shape into a perfect rectangle which he tossed on to the scales where it weighed an exact eight ounces.

There was no sign of Danny so I stepped out into the street where, once again, I was almost swept off my feet by the mass of humanity now surging down the Overgate. I overheard another snippet as I was swept along. 'It's a march against unemployment and the Workers' Movement want as many folk as possible to show up.' I was suddenly worried about Dad. Most of the men I knew, including Dad and his friends, all supported the National Unemployed Workers' Movement. It now looked as if the entire population of Dundee was on the move and converging on the town centre.

By the time I reached the foot of Reform Street, a huge procession of people marching four abreast was heading towards me. As they passed by, they were joined by a fringe of onlookers. A motley collection of women, children and old men tagged along at their rear – whether from sympathy or curiosity it was hard to tell.

I scanned the faces as they swam in front of me like a vast human sea but I didn't see Dad. This was not surprising because, in the general noisy hubbub, it was difficult to see everyone. The fact that they were singing didn't help the noise levels and the street was a seething mass of people.

Then Danny suddenly appeared. He was cycling at the rear of the ragtag hangers-on who were not exactly marching – jumping along was a better description. I stepped out and waved a frantic hand at him. The bike's wheels squealed to a sudden halt on the litter-strewn road. 'I've been looking for you,' he shouted as he quickly manoeuvred his bike between groups of gawking bystanders. 'Granny has just heard about the march and you've got to come home right away.'

I saw that he still had a few packages in his basket. Granny had obviously collared him on his round. 'I've got to see Dad. I think he might be on this march.' I was worried and it showed because a new cry was ringing around the hundreds of spectators.

'The bobbies are coming and they're on horses!' screamed one disembodied voice from the crowd. This remark echoed around the street and, in their panic, people began to run in the opposite direction from the policemen. I knew there had been a lot of unrest over the plight of the jobless and all the poverty that was attached to being out of work and, although a few demonstrations had taken place, this one seemed to be different. It had a feel of desperation which was noticeable in the marchers' faces and now the mention of the police seemed to stoke up this feeling.

We watched in amazement as the crowds surged forwards and we knew we were in danger of being swept along by the crushing hordes. Although the marchers had been peaceful, even singing as they marched along, the mood was now an ugly one. It was as if people's patience had finally run out and all the frustration of deprivation and poverty was now about to explode between the law and the people and the sweating horses.

Danny, afraid that his packages might be looted or damaged, managed to extricate the bike from the mass of bodies. He also grabbed me around my waist. We squeezed ourselves against the wall for a few moments before gingerly edging our way up the street, a few yards at a time. By the time we reached the High School, the crowds had thinned out considerably. A few onlookers stood around, craning their necks in a bid to witness the action while remaining on the fringe – to taste the excitement without the dangers.

Danny stopped when we were clear of the

crowds. 'Now stay here till I deliver these messages to Barrack Street and then I'll come back and we'll go and find your dad.'

I didn't want him to get into any trouble with his job. The manager might take a dim view of his delivery boy slinking away early.

Before I could protest, he said, 'I'll nip into the shop and tell them about this melee and how it's no' easy to deliver anything in this pandemonium. Maybe he'll let me work later – after it's all over.'

He was back within half an hour. 'Mr Gould, the manager, has given me an hour off.'

We hurried up Meadowside, intent on reaching the house safely. As we rounded the corner to the foot of the Hilltown, we couldn't believe our eyes. Hundreds of people were milling around in an angry throng like a swarm of disgruntled bees. The mounted police were also there and some had their batons drawn. The entire area was like some war zone. It was a real fight between the bobbies and the mass of bodies now scurrying in all directions and screaming at the top of their voices as they ran.

To make matters worse, residents who lived in the upstairs houses were either viewing the riot or actively encouraging it. The ones who were alarmed by the dramatic panorama under their noses kept strictly behind the protection of the glass but the hardier souls were hanging out and throwing the odd missile on to the heads of the law.

Three burly policemen were trying to push a crowd of angry youths against a wall but, as soon as they succeeded with one group, another surge of humanity erupted elsewhere. The crowd ran round the horses and the police wagons. The sound of the horses' hooves against the pavement was terrifying but, above this noise, the shouts of neighbourly comradeship could be heard being hurled down towards the heads of the protesters and these grew louder and angrier whenever they could see demonstrators being herded into the police wagon and taken in to custody.

'What a bloody noise you bobbies are making. No' to mention your snorting horses,' shouted one elderly woman whose thin wrinkled face was minus any teeth. She shook a blue-veined feeble arm into the air. 'But never you mind, lads – just give them hell.'

From our vantage point on the edge of the riot we were unable to see if Dad or any of our neighbours were involved and it looked as if we would have to run the gauntlet of the fighting mob. I was scared – not for myself but for Danny because the policemen seemed to be collaring all the young men, regardless of the fact that many of them had been minding their own business and had merely been caught up by accident.

Frightened, howling young children were frantically holding on to their parents but the older braver ones were throwing stones at the horses. They then darted away like thin wraiths into the warren of tenements.

'We're never going to get past that crowd,' I shouted to Danny. 'Maybe I'll be better on my own.'

He shook his head. 'Granny will skin me alive if I leave you here. No, we'll take a shortcut.'

He grabbed my hand and we raced along Dudhope Street. When we reached Dallfield Walk, we skirted around the many washing lines in the back courts to emerge at Shepherd's Pend. This detour brought us out at the Progress Hall and above the riot. The noise was still as deafening but at least our way wasn't obstructed by shying horses and irate bobbies.

Just a few steps from our close, we were appalled to see a human bundle lying against the wall. With a feeling of fright and apprehension, we lifted the coat lapel which was obscuring the face.

'Oh, it's old Mrs Dodds and she's been hit on the head.' I pointed to a two-inch gash above her eye. 'She must have been injured in the riot.'

She lived a few yards from us on the Hilltown and Danny picked her up in an effortless manner while I put an arm around her waist. Fortunately she was a small wiry-framed woman so it wasn't too difficult to make our way slowly towards her house.

Suddenly Rita appeared and I was so grateful to see her. I ran ahead, leaving Danny with the injured woman. I almost bowled them over in my haste.

'We found her lying on the street and we think she's been hit in the riot.'

Rita summed up the situation. 'Better bring her up to my house and we'll have a look at her.'

We slowly made our way up the stairs but before we reached the flat, the old woman groaned and Danny lowered her on to the shabby linoleum-covered lobby. She groaned again, her eyes trying to focus on her small audience.

As Rita knelt down beside her, a loud bellow erupted from the direction of her flat, accompanied by the piercing cries of a child. The man bellowed again. 'For heaven's sake, Rita, will you come in and see to this child or we'll all be deafened.'

She ignored this summons and inspected the woman's cut. 'Oh, it's just a wee graze you have there, Mrs Dodds. How did it happen? Did you get mixed up in the riot?'

Mrs Dodds looked at her with a puzzled frown. 'No, no, lass, I was in the snug bar of the Windmill Bar and I think I had too much stout to drink.' She laughed feebly, showing a row of discoloured teeth. 'What riot are you talking about?'

Rita sounded incredulous. 'Do you mean to tell me that you don't know about the fighting at the foot of the street? The noise alone would waken the dead, never mind the living for that matter.' She pointed behind her where husband and son were now competing for the highest decibel prize. 'Oh, I expect I'd better get in there and calm things down. What a day it's been and what a world. No money and no pleasure in life – just a nagging man to contend with day in and day out.'

Mrs Dodds, who didn't seem too perturbed at missing all the drama, said, 'I was too busy supping my stout in the snug to hear any fighting but, when I got outside, I felt real queer-like and my legs wouldn't hold me up.' She turned to Danny. 'Maybe this handsome young man will see me home. If it's no bother, that is?'

'Mind and give that cut a wee wash,' shouted

Rita as Danny retreated down the stairs with his burden. 'Imagine that old codger. I aye knew she liked her stout but no' as much as would make her legless,' she laughed. Nellie, who had also witnessed this small drama, smiled too.

I didn't comment because I didn't really know the woman that well and I had problems of my own. 'I'm looking for Dad, Rita. Have you seen him?'

Before Rita could answer, Nellie piped up, saying, 'Aye, he's on the march with Joe and the gang.' Nellie looked harassed as the wailing cries of Rita's child echoed in the narrow confines of the lobby. 'If it's no' one thing, it's another.' She sounded fed up. 'I tried to run down to the chip shop for five Woodbines but it's an absolute madhouse out there. But his majesty, my man, will be looking for his fags when he gets back, will he not?'

'Did Dad say when the march will be over?'

She shook her head. 'To be honest with you, Ann, Rita and me don't see your dad often, especially lately – although we've offered to help him out. He says he's managing.'

I bit my lip, unsure what to do.

Nellie continued, 'This march is a protest against unemployment and now it seems our dole money is going to be cut and we're all to be subjected to this awful means test. My Wullie is on the march and I'm hoping he's all right as well. Rita's man wasn't well so she put her foot down at him going. That's why he's like a bear with a sore head.'

Rita appeared and nodded. 'Oh, aye, it's obviously better being out with your pals, shouting and singing and chucking insults at the police.'

'Aye, you're right, Rita. Wait till my man gets back and finds I didn't get his five Woodbines – all hell will be let loose.' She turned wearily towards her house then stopped. 'Heavens, I didn't ask how wee Lily is. I hope she's fine.'

I assured them that all was well with the baby. After the two women had gone I decided to wait for Dad in the house. There was no need for a key because no one ever bothered to lock their doors.

As I stood on the threshold, I almost burst into tears at the sight of the neglected and untidy room. The bed looked as if it had never been made since my last visit. The bedclothes lay in a heap, some on the bed and the rest on the floor, and not only that – they looked grubby.

Grey ashes had built up in the grate before finally spilling out in a lifeless eruption on to the tin fender. Some had even landed on the little colourful rag rug that Mum had lovingly made one winter from a pile of jumble sale rags. Dad's boots had trodden cinders into the fabric, making the colours appear subdued under this ashy cover.

A thick layer of dust lay along the mantelpiece, covering the few cheap and cheerful ornaments that had also been Mum's pride and joy. The wooden kitchen table was minus its oilcloth. There was a stale loaf of bread, a packet of margarine with a knife still sticking in its yellow surface and an almost-empty bottle with an inch of milk at the bottom of it that had long since gone sour and congealed.

The sugar bowl lay on its side, a trail of silver crystals decorating the rough table top in a haphazard pattern before mingling with a dried-up pool of tea stains. Beside this was a brown-stained cup with a thick sugary film clinging to the sides while brown tea drips formed a pattern on the outside. A small teapot lay on the unlit gas ring, holding in its depths something that resembled a petrified fossil.

'Oh, Dad, how could you end up like this?' I thought aloud. 'Mum kept this room like a wee palace.'

Danny appeared back and his eyes opened in amazement. I held up my hand. 'Not a word to Granny about this but can you help me clean it up?'

He cleared the table, throwing the milk down the sink and putting the margarine in the cupboard while I stripped and remade the bed. Finally I filled a bucket with several scoops of ashes and carried it down to the midden in the courtyard.

When I got back Danny was whistling cheerfully. 'Your dad's going to wonder who did all this cleaning for him,' he said, running a rag over the dusty surfaces. 'Now I'm not leaving you here so hurry up – I've to get back to work.'

I was busy laying the fire, placing the kindling crosswise over screwed-up paper. I then picked up the dirty sheets and, with a quick backward glance, we left. Dad had still not returned.

I was feeling so sad as we headed back for the Overgate, retracing our steps through the short-cut because the crowds were still surging around the bottom of the Hilltown. Although the noise had subsided slightly, the racket was still going on. It was the same scene at Albert Square, which had been the venue for the start of the march. There was still a multitude of people and some of the injured were being ferried away. We saw one policeman with two young men, both of whom had blood streaming down their faces.

'Better get them to the Dundee Royal Infirmary,' said a voice from the crowd.

'This was a peaceful march till you lot waded in,' shouted another angry disembodied voice from the heaving mass.

There were groups of tearful women with distressed children. Tearful streaks running down their dirty faces gave them a two-toned striped look.

'You would be better off taking your kids home than have them howling here,' suggested one policeman.

This was met with enraged shouts. 'Take the kids home, did you say? And what happens when we get there. We get cut off from the dole and maybe even the parish relief. What do we feed them on? You tell us. Aye, we'll take them away – take them home to starve.'

The policeman retreated to the far edge of the crowd. He obviously didn't have the answer to that tragic thorny question.

I was still agitated. 'Danny, promise me you'll no' say a word about the state of the house. It'll just worry Granny and she's got enough of that on her plate at the moment. No, I'll just have to look hard for a job then I'll be able to look after Lily and Dad.'

Granny was relieved to see us – so relieved that

she didn't notice the sheets. 'My, I'm glad to see you both. What a night it's been. Some windows in the Westport have been broken and the rumour is that the communists are behind it. Personally I don't believe that. The Establishment will need a scapegoat because they'll not want the riot to be their fault. No, siree.' She suddenly spotted the bundle. 'What's that?'

I looked nonchalantly at them as if seeing them for the first time. I tried to sound unruffled. 'Oh, these? I decided to change the bed for Dad and I'll wash the sheets along with our washing at the steamie.'

She looked disapprovingly at me. 'Your dad will not be pleased. We've all tried to help him but he's that thrawn at times and he says he wants to think things out for himself.'

'I'm no' working out his problems for him, granny – just changing the sheets.'

It was important to keep the secret from her. If she saw how Dad was now living, she would be round to the Hilltown in a flash, packing his things and removing him to her caring and orderly domain.

Although I didn't say it, my plans included a quick visit every week to keep an eye on Dad and on the house.

4

Granny always said Hattie had a lucky streak. She was the kind of person who, should she fall out a window, would go straight to heaven without the initial impact of hitting the pavement.

But that wasn't really true. The one time her good luck deserted her was when her husband Pat died, leaving her a widowed mother at twenty-five. She met Pat during the summer of 1913, a year before the Great War started. Instead of going into one of the numerous jute mills like most of her contemporaries, the fourteen-year-old Hattie had gone into service as a housemaid in a large house near Glamis. Pat had been on a day's hike with a Lochee walking club. The men had stopped for a refreshing drink from a water fountain in the street and he saw Hattie coming out of a shop. When their eyes met, they were both smitten and it was love at first sight. At least that was the story according to Hattie but I always thought it was so romantic.

After a quick courtship they were married. In 1915, two weeks after Pat had left for France, Danny was born. Pat didn't see his wife or son until he was posted out of the army in 1917.

I could well remember Bella going on about it in her usual garrulous manner. 'Oh, he was a poor soul. He lost all his toes on his right foot in a shell blast,' she said, scrutinising her own feet with a sharp glance to make sure her own toes were still intact. 'Well, he got sent back home but, one Sunday morning, after a visit to his family in Lochee, he got killed by a tramcar – fell right in front of it.'

Granny had tried to hush her up but Bella was the kind of person who spoke first and thought about it later. 'Now just keep quiet, Bella. Don't rake it all up again – especially in front of Danny. Hattie has done a good job bringing him up and she's aye had to work hard.'

Bella was unabashed. 'Still, she aye seems to land on her feet. She got a few quid from her man's insurance policy and she has the money to make her house bonny – it's real palace, her flat in Westport. And now she's got another cushy job in another fancy big house.'

Bella sounded jealous of the fact that Hattie was getting on in her life. Granny suspected that Bella would have liked to see Hattie descend the social scale rapidly but, instead, Hattie was climbing the ladder slowly, rung by rung.

Even at Mum's funeral, Bella had been harping on about Hattie. 'I see Mrs Hoity-Toity has landed herself another fancy job – no dole money for her or even working in a dirty jute mill.'

Actually this statement was untrue because her job as housekeeper to an old lady in Forfar Road had been terminated due to her employer's death. That had been over a year ago and Hattie had been doing odd jobs here and there. Then, with her special brand of luck, fate and providence had stepped in – or, to be more accurate, had fallen in.

While out for a walk one cold winter's day in Perth Road, when the pavements were a lethal mixture of ice and snow, she came across a woman in distress. Mrs Pringle had slipped on the ice and was in considerable pain with a sprained ankle. Hattie had escorted the woman home and called a doctor. This was all done with a combination of skill and cheerfulness, assets that hadn't gone unnoticed at the time, and the rest was history. Hattie had landed on her feet again with a job as housekeeper-companion to the Pringle family.

The strange thing was that, like Mum, Mrs Pringle was also in her forties and expecting another baby. Having Hattie around was a blessing for her as they didn't employ any servants.

Hattie did a few light household chores, made a meal for Maddie on her return from school and generally kept Mrs Pringle company until her husband returned home from his solicitors' firm in the early evening. Another important fact was that she was treated as a member of the family instead of the hired help and that, in Hattie's estimation, was worth much more than money.

'I get a good wage but what I like best is they never have a snobby attitude or take sides,' she said.

This statement incensed Bella even more. 'I sometimes see her when I'm carrying my messages up the street.' She gave Granny a ferocious scowl. 'She swaggers towards me, dressed like the lady of the manor, but does she offer to help me? Does she thump.'

Granny was fed up hearing Bella's moans. 'Well, Bella, you should get your messages delivered from Lipton's and Danny will bring them on his message bike. And another thing, Hattie is my lassie and I'll not have you running her down. We think she keeps herself really smart. Especially when she wears her bonny blue frock with the dropped waistline. It goes really well her dark Eton crop hairstyle. She looks like Ann.'

I was appalled. I hated my short dark hair, longing instead to have lovely long golden ringlets. But I had to admit silently that my hair was the least of my worries just now. I was still without a job and another thorn in my flesh was the non-appearance of Dad. Every time I called at the flat in the Hilltown, he was out and I was even beginning to suspect that Rita and Nellie were just as evasive. But maybe I was just being daft.

The flat kept slipping back to its original untidiness and, although I did make attempts to keep some sort of order, I finally gave up. As it was, we had enough worries to think about. Lily was teething and every night was a trial with her noisy bouts of crying. Twin red spots appeared on her smooth cheeks and she looked distressed and wet-eyed.

One morning, after a particularly fractious night, I was sent to the chemist. 'Get a packet of Seidlitz powders for the baby's sore gums,' said Granny.

These powders helped slightly but we started to take it in turn to get up through the night with her. All through this demanding time, I was thankful not to be working because I doubt if I could have got up in time for work in the morning after such disturbed nights. It was lovely to lie in bed in my tiny cupboard after a spell of night duty and listen to Granny as she stirred the large pot of porridge, its aroma wafting through the cracks in the door.

Although the year was almost over and the weather was bitterly cold, Grandad still took Lily for her daily walk in the old dilapidated pram. She loved those trips and Grandad never stopped telling us how much she adored her pram. Not like Hattie – on seeing the pram for the first time, she had threatened to boycott the entire family such was her humiliation at being associated with it, albeit at a distance. In fact, she had almost fainted at the time. This was followed by a strangled cry when she was told where it had been bought. She had stepped smartly backwards as if it would contaminate her, a look of disgust on her handsome, refined face. Still, she had come round in time. Not that she was reconciled to it – no, it was more the solemn promise extracted from Grandad that he would keep well away from the Perth Road with it.

One day, she produced some of Joy's cast-off clothes but, because of the difference in size, nothing fitted Lily except for a lovely knitted yellow pram suit with a matching pixie hood. This had been a present from a relative who had obviously never set eyes on the dainty Joy – hence the fact that it fitted our Lily. Sitting propped up against a thick cushion, she looked like a bright sunbeam in her pram and lots of people stopped to comment on her prettiness – compliments with pleased Grandad immensely. 'Folk aye stop me when I'm out with the baby and nobody ever mentions the scruffy pram.' This was obviously

78

aimed at Granny. He remembered her initial response and Hattie's look of horror.

A few days before Hogmanay, Hattie appeared at the house, a deep frown on her face. 'Mrs Pringle wants me to bring Ann and Lily out to her house for a visit.' She made it sound like a royal command. 'She wants to have a chat with Ann.' The frown deepened as she gazed at me with her dark eyes that were seemingly so like my own.

I was alarmed. 'What does she want me for?'

Hattie screwed up her face. 'I don't know, do I? She gave me this lovely little frock for Lily.' She held up a lovely confection of a dress, all ribbons, rosettes and frills but far too small for our bouncing baby.

Granny looked doubtful. 'It'll not fit her, Hattie. We've told you before that Lily is far bigger than Joy.' She sounded as if my sister was some gigantic wrestler. She held the frothy garment in her gnarled, callused hands. 'Still it's really bonny and maybe I can let it out a bit.'

Hattie turned a haughty eye on Grandad. 'Another thing – I'm not pushing Lily in that monstrosity.' She pointed to his pride and joy.

'What? Not take the pram?' He was affronted. 'Lily loves her pram and she'll cry if she doesn't get her hurl in it.' He retreated to his chair in the corner and sat down with his back to Hattie.

'Well, that may be so but she's not going in it with me,' said Hattie, a steely determined note in her voice, 'even if it means that I have to carry her.'

She turned to me. 'Now, Ann, make sure your hands and face are washed. Oh and make extra sure that there's no dirt under your fingernails. I always think that looks common.'

Up till this point, Granny had stayed silent but now she was highly annoyed at Hattie and set about her in a fierce voice. 'Now you look here, Hattie. You come marching in here with your commands and your dos and don'ts – well, let me remind you that we keep a clean house here and Ann's hands, nails and face are aye spotless.' She stormed over to the sink. 'We maybe live in the Overgate and not the Perth Road but we're no' tinks.'

Grandad nodded in approval as Hattie's cheeks burned bright red but she had the grace to apologise. 'I didn't mean it like that,' she stuttered before dashing out through the door.

I thought that, if she had a tail, it would have slunk between her legs as she departed. Granny, as usual, had brought her down to earth with a bump.

Meanwhile Grandad was still smarting from the slur on his pram. He muttered darkly, 'I'm beginning to think that Bella is maybe right about that lassie being a snob.' He added quickly, 'Mind you I would never tell her that.' We all knew that he never saw eye to eye with Bella.

By two o'clock the following day, we were ready and waiting for Hattie, both of us scrubbed to within an inch of our life and wearing our best clothes. Mainly because I wasn't given any handouts from the Pringle family, I was wearing a white blouse, a dark woollen skirt and a cardigan in a rotten shade of olive green. I felt frumpish in this and I knew I resembled some middle-aged matron because the cardigan had come from

Alice next door who, unfortunately, was my size.

But, if I looked terrible, at least Lily resembled a pink cherub in her frothy frock. Granny had managed to let out the seams and the only thing that wouldn't fasten was the tiny pearl button at the neck. Lily had almost choked when we tried to fasten it.

Granny warned me, 'Now never mind Hattie – mind and leave the neck open, Ann. Hattie is not to touch it and just never heed her if she starts moaning about it hanging open. She would sooner let the baby choke than show herself up in front of the Pringles.'

I promised, hoping and praying that the visit would be a short one. I just knew I would look out of place amongst a load of toffs. The only saving feature in the entire fiasco was the fact that Danny would be there as well. He always went to see his relations in Lochee every Sunday but he was coming along later in the afternoon – hopefully in time to rescue me.

Before leaving, I asked Granny what Mrs Pringle and Maddie were like but she just shook her head.

'No idea, Ann. I just saw Mr Pringle at your mum's funeral but I've never met any of the family. Still, to listen to Hattie, you would think they're royalty so maybe they are snobby. You can tell me all about it when you get back.'

She then turned her attention to the large pile of ironing, a job I usually did when I wasn't socialising with the rich and snobby. She heated the flat iron on the gas jet before tackling the wrinkled garments.

81

We set off on our visit with Hattie holding Lily in her arms. With her yellow coat over her pink frock and a multi-coloured crochet blanket around her legs, Lily looked like a little rainbow. And me ... well, I looked drab and shabby in my old school trench coat.

As we left the high tenements and grubby narrow streets behind us, the houses became more prosperous and spacious with their well-tended gardens and high, multi-paned and richly curtained windows. On a sunny day, these windows would no doubt gleam but on this cold drizzly day they reflected only greyness.

Even the river, which I could glimpse between the houses, echoed this dismal monotone. A chill wind rose from the water and moaned through the leafless trees that stood like silent sentinels guarding pavements and gardens alike. Everything looked dreary on this chilly dismal day except Lily in her bright outfit. She kept twisting her tiny face around as if the scenery was familiar to her – movements that Hattie had also noticed. She muttered darkly, 'I just hope Dad hasn't pushed that pram out here. Even though I warned him, I wouldn't put anything past him.'

I tried hard not to smile and remained silent, knowing for a fact that Grandad regularly pushed Lily out this way. I thought Hattie was making a fuss over nothing. After the noise and bustle of the Overgate which even the Sabbath failed to quieten, the street here was quiet – so quiet, in fact, that the sound of Hattie's tapping heels echoed against the pavement. A pungent smell of the sea lay in the dank, miserable air.

I was unsure about the cathedral-like hush of these lovely houses, each standing alone in their section of landscaped garden. I think I much preferred the Overgate. The Salvation Army had been playing at the end of Tay Street. Standing in a circle, they had been singing their rousing hymns. Rosie was there. She looked downright miserable as I passed by and I felt so sorry for her. Perhaps, like me, she had also been looking for Dad – obviously with the same joyless results as myself.

Children danced around the circle, dressed unsuitably for the cold weather. The small boys were in short trousers, their red raw and skinned knees contrasting sharply with thin white legs. Some of the girls wore thin shabby coats but the majority were dressed in well-darned jumpers pulled over tatty-looking skirts or, in a couple of cases, thin cotton dresses. But they all looked happy with their faces beaming at the music while a few of the girls joined in the singing. In fact, the only miserable face was Rosie's. I couldn't imagine this human tableau taking place in this hushed street with its smell of the river and stark trees. I should think the merest whisper would echo like a deafening bell in the church-like silence.

'We're almost there,' said Hattie, a look of relief on her face. 'I never realised Lily was as heavy as this.' She shifted the child to her other arm.

When we reached the house I was struck dumb by its impressive appearance. There was a high stone wall guarding it from prying eyes and only the top windows were visible – lovely large shining windows under an expanse of red roof tiles.

We entered through a tall wrought-iron gate that

led on to a wide, sweeping gravel drive that sloped downwards. Lights glowed in the downstairs windows, casting soft patches of golden light on to the drive. For a brief moment, I was mesmerised – it was the most beautiful house I had ever seen.

Hattie whispered loudly as we entered, 'Make sure you wipe your feet properly – Mrs Pringle has lovely carpets and I don't want mud all over them.'

With Hattie's commands and my plain outfit, I felt like a six-year-old. We were all used to her enthusing over her job and how it had appeared like manna from heaven but I was quaking at the thought of the imminent meeting. I had no idea what to expect. In my mind, these Pringles were on the same plane as royalty. How well I recalled the picture of a fiercely frowning Queen Victoria in one of my school books. As for the present Queen Mary ... well, she looked as approachable as a stone statue.

Hattie hung my coat up in the small, red tiled hall. She called it the vestibule but it was larger and far superior to the cupboard I called my bedroom. We were then ushered quickly through a large, quiet hall and into the lounge – another new word in my vocabulary. Many years later I was always able to recall my first sight of it and how I had been rendered speechless by the warmth and elegance. A large bay window took up almost the far away wall and I was enchanted by the panoramic view of a wide grassy lawn that swept towards the steely grey river, now flecked with angry, white-tipped waves. Away to the left, just visible, was the iron-spanned Tay Bridge and tiny pinpoints of light shone like gem stones on the far shores of Wormit and Newport.

Although it was barely mid afternoon and not yet dark, three lamps were lit in this grand room. Their deep pink shades with heavily beaded fringes cast a soft glow on the deep rose coloured carpet. Comfy chairs and sofas covered in subdued flowery covers were grouped around the large stone fireplace in which a glowing fire burned bright. Yet, in my opinion, the best thing in the room had to be the electric light. No hissing and spurting gaslamps here and no panic buying of another gas mantle when the old one was so broken that it resembled the long blue flame of a workman's blowtorch.

Suddenly realising that I was standing with my mouth open, I quickly closed it – much to the amusement of a girl who was sitting on a low stool, a large book on her lap. My heart sank as I realised this must be Maddie. She wasn't very tall but she had a slender, fragile beauty with her golden hair and deep blue eyes. She reminded me of Tinkerbell, the tiny fairy in Peter Pan – minus, of course, the wings and bell.

So taken was I with the lovely room and equally lovely occupant that I almost jumped when a voice called from one of the deep armchairs. It was Mrs Pringle.

'Hello, Ann and Lily, I'm so pleased to meet you at last – all the Sunday girls together.'

Lily – I had forgotten all about her but she was being held by Hattie and she was equally fascinated by the lovely room.

Mrs Pringle sat beside a wicker bassinet on a

85

stand. Inside lay a tiny carbon copy of Maddie – her baby sister, Joy. I looked at the woman with uncertainty, trying to mind my manners but unsure amid all this grandeur. To my relief, she didn't look the least bit fierce – not in the way Bella always painted a toff. She was a small, plump woman with a pink complexion and a serene expression. Her dark hair, streaked with some grey, was set in waves so close to her head that they resembled a rigid plaster cast. Hattie said afterwards that this style was a Marcelle wave, done by some posh hairdresser in town and not only fashionable but expensive.

'Come and sit beside me, Ann,' said Mrs Pringle, holding out her hand. 'Let me hold Lily.'

She took the baby on her lap and Lily immediately wrapped her tiny fist around the pearl necklace that lay like an expensive bauble around the neck of an equally expensive-looking jumper. Hattie told me afterwards that it was made from cashmere.

I sat on the edge of my seat. I was frightened the necklace would get broken but Mrs Pringle seemed oblivious to this danger.

'You are a lovely big girl, aren't you?' she said. 'Not like my little Joy.'

Maddie, meanwhile, looked at me with her large blue eyes.

'Is Danny coming today?'

Hattie appeared with a loaded tea tray. She answered for me. 'He'll be here later.'

She handed me a cup of tea with a stern glance that warned me not to let her down with any uncouth behaviour. The cup was delicate and made from extremely thin china and I was almost afraid to lift it from the saucer. Compared to our cups at home, which were thick and serviceable, this china looked as durable as an eggshell. Coping with the plate and the knife, not to mention the sandwich, the scone, the butter and the serviette – another new word – was extremely difficult.

There was also the sugar bowl and the milk jug, plus a pot with hot water and a large oval plate with dainty cakes. No wonder, I thought, that this house needed a housekeeper. Hattie must spend all day just washing up the dishes.

Still the thought of describing all this grandeur to Granny later cheered me up – as did the sight of Danny passing the window.

Maddie jumped up, almost knocking my scone into the cup of tea as she darted towards the door.

Her mother looked amused. 'Danny's her boy-friend.'

I almost choked on a piece of scone and she was concerned. 'I do hope you haven't found a stone in your jam.'

I assured her all was well although I didn't add that I hadn't got round to the jam at that point, such was the disconcerting choice in front of me. I wished the floor would open up and swallow me whole.

Danny bounced in with Maddie. Seeing them together made me feel miserable but I realised I couldn't keep him all to myself as I had done all through my childhood.

Mrs Pringle turned towards them with a smile. 'I'm just saying to your mother, Danny, that I've managed at last to get all the Sunday girls together.' She looked at me. 'I would have done it sooner but I haven't been well since Joy's birth.' Her face clouded over. 'Of course I've been lucky, Ann. Not like your poor mother and we all sympathise with your family. I've been so lucky to have Hattie here to help me – she's been such a boon and a blessing.'

Maddie began to pirouette around the room like some lovely fragile Christmas fairy. 'The child that is born on the Sabbath day is blithe and bonny and good and gay,' she chanted.

Well maybe you are, I thought darkly, but some of us are not so lucky.

A sharp cry came from the bassinet. Joy was awake. Hattie lifted her on to her lap where she sat in her spotless frilly frock which looked pristine and new and I noticed she wore delicate little fabric shoes.

Lily, on the other hand, was showing her upbringing by cheerfully chewing on a dry rusk. Large streaks of rusk mixed with saliva dripped from her chin and landed in thick globules down the open neck of her second-hand frock.

I laid down all the accoutrements of the tea party and walked over to Lily, the paper serviette in my hand, ready to wipe the slavers away.

Mrs Pringle smiled and held up her hand. 'Just leave her to enjoy her rusk, Ann.' She gazed fondly over to Joy. 'Lily has such a healthy appetite and I wish Joy would eat as well as this.'

'She's just a different type and build,' said Hattie before I could answer for this huge child who was my sister. 'Perhaps it's just her nature to be a good eater.'

Mrs Pringle smiled. 'Of course you are right, Hattie. Maddie was the same picky eater when she was young.'

I glanced over at the golden girl and she returned my inquisitive look with such a cheeky, friendly grin that I found myself, much against my will, liking her.

'Play us a nice song on the piano, Maddie,' said her mother. 'Something nice and tuneful.'

Maddie moved over to the grand mahogany piano and proceeded to rifle through a huge pile of sheet music which lay in tidy isolation in the equally grand piano stool.

'Here's something tuneful,' she said, placing her elegant fingers on the keys. 'Horsey, keep your tail up, keep your tail up,' she sang in a clear soprano while her fingers played the melody in a jazzed-up version of the original tune.

Mrs Pringle shook her head. 'When I said something tuneful I meant a lovely melody like Brahms' "Lullaby" or something similar, not that dreadful racket.'

Maddie ignored her and proceeded to the end of the song, her voice growing louder as she reached the last few notes. Then, with a final flourish, she swung round on the stool and began to applaud herself, giving me another lopsided grin. Suddenly I knew beyond any doubt that I liked this golden girl. She had such a good sense of humour and wasn't afraid to laugh at herself. We were indeed the four Sunday girls.

Hattie began to gather up the plates and cups, placing them on a large tray. I made a move to help her but Mrs Pringle stopped me.

'No, Ann, I want a word with you – Maddie and Danny can help with the washing-up.'

Danny gave me a quizzical look as he departed.

After they left, Mrs Pringle said, 'Hattie tells me you haven't been able to get a job, Ann.'

I nodded.

'I was hoping Mr Pringle would be here today but he had an urgent meeting in Glasgow. Anyway, we want you to know that he is still looking for a job for your father as he promised he would. But that isn't the reason for this meeting, Ann.' She stopped and gazed at me with pale blue eyes that looked soft and slightly out of focus in the soft lamplight.

Meanwhile I sat in silence, waiting for her to continue.

'I know of a job that's vacant, Ann,' she said. 'It's similar to Hattie's job here. A very dear old friend of mine lives in Broughty Ferry and, although she has a live-in housekeeper and a cook who comes in on a daily basis, what she needs now is a young pair of hands around the house and we thought it might suit you.'

I was taken aback and took a full minute to answer. 'It's very kind of you both, Mrs Pringle but what I'm looking for is a job I can get back home from every night. Granny needs a lot of help with Lily.' Quite honestly, I couldn't imagine Granny coping with all the hard physical work on her own. Even with my considerable help, she was always tired-out at night with all the extra workload of a baby.

Mrs Pringle nodded. 'I understand and I've discussed this with Eva – Mrs Barrie, the woman you would be working for. Now Eva will give you a Sunday and Monday off each week so perhaps you can look after Lily on those days and give your grandparents a rest. Then maybe your father can help out as well.'

I didn't mention that Dad was never at home these days. In fact he had become invisible during the past weeks but hopefully I would see him on my next visit to the Hilltown.

Mrs Pringle was still talking and I heard the chink of crockery and Maddie's laugh coming from the kitchen.

'Go home and think about this job, Ann, then go and see Mrs Barrie. Make up your mind if it's suitable or not.' She leaned towards me. 'Another thing you must consider is this terrible means test. If you do live at home and have a job then whatever you earn will be deducted from any benefits that come into your house. Now that may not count in the case of your grandparents but it will certainly count should you go back and live with your father.'

I knew she was speaking the truth because everyone was up in arms over this new law that would see thousands of people being cut off from their unemployment benefit.

I made up my mind. 'I'll go and see Mrs Barrie. Thank you for thinking of me for this job,' I said. There was something else I wanted to explain. 'Mrs Pringle, I hope you don't think I'm frightened of work because I haven't shown a great deal of interest in this job. It's just that it's a heavy task looking after Lily and it should be me who shoulders it – not my grandparents.' I couldn't

91

stop thinking how tired they had been these last few weeks with the sleepless nights due to Lily's teething problems.

She looked taken aback and patted my arm. 'I don't think that for a moment, Ann. In fact, we all think you are a very clever and brave girl.'

Well, that was it, I thought, a job – just what I had been praying for.

Mrs Pringle wrote down the address on a card, using a very elegant gold fountain pen. 'This job will bring some much-needed money into your home and then, when your father has a job as well, you can maybe look for something nearer home because the means test won't apply to you then.'

This terrible new law, the means test, had come into force in November and it was playing havoc with people's lives. Folk were being denied un-employment money and were having to apply for parish relief or transitional benefit to give it its proper title. The parish relief was now under the auspices of a certain Mr Bobby Allen and his staff were turning people away in their droves every day with no relief and no money. The vic-tims of the new system were mostly the women who had worked in the jute mills and who were now on the breadline. Danny said that three of his aunts in Lochee who had previously worked in Cox's mill were now jobless and without money coming into the house.

Another unfair barb in this law related to any occupant in the house lucky enough to be in a job. Their wage was then deemed to be enough to keep an entire family so that no parish relief or dole money were forthcoming. In cases like these, it was better if the worker lived elsewhere in lodgings. This terrible law was afflicting the poorer sections of the population, leaving them almost destitute as well as breaking up families – all to save money – and it was being done with a great deal of pride. The unemployment office and the jute mills were even going as far as publishing a weekly total of savings in the local newspaper. And, no doubt, it was all done by Christian men and women who faithfully attended church every Sunday and prayed for the poor wee black boys in Africa – never mind the poor people who once worked for them. Because of this law, I could see that Mrs Pringle's offer was a good one but only if Granny felt she could cope on her own with Lily while I was away.

Then it was time to go home. As we left the house, Maddie ran after us. 'Can I visit you some time, Ann? I would like us to be friends.'

I smiled. 'That would be grand, Maddie. The only thing is your mother has offered me a job in the Ferry so I'll only be at home two days a week. Maybe you could visit us then?'

Although I was genuine in my offer, I was a bit perplexed by her request. Surely, I thought, she would have dozens of pals at her school, the Harris Academy, or even friends from the Perth Road.

'Right then,' she said, 'I'll look forward to seeing you soon.'

She stood waving at the gate until we were almost out of sight. Darkness had fallen and the pale glow from the street gas lamp seemed to subdue her bright golden hair and turn it into a wash of soft silver. She looked ethereal – like a spirit of the night.

It seemed as if the means test had taken over the entire day because Danny began to lament on its injustices. 'It's a terrible thing. Kit, Lizzie and Belle have all been cut off from the dole office and are no' getting any money. Although their men get something, it's no' enough to live on. This government should be ashamed of themselves. Men who fought and died in the war – what becomes of their families? No work and now no money. Barely enough for a pauper to live on, never mind a family.'

Hattie snorted. 'Well, I think your aunts are to blame. If they really wanted a job, then they would find one. Look at me – I've never been stuck for work, have I?'

She stopped and looked at her son. 'I do hope you're not becoming one of those communists that's been organising all the riots.'

Danny loved his mother but, unlike her, he had a social conscience. He gazed at her with surprise. 'Well, I'm not a communist but, if I thought they could help the poor and unemployed, then I would gladly join.'

Hattie's face turned purple. For a moment she was speechless but then she suddenly laughed nervously. 'Oh, you're kidding me on, you cheeky devil!'

Danny gave me a wordless look but I just shrugged my shoulders. Hattie was just Hattie and nothing would ever change that.

'Danny, Mrs Pringle has offered me a job in a big house in Broughty Ferry. You heard me mention it to Maddie at the door?'

94

He shook his head. 'I did hear you but this is the first I've heard of it.'

I then remembered how surprised he had looked and Maddie went up another notch in my estimation. I would have hated it if she had discussed it with him or Hattie before me.

'It means working away from the house for most of the week and it all depends if Granny can cope on her own.'

He was pleased. 'It's a great chance for you, Ann, but you'll have to talk it over with them. The main thing is the money which will be a great help every week.'

'I've got to go and see Mrs Barrie this week so keep your fingers crossed for me. With a bit of luck, I'll get the job and still be able to look after Lily. Still it all rests with Granny. If she could cope with the baby, then I would be able to take this live-in job.'

Alice was in the house when we arrived home. Now that the weather was too cold for a chat at the open windows, the two women resorted to an indoor gossip. Alice was worried about the new rules regarding wages coming in to the house. Once again the conversation was all about the means test. 'I'm really flummoxed over this, Nan. With Rosie still lucky to have her job as a weaver in the mill, do you think my wee pension will be affected by her wage?'

Granny, although not one hundred percent sure, was doubtful. 'Well, I did read in the paper last week that old age pensions and widowed pensions were not to be regarded as a wage coming into the house but you never can tell with these officials.

Their rules are as long as their arms.'

These words seemed to help Alice and she stood up, ready to leave. She placed the thick earthenware cup on the coal bunker lid. This tea-cup was a million miles away from the thin delicate china at Perth Road.

'I'll get away then, Nan. Now that Ann's back.' She looked fondly at Lily who was now fast asleep. 'Just look at the wee soul – out for the count after her party.' She turned to me. 'Did you have a good time as well, Ann?'

I nodded eagerly, not mentioning how different it was to our Overgate flat.

Granny said, 'Is Hattie still there?'

'No, she went home with Danny.'

As we put Lily to bed, I brought up the subject of my new job, fearful Granny would be upset.

To my surprise she was pleased. 'It sounds like a good job, Ann, and the money will be a real blessing – not just for us but for your dad as well. It'll maybe give him a wee lift because he's really depressed at the moment.' She looked sadly at me. 'Still that's to be expected, I suppose.'

She gave a loud sigh and I felt so sorry for all her worry and hardships – and now she had the added burden of grandchildren. Also it was the first time I had heard of Dad being ill. I knew he wasn't looking after himself but it was news to me – his depression. Depression was a well-known con-dition on the Hilltown as well as many other areas in the city. I had often heard the neighbours gossiping about Mr or Mrs So-and-So. I especially remembered Lizzie Hogg, who had been a bright, middle-aged woman when her husband had died

96

suddenly. Over the following months, Lizzie had become mentally ill through grief and destitution. She was a sad figure who regularly walked the streets, speaking to herself. Sadly she was usually followed by a group of grubby-faced children who called out, 'Daft Lizzie, daft Lizzie.'

As Granny tucked Lily up in her ugly old pram – no pretty wicker bassinet for her – I prayed Dad wouldn't come to that and I said so.

'No, no, your dad's not ill, Ann. It's just his way of coping with your mum's death. He blames himself but, if he could get a job, then it would help with his problems. But maybe now that you've got the chance of a job then the extra money will perk him up. At least I hope so.'

I explained about the two days off every week and she promised to leave all the heavy work till then – jobs like humping the weekly washing basket to the wash-house. Also, Danny had offered to deliver her messages or take Lily's pram down the stairs for Grandad – jobs that, up till then, had been my responsibility.

A couple of days later I was on my way to Broughty Ferry. Still dressed in my frumpish trench coat, I caught the bus. Sitting nervously on the hard seat, I gazed out of the window as the bus made its way past tall, dismal and crowded tenements and streets full of noisy children.

Within a short distance, the scenery changed to a more prosperous landscape as we headed towards my destination. I couldn't help thinking that our poverty-stricken streets seemed to be en-circled by wealth – this Broughty Ferry Road, for instance, to the east and Perth Road to the west.

I gazed once more at the diagram given to me by Hattie. Mrs Barrie lived on the edge of the town, on the Monifieth road, and I had asked the conductor to let me know when the bus reached the stop nearest to her house, Whitegate Lodge.

He had rubbed his chin and rattled his money-bag at my request. 'Whitegate Lodge ... now let me think a minute.' His minute was barely twenty seconds. 'That's the big house just past the last stop at the Ferry. Right, lass, I'll give you a shout when we reach it.'

The bus was very quiet and he sat down on the empty seat opposite me. 'You ken something?' he said. 'This was a far better run in the days of the tramcar but they took them off this route and replaced them with buses. Damn disgrace if you ask me but that's progress, I suppose.'

Actually I hadn't asked him but he seemed eager to have a chat. As I said, the bus was almost empty. Apart from me, there were only two more passengers – two young women who were very fashionably dressed in similar smart woollen suits with fur necklines and elegant cloche hats. I had noticed earlier that the conductor had tried to make conversation with them but they had merely held out the fare of a few coppers with identical snooty and disdainful expressions. This was probably the reason I had his full attention and he chattered on about tramcar tales remembered.

I would rather have had the opportunity to sit and view the unfamiliar scenery. In spite of it being intensely cold, the sun shone from a clear blue sky. The elegant houses all had gardens with their winter mantle of stark trees and dark, frosty flowerbeds. Still, I was willing to bet they all looked splendid and beautiful in the summer.

The two women stood up and waited patiently as the bus shuddered to a halt, stepping down with a panache that matched their fashionable clothes.

The conductor snorted. 'Acting like they're blooming ladies or something instead of being housemaids in that big house across the road. Come on the bus every week with their snooty faces as if they owned the blinking Ferry and the bus company as well.'

I was taken aback. Housemaids dressed in the height of fashion and with money to spend as well? The parcels clutched in their gloved hands hadn't gone unnoticed by me – parcels wrapped in paper from D.M. Brown's and Smith Brothers department stores. My mood cheered up considerably and, before long, my stop was in sight.

'Here you are, then,' said the conductor, looking morose at the thought of being alone. 'This is the stop nearest to Whitegate Lodge. It's that house over there. You can see its roof.'

I thanked him and made my way nervously towards two stone pillars holding a large forbidding gate made from thick iron bars. Beyond the gate lay a curved gravel path that meandered through a well-kept garden before sweeping up to a large house that resembled a relic from a Gothic novel.

The Lodge had two round towers, one on either corner of the stone facade. There was an immensely dark and ugly door and large lifeless looking windows that lay under a grey slated roof which held a multitude of stone chimneys.

As for the white gate, well I couldn't see one. Being an avid reader of all kinds of books I could almost imagine this house harbouring an Edward Rochester or even, heaven forbid, a Count Dracula.

I rang the bell and wasn't disappointed when it made a deep booming sound inside the interior. It was just as I expected and in keeping with this creepy house. That was why I was so surprised to find the door opened by a chubby and cheery woman who stood on the threshold, wiping her floury hands on a bright floral apron. I was half expecting, if not Quasimodo, then a hunchback at least.

'It's Ann, isn't it?' she smiled and moved aside to let me enter. 'Come in out of the cold.'

The house was much bigger than the Pringles' house but not so bright or cheerful.

The cheery woman introduced herself. 'I'm Mrs Peters, the cook. I don't normally open the door to visitors but it's Miss Hood's day off.' She showed me into a dark, wood-lined room and smiled. 'When you've finished chatting to Mrs Barrie, come into the kitchen for something to eat.' She gave a small wave before departing down an equally dim corridor.

I glanced around the room and at first thought I was alone because it was so dark and quiet. Then a voice coming from the direction of the fireplace startled me. Mrs Barrie was sitting in an enormous wingback armchair that almost totally enveloped her.

'Come and sit beside me, Ann,' she said.

I was surprised by her voice – it was surprisingly deep and resonant and not in keeping with her fragile look. 'You'll have to excuse me sitting in the dark but I like to keep the light off till dusk. We get so little daylight at this time of year and I don't like spoiling it with artificial light.'

I couldn't understand why the room was so dark because the sun was still shining brightly when I entered the house. I then realised this room faced the back of the house and there were tall trees so close to the windows that the branches tapped gently against the windowpanes.

I sat down opposite Mrs Barrie, my hands clutched tightly in my lap. She was tiny and thin. Almost shrunken in stature, she had a deeply lined face and short white hair cut in a similar but softer version of Mrs Pringle's.

Mrs Barrie placed thin, yellowed hands that showed raised blue veins on the arms of the chair. She wore four rings – all vying with each other to be the most beautiful in the diamonds and precious stones stakes.

'Now, Ann, I'm sorry my housekeeper has the day off – it isn't her normal one but she had unexpected business to attend to. But you've met Mrs Peters. The job consists of helping Miss Hood with the heavy housework because, like myself, she is getting on in years. Some days she will need specific jobs done but, apart from that, the work shouldn't be too demanding.'

She fixed me with a gaze from her bright, bird-like eyes that suggested she liked to laugh a lot. 'Is there anything you would like to know?'

I explained about the need to get two days off each week and she nodded. 'Yes, Jane Pringle has

101

told me about the tragic loss of your mother, Ann, and the fact you bring up your baby sister. Well, if you decide to take the job here, the wage is ten shillings a week. Plus, of course, your bed and board will be free.'

I clutched my hands together even more tightly, trying hard not to shout for joy at the mention of this wonderful sum of money, and I must have given the impression of a statue.

Still she didn't seem to notice. 'I'll let Mrs Peters show you your room and, if you can start on the second of January, that will be fine.' She rang a small bell that was positioned on the wall by the side of her chair. 'Now remember to have something to eat before you leave and you can let me know if you want the job.' She retreated back into the depths of the huge chair.

Mrs Peters led me down the dim corridor then up two flights of stairs and along another corridor before opening a door at the far end. Stepping into the room was a delight when I realised it was in one of the towers I had seen on my arrival. The window faced an expanse of sand dunes that swept down to the sea. I gazed in rapture at it. It seemed as if the sea stretched forever before disappearing on the far grey horizon.

I was mystified as to why Mrs Barrie liked to sit in her dark room while the humble housemaid had all the sunshine and a wonderful view. I said this to the cook but she said Mrs Barrie had a lovely view from her bedroom as well.

Later, when I joined her in the lovely cosy kitchen, I was amazed by the unusual cooking range.

'It's an Aga cooker,' she explained. 'Put in this house at great expense but everything in this house is the best. All except...' She stopped. 'Oh never mind me – I'm chatting here while you're dying for a cup of tea.'

She pottered around the kitchen, opening great cavernous cupboards and still chatting. 'Do you think you'll take the job, Ann?'

She handed me my tea in a nice thick cup and then produced a variety of scones, cakes and biscuits from a selection of large tins. I had never seen anything like it. It was a palatial feast and I wished Granny could have seen it. A fancy treat in our house meant the occasional tin of syrup or jar of strawberry jam – not this wonderful array of goodies.

After I bad munched a thick, floury scone, I said, 'Aye, Mrs Peters, I'll be taking the job.'

A flicker of emotion crossed her face then she smiled. 'Good. It'll be grand to have a young face about the place.'

I went and told Mrs Barrie and she seemed very pleased but afterwards, as I travelled back on the bus, I recalled that strange expression on the cook's face. It had been a mere flicker so I decided I had imagined it. I sat back in my seat, my head buzzing with all the good news I had to give to Granny.

5

It was Hogmanay and I was excited. Danny and Maddie were meeting me later that evening and we planned to see the New Year in together at the city square.

One spot of worry was Dad. I could never find him at home on any of my many visits to the Hilltown and now, on this last day of the year, he suddenly appeared at the Overgate around teatime.

Granny, who had also been irritated by his thoughtless and strange behaviour, now looked with annoyance at him as he sat looking ill at ease in her kitchen. She spoke bluntly. 'I thought you would want to see more of your family, Johnny, instead of less.'

I felt a bit sorry for him. Although never plump, he had now lost so much weight that his old trousers clung to his thin legs and a threadbare jacket hung limply from his shoulders. A thick woolly scarf covered his scrawny neck. Still, he had taken the time to shave which was a slight improvement on his gaunt, stubbled appearance at the funeral.

He looked at Granny, his eyes bright with unshed tears. 'I'll be as right as rain in a wee while and then Ann and Lily can come back and live at home. I don't expect you to look after them forever.'

Granny held up her hands and looked embarrassed. 'It's not that Johnny.'

He opened his mouth to speak but she stopped him. 'As I said, it's not that. It's just that the lassies have lost their mother and they need you more than ever. We know you're still grieving for Lily but we are as well. Ann has tried to see you lots of times but you're never in the house.'

'Aye, you're right,' he said sadly, putting his empty soup bowl by the side of the sink before pouring out a cup of strong black tea. Then he gazed at us with a cheerful expression. 'Never mind, it'll soon be a brand-new year and things will get better – I promise.'

In spite of his cheery remark I couldn't help noticing a tinge of hopelessness in his voice. Still the good news about my job pleased him and his face became alive with eagerness at my good fortune. 'As I said, Ann, things will be much better next year. You wait and see.'

Then suddenly, out of the blue, Rosie spoilt the moment by appearing from next door. She was one disgruntled lady. 'Well, I'm glad to see you at last, Johnny. I've asked you over and over again about getting Lily christened and I can arrange it at the Citadel.'

This was news to me as I didn't know she had been successful in even seeing Dad, let alone discussing Lily's Christian upbringing with him.

His face turned a deep pink, the flush spreading up from the woolly scarf to his hairline. He stared at her. It was a look I misunderstood and what I though was guilt turned out to be anger.

'Look, Rosie, I don't want to discuss it. If I choose to have Lily christened, then it'll be in my own good time and not before.' His voice was hard and he made it clear the matter was now closed.

Rosie however was like a hungry mongrel dog with a juicy marrowbone. 'Well, your mum thinks the baby should be christened. Isn't that right, Nan?' She looked at Granny with her soft brown-eyed gaze and Granny nodded slightly.

Dad's cheeks now turned a bright dark red and his eyes were stormy. 'Well, she's not getting done and that's final.' He pointed an accusing finger at Rosie while inclining his head in Granny's direction. 'My mother doesn't give a toss about a christening. It's just you and your religious mania. What I would like to know is this – where was this ever-loving God of yours when my wife died? Tell me that. Just keep your views to yourself, Rosie, and don't turn us into Salvationists.'

He grabbed his cap, jammed it on his head and hurried through the door. Meanwhile Rosie looked as if she was about to burst into tears and I was shocked by his outburst.

As usual, Granny saved the situation. 'He didn't mean it, Rosie. Grief has to come out in the open sometime – one way or another. His anger is just his way of coping with it. Let the issue of Lily drop for the time being and I'll work on it.'

Rosie took off her glasses and wiped her eyes with the sleeve of her jumper. 'I was just trying to help, Nan, but it looks like I'm the last person he needs.'

I felt so sorry for her as she headed sadly out the door. I now realised how deeply she cared for him while getting precious little thanks for all her trouble.

I was also puzzled about her remarks. 'Granny, has Rosie seen Dad like she says? Every time I go to the Hilltown, he's never there. Even Rita and Nellie never see him.'

I thought about our old neighbours – two women who also had enough on their plates. They had enough problems with money and the never-ending struggle to make ends meet without the added worry of looking out for Dad – especially when he had rejected all their offers of help.

Granny looked evasive. 'Well, I think she goes to the Hilltown quite a lot with the Salvation Army – especially at night – and she sees him with his cronies.'

It was an inadequate answer but I let it drop. I had quite a bit of housework to finish before my exciting adventure into the town at midnight.

Danny was working until ten o'clock with his deliveries and then he had to pick Maddie up at the Perth Road. Mrs Pringle wasn't happy about letting her out so late but Maddie had a way of getting round her parents in a manner that was an eye-opener to me.

'She could charm the devil himself,' was one of Hattie's favourite sayings but the fact that Danny was acting as her chaperone had clinched the deal.

I was waiting on the pavement when they appeared and by eleven thirty we were finally in place at the far end of the High Street, almost in front of the Town House or the Pillars as it was better known as.

The crowd was growing by the minute, milling around the many barrows that were dotted about the street. These barrows were piled high with fancy hats, loud hooters and the favourite first-foot present – the dressed herrings. These were gaudily wrapped in bright, multi-coloured crêpe paper frills. The vendors were doing a brisk trade as good-natured customers jostled forward with their purchases into the seething mass. The air hummed with hundreds of voices. The conversations mingled with shrieks of laughter and the high-pitched sounds from the hooters and whistles. Also, from the far edge of the crowd, the sound of noisy singing erupted.

Rain had fallen earlier but it was now dry although still very cold. Maddie had a fashionable fur hat perched on top of her curls – a hat that made my old woollen headsquare look really frumpish and I was grateful for the darkness. It at least hid my tatty old clothes and put me on the same level as Maddie. This was merely superficial because I knew her clothes were as fashionable as the hat and should some spotlight appear in the darkness, well, I would be shown up for my frumpy look.

Danny was also taken by her pretty headgear. 'Better hold tight to your hat, Maddie, or somebody might pinch it.'

A group of young women who looked like mill-workers stood beside us. They had thick shawls around their shoulders and were lamenting about the threatened demise of the Town House, a demise that had now firmly begun with a partially demolished steeple lying as silent witness to the town planners' dastardly scheme.

This was a source of much chagrin amongst the

population at large and the Overgate residents in particular. 'They've got a bloody cheek knocking the Town House down,' said one of the women while her companions nodded vigorously in agreement.

'When they knock it down what will happen to the shops? Where will the tramcar drivers go to shelter from the rain? It's a grand place to huddle when it's raining,' said one of the women who had prominent teeth that were chattering in the cold.

We all felt the same about these shops that lay in a row under the arches or pillars. It was a sheltered spot for lots of people in wet weather. This fine William Adams building was now being demolished and the Dundee populace were not happy about it.

'We better watch our heads,' said Miss Prominent Teeth. 'Stones have been falling and almost hitting folk.' She laughed. 'Mind you, with the state of some of these folk tonight who are the worse of drink, a stone falling on their heads will not be felt – at least not till the morn.'

Then suddenly the crowd went quiet, the conversations dying along with the singing. The excited buzz dropped away to a low mutter as the bells started to ring. Their sonorous pealing pierced the cold night air and heralded in the New Year.

'Happy nineteen thirty-two,' said Danny, giving us both a quick kiss.

Meanwhile, the women beside us shrieked with mock surprise as a group of young men threw their arms around them and started an impromptu dance. With the crowd now surging

109

around, they were soon whisked away into the darkness, still laughing.

'A happy New Year, Danny,' we said, almost in unison while Maddie kissed him on the cheek.

We tried to escape from this mass of celebrating humanity. Maddie, with one hand on her hat and another around my waist, and I stayed close to Danny who was leading the way and trying to weave through the crowd.

We were at the bottom of the Overgate when I spotted Dad. He was with a group of men but a woman was hugging him. Perhaps some over-eager reveller, I thought, trying to squeeze my way towards him.

'Danny, it's Dad,' I shouted, trying to raise my voice above the deafening din. 'I'm going over to see him.'

I was almost there – just a few yards away. I could see Dad's face clearly when suddenly Jamie appeared in front of me. He was one of Dad's younger pals and he barred my way, grabbing me and planting a wet kiss on my lips. I smelt the beer aroma from his breath and his grip tightened around my waist.

I tried to struggle free. 'I've got to see Dad, Jamie.'

His response was another wet kiss. 'Oh, you don't need your dad when you've got me.' His words were slurred. 'You know I've always fancied you?'

This was news to me and I was aghast. Fear and panic gripped me as I tried to twist away from his ever-tightening embrace. I realised the crowd was so thick that escape was almost impossible and, to make matters worse, Dad had disappeared without ever seeing me.

I thought I would faint in the crowd but suddenly and without warning a strong hand grabbed my coat collar and I was plucked backwards. I almost cried with relief when I saw Danny and Maddie, who had a very worried look on her face.

'You gave us a fright, Ann', said Danny. 'Luckily Maddie saw your headsquare.'

Good old tatty scarf, I thought, mentally apologising to it for calling it frumpish.

Jamie grabbed me again but Danny stepped in beside me and gripped him by the hand. 'A happy New Year, Jamie,' he said brightly, as the youth glared at him. 'Sorry to butt in but Ann has to be home by now.'

Jamie gave another glowering glance at me then to my relief, he nodded. 'Aye, I'll see you around sometime maybe.' His words were more slurred now and I realised he wanted to be home himself or maybe he wanted to be sick. Either way, he pushed his way through the crowd and disappeared into the throng.

I got a lecture from both Danny and Maddie as we made our way along the Overgate. I trudged along, all excitement now gone, and I was deeply disappointed at missing Dad. It would have been lovely bringing in another year with him – just like when Mum was alive.

By the time we reached the house, it was full of neighbours celebrating. As well as Rosie and Alice, all the people from the close had squeezed into the tiny kitchen. I also saw Mrs Watts who lived in the next close. Granny always liked to include her in any gathering and, although there were few occasions for celebrations in this poverty-stricken life, they were all having a good gossip. Mrs Watts was a young-looking widow who had lost her husband at the end of the war. In 1918 she had been just nineteen and looking forward to a married life but there were hundreds, if not thousands, of women like her who had lost loved ones in the carnage.

Then we noticed Bella, sitting on the best chair with a tiny glass of whisky in one hand and a small piece of shortbread in the other. When she spotted Maddie who was a new face to her, she latched on to her like a leech.

'Come over here, lass, and sit beside me and tell me who you are.' She patted a vacant wooden stool.

As Maddie dutifully went over, Danny whispered behind her retreating back, 'We'll rescue you in three hours.'

I looked over to where Granny was presiding over her guests. Although money was in short supply, my grandparents liked to be hospitable at Hogmanay. In order to do this Granny joined her New Year club with the small licensed grocer across the street. By paying a small amount every week she was able to buy a half bottle of whisky, a bottle of ginger cordial, a box of shortbread and a small sultana cake. Some people liked black bun at this time of year but Granny's budget didn't stretch to that.

The noisy chatter had kept Lily awake and she was sitting up in her pram. Grandad was doing his party trick with the spoons. Rattling them together against his arms and legs in a syncopating, metallic beat which, to everyone's delight, was mimicked by the baby as she shook her rattle every now and then.

Maddie seemed fascinated by this co-ordinated, dexterous display with the spoons but Bella was annoyed by this because Maddie's gaze had wandered right in the middle of the tale of Bella's ingrown toenail. Not to be outdone, she raised her voice over all the distractions. 'Now, as I was saying, this nail gives me gyp, I can tell you, and there's no medicine strong enough to help the pain.' She fished a small bottle out from the pocket of her voluminous apron and almost shoved it under Maddie's nose. 'Even this stuff doesn't help and I get this from the chemist's shop.' She gazed at the bottle as if deciding. 'Still, maybe I'll just have a wee drop.' She sounded like a martyr.

Maddie jumped up. 'I'll go and get a glass for your medicine,' she volunteered, only to be forestalled by Bella's big hand.

'No, no, lass, just sit down.' She yanked the cork from the dark brown ribbed bottle and raised it to her lips. 'I'll just have a swig of this. I've been taking this medicine for so long now that my swigs are more accurate than any chemist's measure.'

She then replaced the cork firmly back in the bottle and replaced it in her pocket before picking up her tiny glass and downing the contents in one go. 'That's better,' she said, wiping her lips in satisfaction.

She then called over to Danny. 'Where's your mother, son? Are we no' good enough for her at Hogmanay?'

'Mum's had to work tonight,' he said but she wasn't satisfied with a short answer and wanted the entire version and nothing but that.

Maddie interrupted. 'Hattie is working in our house tonight – or I should say this morning? My parents are entertaining a few of my father's colleagues to dinner.'

Bella gave her a puzzled look. 'Dinner? Surely your dinner was over long ago. We have our dinner in the middle of the day.' She took another swig of her medicine which obviously cleared her head and engaged her brain. 'Oh, I forgot – you toffs have your dinner when we're eating our supper.' The perplexed frown vanished from her face and she looked pleased at solving this problem.

Maddie's face began to twitch and we thought she would erupt in a gale force of laughter but she managed to keep a straight face and she gave Bella a serious look. 'Yes, that's right, Bella.'

Meanwhile, to my dismay and Rosie's apparent anguish, Dad failed to appear.

Another absence hadn't escaped Bella's eagle eye. 'Where's Johnny, Nan? Is he not coming as well? Heavens, what a family! You would think he would want to wish us a happy New Year – especially folk like me that doesn't keep well and will maybe not be here next year.'

She stopped suddenly, warned by the annoyed look from Granny. She looked embarrassed when she remembered my mother who had been hale and hearty this time last year. She lowered her head and muttered, 'Sorry about that but I just thought he might want to wish his kids a happy New Year – especially Ann. He could have wished her well in her new job at least.' She then fell silent.

I thought the same thing myself but maybe I would see him before I left for Broughty Ferry on the second of January.

By now Grandad had finished his performance on the spoons. Then, in the brief interval that usually followed these impromptu recitals, Mary Watts, a normally timid little woman but now fortified with a dram of whisky, began to sing. Her rich alto voice soared majestically in the small kitchen and we were all spellbound. Lily even stopped waving her rattle.

When the song was over, Granny clapped her hands enthusiastically. 'Oh that was great Mary. I've aye liked "The Sunshine of your Smile" – it's a grand song.'

Alice echoed this statement and added, 'You're good enough to be on the stage. You're far better than a lot of singers I've heard.'

Mary blushed but looked pleased. 'It's funny you should say that but, when I left school, my mother was going to get my voice trained but it was the old story of a lack of money. Then I met my man, Willie. Well to cut a long story short, we got married during the war but then he was killed in action. Now of course there's not enough money to live on, let alone have a voice trained.' She gazed down at her hands with a wistful expression on her face, thinking maybe of what might have been.

'Well, that's a shame,' said Grandad. 'A great voice like that shouldn't be hidden under a bushel.'

Bella, who was feeling left out now that the

conversation had swung away from her health problems, said waspishly, 'Maybe you can win a song competition or something.'

Although it was meant as a sarcastic remark, Grandad immediately pounced on it. 'What a good idea, Bella! We'll have to keep our eyes skinned to see if any of the halls have song competitions.'

Bella, puffed up with pride at this unexpected appreciation, tried to look modest but failed. 'Well, as I'm tired of telling you lot, I'm not just a bonny face. I have good ideas all the time but nobody ever listens to me.'

Granny muttered under her breath, 'We do nothing else but listen to you.'

It was time for Danny to take Maddie home and he rescued her before Bella could unearth another ache or long forgotten pain.

Then, to my surprise, he asked if I wanted to go with them. The cold wind smacked against our faces as we stepped out into the street which was still thronged with people celebrating another new year.

'It's a long way to Tipperary,' sang a group of inebriated men as they tried to negotiate a narrow close entrance, their voices suddenly amplified by the vault-like walls.

'Speaking about Tipperary,' said Danny, looking at both of us, 'I'm visiting my relations later on today. Would you both like to come?'

I accepted with such alacrity that I was suddenly embarrassed. I hoped I hadn't sounded too eager. I saw Maddie's face fall.

'Oh, Danny, I would love to come with you

both but my aunts and uncles always come to our house on New Year's Day and I have to be there.'

Danny sounded cheerful, 'Oh, well, maybe another time, Maddie.'

Although I was sorry she couldn't make it, I was still elated that Danny and I would have some time together before I started work. I had another idea. 'What about taking Lily with us? It'll mean pushing the pram instead of taking the tramcar, though. What do you think, Danny?'

Danny thought it was an excellent idea and we strolled on to Maddie's house. This quiet road was such a contrast to the Overgate with its throng of merry revellers and their loud rasping singing and sharp peals of laughter. It was like walking along a hushed road towards a church and most of the houses lay in slumbering darkness, their gardens deep pools of mysterious shadows.

Maddie was silent during the walk, her eyes downcast on the pavement as if measuring each paving stone. Suddenly she blurted out, 'Oh, I wish I was coming with you to Lochee instead of a stuffy day with my relations. They're not as funny and good-natured as your grandparents and their friends. I've got two aunts who look down their noses at drink but make a concession at this time of year. They sit around like two stuffed prunes, sipping a little glass of sherry as if it were poison. I do wish they were like Bella.' She giggled loudly and made a funny face, imitating her aunts' expressions, and we laughed so loudly that a light sprang on in one of the darkened houses. We ran along the pavement in case the irate owner would perhaps open his window and shout at us.

Maddie was still lamenting. 'Then one of my uncles goes to sleep after his lunch and doesn't wake up till it's time for tea. What boring company he is and not like Bella with her numerous complaints and medicine bottle full of whisky. Not to mention her "Dinner at dinner time unless you're a toff".' She mimicked Bella to a tee.

Danny was amused. 'So you noticed that, did you, Maddie? It's supposed to be our family secret – our skeleton in the cupboard.'

'Actually I didn't notice right away,' Maddie admitted, 'but, after a few drinks from her bottle and after finishing her glass, she got tired of waiting for a refill. She gave me this huge wink and poured some of her so-called medicine into her glass and it looked like whisky.'

'Aye, we just love it when she looks so innocent and tells us what a blessing her medicine is,' I said.

Maddie gave another huge sigh. 'It's all right for Joy – she'll sleep through most of the long boring day – but I'll have to play the piano and sing something totally cheerless. Still maybe I'll sing the Horsey song.' This thought seemed to cheer her up.

When we reached her house, a light still glowed in a downstairs window. I remembered Hattie. 'Is your mum coming back with us, Danny?'

'No, her plan was to go home straight after the meal was served. Isn't that right, Maddie?'

Maddie nodded. 'Yes. As Bella would say, us toffs are a dull lot with our boring parties that end early.' She turned to face us. 'Come in for a moment and see Dad.'

118

I was dying to get home to my bed as I had had a really busy day with the housework and a heavy stint at the local wash-house but it seemed churlish to refuse.

We stepped once again into the lovely pink-toned room, now made even softer with a solitary lamp burning. This cast a golden glow, making the room seem mysterious with its shadowed corners. The red embers from a dying fire echoed the warm look.

Mr Pringle sat in a deeply cushioned chair, a crystal glass with an inch of amber liquid in his hand. The room was extremely tidy and devoid of any party traces. Either they had received no 'first-footers' or else Hattie was extremely good at her job.

He greeted us warmly. 'I thought I would wait up for you, Maddie.'

Refusing a glass of ginger wine, we explained we had to be on our way back in case Granny became worried.

Maddie turned an anguished face to her father. 'Can I go with Ann and Danny to Lochee later today?' she implored, her clear blue eyes large and gleaming. 'Ann is going away to her new job and I won't see her for quite a while.'

He shook his head. 'No, Maddie, I'm sorry but you know how much your aunts and uncles like to see you at this time of year.' He turned to us. 'Sorry, Danny and Ann, any other time I would have said yes but you understand, don't you?'

We both nodded while Maddie made a face at him but he was still adamant. Before we left, they both wished me well in my new job, with Maddie adding, 'I'll be out to see you sometime, Ann. We Sunday girls must stick together.'

When we were outside, Danny burst out laughing. 'I thought Maddie would get her own way and get round her dad but she was unlucky this time.'

The wind whipped coldly against our faces and I pulled my headscarf tightly under my chin as we hurried homewards. When we reached the house, the party was still in full swing and Mary was singing again.

Lily had fallen asleep and she had been put in my tiny room where I joined her, leaving Danny to return to the Westport. Within minutes I was fast asleep.

Daylight dawned clear and cold with some thin wintry sunshine but, by eleven o'clock, a thick bank of grey ominous looking clouds appeared as a threatening mass above the tenements.

Granny didn't like the look of the weather. 'I don't think you should take Lily in the pram. Why do you and Danny not go on your own?'

Grandad, who was nursing a headache after the night's celebrations, was in the process of swallowing an Abdine powder. He looked at me. 'Aye, you'd better not let Hattie see Danny pushing the pram. She's never liked it.' He was still obviously smarting from her attitude.

'We don't mind taking Lily and letting you both have a wee rest – especially when I'm off to work tomorrow.'

I put Lily's arms through her little jacket. She looked so bright eyed and lovely in the pram suit with the matching pixie hood, the one Mrs Pringle had given her.

'We can just as easily go on the tramcar to Lochee,' I said.

Danny appeared, looking so handsome that I almost felt sorry for Maddie having to miss our outing. I mentioned the pram and Danny said the walk would do us all the world of good. So the pram was manhandled down the stairs.

Grandad gave Lily a cuddle as he passed. 'Cheerio, my wee pet. You look really bonny and wrapped-up in your new suit. A proper wee toff – that's what you are.'

The street was still as crowded as the previous night and we almost knocked over a small woman who suddenly darted from one of the closes. She was extremely thin with a shrivelled looking face. She was almost wraith-like except for her hands which were encased in an enormous pair of furry gloves that looked as if they had once been the front paws of a grizzly bear. Her thin bony face was wrinkled and her pale eyes were watery from the cold wind. She turned to look at us. 'A happy New Year to you and your wife. What a bonny baby. Is it your first?'

Danny smiled at her. 'Oh, no, we're not married.'

The woman took this misleading statement in her stride. 'Oh, that doesn't matter a scrap these days. Many a bonny baby's born out of wedlock and good luck to you.'

I was appalled at being taken for an unmarried mother so I butted in. 'No, what he means is the baby's my sister and he's my cousin.'

'Oh, I see,' she said, looking quite perplexed.

'Mind, I did think you were both too young to be married with a wee one.' She peered at Danny and recognition dawned. 'I know you. You live in the next close to me. I saw your mother earlier. She seemed to be in a hurry.'

'She's away to work, Mrs Cooper,' he explained to the woman, who looked pleased at being recognised. 'Her boss is having a lot of relations visiting today and Mum helps out in the house.'

I thought Hattie would be wild at this domestic description of her job. Helping out wasn't what she told us she did – no, it was housekeeper stroke companion and not general dogsbody stroke skivvy – but I held my tongue.

As the woman hurried away, I said to him, 'I wonder if Maddie is practising her piano party piece.' I couldn't control the grin on my face.

Danny laughed as well. 'The strange thing is that the Pringles don't think so much of Maddie's rebellious nature as my mum does. She thinks it's terrible not to act like a lady when you've been born to it. If she had her way, Maddie would be dressed in frills and flounces with ringlets in her hair and wearing white cotton gloves all the time.'

I had this absurd picture of Maddie sitting simpering in yards of pink tulle and white gloves and I burst out laughing. 'I don't think I would like her if she was like that.'

We pushed the pram past high tenements. Some had their curtains still tightly drawn but, in others, there were the remnants of Hogmanay and the sounds of merriment floated out. In a dismally grey, unemployed and poverty-stricken world, people had to take their little bits of pleasure when they could.

We soon reached Atholl Street – or Tipperary as it was better known. Like the Overgate, this street was buzzing with activity. Scores of children went whooping past us. Some had scooters and most of these wooden toys had bent wheels which meant the rider had a struggle to keep up the momentum on the grimy pavements. Others were playing with pretend guns, acting out scenes from the latest cowboy picture at the cinema. A group of more fortunate lads had an old cart which was a scrappy-looking box on a set of old pram wheels.

If there was one place I liked as much as the Overgate, it was this street where all Danny's relations lived. In fact, if one should spit, they would shower the entire Ryan clan because their houses radiated around the abode of Ma and Dad Ryan like some gigantic cobweb.

We heard Kit before we saw her. She was busy chastising a small child who had been scribbling on the stairway wall with a piece of chalk. 'Get away from my clean stairs, you wee devil,' she shouted at the now retreating small urchin. 'I washed these stairs last night and now look at them.' She tackled the area of chalked graffiti with a wet cloth. She looked thin and careworn but her eyes were still bright, as was her deep auburn hair which glowed in the pale sunshine. When she saw us, her face lit up with a huge smile, a smile that widened even further when she spotted Lily.

'Hullo, Ann and Danny, and you've brought wee Lily to see us all.' She scooped the baby from the pram and went upstairs ahead of us, carrying Lily in her thin white arms that, come summer, would be a mass of freckles.

'Did you hear me, Lily? Did you hear your noisy Aunt Kit telling that wee tyke off? Did you hear me roaring?' she said to the baby in a soft, soothing voice. 'Come up and meet your other aunts. They're in my house.'

Kit lived with her husband and two children in two tiny rooms which lay at the far end of a dark lobby which was situated at the top of the outside stairs, the stairs with the graffiti. There was a line of similar, darkly painted doors in the lobby and, in the dimness, it resembled a rabbit warren.

Tipperary was an over-populated region that had been built to house the thousands of Irish immigrants who had poured into Dundee at the turn of the century to work in the city's numerous jute mills.

Now, because of the current high unemployment rate, not only in the jute mills but also over the entire country, the entire Ryan clan was on the dole – or that had been the position before the dreaded means test law which had not long been sanctioned by an uncaring government.

Sitting beside a fire that seemed to be all smoke and precious little heat or flames were Kit's two sisters, Lizzie and Belle. Ma Ryan was there as well. She sat in the corner, puffing on an old clay pipe that had once been as white as snow but was now a grimy mixture of brown nicotine stains and black, sooty streaks.

I hadn't seen the Ryan family since the funeral and I was shocked by their appearance. Like Kit, they all were all thin and weary looking but they cheered up when we appeared.

'A happy New Year,' said Lizzie. Shivering beside the paltry fire, she pulled a thin woollen cardigan around her hunched shoulders. 'Mind you, it's not a happy time these days now that we've all been cut off from our dole money.'

Belle nodded gloomily. 'The men are still getting some parish money but it's not enough to keep body and soul together. That's why we're all sitting here moaning about our trials and tribulations.'

Danny was quite upset. 'That's terrible. Now, you all know I've got my job at Lipton's so you've only got to ask if you need any more help with money.'

Kit was aghast at this. They all knew Danny helped out a lot with the families. She glared at Belle who blushed under the fierce gaze. 'Don't be daft, young Danny. It's just that we've had an unpleasant encounter with one of those snotty-nosed devils who check on your circumstances before you're allowed to have any money from Bobby Allen and his gang of merry men from the parish relief.'

'It's not just us,' said Lizzie. 'Mrs Flynn across the lobby was wakened up one morning last week. "I'm just making sure none of your family are living here and helping out with the house-hold bills." She put on a snooty voice, obviously imitating the official interrogator.

Kit was equally cross. 'Just imagine if any of your family are lucky enough to have a job – and there's damn few around here, I can tell you – well, then they have to move out to lodgings or else the dole or parish money is stopped. I mean, they have to pay for their lodgings so where's the sense in that?'

'Aye,' said Belle, 'Would it no' be better to let them stay at home and help out with their wee bit wages instead of treating them like the main breadwinner? It's really crazy.'

By now, the fire had sprung into life with a small spurt of flame and we had a cup of tea which warmed us up. There was no sign of the men or the children. They were all otherwise engaged. Perhaps the children were all outside with home-made scooters or carts.

'Another thing that annoys us all,' said Lizzie angrily, 'is, when the officials come into the house, they start poking around in cupboards. Just to see what we've been spending our few shillings on every week. Maybe they think we splash out on luxuries like an extra loaf of bread or a pot of strawberry jam.'

Kit's laugh was without humour. 'Aye, it's bread and margarine for the poor and strawberry jam for the rich.'

She certainly had a bee in her bonnet but she was quite right in her indignation as this behaviour was happening all over the country. The majority of officials were decent and sympathetic but, human nature being what it is, some of them had let the job go to their heads and they now acted like apprentice dictators.

She refilled our cups and sighed. 'Oh, it's not just us that gets bothered. I heard that two of Mrs Murphy's kids were on their way to the Royal infirmary when the man from the parish arrived. He was coming in the door as they were being carried out. He was having his wee poke around when he heard the kids were suffering from suspected TB. Seems he hot-footed it out of the house like a scalded cat.'

The women all chuckled at the memory.

'Was it tuberculosis?' asked Danny.

Kit rubbed her nose as if thinking. 'Well, no one is sure but I would say it is. In fact, judging by all their hacking coughs, I would say the entire family have it.'

We all pondered this terrible affliction, just glad we had our health if nothing else.

Lily had fallen asleep on the big double bed but she awoke with a frightened cry when a gang of children swooped into the room. The children were Danny's niece and nephew plus their pals and they swarmed around him like a flock of vultures. Even Ma Ryan, who had remained silent most of the time, now chuckled.

Danny produced a big paper bag full of sweets. He handed them to a miniature Kit clone. He ruffled her red hair. 'Here, Kathleen, you can share them out but mind it's not four to you and two to the rest.'

Kathleen grinned, an impish expression on her face. 'Cross my heart, Danny.'

'Well, it's not your heart that needs minding,' he said, 'it's your multiplication tables.'

Kathleen was obviously the spokeswoman for the group. She looked at her mother. 'Can we get a piece with margarine and sugar, Mum?' She said, crunching a sweetie.

Before Kit could answer, a small voice piped up. 'I want condensed milk on my bread.'

'Oh, you do, do you?' said Kit sarcastically.

'Well, your majesty will have to get bread and margarine like everyone else.'

While Ma sat puffing her pipe, Kit manhandled a loaf of bread, dishing out thick slices to the assembled children. As they ran off to play again, she shouted after them, 'Mind now, we don't want to see you lot again until teatime.'

She sat down on a chair and sighed loudly. 'Heavens, what appetites the kids have. They eat like a pack of Clydesdale horses.'

'Isn't it a blessing we all have our hidey-holes?' said Belle who, like her sister Lizzie, was childless.

Lizzie laughed. 'I aye hide an odd five Woodbines and sometimes a tin of syrup or condensed milk in my wee hideyhole. Ned cut a wee section from the floorboards and that's where I stash my few wee extras.'

Ma Ryan said, 'Aye, you're quite right. Then, when the snoopers come along, the cupboards are like Mother Hubbard's.

At the mention of Ned, Danny asked after the men in the family.

Lizzie rolled her eyes heavenwards. 'Well, maybe they're with their pals in the street or else they're with Dad in his house.'

Kit looked annoyed. 'That's the best place for them – it keeps them out of mischief.'

We looked mystified but Kit was too annoyed to keep silent. 'My George was in the Nine Bells pub last night. Just for a quick pint before the bells. Then at twelve o'clock what do you think we got for a first foot? A man with a black eye as big as a soup plate – that's what.'

Danny and I looked nonplussed but she gave us a knowing look as if, like Ma Ryan, we were also clairvoyant.

'"I walked into a lamp post," he said, with a shifty look in his eyes. "A lamp post?" I said. "Pull the other foot, George." "No, no," says the big man, "I'm not joking – I was coming out of the Nine Bells when it happened."'

Danny laughed. He was fond of all his uncles but he was especially fond of George, a tall, well-built man who was well known for his gentle nature and good humour. A popular man in this warm and caring albeit poverty-stricken Irish community, if he had arrived home on Hogmanay with a black eye, then something was far wrong.

Before we could ask, Ma Ryan leaned forward. 'He might have walked into a lamp post as well but the story that's going around is that he walked into Billy Murphy's fist – that wee troublemaker. The fist was meant for Billy's brother but George just happened to be in the middle of it.'

Kit was still annoyed. 'Those two Murphy brothers should be belting it out in a boxing ring because they're aye fighting with each other or anybody else who gets in the way.'

'Aye, you're right, Kit,' said Ma. 'I hear they're now walking about like the best of pals while George is walking about with his black eye.'

A howl from the direction of the bed stopped the conversation. Lily had become quite fractious.

I stood up. 'I'd better go.'

I didn't want Danny to curtail his visit so I said, 'I'll manage down the road on my own, Danny.'

He stood up. 'No, I'd better be getting back as

129

well. Mum will be back from the Pringles' house. They were just needing her help with the luncheon.' He stopped, trying to get his tongue around this strange, new word while the women looked at him in amusement.

Kit put on her haughty expression but fortunately Danny didn't see it. Poor Danny. He was just like his uncle George – caught in the middle. He loved his mother as much as he loved his dad's relations but it was obvious they didn't like Hattie.

We all knew she was a bit snobbish and had always been this way but surely this human failing didn't warrant all this hostility.

Danny went over to Ma and placed something in her hand. 'A happy New Year, Granny.' When she protested at his present of a few shillings, he replied, 'Put it aside for a few messages for your hidey-hole and pray the snoopers don't find them.'

We were going through the door when he said, 'We almost forgot to say Ann's got a job and she starts tomorrow. Isn't that good news?'

They all looked pleased. 'Oh, that is good news, Ann. Maybe you can keep your eyes skinned for jobs for us.' They laughed.

I told them about the job and how Mrs Pringle had found it for me. 'I'm really happy with it but still a bit worried about leaving Lily with Granny. They will have to cope with her on their own – she's getting heavy to carry now plus there's all the extra work.'

Kit spoke for her sisters and herself, 'Now, you're not to worry because we'll help out with Lily. Maybe Danny can bring her here while your grandparents get a rest. Just say the word.'

While Danny negotiated the bulky pram down the stairs, Kit whispered to the women. 'Maybe Hattie can lend a hand as well. It'll make a change from serving luncheons.'

I thought it a bit unfair but, before I could say so, Ma Ryan appeared at my side. 'I knew you would get this job, lassie, but watch out for the bird that's black.'

I opened my mouth to ask her about this cryptic statement but she merely nodded knowingly. 'I can't tell you any more except to watch out for the blackbird. Watch your step and be very, very careful.'

Danny and I walked back in companionable silence until we reached the entrance to Dudhope Park.

'Let's walk back this way,' Danny suggested. Then he turned to me and asked, 'Ann, you're the clever one – what is a luncheon?'

I paused for a moment. 'I think it's what posh folk call dinnertime. After all you can buy luncheon meat at Lipton's and, if you read the advertisements in the *Courier* and *Evening Telegraph*, you often see Draffen's or D.M. Brown's mention luncheons.'

He laughed. 'I wonder if Maddie is entertaining her relations?'

'Well, if she is, she'll soon wake them up from a post-luncheon nap when she belts out "Horsey, Keep Your Tail Up"!'

As we discovered later, she went even better than that, singing a medley of songs in such a common and coarse accent that one uncle almost had an apoplectic fit. At least that was the story according to Hattie who was equally horrified. Fortunately all the other members of the family had thought it hilarious and were unanimous in their verdict that Maddie was talented if somewhat high-spirited.

Before we reached to Overgate I asked Danny about Ma Ryan.

'Aye, she's supposed to have the second sight and she can tell the future. Mum says it's all hogwash but I don't really know,' he said, shrugging his slim shoulders.

'She told me to watch out for a blackbird, Danny. Said I had to be very careful. What did she mean?'

Danny shook his head and looked as perplexed as I felt. 'I'm not really sure, Ann.'

We then said cheerio and went our separate ways.

6

Early on Friday morning, the second of January, I said my goodbyes to the family and, by seven o'clock, I had boarded the bus for my journey to the Ferry and my new job.

Thankfully the chatty conductor from my previous trip was missing. In his place was a surly looking character with a snappish, offhand manner which may or may not have irritated his passengers. As for me, I was just grateful for the lack of eye contact or cheerful conversation. The windows were steamed up with condensation and an air of misery was so tangible that I felt I could almost grasp it. With the New Year festivities now well and truly behind us, it was as if people had fallen back into a humdrum and dismal existence after burning briefly for a few short hours – like a Roman Candle firework with its exploding shower of light and stars then nothing but putrid smoke hanging in the air like a half-forgotten memory.

Although I was looking forward to my new job, I was still feeling sad at having to leave Lily and my grandparents – and Dad and Danny.

Granny, as usual, was her practical self as she watched me pack a tiny suitcase with my few belongings. 'Heavens, lassie, don't look so sad. It's just the Ferry you're going to, not the North Pole. We'll see you every week.'

Maddie had sent me a home-made card via Hattie and I smiled at the memory of it. On the cover she had drawn an elegant looking maid with a feather duster in a slim white hand with its red painted fingernails. Inside she had also drawn a good likeness of me surrounded by an assortment of cleaning aids at my feet. Needless to say I was minus the red nails or the elegance and the caption read, 'Ann buzzes through the chores like a busy bee.' It was signed in her large flourishing style but had a postscript. 'Wish I could be joining you instead of going back to the boring school.'

On seeing this last night, Hattie had pursed her lips together, disapproval written all over her face. '"Boring school", indeed! Imagine saying that about the Harris Academy. Most of the scholars there live in posh houses or in flats with tiled closes.'

Granny and I had been amused at her. Hattie's big dream was eventually to move to a house with a tiled close. Should this ever happen, it would be the apex of her life.

'I don't think Maddie is running down the school, Hattie,' said Granny. 'It's just that she feels Ann and Danny are getting more grown-up than her, even though she's almost the same age. She's right of course. The one thing about being poor is that you have to put your childhood behind you and grow up fast.'

She bustled around my suitcase, smoothing down the meagre contents. 'I suspect, if you were lucky enough to be a pupil at a posh school, you would be delighted, wouldn't you, Ann?'

She was right. If circumstances had permitted, I would have loved to remain at school with my beloved books.

Still, as I sat on the bus, I knew my schooldays were just a memory. I rubbed the steam from the window and peered out into the darkness, fearful that I would miss my stop and maybe be carried on to Monifieth which was just a name to me.

I didn't want to ask the conductor where I should get off because his face had turned increasingly sour-looking as the journey progressed. Woe betide any hapless passenger who didn't have the required pennies ready for their fare.

'Any more fares?' he snapped, almost shouting the words as he clumped heavily up the aisle behind each new batch of travellers who scrambled on board with all the finesse and dignity of an invading army.

Thankfully, I spotted a landmark through the morning gloom – a certain shop on a corner. I knew my stop was near. Sleet was falling as I stepped down from the bus and I watched it rumbling away, my head filled with a mixture of emotions. I found myself suddenly wishing I could be back inside my cosy haven at Granny's house, instead of standing alone on this alien pavement which was very slippery.

Dawn had arrived very grudgingly with a fractional layer of light which was unable to push the darkness away entirely. The sea and sky were the same colour. The horizon was a grey smudgy blur while the swell of the sea pulsated with huge amounts of water rushing towards land and the cold wind pushed massive waves on to the beach with a growling sound. It reminded me of some monster, fiercely rabid and foaming and straining to escape. This flat and overwhelming landscape was a fearful sight. Compared to the over-crowded Hilltown and Overgate, it was like being stranded on the moon or on some vast ocean.

Whitegate Lodge looked even more Gothic and bleaker than I remembered. Its grey stone walls blended so well with the monotones of sea and sky that it was a wonder it wasn't invisible. It was a perfectly camouflaged backdrop except for the trees which stood like black silhouettes, their bare branches stretching up like pleading arms.

It was a bleak house in a bleak landscape and my heart sank when I saw the rows of windows, the glass glinting like gunmetal steel in the half-light of this winter morning. Granny always said the windows were the soul of a house and, if this pithy saying was true, then I was looking at a pretty depressing and heartless house. Although we had no luxuries at home, our basics at least included cheap and cheerful flowery curtains.

I walked up the drive, wondering if I had got the date wrong but I recalled Mrs Barrie had specifically mentioned the second of January. Because the front of the house was so dark and unwelcoming, I set off along a side path which wound through the shadows of the trees. Thankfully I saw one window showing a rectangle of golden light.

I rang the bell on the solid wooden door and its sound reverberated like a chiming gong in a cavern. I could well imagine this bell echoing right up to the attics. There was a moment of silence. I was wondering whether I should ring once more when the door was suddenly yanked open by a tall, thin woman, annoyance deeply etched on her face. She wore a bottle-green sleeveless pinny over a mud-coloured dress, a combination of colours that, even to my untrained and unfashionable eye, was depressing.

She wiped her hands on a cloth and glared at me. 'Well, what do you want?' she snapped like a whippet chasing a rabbit and angrily realising the rabbit was winning.

This must be the housekeeper, I thought, forgetting, in my confusion, her name.

'I'm Ann Neill,' I said, trying to sound cheerful and competent but obviously failing miserably on both counts. 'I start my new job today as a housemaid.'

This admission was met with a bad tempered

grunt. 'Well, I suppose you'd better come into the kitchen.' She turned away and walked down a long corridor towards a patch of light that shone as a yellow square on the dark but highly polished linoleum.

Before we reached the door, a putrid smell of burning toast wafted out to meet us in a blue hazed cloud. The housekeeper darted forward with a howl of rage. 'Look what you've made me do, now!' she shouted, pulling the grill pan from the gas flame. Two pieces of toast lay on the rack, their black shapes not so much burnt as cremated.

She turned to me with a snarl. 'If you hadn't arrived at this unearthly hour, then this would never have happened.'

I almost apologised but instead I said quietly, 'I was told to report for work today at 8 a.m. and I'm just doing what Mrs Barrie told me to do.'

She looked at me, her pale, fishlike eyes summing me up and I knew without a doubt that I had made an enemy.

Wonderful, I thought, ten minutes into my new job and I had already antagonised Miss What's-her-name.

Her summing-up complete, she snapped again, 'Well, young madam, you can start by cleaning out all the fireplaces – there's one in the lounge and another in the morning room. Then, when Mrs Barrie has finished her breakfast and I mean when...' she drove home the point by slapping another two slices of bread on the pan, 'you can clean out her bedroom. Then light the fire in the bedroom and the morning room but just set the one in the lounge.'

My head was spinning with all these rooms and I suddenly wished I was back at the Overgate. I was thinking that living in a house with one room and a converted cupboard was perhaps no bad thing.

She handed me a heavy housemaid's box filled to the brim with polish, Brasso, Zebo black lead, emery paper and dusters. 'The grates all get black-leaded before you light them and all the brassware gets cleaned. Now away you go and I'll be along later to inspect your work because there will be no slacking here, girl.'

She picked up a massive wooden tray but turned as she reached the door, a self-satisfied smirk on her face. 'Oh, by the way, I will be deducting the price of the burnt toast from your wages.' This remark seemed to cheer her up and she smiled to herself. Her thin lips were clamped together in a straight line but the smile failed to reach her eyes. 'Yes, indeed, my girl.'

I watched as she made her way down the passage. A cold feeling grew in the pit of my stomach. I had seen a smile like that before in one of my library books – on a shark.

The passage led on to a large hall that I remembered from my earlier visit and I was able to find the morning room as this was where I'd had my interview. The room was in darkness and I pulled the thick chenille curtains apart but little light penetrated this dismally dark room. I saw the ugly, leafless trees through the rain-streaked window and I thought they held a hint of menace in their wet branches that were encrusted with a creeping green moss.

The fireplace was a small one and I worked quickly – after all, it was a job I had tackled hundreds of times. I did notice the brasses were brown and dingy with the accumulation of smoke and, if the housekeeper said these were cleaned every day, then she was lying.

After finishing my chores in that room, I went in search of the posh-sounding lounge. Maddie's parents had a lounge as well and it seemed that only the rich people had this superfluous room in their houses. The rest of us spent our lives in one room where every human need took place – sleeping, eating, washing and laundering, also cooking and recreation – all within twelve feet or sometimes even smaller.

There were two other ornately carved doors in the hall and a grand staircase that swept upwards in a positive delight of russet-coloured carpeting and deep brown polished banisters. I poked my head round one door only to discover it was a large dining room. It had a fireplace but a huge ugly embroidered fire screen, with enormous claw feet, stood on the tiled hearth. It looked like it was guarding some hidden treasure.

Right, I thought, it must be the other door so I carried the heavy box towards it. Years later and long after Whitegate Lodge was just a memory, I was always able to recall my delight at my first sight of this wonderful room. Whilst the morning room was dark and sinister, this room was all light and beauty. The large bay window overlooked the sea and a large ornamental mirror which stretched from the skirting board to the picture rail on the opposite wall reflected this seascape. It was like being on an ocean liner. The assorted settees and chairs were all covered in a fabric riotously printed with huge cabbage roses in a kaleidoscope of colours ranging from pale pink to deep crimson. The matching crimson carpet felt thick and luxurious under my feet and I had never seen such luxury before. Even Mrs Pringle's lounge faded into insignificance compared to this splendour.

A compact baby grand piano stood in one corner, its dusty surface covered with silver-framed photographs. The best part of this room however was the bookcase which filled one entire wall. It was filled with lovely leather-bound books. There were none of the usual dog-eared books in this collection and I thought of old Mr Jackson who owned the second-hand bookshop on the Hill-town. How his eyes would have brightened at this display.

I walked towards the bookcase, my footsteps muffled by the thick carpet but thankfully I heard the clatter of the breakfast tray outside the door so I hurried over to the very ornate fireplace with its cold-looking marble mantelpiece. I was scooping the dead ashes into my pail when she appeared. Pretending I hadn't noticed her, I carried on with my chore. She stood for a moment then left, closing the door silently behind her. I had the impression that this would be the pattern of my work here with her creeping up behind me, checking and watching. At that moment I was grateful for my acute hearing. It had always been a family joke, this ability to hear the slightest sound and this talent, if that is what it was, had got better since Lily's birth. It was as if my ears had become finely tuned to the baby. She only had to give the slightest whimper and I would hear her. I was happy to sit up at night and feed her with her bottle of milk – it enabled Granny to have a well-earned rest.

Suddenly I felt homesick as a surge of misery swept over me. I missed our small kitchen and the warm presence of my grandparents. How would they cope on their own? Still my financial help would be a blessing and I knew that everyone in life had their ups and downs.

The good side of this job, apart from the money, was Mrs Barrie, Mrs Peters the cook and this lovely book-filled lounge. The bad side was definitely Miss Hood. I wondered where the cook was as I hadn't seen her but maybe it was her day off.

Rising from my knees, I was about to leave the room when I saw a blackbird reflected in the mirror. Almost fainting from fright, I wheeled round to see it standing with a cheeky expression on the windowsill. It peered at me briefly before flying away. Although I hadn't worried unduly about Ma Ryan's warning at the time, it now came back to me with such clarity that I was transfixed to the spot. This is stupid, I thought, giving myself a mental shake. It was only a small bird, for heaven's sake, and not a man-eating tiger. Still the warning niggled me, lying in my mind like a dormant seed only to explode into a panic-filled moment on seeing the bird.

The spectre of Miss Hood forced me to move and I met her in the kitchen. To my immense relief I saw Mrs Peters in her bright flowered overall which stretched over her ample girth. She

141

was standing at the sink, humming a cheery tune.

She smiled when she saw me, much to Miss Hood's annoyance. 'So you've started then, young Ann?' she said as she busied herself with a collection of pots.

This clattering noise almost drowned out her singing and this mixture of sounds obviously irritated the housekeeper. She pursed her lips tightly and her whole face screwed up, turning the fine lines into deep wrinkles.

It was clear she wanted to be out of the kitchen so she called me over to another smaller sink which was full of vegetables. 'You can peel these then, afterwards, come and report to me. You have your lunch at midday and your supper at six o'clock. After washing the mistress's dinner dishes at eight o'clock, you will be free till six o'clock tomorrow morning.' She turned on her heel and took her colourless personality away.

Mrs Peters made a derisive snort, like a pig searching for scraps. 'Heavens, she's got your day mapped out for you, hasn't she?'

I turned towards the sink, a dull feeling of hunger making me feel sick, and I now wished I had eaten the bar of chocolate that had been Danny's goodbye gift to me. This hunger was made worse by the smell of toast and the sound of the kettle boiling, sending waves of steam in my direction.

The cook called over, 'Stop what you're doing, Ann, and come and get a cup of tea.'

Without further ado, I hurried over to the square wooden table which held a plate piled high with toast. Butter and marmalade in small earthenware pots lay beside this plate. I sat down and quickly munched a piece of toast, trying to ensure the hot butter didn't run down my chin.

The cook looked at me with a questioning eye. 'You'll have had some breakfast since you arrived?'

I shook my head. 'No, not even a cup of tea,' I replied, trying to mind my manners and not talk with my mouth full.

She looked annoyed, an angry glint appearing in her eyes. 'Well, that's typical, I can tell you. That miserly old besom – in fact, she's an old witch. Imagine having a young lassie arriving at the crack of dawn and not offering her something to eat.' She shook her head slowly and took a large frying pan down from the shelf. She laid strips of bacon in it, followed by one of the brownest eggs I had ever seen.

I thought this was for Mrs Barrie but, when it was cooked, she placed it in front of me with a terse, 'Eat that.' She then laughed and patted her ample waistline. 'I'll soon have you as big as myself!'

She gave me an exaggerated wink and when she saw my hesitation, she waved her hand over the plate like a conjurer. 'Eat it up before it gets cold.'

I was dipping a piece of toast in the runny yellow egg yolk, prior to popping it into my mouth when Miss Hood appeared. I heard her step on the lino-covered passage but there was nothing I could do apart from maybe shoving the plate under my jumper.

Like an avenging angel full of anger and outrage, she stood on the threshold, quivering with rage. 'What is the meaning of this? You are allowed a cup of tea in the middle of the morning and not this...' Her mouth moved convulsively as she searched for the words. 'This, this beanfeast!' She shouted so loudly that little drops of spittle shot from her mouth. It wasn't a pretty sight.

She put her hand out to yank the plate away but Mrs Peters sprang forward and pushed her hand away. 'Excuse me but I gave the lassie something to eat which was a damn sight more than you did. When she's finished and not before, then she'll return to her chores.'

The housekeeper glared at both of us before turning on her heel and marching out, twin spots of red on her cheeks.

Needless to say, this confrontation took away any remaining appetite but the cook was un-repentant. 'I don't take my orders from her and fine she knows it. Heavens, she runs this house as if every penny was a prisoner and coming out of her own pocket.' She gave another snort of deri-sion and then joined me at the table where she calmly finished her cup of tea.

I dutifully ate the rest of the egg, which was now cold, but my heart wasn't in it. Once again I had been the victim of Miss Hood's malevolent stare and I just knew from now on my life at Whitegate Lodge would be difficult. At least I had an ally in the cook but she didn't live in and I knew I would be at the mercy of the housekeeper.

As if reading my thoughts, Mrs Peters leaned over and patted my hand. 'Now don't you worry about her. She gets the whole day Saturday and a Sunday morning off every week while you and

I get a Sunday afternoon and Monday off so she'll only be around for part of the week.'

Relief flooded over me. 'So we get the same days off every week?' I was puzzled by this arrangement.

'Aye, we do.' She refilled our cups and leant back in her chair. 'Mrs Barrie aye goes to visit friends on a Monday. She gets a taxi at ten o'clock and the taxi then brings her back in the early evening. She has her lunch with friends, usually in Draffen's restaurant, and she goes to one of the friends' houses to play bridge in the afternoon. Miss Hood aye does the breakfast anyway and she makes a snack for their supper so we're not needed.'

'I don't think I'll get my days off this week with me just starting on a Friday but it would be great if I did,' I said, more in hope than anything.

'Well, make sure you ask Mrs Barrie before her ladyship gets to her first,' she advised.

As it turned out, I didn't get the chance. Miss Hood, incensed by my so-called earlier insubordination, kept me so busy that, by supper-time, I was almost asleep on my feet.

She had placed three very heavy rugs over the washing line and she sent me out in the cold wind, a wind that held slivers of ice in its breath like sharp needles. 'You can beat these rugs till all the dust is gone,' she said, rubbing her hands while standing in the sanctuary of the back door.

It took me two hours before she was satisfied that no more dust remained. By this time, the rugs were as wet as I was and I struggled to carry them indoors. She wanted them put in a roomy airing cupboard that had slatted shelves all round the walls and a huge pulley with a rope so thick it would have held a ship tight-fast. Still, I was fortified by Mrs Peters' cooking and home-made baking and the thought of my lovely little room under the eaves of the tower kept me going.

By nine o'clock, I was stretched out on my bed with its comfy mattress and pretty eiderdown. I gazed at the fresh bluebell-printed wallpaper and I had a strong notion that this pretty bedroom had been Mrs Barrie's idea. If it had been left to Miss Hood, then I would surely be reclining in the cellar or maybe even the outside wash-house.

I propped Maddie's card up against the small lamp on the bedside cabinet and placed Danny's bar of chocolate beside it. Strangely enough, I found it difficult to get to sleep in spite of my tiredness. The silence was unnerving. Apart from the sleet hitting the window and the ominous roar of the sea, no voices carried up from the road. It was so unlike the Hilltown and the Overgate, with their teeming masses – people who regularly shouted, sang, shrieked or even fought in the street, sometimes even until the early hours of the morning. It was a street lullaby that over the years had become so normal that I had simply stopped hearing it – until now, when faced with these unusual night noises.

The alarm clock that Rosie had unearthed from the depths of a cupboard ticked merrily away. She had brought it in before I left, offering it almost apologetically. 'It's a wee bit bashed but maybe it'll come in handy.' She looked dubiously at the face. 'Heavens, the two hands have broken

146

off. I wonder how that happened?'

The hour and the minute hands had indeed both broken off at precisely the same spot and they now lay at the base of the dial, entrapped forever in the glass cover. This left two stumps about half an inch long with gave the clock a comical appearance. Still it was functional and I had accepted it gracefully.

Now that I had met the housekeeper, the last thing I wanted was to be late. I thought about the library downstairs and I wished I had been allowed to borrow one of the books to read – not that I would take one without permission. Miss Hood was also an uncomfortable thought. Although her room was next door to Mrs Barrie's, I was still afraid her ever-watchful fishy eyes would be wakeful – even during the night.

I lay and let the crashing sound of the waves wash over me, hypnotising my brain with their soothing sound. I didn't know I had fallen asleep until an ear-splitting racket awoke me. ☙

It was five a.m. and the alarm clock was clanging furiously, accompanied by a series of whirring noises and metallic scrapings. For a brief moment, I couldn't think where I was but my main concern was to halt this deafening clatter. I was certain that this noise must surely have echoed into every corner of the house. The stop button wouldn't work so, with fumbling fingers, I jammed the still-protesting clock under the blankets and threw the pillow over it. It made a sound like a caged bear before finally stopping. By now, I was fully awake and I stumbled in the darkness to switch the light on. This in itself was a delight – so unlike the gas lamps that I was familiar with.

Another pleasure was the small bathroom at the end of the lobby. The lino felt cold against my bare feet but the water, much to my surprise and joy, was piping hot. Perhaps to the occupants of this house who were used to such modern facilities, this bathroom would seem quite basic. The deep, not quite white bath stood on heavy claw feet while the ornate wash basin had lovely scallop-shaped soap dishes. The toilet, with its heavy wooden seat, had a brightly pattered ceramic handle at the end of the cistern chain. To me it was pure, unashamed luxury.

Miss Hood was waiting for me in the kitchen. She was wearing the same bottle-green apron but this time it was over a sludgy-green, long-sleeved dress. The unfortunate colour cast a greeny tinge on to her face, making her look slightly seasick.

Her tongue was still as sharp as ever. 'Now, today and tomorrow are my days off and on these days your first duty will be to make the mistress's breakfast.' She placed a dainty traycloth on the large tray and set it with very fine, exquisitely made china that looked expensive.

I was making the tea and toast when she called me over. 'The mistress has a half of a grapefruit every morning and this is how you prepare it.' She took a small, sharp knife and proceeded to jab it into the fruit in a line of V-shaped cuts. When she pulled it apart it certainly looked pretty and much nicer than a straight cut.

'Now put the sugar sifter on the tray, girl,' she demanded.

I gazed around the kitchen in dismay. I had

148

never even heard of a sugar sifter before and had no idea what one looked like. She saw my dismay and she marched over with a large silver container that resembled an overgrown, albeit luxurious, salt cellar. She placed it triumphantly by the side of the grapefruit like a victorious general placing the winning flag. She said loudly, 'Imagine not knowing what a sugar sifter looks like! What kind of upbringing have you had, madam?'

For a brief moment I almost retaliated. I thought about all the poor people I knew – folk like my grandparents, the Ryan family and Rita and Nellie – plus the thousands like them who struggled daily to get enough to eat without worrying about special containers for the bloody sugar. These were people who, in spite of their dire poverty, were still charitable enough to offer a visitor a cup of tea and not act like this genteel dragon's welcome to me yesterday. But I remained silent.

The thought of my ten shillings at the end of the week acted as a silencer on my tongue so I concentrated on carrying the tray upstairs, gingerly feeling for each tread in case I tripped.

Miss Hood had gone ahead and my cautious attitude annoyed her. She called from the top of the stairs, 'Will you hurry up, girl? Everything will be stone cold by the time we reach the bedroom. Anyway this is my day off and I'm staying behind to show you your duties.'

She made it sound as if she was doling out a knighthood and I made a rude face at her retreating back. And she was also a liar, I thought, as Mrs Peters had told me that Miss Hood's day off began after Mrs Barrie's breakfast.

149

Mrs Barrie lay in a huge and highly decorative bed. I realised her room lay above the lounge because it had the same large bay window.

Miss Hood marched over and opened the thick velvet curtains. 'Good morning, Eva,' she said, helping the old woman into a pale blue bedjacket. She also plumped up a pile of fluffy pillows. There must have been ten pillows at least and I wondered anew at this world of wealth and plenty.

I took the tray over and looked around for somewhere to put it. Miss Hood saw this and I knew from the angry glint in her eyes that I was in for another telling off.

Before she could reach the bed, however, Mrs Barrie gave me a kindly look. 'The tray has little legs on it, Ann,' she explained, helping me pull the hidden part down. This was another revelation – a tray that turned into a miniature table. I wondered how many more secret and wonderful gadgets lay in store for me in this grand house. I made a mental note to ask Mrs Peters.

Mrs Barrie gave me another kindly look. 'Are you settling in all right, Ann?' When I nodded, she continued, 'I know that Lottie will show the ropes and, as it's her day off, perhaps I'll see more of you.'

Judging from Lottie's expression, this wasn't what she was expecting and I was positive that she was on the point of forsaking her time off in order to keep me well hidden and doing all the menial tasks.

She opened her mouth but Mrs Barrie turned to her. 'Now do have a rest, Lottie. After all, we're both getting on in years and I'm sure young

Ann will be a boon to you.'

Later, as we stood in the kitchen, Miss Hood handed me a list of chores. It almost filled two sides of the paper and she looked so satisfied with herself as she scrutinised the list before placing it in my hand.

'Apart from running the mistress's bath and taking in her meals, you will have no more dealings with her,' she almost spat at me. 'That is my job. Do you understand?'

I had been toying with the idea of asking for a few hours off – either on the Sunday or the Monday – just to check on Lily. As she swept through the door, she turned with a malicious look and said, 'Oh, by the way, you won't be getting a day off this week. Mrs Barrie said you'll have to wait till next Sunday.'

On that final note, she went out of the kitchen and I heard her moving around for a short time, then silence. There was no sign of her as I went upstairs to start my jobs.

Mrs Barrie was on her feet and was getting into a thickly quilted dressing gown. When she saw me, she said, 'You can maybe run the bath for me, Ann. That would be a big help.'

Compared to my tiny bathroom upstairs, this one was enormous and, like the rest of the house, it was luxurious. A large selection of glass bottles lined one of the glass shelves and, when she came in, she chose one. 'Put this in the water. It's one of my favourite bath oils.'

I did as I was told and the most wonderful perfume filled the air. It was a mixture of flower scents, just like a summer garden, and such a

151

contrast to the bar of carbolic soap that lay in my bathroom upstairs.

Miss Hood had left stiffly starched sheets to change the bed. It was such a struggle to tuck them under the giant-sized mattress. Unlike our beds at home, which were a doddle to change, this was more of a marathon task. Running around it, I tucked the sheets under each corner and followed them with a mound of soft blankets. The fat pillows were another problem because of their plumpness. As it turned out, my earlier assumption of ten pillows was wrong. I counted eight. Like a contender in a boxing match, I resorted to punching them into their soft fine covers. By the time the bed was made, I felt I had run a ten-mile race.

Like the rest of the house, either because of the open fires or Miss Hood's neglect, a thick dust had settled on all the surfaces and over the numerous ornaments and bric-a-brac. The room was pretty well cluttered up so I decided to work systematically, doing one area at a time. Scores of silver-framed photographs stood everywhere and they all showed a still-recognisable Mrs Barrie, albeit in her younger days. The poses were all in different costumes and showed her as a beautiful young woman with dark curly hair and large doelike eyes.

I dug out the tin of polish from the box and noticed with dismay that the contents were all dried up. It had obviously not been used for a long time. In spite of this, I worked as quickly as I could and was almost finished when Mrs Barrie came out of the bathroom, wafting in her flower cloud.

She saw me looking at my list and she asked, 'I hope Miss Hood hasn't left too many jobs for you, Ann?'

Under her kindly gaze, I almost blurted out the truth. Still, not having worked as a housemaid before, I didn't know if the list was long or not. I thought there was a lot but perhaps other house-maids did as much – or even more – so I shook my head. 'No, everything's fine, Mrs Barrie. There's just one thing. Do you want the books in the lounge dusted when I clean in there?'

She looked thoughtfully at me. 'You love books, don't you?'

I nodded eagerly.

'These books belonged to my late husband but, if you promise to treat them carefully, then you can certainly dust them.'

My face lit up, an expression that didn't go unnoticed.

'Another thing, Ann, if you promise to look after them, then you can borrow them to read.'

I was almost singing as I finished off all my jobs in her room. As I turned to leave, she called out, 'Oh, by the way, Ann, I was going to let you have this Sunday off but Miss Hood tells me there is a tremendous backlog of work to do and she can't spare you. I hope this doesn't spoil any plans you made for your sister?'

I could do nothing but shake my head. 'No, Mrs Barrie, I did say to my granny that it might be next Sunday before I saw them.'

By the time I went downstairs, I was on the verge of tears. That old besom, I thought, acting like she was the owner of the house – queening around in her awful manner. If Mrs Barrie wanted me to have one day off, even just a few hours, what right did this crabbit housekeeper have to overthrow the plans?

Mrs Peters was at the back door and, when I saw her cheery face, all my anger evaporated like morning mist. Miss Hood created this dismal fog around her then along came the sunny-natured cook and dispersed it.

Mrs Peters was throwing a handful of crumbs into the courtyard. Within seconds, a flock of birds appeared and strutted around. Two blackbirds with their shiny black coats and bright yellow beaks pushed their way in, scattering the tiny birds in their haste to gobble up the food. I drew back in alarm when I saw them.

The cook, looking mystified by my action, reassured me. 'They'll not bite you so don't be frightened.'

I wasn't taking any chances. 'Would these blackbirds attack you? Say if I was outside here in the courtyard?' I asked.

She laughed. 'Don't be daft, lassie. You've been reading too many nursery rhymes.'

I was on the verge of telling her about Ma Ryan's warning when a bell rang in the hall. 'That'll be Mrs Barrie. She must want something,' said the cook, still chuckling.

Mrs Barrie was sitting in front of a mahogany dressing table and she looked at me through the mirror. 'Ann, I'd like you to go to the post office in the village for me and post these letters.' She held up a large pile of white envelopes. 'Mrs Peters will give you instructions on how to get there.'

154

She turned round on the dressing stool. 'I do have another favour to ask you. I enjoy reading as well but I find the print is very small and difficult to read. Can you read to me this afternoon? About three o'clock? I normally go out for the day but I don't feel like it this week so a good book will cheer me up.'

My face lit up. 'Of course, Mrs Barrie – I'll enjoy that.'

The air was cold and bracing when I stepped through the gate – a fresh tangy wind that swept in from the sea with a tinge of salt in its breath. A pale winter sun shone on the sands and on the windblown patches of dune grass – grass that was almost bent double in its struggle for survival in the harsh salty conditions. Large cotton-wool clouds lay in a bunched-up mass out at sea, obscuring the horizon and bringing the promise of another storm. Since my arrival yesterday, the rain and sleet had been incessant and now another bout of bad weather was heading our way.

Still it was pleasant to stroll in the calm, cold sunshine I could hardly believe that I had been there just a little over twenty-four hours and, during that time, I had come to know how kind Mrs Barrie was. I had also discovered that Mrs Peters had originally come from Dallfield Walk in Dundee and Miss Hood, for some unknown reason, hated me intensely. I'd also come to know that the house seemed to be surrounded by blackbirds.

The post office was busy and I joined a queue of women who all looked comfortable with one another due, no doubt, to an intimacy born from

155

long acquaintance and neighbourly friendship.

I pushed the money for the stamps through the slit of the mesh screen and the middle-aged assistant commented on the weather, giving me the cosy impression that I was already part of this small community. It was like being at home. I was almost out of the shop when I spotted the wire stand full of postcards. Not sure how much money I had in my purse, I did a quick calculation. I had enough to buy three cards and three stamps. I bought a humorous one of a small kilted girl playing the piano for Maddie while Danny got a picture of an old Highlander with a crooked stick. This stick looked similar to the one carried by Harry Lauder and the man looked as bow-legged as Jeemy from the Overgate emporium. Granny got a nice one of Gray Street and, as for Dad, well, I didn't buy one for him because I could see it in my mind's eye, lying behind the door in the cold, neglected flat, unread.

Back at the counter once more, the woman, who wore spectacles similar to the ones worn by Rosie, smiled. 'Are you on holiday, dear?'

'No, I've started work with Mrs Barrie at White-gate Lodge,' I replied, handing over the correct money. It included quite a few halfpennies and was all the money I had.

She looked surprised. 'Has Miss Hood retired?'

I shook my head and explained that I was an extra pair of hands around the house. As I left, I overheard the woman standing behind me whisper to her companion. 'I didn't think yon old battle-axe had retired. She likes to give the impression she's the owner of the house and does she not like

156

to rule the roost?' In a curious way, this statement cheered me up and I was glad the housekeeper wasn't generally liked. I thought it was just me that didn't get on with her.

Later that afternoon, when the storm clouds moved overhead and thin streaks of sleet splattered against the windowpanes, Mrs Barrie settled back in her large armchair while I sat on a low stool, not quite at her feet but close enough for her to hear.

After the trip to the post office, I had spent a lovely two hours dusting all the books in the lounge. I noted all the authors – wonderful writers like Dickens, Walter Scott and Jane Austen – as I went.

That was why I almost fell of my stool in surprise when Mrs Barrie pointed to a bookcase in the corner of the dark morning room. 'You'll find the latest novel by Agatha Christie over there, Ann. I just adore mystery novels.'

After an hour and a half of reading, she stopped me. 'You will be getting tired, Ann, but I'm dying to know the ending. Maybe you can read to me tonight?' She hastily added, 'At least if you don't mind?'

'Oh, no, Mrs Barrie,' I assured her, almost adding that I was also keen to know how the story ended.

She smiled. 'It's easy to see you love books, Ann, because you have the talent to bring the story alive when you read the words.' She shook her head and added, 'Not like poor Lottie who hates the written word. Listening to her is such a trial as every word comes out with no expression.

To be honest, I resort to using my magnifying glass to read the book myself but that is our little secret. Perhaps you don't realise it but, when you read the text, your voice takes on a different tone for each character. If you got your voice trained, you would make a good actress.'

I went pink with pleasure at this compliment and, although I had no inclination to be on the stage, I relayed it to Mrs Peters when we sat down for our tea.

'Well, that is praise indeed, Ann, coming from Mrs Barrie. She was a famous actress in her younger days – even acted in films,' said the cook, spreading a floury scone with a huge dollop of jam. This was news to me but it explained all the photographs in the house.

The cook wiped a floury smear from the front of her ample bosom. 'Aye, she was on the stage in the West End of London for years and she even appeared in some silent films in Hollywood. She was called Evaline Bay in those days. That was her stage name because she was married to Mr Barrie by then.'

I couldn't understand why she had given up such a glamorous and exciting life to come and live so far from the scenes of her triumph. Especially with someone so sour-faced as Miss Hood. I said so.

'Well, she never had good health, even as a lassie, and, about ten years ago, they came here to help her recuperate after a bad dose of influenza. Then, just a month later after moving in, Mr Barrie collapsed and died. It was so sudden and so sad. I remember it well because I had just started working here.' She looked sadly at the half-eaten scone in her hand, almost as if reliving that sad time.

'Then that old besom Miss Hood wrote to her to commiserate on her bereavement and giving Mrs B. some hard luck story about some man she'd met but he had buggered off. And who can blame him, being shut up with her? She had been Mrs B's wardrobe mistress in the days of the theatre and the upshot was she was invited to come here as companion-stroke-housekeeper.' The cook stopped, a hard look in her merry eyes. 'Within a week of arriving, she was throwing her weight around like she was the owner of the house.'

'Does Mrs Barrie know what a horrible person she is?'

The cook almost choked on her scone. 'Not on your nelly. She makes sure she puts on her charming side upstairs but, down here, it is another matter. Still we don't have her company today or tomorrow although you will have her this week on your own.'

When she saw my worried look, she patted my hand.

'Never mind. It's just for this week and then we'll have our time off together.'

Later that night, after a companionable evening with Mrs Barrie and Agatha Christie, I had a lovely bath in my own private chamber. Then I went off to bed with a book from the lounge.

The small bedside lamp cast a warm glow over the quilt and a warm feeling of happiness spread through me as I snuggled into my pillows. On many occasions in later years, I was able to recall that happy night – that brief hiatus of pleasure. As a child, I had read somewhere that happiness is nearly always followed by sorrow as surely as night follows day. One thing was for sure – whoever wrote that certainly knew what they were talking about.

7

Trouble descended on me on the Monday like a thunderclap. Actually the blue touchpaper was lit on the Sunday afternoon with the return of Miss Hood.

Mrs Barrie and I were closeted in the morning room. Our reading session with Mrs Christie having finally come to a denouement, we were now engrossed with Dorothy L. Sayers – so engrossed, in fact, that Miss Hood's arrival had gone un-noticed until she swept towards us in a cold cloud of hate. I thought she was about to have a seizure. Her cold eyes like grey slate swept over me with such loathing that I could almost swear the temp-erature of the room dropped a few degrees.

Mrs Barrie, being short-sighted, missed this terrible look but she heard the footsteps. She turned in her chair, a bright smile on her face. 'Oh, you're back, Lottie. Did you enjoy your time off?'

Miss Hood tried to smile gaily at her but it only emphasised her fury. The bottom half of her face held a shark-like grimace – a so-called smile which, as usual, didn't reach her eyes and

160

stopped at a point midway across her nose.

She pulled off her long woollen coat that was neither beige nor brown and was another unfortunate colour for her to wear. She had such a strange complexion, I thought. Just as it had done when she was wearing her green dress, her skin seemed to echo the colour of whatever she was wearing. On this particularly cold Sunday evening, she looked as if she was suffering from a bad dose of jaundice. She snatched the detective novel from my hand and, if I had been standing instead of sitting on the low stool, I just knew she would have pushed me towards the blazing fire.

'That's fine,' she snapped. 'I'll take over the reading and you can go back to your chores.' As if to emphasise any laziness, she drew her gloved finger along the edge of the side table and looked at it in disdain.

If I hadn't been so alarmed, I would have laughed at her comical image. In her haste to oust me, she sat down on the stool still completely dressed in her hat, boots and gloves.

Mrs Barrie was taken aback by this display of brusqueness and, for a brief second, she looked angry. Suddenly she shrugged her slim shoulders and said softly, 'I think I've had enough reading for one day, Lottie.' Then she turned to me. 'Ann, will you bring in the tea tray please?'

I spent the rest of the evening dreading meeting Miss Hood but, for some reason, she stayed with Mrs Barrie for most of the time.

After a rotten, sleepless night, I crept downstairs and began my morning chores. I was kneeling on the stairs, dusting the banisters when she suddenly appeared from nowhere and swooped down on me. She gave me such a hefty shove that I almost toppled backwards. In fact, if I hadn't had a good hold of the banister, I would have landed in an untidy heap on the hall floor. With her mission unaccomplished, she walked back up the stairs, giving me another hefty shove that was so hard that I banged my shoulder and arm on the carved wood. A sharp pain surged through my arm and I cried out in agony.

She placed her face a few inches from mine and her fury was plain to see. At first I thought she was going to prise my arm away from its hold on the banister and perhaps that was her original intention. Instead, she hissed like a deadly cobra, 'You stick to the cleaning jobs around here, madam, and don't try and ingratiate yourself with the mistress. Is that perfectly clear?'

Although fear made me feel queasy, I suddenly remembered Mrs Peters and how she had stood up to her. I looked right at her. 'If Mrs Barrie wants me to do anything for her, then I will do it. She's my employer – not you.' Her face convulsed with anger but the unexpected sound of a voice calling from upstairs made her turn on her heel.

She gave me a backward, malevolent stare. 'Your job here depends on me.' She pointed a bony finger to her chest. 'And don't you ever forget that.'

She then climbed the stairs, calling out softly, 'I'm coming, Eva.' Her dulcet tones must have fallen on Mrs Barrie's ears like honey. Who could blame her for thinking everything was sweetness and light down here?

As that dreadful day progressed without the comforting presence of Mrs Peters, my chief ally, Miss Hood had me working every minute with no respite for a cup of tea or a meal. I stood in the yard with another pile of carpets. I could hardly hold the big carpet beater because of my increasingly sore shoulder. The cold wind didn't help either – it seemed to penetrate every muscle. The wind also whipped up the edges of the carpets, making it difficult to get any direct aim with the beater. I resorted to holding the corner with my bad arm and beating with my weaker left hand.

For a short time, I considered going upstairs and packing my small suitcase and going back home to the Overgate. Then the spectre of no money floated in front of me like a grey financial ghost and I knew I had to grit my teeth. I also had the horrible impression that Miss Hood was behind one of the dark windows, watching and gloating and rubbing her thin bony hands in glee.

After two hours, I struggled indoors with the heavy rugs and left them in neat rolls in the back lobby. One blessing, if it could be called that, was the fact that, although the wind was freezing cold, it had at least been dry – not like the other day when we, the rugs and me, had got a proper soaking.

There was no sign of the housekeeper so I put the kettle on to have a warming drink but, before it could boil, she was back in the kitchen with a huge mound of bedclothes. She marched me right out to the wash-house in the yard where she deposited the huge pile on the stone floor.

'These have to be washed right away so get on

with it,' she snapped, like some third-rate tinpot dictator.

I spent ages lighting the fire under the copper boiler. It had a look of neglect, as if it had been years since it had last been used but, once the fire was glowing, the water soon heated up.

I sorted through the pile and separated the sheets and pillowcases from the blankets, not to mention at least ten huge bath towels. By the time I pushed the first lot into the hot soapy water, darkness had fallen and, because I didn't know where the lamps were, I just kept working in the dark. It was so scary in the small vault-like building and I kept a wary eye out for the house-keeper – after all, she had injured me once already that day. I also kept an eye on the door in case any stray blackbirds flew in as the yard was their happy eating area.

By now, the pain had spread right up to my neck and down to my hip. Whether this was from the knock on the stairs or the manhandling of the heavy rugs and wet washing, it was difficult to say but I was grateful when the last load was done and I stumbled into the warm kitchen. I noticed with dismay that it was nine o'clock and supper was now long past.

Because the airing cupboard was still full with the wet rugs from the previous day, I had to drape the wet washing over a large clothes horse and I placed this in front of the warm Aga.

Starving with hunger because I hadn't eaten anything all day, I decided to cook something for myself. I scouted round the pantry, finding bacon and a large bowl of eggs plus a large white loaf.

Mrs Peters had told me to help myself to anything if I was hungry but I was unsure of Miss Hood. What if the tantalising smell of bacon wafted upstairs to her room? Would she descend like a Valkyrie? I thought for a moment that, if this should happen, then I would tell her to leave me alone – either that or I'd hit her with the frying pan. Having been brought up to respect my elders, this action was a mere rebellious thought but, in the end, I settled for tea and toast.

The atmosphere in the kitchen was damp from the warm steamy mist that arose from the wet washing. As I chewed my toast, I wondered idly where all the washing had come from. The pain in my shoulder was now throbbing as I made my way wearily to my room, remembering how happy I had been on Saturday night.

The upper stairs and lobby were normally lit by shaded ceiling lights and the old gas lamps on the wall were just silent reminders of the house's previous energy source. Tonight, however, everything was in darkness but, because I now knew my way around, I navigated the lobby in the dark. I was almost at my door when a figure materialised out of the gloom like a ghostly blur. To my horror, it was Miss Hood and she was waiting for me. She snapped the light switch on in my room and I saw the copy of the book in her outstretched hand.

'You little thief,' she snarled, her lips curling with satisfaction. 'Right then, madam, first thing tomorrow morning, you are going to see Mrs Barrie and you'll explain why you have one of her books in your room. Then I'll make sure you get your marching orders.' As she stormed off down the corridor, I wished she would trip over her feet but the footsteps receded down the narrow stairs.

I gazed unbelievingly at my bedroom. The bed had been stripped and she had moved the mattress for some reason – maybe to search for some more so-called stolen goods. I now realised where some of the washing had come from – from this room and there was no sign of any replacements either. There was also no sign of Danny's chocolate and Maddie's card had been torn in half and it lay on the floor. With a feeling of weariness and a very painful shoulder, I got down on the bed and lay my head on the scratchy blue-striped pillow.

My one consolation was the fact that I had permission to read the book but, just on the point of sleep, a horrible thought erupted in my dozy brain. What if Mrs Barrie couldn't remember saying I could borrow the books? After all it had been a pretty casual permit. Ma Ryan had predicted the blackbirds but not the housekeeper. Between that thought and the cold bed, I spent another miserable and sleepless night.

The next morning, on seeing Mrs Peters' motherly face, I almost fell into her arms.

'For heaven's sake, what's been going on here?' she asked, gazing open-mouthed at all the bedclothes drying in her kitchen.

I told her the whole sorry story. Pulling up my jumper to show her the large bruise which had now spread, in a multicoloured patch, from my shoulder almost to my waist.

She pressed her lips together. 'Right then, we're

going to tell Mrs Barrie about this.'

I was mortified. 'Please don't say a word. Promise me. I need this job and what if Mrs Barrie doesn't believe me? After all her housekeeper has been here years and I've only been here a few days. She'll maybe call me a troublemaker and you did say yourself that Miss Hood puts on a different face upstairs.'

She looked dubious for a moment then nodded. 'All right but, if this happens again, then we're telling her.' She pointed to the still-wet washing. 'I mean look at this. No washing is ever done in this house. Everything gets sent to the laundry in the Ferry. The man collects it every Wednesday.'

There was one small blessing I was grateful for. 'At least we'll both be off on the same days after this. I'll not be left on my own with her again.'

The cook said loudly, 'Damn right you'll not.'

I waited all morning for my summons about the book but, by evening, I still hadn't heard any word – either from the housekeeper or Mrs Barrie.

The cook had her own idea about it. 'You mark my words, you'll not hear another cheep about it because Mrs Barrie will have put her right about the book. That old witch will be left with egg all over her face and she'll not be happy to admit that.'

She pulled a pair of rubber galoshes over her shoes and put on her hat in readiness to go home. It had been another day of heavy rain and a miniature river swept down the drive towards the road drain where it disappeared with a loud gurgling sound. A cold wind swept in the open door and sent a smattering of raindrops over the patterned linoleum. I watched Mrs Peters as she departed into the darkness, skirting round the deep puddles.

I turned round with a deep sigh and almost fell over Miss Hood. She had obviously chosen her time to summon me upstairs. I held my breath for so long that I almost choked but she just glowered at me. She was certainly a sly one.

I waited in terror but, to my immense surprise, she crossed over to the Aga where a kettle simmered gently and filled two puggy hot water bottles. Without a word, she moved out of the kitchen as silently as she had entered, stopping briefly to place a slip of paper on the kitchen table.

It was a list of tomorrow's chores and I was dismayed to see the list grow longer with each passing day. Still I could cope with it and I hoped this silent treatment was to be in operation all the time. How wonderful if our only communication was to be through a slip of paper.

As it turned out, this was to last till Sunday lunchtime when another confrontation loomed out of the blue. I was eagerly getting ready to go home and was packing a bag of the cook's scones into my suitcase. They were a present for my grandparents. One niggling worry was the non-appearance of my wages so I went in search of Miss Hood.

Her pale eyes opened in surprise when she saw me. 'I would have thought a girl of your class would be out the door like a shot instead of hanging around her job.' She sounded so sarcastic.

I was determined to be polite. 'I've come for my wages, Miss Hood – my ten shillings.'

A sudden but triumphant expression flitted over her wrinkled face. 'Your what?'

I repeated it. 'My ten shillings.'

'Well you're out of luck madam. You get paid monthly here and I haven't forgotten about the burnt bread. It had to be thrown in the bin and that costs money. I'll be deducting that plus the beanfeast you had here on that first morning.' She smirked and it wasn't a pretty sight.

I couldn't believe that anyone could get so much pleasure from cruelty but this woman could. I did a mental count of my finances which were nil and apart from having to walk all the way home to the Overgate because I didn't have the bus fare, this all paled into insignificance against the thought of Granny's face. She was depending on this money.

There was no way I was going to throw myself on the housekeeper's mercy but, on the other hand, I needed my wages desperately. I was really angry with this old dragon because I had worked so hard and had done all the chores she set before me.

Her cold unblinking eyes stared at me and I realised where I had seen a look like that before – on a dead cod on the marble slab of Horatio Leslie's fishmonger shop.

With tears pricking the back of my eyes, I picked up my suitcase and headed for the kitchen. Mrs Peters was still busy. She normally left a hot Sunday lunch for the two women plus a cold supper for later. She tossed some diced carrots into a large pot of soup on the stove. She turned brightly when I entered. 'Well this is your first day off, young Ann, and you'll be looking forward...' She stopped when she saw my face. 'Don't tell me she's not letting you off?'

By now, because of the sympathy, tears began to trickle down my cheeks and I brushed them away with an embarrassed hand. 'It's just that Miss Hood tells me that I'm on a monthly wage but I can honestly swear that Mrs Barrie mentioned ten shillings every week and there was no mention of getting it every month.'

The cook pursed her lips, an expression she constantly used every time Miss Hood's name was mentioned. She went over to her coat which hung from a peg on the back door.

Taking her purse from her pocket, she said, 'I can let you have five bob, Ann. I know your granny is depending on it.' She took out two half crowns and handed them to me.

I was mortified and wished I had kept quiet. I put my hands behind my back. 'Oh, no, Mrs Peters, you need your money as much as I do. Don't worry, we'll manage somehow and Granny is aye short of money so another three weeks won't take too long to pass.' Although the words sounded brave, I was almost on the point of despair. Lily was growing bigger every week and she now needed to be fed on something more substantial than milk. She was also growing out of her clothes and, although Granny bought most of these from a small, second-hand shop in the Westport, they still cost money.

The cook looked doubtful. 'I wish you would

take it, Ann. We've a few bob saved up and I hate the thought of you not having any money for three weeks. It's a bloody disgrace, that's what it is. After all, I get my wages every week and it's been like that since I started here.'

I tried to smile at her. 'It's really good of you offering but we'll manage somehow.'

I waited till she hung up her dishcloth and collected her coat and message bag. As we opened the back door, Miss Hood appeared with a smirk as she headed for the soup pot. No one said a word but I was secretly pleased that I managed to hold my head up high.

Outside in the yard, the cook exploded. 'You know there's times when I could cheerfully throttle that old besom. I bet you a tanner, Ann, that Mrs Barrie doesn't know a thing about your wages. She seems to leave everything to her precious Lottie.'

She stopped to tie her scarf over her head. 'You mark my words, that Miss Hood has been feathering her nest since she came here. She's bought a wee cottage in Monifieth on the strength of living here and saving all her wages.'

'Oh, if only she would go and live there,' I said, with little charity.

We went down the path that skirted the front garden. Someone was sitting on the edge of the wall and I was delighted to see it was Danny. Although it was a pleasure to see him, I wasn't unduly surprised because I had an idea he would be here – our personal telepathy again. He turned round when he heard our voices, his delightful smile washing over his face like a summer sun.

Even Mrs Peters was bowled over by it. 'So you're Danny?' she said. 'I've heard all about you from your cousin. She did say you looked like a Greek god. I didn't believe it but she was right.'

Danny blushed so hard that his face almost matched his auburn hair.

The cook laughed. 'I'm just teasing you, son. Never mind me.' She pulled a pair of furry gloves over her hands, put her message bag over her arm and smiled again. 'Well, Ann, I'll leave you with Danny as you'll want to have a blether. I'll see you on Tuesday morning.'

Her plump figure departed down the road and I was once again grateful that she was a safety buffer for me. My nightmare with Miss Hood was still fresh in my mind and I had the bruise to show for it. My shoulder still throbbed painfully.

Then suddenly, a voice called my name. We both turned to see Mrs Barrie at the upstairs window. She called again and beckoned me. 'Come up, Ann, I want to see you. Use the front door.'

Danny raised his eyebrows as I darted up the path and, as I went through the front door, my heart was pounding as I was scared that I might meet Miss Hood. I ran swiftly up the stairs in case there was an emergency but I still dreaded the thought of running into the housekeeper.

Mrs Barrie was sitting in her high-backed chair, looking quite normal. If there was an emergency, I couldn't see it. She called me over. 'Come and sit down for a moment. I won't keep you long because I see your boyfriend is waiting on you.'

I did as I was told, explaining that he was my cousin but I didn't add that he was well liked by

172

Maddie, who I later found out was her god-daughter.

Mrs Barrie opened a capacious handbag and withdrew a tapestry purse from its depths. 'Now, Ann, I want to give you an extra half crown for your sister,' she said, handing over the coin.

I hesitated for a moment before gratefully accepting it. 'Thank you, Mrs Barrie. I'll give it to my granny and she'll spend it on Lily.' I stood up to leave but suddenly I had the courage to speak – a courage born from desperation. 'Mrs Barrie...' I stopped, my throat tightening with apprehension. 'Mrs Barrie, I didn't think I would be on a monthly wage when I came here to work. I thought it was weekly but Miss Hood says it's not.'

The sweet placid look shifted slightly and a glint came into her soft eyes. Oh, no, I thought, I've said the wrong thing. I prayed that I didn't get dismissed on the spot. But, to my utter surprise, she withdrew a crisp ten-shilling note from her purse and handed it to me.

'No, Ann, you're right – I did say it was a weekly wage but Lottie doesn't realise this. What we'll do is this. Every Sunday, come up here to be paid and, when Miss Hood gives you the wages, then you can repay me.'

It took all my willpower to stop me running over and giving her a hug but instead I simply thanked her.

She had an impish look on her face, like a small child with a great secret. She tapped the side of her nose and said, 'This will be our little secret from Miss Hood.' She laughed heartily. 'Now run

173

along for your time off and get down the stairs before she calls me for my lunch.'

I could still hear her laughing when I ran downstairs, still keeping a watchful eye out for Miss Hood. I was in the small vestibule when I saw her through the pane of glass in the inner door. She swept into the hall, a smug, self-satisfied expression on her face. It gave me great pleasure to see her looking like a cat with the cream instead of the cat that lost the mouse – a mouse, moreover, that had twelve and a tanner in her hand.

Danny was admiring the scenery when I came back down the path. It was another grey day with a sharp, strong wind that pushed gigantic waves on to the beach with a muffled roar. It was like the sound of thunder.

He tucked my arm in his and we set off for the bus stop. 'This is a different world from the Overgate, Ann – nothing but the sound of the sea.'

I turned sharply to look at him, my senses alert. Although his voice was light, I sensed he was worried about something.

'It's Lily – she's not well,' he said when I tackled him. 'She's had a very bad cold and Granny thought she was also teething but she's not eating or sleeping very well.'

I was suddenly grateful for the money in my pocket. If we had to call out a doctor, then we could pay his fee, even if it meant putting other things on hold.

By the time we reached the Overgate, my imagination was working overtime but I was taken aback by the explosion of noise that hit me like a slap on the face. After ten days at the Ferry with only the sounds of the sea, wind and rain, coming home to this cacophony of noisy humanity felt alien somehow. Then I realised I would have the same feeling in reverse when I left on Tuesday morning.

Lily was sitting on Granny's lap and I could see she had been crying. Tear streaks were still visible on her little cheeks and small bubbles of mucus erupted from her red nose. She didn't hold out her arms when she saw me and I had a terrible thought that she might have forgotten me. I was also alarmed to see how tired my grandparents looked so I went over and picked her up.

Granny looked relieved when she saw me. 'Oh, it's good to see you, Ann. Poor Lily is not herself these days and she's had this awful cough. I was convinced last week that she had whooping cough but it's not that and she's a wee bit better now.'

Another worrying fact was the coldness of the room, especially after the warmth of Mrs Barrie's house. Although a fire was lit, it wasn't a big blaze. On seeing my expression, Granny explained, 'I have to eke out the coal. I was expecting your dad to hand some money in over the last week but he hasn't shown up.' She sounded as evasive as Danny had been on the journey home. I was sure of that.

Grandad lay asleep in his chair by the fire. Every now and again a sleepy grunt would escape, followed by a melody of snoring ripples.

Danny shoved his hands in his pockets and looked at his feet before saying, 'I'll get away now, Ann. I have to visit Ma Ryan and Kit this afternoon but I'll see you later.' He stopped at the door. 'Oh, by the way, Maddie wants to see you so we'll both come over tonight.'

I ran after him. 'Danny, before you go. Do you remember I mentioned Ma's warning about a blackbird? Well, there's loads of them at the Ferry and I'm really scared of them. Can you ask her what she meant?'

He promised he would and, for the first time ever, I suddenly realised he was thankful to be leaving. Something was going on and I intended to get to the bottom of it – only don't let it be Lily, I prayed silently.

I made some milky Farola for her and began spooning the creamy mixture into her mouth. She cried and stretched, almost knocking the spoon from my hand but slowly, as she focused on my face, she relaxed and ate it all. Afterwards she fell sound asleep.

'Well, that's unbelievable,' said Granny. 'I could honestly swear it's you she's missing, Ann, and, now that you're back, she's settled.' She went over to the gas cooker only to find the meter needed pennies. 'Honestly, if it's not chucking coal on the fire, it's stuffing this meter with money. But Danny's been good to us. He bought a bag of coal last week for us but, with Lily not being well, we had to keep the fire burning day and night.'

She stepped down from the chair after placing three pennies in the meter which lay on the top shelf above the sink. She lit the flame under the kettle. 'Still we'll feel better after a strong cup of tea and you can tell me all about your grand job.'

I handed over the big bag of scones that had

been a present from Mrs Peters and I noticed she had also included a small slab of butter. Granny was overcome by this unknown woman's kindness and I was instructed to make her thanks known on Tuesday.

Later, with Lily asleep in the pram, I gave Granny the twelve and sixpence and the look of delight on her face was a joy to behold. 'Oh, Ann, this is a godsend and no mistake but you'll need some money for yourself.' She sounded evasive. 'And what about some for your dad?'

'No, Granny, maybe when you're a wee bit better off, then I'll take something for myself but all I want is my bus fares for next week.' As for Dad, well I was angry at him for not supporting Lily. 'I'm not sure about Dad. He should have brought some of his dole money to you and Grandad.'

Granny murmured sadly, 'Well, we all know what he's like so we'll see.'

Later that night I got Lily ready for bed. Granny had placed the bottle of camphorated oil on the fender by the fire. I rubbed a few drops into her chest and back. Its pungency almost made my eyes water but it was good for chesty colds and was nearly always used on children during the winter months. Grandad made a huge bowl of saps for her – a large slice of bread covered with hot milk and sugar. Although I hated this dish, Grandad assured me that this delicacy was a huge hit with Lily.

By now, I was beginning to think I had imagined the tension and I put the evasive feeling down to my over sensitivity which itself was a legacy of

Miss Hood's strangeness. Anyway, one minute there were just the four of us in the room and I was beginning to relax and the next Bella bounced in, followed immediately by Hattie. As usual Bella got to the comfiest chair first. On seeing two visitors, Grandad said he was going to the toilet at the end of the lobby. I thought of my own little bathroom at the Ferry and wished my grandparents had a lovely house with all the amenities instead of this constant struggle for survival.

Hattie was behaving strangely. She was making signs to Granny but stopped suddenly when she saw me looking at her. She fiddled with the piece of fur around her neck. This long-dead animal was a loathsome-looking thing with glassy, beady eyes that gazed unblinkingly at me. Bella, on the other hand, was looking at the two women with a malicious gleam and I realised that, for some unknown reason, she was thoroughly enjoying herself.

As for the tension, well, it was so thick that I could almost cut it. No sooner had I started to speak than Hattie began in the same instant. We both stopped but, when I looked at her, she remained silent. She looked at Granny with a will-I-or-won't-I-tell-her look. To say I was now truly worried was an understatement and I looked at Granny with my puzzled face. Bella didn't quite rub her hands together but I got the feeling she did it mentally.

Granny squared her shoulders, took a deep breath and looked straight at me. 'Ann, there's something I have to tell you.' My heart thumped painfully at the thought of bad news. 'It's about your dad.'

I jumped up from my chair and ran over to her. 'He's all right, isn't he? Has he been ill or hurt?' I shouted, aware my voice sounded loud in the confines of the small room.

Granny held up her hand. 'No, he's fine. It's just that...' She stopped and looked helplessly at Hattie. 'It's just that he's getting married again ... to a woman who lives in Ann Street – a Mrs Davidson.'

'Better known as the Merry Widow,' said Bella gleefully.

Hattie pursed her lips and looked at her in disgust. 'You would say that, wouldn't you?' she said sharply.

But Bella wasn't going to be ousted from her moment of glory. 'Well, that's what she is. She's put three men under the ground and collected their insurance policies. That came to few bob, I bet.'

Granny was now annoyed. 'For heaven's sake, you both make her sound like Dundee's version of Lucrezia Borgia. Mrs Davidson's men were hardly murder victims. The first two died in the war and the last one fell overboard from a boat and was drowned.'

Although I didn't contradict Granny, I couldn't see how these tragic deaths could possibly be classed as natural causes.

'She's a scarlet woman,' said Bella, obviously with a bee in her bonnet about this woman who was still unknown to me. 'She's the one that wears her lipstick right up to her nose and she plasters on the powder and rouge – a real painted-up

179

madam if ever there was one. Trying to attract a man by false pretences and now she's landed another sucker.'

Poor Bella, I thought, she was certainly jealous of the other woman's prowess on the attraction scales. I felt sorry for Bella – all the rouge and powder in the world wouldn't improve her plain looks.

Although shocked by this news, especially so soon after Mum's death, I still couldn't understand all the hostility. Surely they all wanted Dad to be happy.

Hattie had remained silent after her abortive attempt to speak but she now butted in. 'She's a really common person and her neighbours all say that her house is a pigsty. Mind you, if she's always on the lookout for a man, then she'll not have time to clean the house.'

Bella, who waited impatiently for Hattie to stop speaking, now produced her trump card. She looked at me slyly. 'Of course, she doesn't want any dealings with you or Lily. It's just your father she wants – no encumbrances is how she's putting it around the Hilltown. Another thing, she doesn't think your father should pay a penny towards Lily's upkeep. It's your responsibility now that you've got a job, Ann.'

Anger exploded inside me like an erupting volcano. I looked at Granny but she just shrugged her shoulders and glared at Bella. 'Well, maybe the woman didn't say these things, Ann. You know what the gossip is like on the streets.'

'But Dad can't shunt his responsibilities on to Granny, Grandad and me.' I knew I was shouting but I couldn't help it. 'My mum died giving birth to Lily and now he just wants to forget all about us...' I stopped, a forlorn thought flitting through my brain. 'Still, as Granny says, maybe it's just gossip.' I didn't believe it was all gossip but maybe a lot of it was exaggerated nonsense.

Grandad appeared just as Bella began to pour cold water over my suggestion. 'No, it's true right enough. Joe, your father's crony, came and told us last week – just after you left for the Ferry.'

I looked at Granny and she nodded.

Bella smacked her lips. 'Then Nan got a frantic visit from Nellie and Rita. They've tried to tell him he's making a big mistake but he'll not listen.' She stopped and the gleeful look was replaced by a sour expression. 'Women like the Merry Widow can be like syrup over a hot pancake, I can tell you.'

For the first time, Grandad ventured an opinion. 'What do you know about men, Bella, seeing you've never had much success in that way? As far as we're concerned, if Johnny doesn't want his family, then we don't need him or his fancy woman. We'll look after Ann and Lily with or without his help.'

At that moment, I felt so proud of my grandparents that I almost burst into tears.

Meanwhile, Hattie was still bemoaning Mrs Davidson's common personality and lack of housewifery skills. 'How could Johnny be attracted to such a common woman? I saw her in the street the other day and she still had her Dinky curlers in her hair and it was covered by a manky-looking headsquare – and it was teatime.' Hattie shud-

181

dered. 'She then had the audacity to wave to me like she was already a relation of mine.' She gave another slight shudder but whether this was because of the tatty scarf or the fact she was common wasn't clear.

I looked at my grandparents, noting, once more, their tiredness and I was furious with Dad for putting the care of a young baby on their shoulders. 'Right then,' I said, my mind made up, 'I'm having a word with him tomorrow about all this.' Although my words sounded brave, I knew within my heart that, if he was indeed smitten with his new love, then my words would fall on deaf ears.

Bella brightened up. 'That's right, Ann, you knock some sense into the daft bugger's head.'

Hattie placed the dead animal around her neck and prepared herself for the final word on the unsuitability of her intended sister-in-law. 'I wouldn't mind him getting married again if she was a nice person with a bit of class.'

There was no mention as to whether this so-called nice woman with class would also be selfish enough to persuade a man to abandon his family, but clearly this was not important in Hattie's view. Hattie would forgive anything from someone who lived up a close with a tiled wall.

Granny shook her head sadly. 'What a family – a son that acts like an idiot and a daughter that acts like a snob.'

Then, at that point, Danny and Maddie arrived into the fray and Hattie almost had a fit. She didn't like Maddie visiting the house in the Overgate, what with the dilapidated pram, the worn lino and the equally ancient looking furniture, not to mention the outside toilet. For the thousandth time she earnestly wished her parents lived in a nice house in a classy location.

Maddie gave me a warm smile and wanted to hear all about my job but, when she realised there had been a family crisis, she stopped in mid sentence and stayed silent – not that I would have mentioned Miss Hood to her. I know I didn't have to explain my unhappiness to Danny, he had already sensed it and that was the reason for him coming to the Ferry this afternoon.

My one blessing was that Lily seemed to be over her illness and Granny had some money to help with the daily grind of life. Because of Maddie's appearance, the topic of Dad's intended marriage was dropped.

Bella now began her long catalogue of illnesses – real and imagined. As usual, Maddie was her confidante and, years later, Danny and I maintained that Bella was the main reason for Maddie becoming a nurse. After all, there wasn't a complaint or illness under the sun that Bella hadn't encountered first. In fact, the doctors at the Royal Infirmary should have awarded her a badge.

I didn't walk back with them to the Perth Road because I was tired but Danny appeared later. 'Come out for a quiet walk, Ann,' he said.

The street was as busy on a Sunday as any other day and, once again, I was struck by the clamour. The open shops and upstairs windows all looked dim in the subdued glow from the gas lamps, especially after the brightness of the electric light at Whitegate Lodge.

'Are you going to see your dad tomorrow, Ann?' he asked.

I nodded.

'Well, although nobody knows much about it at the moment, your dad is drinking a lot with this Mrs Davidson. Joe told me in confidence that his pals are worried about him. He never buys any food for himself and although Rita and Nellie do their best for him, they're hard up with this means test and they've bairns to feed as well.'

A feeling of despair washed over me. 'Oh, Danny, what will I do? He'll not listen to me but he's got to realise that Granny can't look after Lily forever. I can't give up my job although I hate the housekeeper.' And I went on to tell him the details of my treatment at her hands.

Danny was furious. 'You've got enough on your plate as it is, Ann, without that tyrant but I did get the feeling something was wrong. Still, jobs are hard to find and I'm grateful for my job with Lipton's.' He stopped as if a thought had entered his mind. 'Why don't you tell Mrs Pringle or Maddie about the rotten housekeeper?'

This was the last thing I wanted and I said so. 'What if Mrs Barrie asks me to leave if there's trouble? No – I'll just have to not let it bother me and I have Mrs Peters on my side.' At that moment, the thought of the motherly cook filled me with confidence. Then I suddenly thought of Rosie. I hadn't seen her that night.

Danny explained why. 'She's heartbroken about your dad. She also knew about this big family meeting and she's keeping out of it. The strange thing is, she knew about your dad long before Joe and the neighbours. She told me she kept seeing him and Mrs Davidson in the snug bar of the Windmill pub every time she went in with the *War Cry* paper. Again, in confidence, she told me that he was always drunk and that this woman was always hanging around him, telling all and sundry that they were getting married. Poor Rosie.'

I was appalled. 'Don't tell me this woman drinks as well? Maybe it's a blessing that Lily will not be going to live with them. I couldn't bear the thought of her being ill-treated and neglected.' A surge of anger swept over me at this thought.

We walked back up the stairs in the semi-darkness. Because the gas mantle was partially broken, only a thin blue flame erupted from it, illuminating a few inches of wall but failing to cast any light on the well-worn stone stairs.

'Just think how great it would be if Dad married Rosie – she's such a treasure,' I said.

Danny agreed, then added, 'Oh, I almost forgot – Ma Ryan said to watch out for a blackbird, Ann, and that you're in danger from it. The only thing is, she doesn't know what the danger is.'

He looked so worried that I smiled and reassured him. 'Don't worry, Danny, I promise to look out every time I hang out the washing and I'll not end up like the maid in "Sing a Song of Sixpence" – I'll not lose my nose,' I said, trying to sound cheerful.

Later in bed, cheerful was the last word for how I felt. I still had this onerous task ahead of me tomorrow and I couldn't help but ponder on the unfairness of life. Dad could have married Rosie with all her motherly qualities but instead he had chosen a woman who wore her lipstick right up to her nose. In the attraction stakes, it seemed as if the lipstick had won by a few miles.

8

It was only 11.30 a.m. and dad was in the Windmill pub – at least that was the story according to Rita. I was sitting in her tiny kitchen, having a cup of tea and listening to her toddler son wailing with indignation at not being allowed out of the old, paint-chipped playpen which took up half the floor space. Lily was also in it, sitting in the far corner with an old rattle in her hand and a mesmerised expression on her face at the antics of the red-faced toddler across from her.

Rita had collared Joe who had been standing with his usual gang of cronies. She had dispatched him with the message that I was here and waiting to see my father. Joe set off up the hill like a puffing steam train.

Once again I had poked my head into our flat and again I was dismayed by the forlorn neglect. Either Dad was just using it as a place to sleep or else he was living somewhere else. I was hoping he would hurry up and come to Rita's house as I had promised to take Lily for her usual walk along the Esplanade. I was also feeling tired, having not long spent the early part of the morning at the wash-house doing the weekly wash.

Either way, I was fed up and annoyed at Dad for avoiding his responsibilities. As a result I was only listening to Rita's chatter with half an ear.

Suddenly she stopped, bringing me out of my reverie. 'That's Joe now.'

Joe sat down, trying to regain his breath. 'I'm getting too old to be living on this hill,' he panted, as if he had run a five-mile race. He gave me a sheepish look. 'Your dad doesn't want to come to here but he says he'll meet you at the Plaza door.' He sounded apologetic – as if this bad news was his fault.

Rita opened her mouth as if to protest but I was too tired for any more arguments. I stood up. 'That's fine, Joe – I'll go and meet him.' I turned to Rita who stood with an angry look. 'Can I leave Lily here for a wee while?'

'Of course you can, Ann.' She gazed with weariness at her son who was now shaking the bars of the playpen like some demented gorilla at the zoo. She bent down and lifted him up. 'All right, you wee toerag. Do you know you're giving Lily a fright with all your roaring?'

It was another cold day but it was now dry, the earlier rain having stopped. I jumped over deep puddles of dark rainwater and skirted around the miniature river that was running down the gutter. I noticed, with amusement, the clutch of young children squealing with delight as they ran alongside a flotilla of pretend boats made from sweetie wrappers. They all clapped their hands with joy as these fragments disappeared down the drain, along with the swirling, dirty water.

As usual, the street was abuzz with people. They

were standing on street corners or in shop doorways. Being unemployed, they had lots of time for gossip. I rehearsed all the things I had to say to Dad – most of them were angry accusations. My anger wasn't helped by the fact that the entrance to the Plaza cinema was devoid of people and there was no sign of him on the street.

I stepped into the shelter of the large doorway, tightly pulling my coat in an effort to keep warm. The cold wind swirled around me, gently rattling the glass doors of the picture house and pushing a pile of discarded debris into the far corner where it lay in a cigarette packet mountain. After ten minutes, I was really furious. Joe's message had been delivered thirty minutes earlier and there was still no sign of him leaving the pub.

I walked up as far as the Windmill door but my view inside was restricted by the inner swing doors. I hesitated on the threshold, almost willing Dad to appear – nothing.

Suddenly the thought of Lily being left with Rita, who had enough to cope with without the added burden of my problems being dumped on her lap, leapt into my head and I made up my mind. I pushed open the door and entered the inner sanctum. I was in a long low-ceilinged bar with the warm stale smell of beer. A bluish haze was hanging like a cloud over the assorted chairs and tables. This smoky residue was almost certainly from the previous evening because the place was deserted except for the barman, a plump, cheery-faced man who was washing glasses behind the shiny-topped bar. He was whistling something totally tuneless but stopped in amazement when I rushed into the middle of the room. He gazed at me with his smooth round face, unsure if I was a customer or had perhaps been catapulted from a giant sling to land at his feet, so sudden was my entrance. My courage evaporated like morning mist and I turned, prior to running back outside.

'Can I help you?' he said, his face still puzzled. 'I mean are you looking for somebody? Because you're too young to buy a drink in a pub.'

I looked at him, my face red with embarrassment. 'I thought Johnny Neil was in here,' I stuttered.

His eyes opened wide and I could almost hear him thinking, 'Now what does she want with him?'

Instead, he nodded his head towards the door and I thought for one awful moment that Dad had left without seeing me. He nodded again. 'He's in the snug bar – just through the door and it's on your left.'

With my anger now threatening to erupt like some distant earthquake, I pushed my way into the snug bar which was well named because it was so tiny. A small hatch looked on to the main bar and there was just enough room for a well-worn, tatty-looking bench to be placed along one wall, under the window.

Dad sat on this bench and suddenly all my anger disappeared to be replaced by a feeling of pity. His weight had dropped so much that his threadbare jacket now looked two sizes too big for him and the week-old stubble didn't improve his neglected, dishevelled appearance. Still, I was relieved to see he was sober but the pub hadn't

189

been open for long and it was a long day into night. He looked up in surprise as I entered, along with the cold, swirling wind.

He smiled – a lovely smile that, up until last summer, had captivated everyone. 'Hullo, Ann. What are you doing here? How is the job going?' I could tell he was trying to be both cheerful and carefree but he failed on both counts.

I looked at him reproachfully. 'Dad, for goodness' sake, what's the matter with you? You look terrible and you were supposed to meet me at the Plaza door.' I hadn't meant to be so forthright so, in an effort to cover up my brusqueness, I said gently, 'Come home with me. You can see Lily while I make your dinner and I'll get some messages in for you.'

To my surprise, he backed away from me. 'No, I'm not going back to that house. It has too many unhappy memories for me.' Tears appeared in his eyes but he brushed them away with an angry hand. 'No, away you go back to Granny and your new job and don't worry about me.'

Then, before I could answer, the door opened and a woman came in, tottering on uncomfortable-looking high heels. She was small and very thin and in her forties, I thought, with dark blonde curls framing a white, pinched-looking, sharp-featured face.

There was no sign of the Dinky curlers or the manky headsquare and, although no lipstick was evident, the pinky remains of the last application was still visible. It gave her mouth a round 'O' look as if she was permanently surprised by everything.

190

'Johnny...' She stopped when she saw me and began to do a funny reverse movement through the narrow door. She wobbled on her high heels and for a moment it looked as if she would topple backwards but she managed to regain her balance. She gave me a small, apologetic smile before backing out.

Dad had stayed silent during these manoeuvres but I noticed an amused glint in his eyes. 'That's Marlene and no doubt Rosie has told the entire Overgate about her. She must see some awful sights, our Rosie, because of her habit of shaking her can under our noses in the pub, selling her Sally Ann papers.'

'No, Dad,' I said quietly, 'it wasn't Rosie. She never said a word. It was your pals and your neighbours who are worried about you.'

He looked surprised. 'So it wasn't Rosie?' he said thoughtfully.

'Granny says that Rosie wishes you the best of luck with Mrs Davidson.' I stopped. I'd almost said 'the Merry Widow'. 'Rosie says if she makes you happy, then good luck and she'll not bother you again about getting Lily christened.' I looked him straight in the eye. 'Is it true you're getting married again, Dad?'

Once again the amused glint appeared. 'Och, Ann, you're not to listen to old women's gossip and neither has your granny. I just like Marlene's company and we have a good laugh together.'

I doubted that because he looked as if the last good laugh he had was over a year ago – when Mum was still alive.

As if he read my mind, the amused glint van-

191

ished to be replaced by a terrible sad look. 'I can't go back to the house, as I've told you, because of all the memories. Maybe if I had a job it would be better but hanging about day in and day out without your mother is terrible.'

I suddenly knew how he felt and there was nothing I could do about the situation. We all missed Mum terribly but we had Lily to look after so maybe we were coping better with it. As for Dad, well, as Granny said, he had to come to terms with his own private grief and made his own life for himself.

'So there's to be no wedding, then?' I said.

He looked over his shoulder towards the door, placing a finger to his lips. 'Not so loud. Don't let Marlene hear that —she thinks there is but there's many a slip 'tween the cup and the lip,' he said, giving me a huge wink.

I had to laugh in spite of my earlier anger. 'Oh, Dad, you're a right charmer. First Rosie and now Marlene.'

As I made my way out of the snug bar, he called after me, 'Tell Rosie I'm asking for her.'

'No, Dad, that's something you'll have to do for yourself.'

I gave him a final sad wave just as Marlene's head appeared from the door of the main bar. She was patting her curls and she had an odd, anxious look on her face. Another thing I noticed as I quickly left was the fact that she had put on her make-up. Her face had a curious orange tint and, as Bella had succinctly put it, cherry-red lipstick right up to her nose in an exaggerated Cupid's bow.

Joe was waiting for me at the foot of the Hill-town. When he saw me, he detached himself from the large group of men. I saw Jamie amongst the group but fortunately he was too busy trying to extract the last few puffs from a half-inch cigarette stub. His thin cheeks were sucked in with the effort and I wondered if he was using the old ploy of holding the cigarette with a Kirby grip in order to get a few more puffs. As it was I was just grateful that our Hogmanay encounter had obviously been forgotten. Joe didn't speak. He merely lifted an eyebrow but I knew he was worried about Dad.

'I've seen Dad, Joe. He looks terrible but there's nothing anybody can do for him. He'll sort himself out in time, I hope.'

Rita wasn't alone when I knocked and entered. She was standing by the side of the playpen, her arms crossed as if she was feeling the cold through her thin, shabby cardigan. She also looked annoyed. A small plump man was standing in front of the cupboard which was wide open, exposing the wooden shelves which had faded paper on their surface. In one corner lay a few items of food. It wasn't exactly Mother Hubbard's cupboard but it was a close cousin. The man had round grey eyes and rosy cheeks and looked well nourished. He looked like an overgrown gnome but, when he spoke, all the chubby cheerfulness of an elf disappeared.

He squinted at me as I bent over the playpen to pick up Lily, his saucer-shaped eyes now like steel slits. 'Right, then, you'll be the daughter of this house,' he yapped. For such a small man, he had a deep gruff voice – one more suited to a giant in a fairy tale than a gnome. He gave us a 'holier than thou' look, licked his pencil and proceeded to write in his notebook. 'Now, let's see. What's your name and the bairn's name so I can put it in my book?'

Rita launched herself across the room. Placing her thin body directly in front of him, she turned to face me. 'This is the man from the means test. He's come to check if we've any caviar in the press. He seems to think he's got the almighty right to come barging into the house and rake through our cupboards like we're common criminals.'

The man stood silent, letting this tirade pass over his chubby head. He poised the pencil over his book and said, 'I think I asked for your name and the name of the bairn?' He snapped at me like I was some deaf mute and hadn't heard his request the first time.

I was angry – not only at this intrusion into the lives of decent people whose only crime was to be jobless but also at his assumption of my marital status, as if he had been sent ahead from heaven in preparation for the judgement day.

I glared at him as I hugged Lily. 'I don't have to answer any of your questions, mister, but I'll tell you this – not only am I not married but this isn't my bairn.'

His face lit up and I was suddenly reminded of Miss Hood. Perhaps it was the same malicious pleasure in other people's misfortunes. Like Miss Hood, this was another person who obviously relished their job.

Although now near to tears at this heavy

handed and needless treatment, I put on Lily's pixie hood in preparation for leaving but not before the last defiant parting shot. 'You can just score out all your writing because I happen to have a job. I'm a housemaid at Broughty Ferry and I not only support myself but my baby sister here. I'm not on the dole so I don't get paid a pittance from them.'

The man jumped forward and, for a split second, I thought he was going to bar the door. 'Now, just a minute, I think you belong to this house. That you're supporting the occupants here and I don't want any messing around.'

It was at this point that Rita's son, who had been asleep after his initial bout of temper in the playpen, awoke with a loud wailing cry. He was hungry but the man glanced at him with extreme annoyance. 'Just be quiet, sonny, till I fill in my forms.'

This plea fell on deaf ears and he cried even louder. Rita, desperate to get him fed, said quietly, 'Just tell him where you live, Ann.'

Much against my will I told him, not mentioning the house next door to Rita's in case Dad got questioned as well.

He glowered at me, shaking his head slightly as if it was all a pack of lies. 'I don't believe you,' he said, his officious manner now more pronounced. 'I think you're the lassie of this house and, if you're not, then you're the lodger and your landlady here is also a childminder.' The thought of the two misdemeanours seemed to fill him with joy and he turned to Rita. 'You know what the penalties are if you keep a lodger. Your money will be reduced in lieu of it and, if you're also taking in bairns to look after, then there will be another reduction.'

Rita had had enough. 'Look here, you slimy wee toerag, you officious wee swine, my man fought in the war as a sixteen-year-old laddie to keep folk like you from living under the Kaiser. And another thing – he went for a job last week and do you know what? When he got there, two hundred other men were ahead of him in the queue.' Although her stance was defiant, I could see she was close to tears. The child was still howling as she marched over to the bed to pick him up.

'I'll see you to the door, Ann,' she said striding ahead of me with a determined air.

The man took the hint as well but not before issuing a final warning. 'I'll be back to check on this close, mark my words.'

As he glanced along the passageway towards our house, I held my breath. 'I never seem to find that occupant in but I'll be making enquiries about them so you'd better tell them.'

We stood in silence as he swaggered off down the stairs. When he was out of sight, tears ran down Rita's cheeks. 'What a life, Ann, isn't it? No money and no work and now we're being hounded like we had robbed a bank or something equally dramatic.' A weak smile flitted across her mouth. 'Mind you, not that I haven't thought about robbing a bank.'

I knew she was joking because she was an honest woman but I felt sorry for her. She had all this worry on her shoulders but we were all in the same boat. I at least was lucky to have my job and once again I was grateful for Mrs Pringle's help.

'What job did your man go for, Rita?'

'Well, he heard a whisper that a foundry in Dock Street was looking for a labourer but half the bloody town must have heard the same whisper. There was a huge queue of men already waiting but nobody seems to know who got the job. That's the worst of it.'

I nodded sympathetically.

'Never mind,' she said, wiping the tears away. 'How did you get on with your dad?'

I told her about his reluctance to return to the house but I didn't mention that I had met him in the pub – that would have really riled her.

'Is he getting married to Marlene Davidson?' she asked.

I remember the amused look and the huge wink. Maybe during a weak or lonely moment the Merry Widow would succeed but I hoped not. Instead I replied truthfully, not wanting to deceive a good neighbour. 'Well, he said not to listen to gossip, Rita.'

'Well, we'll keep our fingers crossed that it doesn't happen,' she said as she turned to go back into the house. 'I'd better get the bairn's dinner ready or he'll bring the house down with his girning. The worst thing is, there's another bairn on the way.' She patted her stomach, an unhappy look on her face. 'Tell your granny we're both delighted.'

As I went downstairs, I knew she was being flippant. No doubt delight was the last word Rita and her man would use to describe having another mouth to feed in a few months.

Granny was full of pity for her when I relayed this news to her. 'What a shame – as if Rita doesn't have enough to put up with.'

She was a bit more annoyed about Dad. 'What a devil he is and has always been. I remember when he was a laddie, the amount of lassies he knew was enormous. Then he met your mother and he settled down but now it looks like it's all starting up again with Rosie crying every night and now Marlene with her high hopes.' She shook her head in wonder.

I saw, in my mind's eye, Marlene's white pinched face with its anxious look and Dad's unkempt and unshaven look and I wondered where the attraction lay. I said so.

Granny gave me a knowing look and laughed. 'Never mind, young Ann. Wait till you're older and you'll know all about it.'

Oh, I hope not, I thought. Dealing with Miss Hood was troublesome enough.

Later, as I pushed Lily along the Esplanade, I was worried about going back to the Ferry and the tyrannical housekeeper. Being at home with my family and friends made me realise what kindly people they were – not like the horrible Lottie.

Then I saw with dismay that Lily was fast out-growing everything, including her pram. Although it was still rickety and squeaking with every push, it had been a boon for her and Grandad. He had picked up a pair of dilapidated-looking reins with a faded rabbit embossed on the front and I secretly hoped they hadn't been purchased from

Jumping Jeemy but they kept her securely in the pram which was a blessing because she was now able to lean out and study the wheels or the pavements, both of which seemed to fascinate her.

The air was fresh and salty as we walked along beside the river. A group of men with home-made, crude-looking fishing rods were hanging over the seawall. They looked as if they were almost willing any passing fish to take the worm bait.

Beyond them, through the tracery of the Tay Bridge, white puffs of smoke from a south-bound train soared into the air. I turned the pram so that Lily could see the train, hoping that maybe some of the passengers heading out of the city would wave to her. She was such a pretty little girl and I made up my mind, there and then, that, come what may, I would try to like Miss Hood – after all, Lily's future depended on it.

The next morning, when I turned up at Whitegate Lodge, my resolve faltered when I saw the housekeeper was as sour-faced as usual. I knew it was going to be an uphill struggle either to like her or ignore her.

I inwardly dreaded another hefty shove from her and I tried hard not to cringe every time she passed by. But, thankfully, for some unknown reason, she ignored me and I breathed a sigh of relief.

I gathered up my housemaid's box and began my morning chores. Later, I was sitting down to lunch with Mrs Peters, who said I was to call her by her first name, Jean. As we were eating, Miss Hood skulked in and lifted a tray without her usual snide or sarcastic remarks.

'What's the matter with old sourpuss?' Jean asked, astonishment written all over her face. 'I know – you've threatened her with yon big bread knife, Ann!'

I laughed although I was a bit shocked. 'Oh, I'd never do that.'

Jean laughed. 'Och, I'm just kidding you. But I will say this – I bet she's had an earful from Mrs Barrie about how to treat you.'

Just prior to Miss Hood's appearance, Jean had been telling me how she arrived at the Ferry. 'Well, it was like this. Three or four of us young lassies used to come here to the beach every Sunday during the summer months to have a wee paddle in the water but mainly to find a click.' She saw my puzzlement and explained. 'A click – you know, a young man. In those days I was quite bonny and slender even though I say it myself. I didn't have this.' She patted her ample stomach and I was reminded of Rita and wondered how her pregnancy would go.

The cook continued, 'Well, one Sunday we got in with this group of folk on the beach and, after a lot of sand throwing and general banter, Will and I started to go steady. His father had a wee joiner's business in Long Lane and they lived above the workshop. The business wasn't big enough for two families so we stayed in Dundee at Dallfield Walk. We got a house right next door to my mother and Will landed a good job at the docks as a stevedore – at least it was a good job if the boss picked you to unload one of the ships but it wasn't so good if you didn't get picked. Of course, we were never blessed with bairns...' Her face clouded briefly but then she became her usual cheery self again. 'Oh, well, that was a long time ago so there's no use lamenting over it. Then, twelve years ago, Will's father died and his mother followed a couple of months later. So Will inherited the business and the house – him being the only child – so here we are.'

'Do you ever go back to visit your mother?' I asked. I thought she could maybe visit Granny and Lily. I felt so sad for her. I had seen the flicker of unhappiness when she mentioned her childless state. On the other hand, I could well imagine Rita saying, 'Lucky you!'

'Hardly ever,' she said. 'My mother is dead as well and we never seem to have the time. Anyway, I love it here at the Ferry. The air is so fresh and tangy and not like the jute smell in Dundee.'

Then Miss Hood put her head around the door and snapped at us, 'Mrs Barrie is expecting visitors tonight. She wants the lounge fire lit at four o'clock and you will be required to work an extra hour tonight to serve refreshments when they arrive.' She glared at me before stomping off, looking as if she had lost a half crown and found a tanner.

Jean looked at me over the rim of her cup but she was as nonplussed as I was. It was the first time I had heard of these visitors but, whoever they were, their visit was certainly arranged quickly. One thing I had learned while working in the house was the fact that the social calendar was usually well mapped out in advance. Because of this, I was full of curiosity – as was the cook.

As she was leaving, she whispered furtively, 'You can tell me who the visitors are tomorrow. Maybe it's film stars!' She stopped and gave this notion another thought. 'No, it'll not be film stars because they would stay for a meal and this lot are just having refreshments. Oh, well, you can tell me all about it tomorrow, young Ann.'

She was no sooner out the back door than I was sent to the lounge to plump up the fat feather cushions and draw the curtains. I had lit the fire as instructed and once again I let the beauty of the room wash over me. It looked so different at night with the glowing red flames in the ornate fireplace. A selection of lamps dotted around the room also added to the cosy glow, shedding light on the silver photo frames and reflecting off the shiny polished furniture.

Then there were the books, all now lovingly dusted, and, although I still admired them daily, I hadn't borrowed another one since that awful night when Miss Hood had accused me of stealing one.

The doorbell clanged loudly and I went into the hall but Miss Hood scurried ahead of me to open the door, bestowing on me a look of utter distaste, almost as if a beetle had crossed her path. When the door was opened, I almost fell over in surprise as Maddie burst in along with a flurry of raindrops and a gust of cold wind. She was followed by her parents and I heard them tell the housekeeper that Hattie was looking after Joy for the evening.

The change in Miss Hood's manner was astonishing to say the least. She didn't exactly curtsy but she fawned, for the want of a better word, over them. Maddie gave me a quick wink before being ushered into the lounge by Miss Hood.

I was still standing slightly dumbstruck when Miss Hood reappeared and snarled quietly in my ear, 'Go and bring the tea tray, you stupid girl.' She then swept regally away towards the door, just behind Mrs Barrie who was leaning heavily on her stick.

Before entering the lounge she snarled again, 'I've been asked to join the company tonight.' A gleam of smugness was visible in her pale eyes.

Being well aware that Mrs Pringle had found this position for me, I hoped desperately that I hadn't done anything wrong in the job. Something must have happened for them all to appear so suddenly. My mind was churning with worry as I manoeuvred the heavy tray on to the table beside one of the sofas.

'Ah, here is Ann, my lovely new housemaid,' beamed Mrs Barrie while the housekeeper tried to keep her social smile intact.

I could see she was finding this difficult and, in other circumstances, it would have been comical but I knew she would exact her punishment at some future date.

I was also aware that Maddie was gazing wide-eyed at me but I daren't look at her in case I burst into laughter.

Mrs Barrie leaned towards Miss Hood, 'That is all we'll need tonight, Ann. Perhaps Lottie can remove the tray later, once we've finished our tea?' She looked at the housekeeper with a smile and Lottie nodded, like an old dowager dishing out favours. 'Well, that's fine,' said Mrs Barrie. 'Just finish off now, Ann, and we'll see you tomorrow.'

I murmured my goodnights and escaped up the back staircase to the sanctuary of my room. From the window, I saw the Pringles' Baby Austin car. Its gleaming paintwork, highlighted by the street lamps, was peppered by raindrops.

A sudden light footstep on the stair made me whirl around in alarm but it was Maddie. She carried a large bag in her hand.

'Hullo,' she said brightly, 'are you surprised to see me?'

'Maddie, what's the matter? Am I losing my job?' Fear had added an edge to my voice although I tried hard to control it. I was remembering Miss Hood's queer silences. Maybe she had succeeded in putting forward all her complaints about me – real or imaginary.

Maddie's eyes widened in surprise. 'For heaven's sake, Ann, of course you're not losing your job. What makes you think that?' She was puzzled.

'It's Miss Hood, Maddie. She hates me and is so nasty to me.' I then told her everything, holding nothing back.

I also got her to promise to keep quiet. 'I need this job Maddie and after all she is the only nasty person here. Mrs Barrie and the cook are lovely people.'

She looked angry, her blue eyes darkening with disgust. 'I always thought she was a creepy-crawly sort of a person and I've never really liked her.' She laughed. 'Maybe we should call her Miss Creepy-Crawly.'

Getting into the spirit of the conversation and

now so thankful that my fears were unfounded, I put on a pseudo posh voice. 'Can you creep down here Miss Crawly or maybe you would rather crawl into the kitchen Miss Creep?'

We both sat on the bed and laughed so much that my sides ached. I looked at Maddie. 'Well, what did bring you here so suddenly tonight?'

'We often come to visit,' she explained. 'Eva is my godmother and one of my mother's oldest friends. I never got much of a chance to see you on your day off so I persuaded my parents to come tonight. That's why the housekeeper is having tea with them – so we can have our private chat.'

I was suddenly amused. 'What a fuss Miss Hood made over this visit, Maddie. In fact, the cook thought you might turn out to be film stars and the housekeeper was almost dancing with delight.'

'Well, our secret is out,' said Maddie with an exaggerated sigh. 'My mother was also on the stage and in films. Although she's much younger than Eva, they often starred in the same production. Also, like Eva, my mother was quite famous in her younger days before she gave it up to marry my father. Miss Hood worked in the wardrobe department of the theatre and she also travelled to America with Eva for a short spell.'

I sat enthralled on my bed, visualising this wonderful glamorous world so far removed from my own.

Maddie went on, 'Although nothing has been said to me, I heard a whisper one day that Miss Hood carries a dark secret.' She stopped to let this statement drop like a brick between us. I gasped and Maddie lowered her voice to a whisper. 'Yes, it was some kind of scandal or a mysterious secret that happened in America – or maybe it was in London. At least that was what I gathered from the snippet I overheard years ago.'

'A secret scandal,' I said, not believing a word of it. I could never imagine the colourless house-keeper with a scandalous past – not in a million years.

Maddie placed her chin on her hands and gazed unblinkingly at me. 'Well, that's the story. Anyway, that's not what I came to see you about,' she said, changing the subject. 'I want to hear all your news.'

I told her all about the sad saga of Dad and Marlene. 'That was what all the fuss was about when you came to the Overgate on Sunday night, Maddie.'

'You know something, Ann?' she said. 'We're almost the same age but you have so much on your shoulders – so much to cope with. I led such a sheltered life until Danny appeared and showed me a different world. That's why I'm going to be a nurse when I leave school.' She looked at me. 'You can be one as well. We'll do our training together.' She sat cross-legged on my eiderdown and looked at me with a serious face. 'Well, what about it?'

'Oh, no, Maddie, I could never be a nurse. No, my ideal job would be with books. A job in the library would be a dream for me.'

She smiled, her blue eyes crinkling at the corners. 'All right, then, I'll be caring Nurse

Pringle and you'll be the wonderful Brainy Book-worm Neill. There now, that's settled.' She delved into her bag and produced a pile of dressmaker's paper patterns. 'Look at these lovely clothes Ann. Mother has bought a new treadle sewing machine and I'm allowed to use it. I have a dentist's appointment next Monday so I'll be off school. Let's meet up afterwards and look at material. We can soon make a fashionable wardrobe to wear.'

The patterns were certainly fashionable and there were clothes for every conceivable occasion.

'How do you fancy starting off with a pair of camiknickers?' she said, holding aloft the packet. 'I think we'll start off with these. After all, how can Danny resist me when he sees these?'

I found myself blushing. 'Maddie, that's terrible.'

'No, it's not. I know he likes me but he also likes you.' Her face dropped. 'Can cousins get married?' She sounded doubtful.

I gave her a playful push. 'Even if they can, Danny and I are not planning a big step like that. Anyway we're too close and we can read each other's minds. No, he's my best friend and he'll always be that – even when we're old and grey-haired.'

This pleased her. 'Right, then, Danny's mine and the first plan is the camiknickers. Agreed?'

I shook my head at her. She was incorrigible. Suddenly a low whistle came from under the window. It was Mr Pringle standing with his overcoat collar up and his soft hat catching a mini torrent of rainwater as it gushed from the guttering. He shook himself like a dog emerging from a river.

'We're leaving now, Maddie. I'll nip in and tell

207

Eva about her broken rone pipe.'

Maddie jumped up. 'I'll meet you at two o'clock at D.M. Brown's door on Monday.'

On that command, she ran quickly from the room and I watched as they made their way to the car. At the gate, they turned and threw a cheery wave in my direction and I was grateful for all their help and concern. I prayed that Mr Pringle would perhaps find a job for Dad but, after all, he was a solicitor, not a miracle worker.

I lay in bed, trying hard not to think about Dad and all his problems but he kept popping into my mind. Still, Lily was over her bad dose of the cold and it wasn't the dreaded whooping cough as Granny had suspected.

Needless to say, Miss Hood hounded me every day until Friday when she appeared in the kitchen, all dolled up in a matching ensemble of skirt, jumper and long-line cardigan. It was very smart except it was in the most unflattering shade of beige. Set against her grey hair and pale complexion, it made her look absolutely washed out – as anaemic as a stick of seaside rock with all the colour sucked out, as Granny would say. She slapped a list on the table and snapped, 'That's your list of chores.'

Jean lifted her head from the stove and squinted at it. 'You're not leaving much time for eating and sleeping and breathing, are you?'

She ignored her and swept out through the door. I gazed at the list and my heart sank even although I was expecting it. She seemed to find more work with each passing day. Still there was one consolation – she wouldn't be here and peering over my shoulder all the time. Later, as Jean was busy in the kitchen with her baking, Mrs Barrie and I sat in the morning room, following the exciting adventures of Lord Peter Wimsey.

When I reached denouement, she shook herself as if cold and said, 'I didn't think that he would turn out to be the murderer, Ann, did you? I love exciting mystery stories. They add a bit of sparkle to my dull life,' she laughed.

I agreed with her as I had also thought the culprit was someone else. She stood up and I helped her up the wide staircase. She always had a short nap before tea.

'I'm glad we have this time together, Ann,' she said, as we entered her bedroom. 'I'd better pay you now instead of on Sunday – just in case Lottie gets wind of our little arrangement.' She handed over a crisp ten-shilling note and a half crown.

I protested about the extra money but she smiled. 'No, I want your little sister to have something – children need so much when they are growing up.'

'Oh, she's getting so big now, Mrs Barrie. Granny says I've to make sure and thank you for all your kindness. Lily isn't walking yet and Aunt Hattie keeps on at Grandad for letting her stay in her pram. Hattie says she'll never walk at this rate but Granny thinks she's just ashamed of the pram because it's scratched and scruffy.' I was quite happy to chatter on about Lily because I knew Mrs Barrie was always interested in her well-being. It wasn't just a polite act but a genuine interest.

She moved over to the large, ornately carved

wardrobe which almost covered an entire wall. 'Now, Ann, I don't want to insult you by thinking you only have one coat – your trench coat. I would like to give you an old coat of mine which I never wear now. We're about the same height and shape so it should fit you.'

My heart sank. I knew I couldn't turn down this unexpected gift and she would expect me to wear something old and frumpish – a coat suitable for an old lady. Because of this preconceived notion, I almost swooned with delight when she produced the most wonderful coat I had ever set eyes on. It was a deep russet shade, similar to a ripe autumn apple, made in soft wool with pale apricot fur collar and cuffs. I tried it on in front of the long wardrobe mirror and it looked fabulous. I turned, my eyes shining. 'Mrs Barrie, it's lovely but I can't take it. This coat must have cost a lot of money...'

She didn't let me finish and held up her hand. 'Shush, now. I want you to have it as it's just cluttering up my wardrobe.' She bent down and brought out a shoebox. 'These are a matching pair of shoes and a handbag.' She extricated a pair of russet coloured shoes with a small heel and a bag which was no bigger than an average sized purse. They matched the coat exactly.

We obviously had the same foot size because the shoes fitted like a glove and I preened myself in front of the mirror, first turning one way then another. No matter which side of me was mirrored, I looked elegant. I was still doubtful about taking them but, when she mentioned maybe putting them into the church jumble sale, I smiled my thanks. 'Thank you very much, Mrs Barrie.'

'No, thank you, Ann, for giving me so much pleasure with your reading. You bring the story alive – so much so that I can almost imagine the murderer is in the room with us.' She lay down on her bed. 'We'll start another story tonight if that's all right.'

She closed her eyes and I ran down the stairs with the lovely coat over my arm. Jean looked at me with surprise as I almost careered into her. Her eyes opened wide when she saw my goodies. 'Oh, it fair suits you and it sets off your bonny black hair. You look like Pola Negri – she's a film star.'

She looked on in admiration as I twirled around the room. 'Aye, she's a right generous woman is Mrs Barrie. She offered me some clothes when I started here but of course I was too plump so she gave me some lovely ornaments for the house – just bonny wee knick-knacks but I treasure them because they've been given with a good heart. Not like Lady Snootynose.'

I explained how Maddie had christened her Creepy-Crawly and Jean laughed so much she had to sit down.

'It's time for our afternoon tea and some hot home-made scones,' she said, buttering a large scone and placing a dollop of jam on the top. 'Maybe I should stop eating fattening things like these and I could fit into a lovely coat like that.' She ate the remains of her calorie-laden scone and licked her fingers. 'Or maybe I'll not bother – I like my food too much.'

As I carefully carried my coat upstairs to my

room, Jean called after me, 'Make sure you hide it from Her Ladyship, Ann. Don't let her see it.'

That was my intention. Although I planned to wear my new outfit on Sunday, I was going to leave the house dressed in my old trench coat. Then, when out of sight of the house, I would change into my fabulous fashion creation.

What Creepy didn't know wouldn't harm her, I thought.

9

When I was in the isolation of my bedroom, I wondered where I would hide my coat. The black spectre memory of Miss Hood was still fresh in my mind and I wondered what her reaction would be should she spot it. Would she, in one of her dark rages, assume that I had stolen it and perhaps tear it from my back causing havoc, as she had with the book? This image made me all the more determined to hide it from her and not let her cold, fishlike eyes ever see it. Still, in spite of this secrecy, I couldn't resist the urge to try it on again. Once again I was entranced to see the instant transformation from a gawky thin girl to a svelte creature who could well have graced the stage or screen – at least I thought so.

I grinned at the mirror. 'Don't be daft,' I told my reflection, mentally scolding myself for my foolishness. But one thing was crystal clear – the feel of this luxurious coat was no dream. It must have cost Mrs Barrie a fortune and she had given it to me. I couldn't believe my good luck.

That night I came to an arrangement with Jean. The next day, she would bring her largest message bag into work and she would smuggle out my treasures, leaving me to sally forth in my ancient trench coat.

But there was another financial worry looming on the horizon – the folding pushchair. Jean had seen it advertised in the post-office window. 'It'll be just the thing for your wee sister,' she had told me that afternoon, her mouth full of delicious home-made cake. 'I know Mrs King, the woman who's selling it, and she keeps a right clean house so it'll not be in a dirty condition. In fact, it'll be a right good buy, Ann.'

I had almost burst out laughing at this glowing testimonial, the memory of Lily's first pram still fresh in my memory. However I remained silent.

Jean chattered on. 'I think she's asking seven and a tanner for it but maybe she'll let you pay a wee bit every week till it's paid up.'

I didn't want to tell Jean that the sum of seven and sixpence was well nigh impossible for me to find but, on the other hand, I didn't want to hurt her feelings. That was why, after the Saturday night chores were finished and before Mrs Barrie and I started another detective novel, we both made our way to view the pram.

Mrs King eagerly pointed out all its sterling qualities and I had to admit it was in excellent condition. In fact it looked quite new and well worth the asking price. The pushchair's pristine condition was probably due to the fact that it hadn't been hauled up a couple of flights of stairs because the front door of Mrs King's cottage led directly on to the street.

We sat in her tiny front room on fireside chairs that were as hard as a board, almost as if the original cushioned padding had long since disappeared into the blue yonder.

'I did say I wanted seven and sixpence for it but I'm willing to drop the price to six shillings if you're interested.'

She pushed the pram back and forth over the well-polished linoleum as if further extolling its virtues. She nodded to Jean who reclined in her chair with a comfortable expression on her face. Maybe, I thought, she didn't feel the hardness because of her natural padding.

The woman said, 'I can keep it aside for you if you like and you can pay me a shilling or whatever a week.' She glanced once more at Jean and I realised they had discussed my financial circumstances but I wasn't angry. No one could ever be angry at Jean's kindness and, after all, beggars couldn't be choosers. So we struck a deal there and then.

'I'll be here with the first shilling tomorrow, Mrs King, before I go home.'

I had done some quick thinking and I had already made up mind on how I could pay this money up. I would walk home to the Overgate and walk back to Whitegate Lodge every week. That way, Granny wouldn't be burdened by trying to make ends meet on less money.

There was also the worry about Grandad having to manhandle the big pram up and down the stairs every day. Now, with this lighter, folding model and the thought of the approaching warmer weather, it would prove to be a real boon to the family.

The following afternoon was nerve-racking. Miss Hood appeared, dressed in a bilious green outfit. She almost had a purple fit when I marched out with no mention of wages.

Jean was waiting for me in the courtyard, surrounded by a clutch of blackbirds who were gorging on the scattered crumbs. She was clutching her outsize bag. She laughed. 'I thought her eyes were going to pop out of her head – speak about having apoplexy! And did you hear yon strangled wee cry she gave?'

I hadn't heard a sound and I said so, my mind concentrating on walking away from the birds.

'Well, maybe she didn't,' Jean conceded with a deep chuckle. 'But I bet she mentally said it and did you see she almost burst into tears? I'll bet a tanner on it.'

Danny was waiting for me once again and, to my delight, he was carrying Lily. She seemed to be fascinated by the sound of the sea and her clear blue eyes were transfixed in puzzlement as she twisted her head in its direction.

'Oh would you look at the lovely wee babby?' crooned Jean, holding out her arms to take her.

Lily responded by blowing a stream of frothy bubbles. Meanwhile I could hardly contain myself as I wanted to tell Danny all about my lovely new coat and also the imminent purchase of the pushchair.

Almost as if she read my mind, Jean said, 'Ann,

215

let me buy the pram for Lily now and you can pay me just as easily as Mrs King.'

I was mortified. 'Oh, no, Jean, six shillings is a lot of money.'

She was adamant. 'Honestly, if I couldn't afford it I wouldn't have offered. Let's go round and pick it up right now.'

Danny looked at me in puzzlement as we trooped round to the cottage. We all stood in a circle on the pavement at Mrs King's front door as the woman wheeled it out. Jean strapped Lily into it while Mrs King produced the gabardine cover that hooked on to the hood to keep out inclement weather. She then added a bonus of three cosy checked blankets, pocketed the money and gave us a cheery wave.

Before setting off down her lane, Jean handed over her bag while I paid the first instalment of a shilling. Now we had this new pram, the world was our oyster.

Hattie was at the Overgate when we arrived. Her expression beamed approval at the new acquisition. 'Compared to that monstrosity over there, anything would be an improvement,' she said, nodding towards the big pram that lay beside the bed.

On the other hand, Grandad was so impressed that he immediately put on his overcoat and cap and headed off with Lily.

Then Hattie spotted my coat in the bag. Her eyes widened with undisguised delight and she swooped on it with a cry of joy. 'Let me try it on. It'll fit me, I'm sure.' She slipped the coat over her slender shoulders and almost purred. 'What

216

did I tell you? It fits like it was made for me.'

The shoes also fitted and she pranced around the kitchen almost crooning. 'I've always wanted a coat like this. It's cashmere, don't you know? And real fur. None of your ordinary rabbit fur here. I'm sure it's fox fur or it could even be sable although that's usually a dark fur.' Her voice dropped to a whisper as she mentioned the word sable.

To say I was annoyed was an understatement. I quickly took the coat from her. 'Well, it's mine, Hattie,' I said quite firmly, making sure she was in no doubt about it.

But she was determined to have my present and she pleaded. 'I'll swap my new grey woollen coat and a new pair of shoes and a good hand-knitted cardigan.' Her voice held a strange wheedling tone that I had never heard before but I was determined to stand firm.

'No, Hattie, they're gifts from Mrs Barrie and she says I've to wear them because she'll get pleasure from seeing me in them.' I knew this was a white lie but I could visualise my lovely gifts being swept away in front of my eyes by my auntie.

Suddenly, as if tired of all this female bickering, Danny stood up to leave. 'Honestly, you women are crazy about clothes. Imagine argy-bargying over a coat.' His eyes were full of wonder at the secret minds of his womenfolk. 'Mind you, I think Ann suits the coat better than you, Mum.'

He ducked under her hand as she went to give him a playful push but her face looked annoyed. 'Well,' she said, 'if you change your mind, you know where to find me.' She moved towards the door, her face like thunder, with Danny tagging on behind.

Granny, who had been slicing vegetables for her huge pot of soup and keeping out of the argument, sighed. 'Now look what you've done, Ann – you've put your auntie into a huge huff.'

I was mortified until she burst into laughter, loud guffaws that echoed around the small kitchen. She stopped stirring the soup and wiped her eyes dry with the corner of her apron. 'Good for you, Ann. It's about time somebody stood up to her grabbing ways. Of course, she's just green with envy that you happen to be the same size as your employer. With Mrs Pringle being plump, it means that her cast-offs are far too big for our Hattie.' She erupted into laughter again. 'Otherwise she would make sure she fell heir to them. No, Ann, don't you feel guilty. Just you enjoy wearing your bonny coat because it makes such a difference to your appearance. You look like a real rich toff.'

The next afternoon found me at the entrance to D.M. Brown's department store. Maddie appeared and walked right past me without recognising me in my new finery.

'Hullo, Maddie,' I called out to her retreating back.

She swung round with a look of puzzlement. 'Ann, I didn't see you. Where did you get that swanky coat?'

I put my arm through hers. 'I'll tell you about it inside. Did you bring your patterns?'

The dressmaking department, much to my

surprise, was almost an entire floor given over to lovely fabrics. There were rolls and rolls of material in every colour under the sun – a colourful kaleidoscopic chamber with everything from the finest sheer silks to the heaviest of knobbly woven tweeds.

Maddie was studying her patterns when an assistant appeared, dressed in a smart black frock with a white lacy collar demurely buttoned at her thin neck. Her glossy black hair, which looked as if it owed more to a Tonirinse than mere nature, was swept back in an enormous bun. She had a patient, fixed smile on her middle-aged face and this seemed to be a requisite of the job.

Maddie was obviously well known in this treasure trove of home-dressmaking. 'Miss Pringle, can I help you?' She gave her a deferential smile and, much to my surprise, bestowed the same smile on me.

It suddenly dawned on me that this was the result of the expensive coat. I was being treated like a valued customer. If I had come in with my old coat and scruffy shoes, would I have had this same service? Probably but the assistant would have summed me up as having no money to buy anything and she would have been correct.

Maddie explained what she wanted, showing the pattern to the woman. To give her her due, she was a well-trained expert in her job because she guided us towards a display of materials in a selection of cotton, silk and crêpe de Chine.

'What do you like, Ann?' asked Maddie. 'I thought we could make a frock for the summer.' We gazed in awe at a dressmaker's dummy that was draped in something green and expensive.

'What? No camiknickers?' I whispered. She laughed. 'We'll get the material for them today but we'll make them later.' She rummaged through her bundle and produced the relevant pattern.

'Oh, yes,' said the assistant in her cultured voice that somehow sounded far posher than Maddie's, 'they are very popular this year and I would recommend these fabrics.'

We spent ages browsing around while the assistant floated away to attend to another potential customer. Maddie kept referring to which materials I liked and I was beginning to get worried.

'Maddie, I can't afford to buy anything just now. Just because I've got this posh coat doesn't alter my financial state.'

She looked at me in dismay. 'Oh, you're not paying for the material, Ann, and neither am I. It's mother's treat and we can both use the sewing machine.'

I was dumbfounded. 'Maddie, I can't let your mother buy things for me. No, just you buy what you want and I'll save up for something later.'

Much to my surprise, Maddie was firm – almost as firm as I had been with Hattie. She put on a frantic looking face. 'It's the only reason I'm getting to use the machine – if you help me.'

I doubted that very much because what help could I give but I then had a mental image of Mrs Pringle and all her kindness so I relented and we spent a glorious hour choosing while the assistant appeared like magic to measure and cut our fabrics in her expert manner.

As she wrapped our purchases, she enquired, 'Shall I put these on your mother's account, Miss Pringle?'

Once again I marvelled at how the other half lived.

We emerged from the store with our paper parcels all tied up with tape that had the store's name running along its narrow width.

Maddie took my arm as we hurried along the busy street. 'We must celebrate your new outfit so let's go to Draffen's for afternoon tea.'

I had never been inside this grand shop before, this haven of Mrs Barrie and her friends. I found myself being propelled to the back of the ground floor towards the lifts.

Smart looking assistants hovered at all the counters and I stopped in wide-eyed fascination at the hosiery counter. The young assistant slipped an elegant hand inside a silk stocking then drew her hand up the entire length, much to the approval of a well-dressed customer. I marvelled at the girl's smooth hands. If I had tried to do this, my roughened hands would surely have snagged the delicate stocking.

'I'll take three pairs of those stockings in that colour, size nine and half please,' said the customer and the assistant smiled as she placed the stocking back in its cellophane packet.

I almost collapsed when the price was mentioned. It would have kept us for a couple of weeks at least. Maddie tugged at my arm, urging me away from this new experience – this insight into a totally alien lifestyle.

'Coffee lounge, please,' said Maddie to the

smartly uniformed man who operated the buttons on the lift.

We glided upwards with three other like-minded women. At that point, I wouldn't have been surprised to find myself in heaven but the coffee lounge was noisily down to earth and packed with customers, men and women all laughing and gossiping together while the waitresses darted between the tables as if to escape from the noisy conversational babble. They carried large trays with silver tea- and coffee pots while large, unwieldy-looking, three-tiered cake-stands were placed beside each table.

The air was a mixture of heady expensive perfume and cigarette smoke with just the merest trace of the more homely aroma of baking. We found an empty table and sat down, placing our parcels at our feet.

'Let's have Russian tea, Ann,' said Maddie. When I looked puzzled, she winked and placed the order.

This Russian tea arrived in tall tumblers that were encased in silver filigree holders. There was no milk but a slice of lemon floated on the surface of the anaemic looking brew. Granny would have thrown this concoction straight down the sink. She liked her tea strong, even slightly stewed, with the addition of a dollop of condensed milk and two spoonfuls of sugar. Mind you, I had no intention of telling this to Maddie so I sipped my tea and ate a tiny but very delicious scone. It was not as good as Jean's baking but not far off it.

Once again I couldn't get over how some people lived. It was a real eye-opener. I thought about Rita, Nellie and the Ryan family plus the thousands like them who lived every day under the spectre of poverty and the never-ending struggle with money.

With the dreaded transitional benefit or parish money now paying the paltry sum of only £1 7s 3d a week for a family with two children, there was no room and even less inclination for a Russian tea or a pair of silk stockings. This weekly amount was less than half of what two adults and two children would need just to subsist.

Now, thanks to my super – albeit hand-me-down – coat, shoes and handbag, I had, for the moment at least, entered this privileged world. What made matters worse was the guilty feeling that I was enjoying it immensely.

'Want to know something, Maddie?' I said, glancing around the noisy lounge. My eye finally rested on a very elegant woman who was smoking a black cigarette which was perched on the end of long black holder. 'This is just like having a birthday. First the coat then the pushchair and now the lovely dress material and this tea – everything given by other people.'

She leaned over. 'Well, Ann, they do say everything comes in threes.' She fiddled with her teaspoon. 'Talking about birthdays, Mum was planning to have a small party for Joy and she was wondering if you would like to come with Lily – also your dad and grandparents and Danny's relations at Lochee.'

I almost choked on a crumb. 'Oh, Maddie, your mum will have enough to do with your own relations without having us as well.'

She shook her head. 'It won't be any bother. My mother says also to ask Kit and her sisters and their husbands if they want to come. It'll be held on a Sunday in July. I'll let you know later.'

On that worrying note, my magical day ended. Back at the Ferry, life went on as normal. Miss Hood still threw her weight around but, for some reason, it didn't bother me as much as in the early days. In the end, she simply ran out of jobs to give me and I settled down to a weekly routine that was extremely happy on her time off but a bit more difficult when she was skulking around.

The garden, much to my delight, soon exploded into a riot of colour. Even the dark, gaunt trees at the back of the house burst forth with wonderful green foliage that cast shady spots on the grass.

As the weeks passed, Mrs Barrie and I spent a great deal of time sitting under these shady trees with her favourite detective novels. On two days a week, an old gardener appeared and pushed an ancient, squeaking mower over the lawns. He looked about eighty years old, with skin the same colour and texture as Granny's chamois leather which she kept for washing the windows.

He was also a man of few words. 'Roses need deadheading, missus,' he said as he pushed the protesting mower around our haven under the trees.

As charming as usual, Mrs Barrie replied, 'Of course, Mr Potter. I leave the garden in your very capable hands.'

Mr Potter's mouth moved fractionally into a semblance of a smile. 'Aye, just so, just so,' he said, without lifting his head.

As he passed by our chairs, Mrs Barrie held up her hand. 'Do tell me, Mr Potter, why don't you use the brand new mower I purchased? It's the very latest model.'

He did a quick side-step, his face screwing up in disgust. 'No, I've never liked anything new fangled, Mrs Barrie, no, never.'

Mrs Barrie smiled at me. 'Well, I must get Miss Hood to go out to the shed with the oilcan because that squeaking is driving me crazy.'

On my time off, I still paraded around in my gorgeous coat. In spite of the warmer weather, Hattie's envy was still evident although she pretended not to be interested.

Granny assured me it was all an act. 'I'm telling you, Ann, she's wild. She can't see green cheese but she's got to have a bit.'

Meanwhile Maddie and I spent hours in her mother's sewing room, a tiny but very pretty room right under the eaves. Every Sunday evening after all my chores were finished at home, we sewed, snipped, cut and planned. In spite of what she said in the store, Maddie changed her mind and started on the camiknickers before the frocks. I would have preferred it the other way round but I kept quiet.

As it turned out, they were a huge success. Maddie kept chirping on and on about them as if this was the only garment she owned. 'Look how lovely they are,' she said for the umpteenth time. She held the finished garment aloft where the evening light caught the subtle sheen of the pale blue crêpe de Chine.

225

My plan was to keep my camiknickers aside until I made the frock but I had the sneaking suspicion that Maddie was hoping to be wearing hers when some dramatic event happened outside Lipton's shop door – something just eventful enough for Danny to catch an admiring glimpse or, even better, an entire eyeful. The ideal situation would be a sneaky, blustery breeze, swirling perhaps in gusts at the shop door – not too strong a wind but one sufficiently playful to lift her cotton frock into the air. In her fantasy dreamworld, Danny would immediately be struck dumb with admiration at the sight of frills and lace, not to mention her needlewoman's skill.

But, as it turned out, the real world can be so cruel. When this did in fact happen a few weeks later, her sole audience was three old men standing outside the Swan tavern. They were venting their outrage at the demolition of the Town House but their simmering anger seemed to be directed at a meeting in Bonnethill church hall the previous February, a meeting organised to abolish the means test.

'Bloody disgrace,' said one old man, shaking his head so hard that his jowls wobbled. 'Imagine just the one head-bummer, that Baillie Fraser, having the gumption to appear.'

'Aye, it's always the same with the poor jobless folk – the toffs and head-bummers don't want to know. Just shunt the workless off to the street corners and let us do our moaning there,' said his pal.

Suddenly, in the middle of this soiree, a breeze, sharpened by the funnelled shape of the side street, swept down on the men and Maddie, who was passing at the time. The wind tugged at the hem of her frock and sent it flying upwards. The men fell silent, their moans about the means test dying on their thin, bloodless lips as Maddie tried furiously to gather her dignity together.

One old man tried to whistle through toothless gums but failed. He winked at his cronies. 'Yon's the best sight I've seen in years and years, lass,' he called after her indignant, retreating figure.

With their jesting comments still fresh in her ears, a red-faced Maddie made her escape, lamenting her bad luck that the incident hadn't taken place a few hundred yards further down the road in front of Lipton's shop.

As Lily's birthday approached, we were filled with a great sadness as it was the anniversary of Mum's death. Dad was absent for most of this time although he had been told about the coming party for Lily and Joy.

Fortunately, out of deference to this sad time, Mrs Pringle held the event a couple of weeks before the actual date. That way, we could all be cheery for Lily's sake. She was now at the crawling stage and forever moving across the floor in her search to explore her new world. The coal bucket was her favourite spot. Her dark hair, although not thick, lay in soft curls against a pink scalp and was forever getting washed, as were her chubby arms and legs.

This grubby situation was viewed by Hattie with a look of distaste. 'She's always getting dirty, is she not? My Danny didn't crawl around like this and he was always clean.'

'Och, away you go, Hattie,' said Granny with annoyance. 'You're just looking at Danny's infancy through rose-coloured specs. I mind fine when he was a lot dirtier than Lily.'

Hattie ignored her mother and produced a parcel from her fashionable bag like a magician pulling a rabbit from a hat. 'This is another frock and shoes from Mrs Pringle. She wonders if they're any use to Lily as Joy has never worn them. It seems such a shame not to get any wear out of them,' she added ruefully.

We studied the gifts and, lovely as they undoubtedly were, it was obvious that Lily was almost twice the size of Joy. Granny shook her head. 'That's the second time Joy's cast-offs haven't fitted. It must be grand to have such pretty things and never need to wear them. Our problem is keeping everything patched and mended till they're almost falling off our backs.'

Although I hadn't said anything at the time, I had bought a summery cotton frock for my sister to wear at her party but, compared to the gossamer quality of Joy's frock, it suddenly looked cheap and tawdry. The middle-aged owner of the small clothes shop in the Ferry had been very helpful, pointing out that the dress had the added bonus of a pair of matching knickers but now the material had a coarse and shoddy look.

Hattie reluctantly parcelled them up again when it was evident that even the little shoes wouldn't fit. Not that she hadn't tried – tugging them on to the feet of a now loudly protesting Lily, like Cinderella's slipper on one of the ugly sisters.

Then the day of the party dawned hot and sunny, almost like a carbon copy of the day when Lily and Joy were both born. Most of the Pringle relations were already gathered on the grassy lawn. They were facing the river and sipping sherry from crystal glasses.

Granny was dressed in her best brown wool frock and, although it was not really suitable for the hot weather, it was, nevertheless, smart enough to wear when mixing with the toffs, as Bella kept referring to the Pringles.

Grandad had decided right from the start not to appear because he felt he didn't own anything good enough to wear. Rosie had offered to find him a suit from the Salvation Army's charity box but he was mortified by the suggestion – as was Hattie. 'No, I'll just stay here and you women go and enjoy yourselves,' he said before planting a kiss on Lily's head. 'Now, you go and have a great birthday, my wee lass.'

Rosie had put a score or more Dinky curlers in Granny's hair the night before and she was now combing it out. As a final touch, she pinned it into a topknot which gave her the appearance of a dowager, a look that pleased Grandad. 'Aye, you look real regal, Nan.'

Granny had tried to keep the party a secret from Bella but, with her unerring nose for gossip, she soon cottoned on. 'I suppose I'm not on the invitation list?' she said peevishly.

'Well, no, Bella, it's just the close family,' said Granny.

How Bella found out about Grandad's planned absence was one of life's little mysteries but she was in like a rocket with her offer to act as a substitute. The upshot was that we all set off for the Perth Road with Bella wearing something striped and voluminous, an unfortunate choice because she resembled a Bedouin tent.

'Here come the pirates,' said Danny jokingly as we were ushered on to the lawn.

Kit and Lizzie were standing beside Maddie but there was no sign of the rest of their families and Ma Ryan was also missing.

'It could have been worse, I suppose,' whispered Hattie to Granny. 'At least the husbands and snottery-nosed kids are all left behind in Lochee and Belle is seemingly under the weather – more like under the influence, if you ask me.'

I had a mental picture of Ma Ryan sitting on the lawn with her clay pipe, blowing putrid smoke into the faces of the sherry drinkers who were all decked out in their expensive Sunday best.

Mr Pringle, ever the gentleman, greeted us like long-lost but cherished friends, even making sure Bella got a good seat – a gesture which warranted her beaming gratitude and she eloquently expressed this to Hattie. 'Your boss is a real toff and, if I ever need a solicitor, then he'll get my business.' She smacked her lips as the drinks tray was carried towards her.

Hattie visibly winced as Bella frowned at the tiny glasses. 'Have you got a bigger glass, Maddie? For my medicine, you know,' she added in a stage whisper.

As Maddie hurried away, no doubt in search of a pint glass, Hattie still looked annoyed as she served the dainty sandwiches. She reserved a special glare for her sisters-in-law.

'You've got a braw cushy number here, Hattie,' said Kit. 'It must be great working in a grand house like this.'

Hattie gave her a look that suggested the silver was well counted before she passed on towards a couple of Maddie's relations. Her body posture immediately changed, becoming more deferential.

'That bloody woman's going to topple over one of these days with all the crawling she does,' said Kit to her sister.

Although it was a whispered comment, it was loud enough to reach Hattie's ears. She turned with a glare, twin red spots visible on her cheeks. She started to walk towards Kit and Lizzie but fortunately two things happened almost at once to take the unpleasantness out of the situation. Lily started to pull at a small string of beads around Joy's neck. Taking umbrage at this, Joy started to howl with a series of high-pitched shrieks. At the same time, the doorbell pealed.

As Mrs Pringle and Granny separated the two squabbling toddlers, Maddie made a beeline for the door, overtaking Hattie in the process. Which was perhaps just as well because Dad was standing on the doorstep.

Hattie jumped out the door like a jack-in-the-box, looking up and down the street.

Dad grinned. 'It's all right, Hattie, Marlene's not here.'

When I saw him, I ran over. 'Dad, I've been looking for you every week but you're never at the Hilltown.' I knew I was chastising him again

231

but he made me so angry at times. Still I was grateful to see he was reasonably tidy and had taken the time to shave. His blue knitted pullover looked new until I noticed the small patch on the elbow which had been darned in a slightly different shade.

Mr Pringle came over. 'Johnny, how nice to see you. Come over and see the birthday girls before you meet my brother John. I'm hoping he'll find you a job in his warehouse.'

With Dad now whisked away, I felt at a loose end. Granny was sitting beside one of Maddie's aunts and, judging by their animated conversation, it was clear they were hitting it off.

Maddie was helping Hattie with the food while Danny was talking to an old man who had the bushiest set of whiskers I had ever seen. I moved towards them.

'I'm telling you, young Danny, at your age I was at sea, sailing right round the world,' said the old man. 'I've been in all kinds of storms – I was almost shipwrecked by a typhoon in the China Seas and I almost drowned in the Atlantic Ocean but shall I tell you the worst sight I ever saw?'

He stopped as Danny nodded wordlessly.

'Well, one night in a house not very far from here, where I lived at the time, I saw the Tay Bridge collapse.'

We both gasped and he looked pleased.

'Aye, it was in December 1879 and my father and I were outside in one of the worst storms we could ever remember. We saw the lights of the train as it started to cross the bridge and my father remarked that he was glad he wasn't a passenger on it on a night like this. Suddenly the lights disappeared and we didn't know what had happened. At least not until the following morning when the full tragedy unfolded.' He shook his head as if still experiencing that sad moment.

'That's terrible,' said Danny.

'Aye, it was and I'll tell you something – I've seen storms all over the world but the storm that night on the River Tay was one of the worst I've ever encountered. The middle of the bridge and an entire train with passengers all disappeared under the cold waves – poor souls.'

I looked at the river which was calm and peaceful on this sunny Sunday but I could well imagine the scene of over fifty years ago when the magnificent iron bridge collapsed – the high girders falling into the foaming river with the appalling loss of life. Shaking off the morbid thought, I now noticed that Lily and Joy were the best of friends again but I was surprised to see Kit and Lizzie preparing to leave.

'Och, we just came to see Lily and yourselves, Ann,' said Kit as I walked to the front door with them. 'Not to mention putting Hattie's nose in a sling – the snotty besom.'

As I watched them hurrying away, I was once again struck by the open hostility between them. The reason must lie in the past, I thought, because Hattie hardly ever visited Lochee and she didn't have enough contact with them to warrant this hatred. Perhaps it was Hattie's high-and-mighty nature. I knew it annoyed a lot of people and maybe, during the early days of her marriage, she had flaunted herself at Lochee. Still, this thought, along with the Tay Bridge disaster, was banished from my mind when I noticed Dad was also on the verge of leaving – much to Hattie's relief. It would appear she was getting rid of all her embarrassments at one fell swoop.

Mr Pringle stood at the door with him as I hurried over. Dad wasn't going to escape from me this time as we had a lot of talking to do.

'Well, the job will be yours when Willie retires,' said the man standing next to them. He was obviously John Pringle. I thought Dad would seem pleased at this news but John went on, 'Unfortunately, Willie doesn't retire for a while yet but, if something else comes up, I'll let you know, Johnny.'

Dad smiled, a smile which, as usual, enhanced his handsome face. 'You've all been so good to me and my family, Mr Pringle, and I really appreciate it. I'll hang on till the man retires. After all, I've been without a job for years.'

Hattie appeared at my shoulder, her mood now brighter with the disappearance of her tiresome relations. In the second it took me to turn at her appearance, Dad was gone. I was vexed but Hattie needed help with the dirty dishes and glasses. I sighed, fully expecting another row over the coat.

Instead, she said quietly, 'Do you know your dad hasn't paid the rent for weeks and now the landlord is evicting him from the house?'

I almost burst into tears. 'Oh, no, Hattie. How could Dad have been so stupid? Where is he going to live?'

I rushed from the kitchen but he was gone. Mr

Pringle passed on Dad's message to say cheerio to us all.

I tackled Hattie. 'When did you hear about this?'

She looked at her hands. 'Well, I expect he mentioned it to me today because he wanted a loan of money to pay the back rent but I'm not giving him a penny while he's still seeing that Marlene woman.'

Her face was set firmly and I realised Dad must have been desperate even to ask his sister.

Hattie continued, 'And he's drinking, Ann. The money would have ended up in the pub. I just know it. The factor would never get a sniff of it.'

I gazed at her with dismay. Although I knew she was right, it would seem that Dad's famous charm with women was lost on one – his sister.

10

There was little sleep in the Overgate house that night. As I lay awake in my tiny room, afraid and full of apprehension at Dad's downhill lifestyle, I heard Granny pottering around in the kitchen. The distinctive plopping sound from the gas cooker was a sign that she was also worried. Drinking tea in the middle of the night, in this house at least, was a sure sign of a crisis.

I padded through the lobby in my bare feet. In spite of the earlier hot sunshine, the lino felt cold under my feet. The kitchen felt warmer but it was very dim. Granny had lit the gas lamp but she had turned it right down.

When she saw me, she put a finger to her lips. 'Shush, now – I don't want your grandad worried.' She looked over to the large bed in the corner where he lay blissfully asleep. He was snoring – not loudly but just gentle grunts that escaped from his open mouth to ripple like waves along the surface of the home-made patchwork quilt where it seemed to rise and fall like waves on the ocean. I was reminded of the sea at the Ferry, which either pounded or lapped against the shore, depending on its mood.

Granny motioned to me as she placed the two cups of tea on the coal bunker. 'Come over here. I don't want to waken your grandad.' Through the half-lit gloom, I saw her tired lined face and once again I was very angry at Dad. Along with this anger was the knowledge that Hattie would no doubt be fast asleep and not worrying one jot about her brother. She had said as much at the party.

Granny shuddered slightly. 'I'm just thinking about that scene at the party. What will Maddie and her parents think about us? And although Bella hasn't said anything, you can rest assured that it'll be the topic of conversation for ages. Did you notice her face? It was full of curiosity and I thought her eyes would pop out of her head.'

Although I didn't answer, the scene was also vividly etched on my mind. After Dad's hurried departure, Granny had turned on Hattie. 'Honestly, Hattie, could you not have arranged a family meeting at least? He turned to you for help and you let him down.'

Granny was so incensed at her that Lily, perhaps picking up the angry feelings, began to cry. This distraction gave Hattie the chance to make her escape but not before throwing a parting shot at us. 'Johnny has had all the help this family can give him. Look at him – living like a tink with a widow and not giving one jot of thought for the welfare of his kids.' Her dark eyes blazed. 'And I suppose he's never as much as put one flower on his wife's grave.'

On that final note she then darted through the door, almost knocking over Maddie and Danny in her haste. If she was regretting anything this night then it would be that her actions were witnessed by the Pringle family.

Granny had sat down, her face white. She looked as if all the stuffing had been knocked out of her. I was alarmed but Mrs Pringle had come over with a cup of strong sweet tea. Meanwhile Maddie tried to soothe Lily while Danny stood beside her, utterly speechless.

Granny gave a huge sigh. 'She's right of course. Hattie is the only one honest enough to tell the truth – it's maybe because she's a bit selfish herself but she certainly hit the nail on the head.' She turned to me, wishing no doubt that Maddie and her mother weren't there but they were, much to everyone's embarrassment.

Then, from across the grassy lawn, a voice called for Mrs Pringle. She patted Granny's hand and said, 'I'll be back later.'

Maddie blushed. 'I'd better go as well and let you speak privately.'

Granny said, 'There's no need, Maddie. Everything that's been said has been overheard so just stay here with Danny and Ann. The whole truth is that Ann's dad has never got over the death of his wife.' She looked at me. 'But Ann will go and see him tomorrow to get this mess sorted out.'

I was suddenly filled with dread because I didn't have a clue about his living arrangements and I certainly didn't want to go to the Windmill bar again.

Danny had come over and put his arm around my shoulder. 'Wait till I finish work at night, Ann, and I'll come with you.'

I squared my shoulders. I knew Danny would help all he could and I also knew my grandparents were strong characters but they couldn't be expected to shoulder all this burden and nor could Danny.

'Thanks, Danny, but I'll go to find him early in the morning. You know before he...' Before he goes to the pub, I almost said.

Maddie's eyes were full of sympathy and I knew she was on the point of tears. I also felt hot tears sting my eyes – tears of helplessness at Dad's incompetence, especially as the anniversary of Mum's death was near.

Granny's voice brought me out of my reverie – back from the nightmare of the afternoon. 'Another thing that Hattie was right about is the fact that your dad never goes near the grave.'

Perhaps he couldn't face it, I thought, but, on the other hand, Danny, Lily and I made regular visits to the Balgay cemetery. Sometimes we'd gone with just a handful of wild flowers but once or twice we'd had a large bunch of blooms from

Mrs Barrie's garden, placing them on the unmarked and desolate spot.

Then the dreaded thought of hunting for Dad emerged again as an ugly image in my brain. I had said tomorrow but that had been yesterday and now the moment of reckoning was almost upon me.

'Granny, have you any idea where Mrs Davidson lives?'

'Well, Hattie did say it was somewhere in Ann Street, did she not?' She sounded dubious. 'But, there again, maybe that's not right.'

Grandad stirred in his bed. She moved over to the gas lamp and turned it off. 'I don't want your grandad to know about the stushie this afternoon, Ann.'

I nodded. I didn't want anyone to be worried about Dad – just myself. Granny rinsed the cups under the cold-water tap. 'Time to off to bed, Ann. It'll be a busy day later on.'

I stood by the window, dreading the thought of what lay ahead. The moon rode high in the sky, a pale imitation of the earlier golden sun but its subtle silvery light matched my mood. Outside on the street, closes and crannies lay in deep shadow which was a sharp contrast to the shimmering tenement roofs. The slates, bathed in the moon's milky light, had an opaque sheen which lent enchantment.

I sighed. My life was like this moonlit night – silvered parts in the shape of Lily, my grandparents, Mrs Barrie, Jean and Maddie. Then there was Danny. Until Lily's birth, he had been the zenith of my heaven and, although the axis had slipped slightly, he was still my moon. Dad, on the other hand, was my shadow, his deep unhappiness casting a dark cloud over all our lives, and I was at a loss to know how to deal with it.

But, in spite of my worries, within minutes of going back to bed, I was fast asleep. Dawn brought another golden day. It would be another scorcher by the feel of it although the sun's breath was just pleasantly warm by the time I set off in search of my father.

As usual, the Hilltown was crowded with people – a multitude of human beings either going about their daily chores or merely lounging in the sunshine. Hordes of children spilled out on to the pavements – thin, hungry-looking children in faded, patched clothes and white arms and legs. A boy, with a paper eyeshade that dominated his pinched, white face, was busy playing with another boy who had one leg shorter than the other, the difference in height being made up by an iron calliper which encased his leg and shoe. But these deprivations went unnoticed as they whooped and shouted and threw themselves into their game of cowboys and Indians.

There was no sign of Rita or Nellie but I only gave them a fleeting thought as I hurried upwards. I had no plan of action as such. I suppose I was hoping that Dad would somehow materialise out of whatever abode he currently occupied. But, as I had long since discovered, life was not like a scene from my *Arabian Nights* book. Life did not have marvellous miracles or a genie in a bottle and nor did it have my father stepping out at my feet. There was no sign of

Marlene either.

I walked along both sides of Ann Street, right to the perimeter of Bonnybank Road but, in spite of it being busy, everyone I met was a stranger.

It was too early for the Windmill bar to be open but that had been my intention – to arrive before opening time – and I now realised that this had been an unwise move. Mrs Davidson could live anywhere amongst this warren of tenements and humanity.

I paused outside a small shop that was obviously linked to St Mary's Chapel in Forebank Road, a chapel that was situated about fifty feet from where I was standing. The window was adorned with crucifixes of every size. Religious pictures and rosary beads were also very much in evidence.

I wondered if Marlene was a member of the chapel and then decided she was not. During our brief meeting, I got the impression she had long ago embraced Bacchus as her spirit instead of Jesus. The tiny 'jenny-a'-things' shop across the road seemed a better bet. I stepped inside the minuscule shop, noticing with amusement that the huge bell nailed to the door was well out of proportion to the size of the shop. The metal bell shivered in excitement, almost shifting the film of dust on its surface but not quite. A shaft of sunlight, filled with a million dancing particles, somehow managed to squeeze through a gap in the many posters that decorated the door, falling like a stage spotlight on the dusty wooden counter.

At this point, the reason for the noisy bell became apparent. The owner was a bit deaf. I spoke in a loud voice, mouthing my words in an exaggerated manner, almost as if the old lady was daft as well as deaf. 'I'm looking for a Mrs Davidson. Do you know where she lives?'

The old woman looked puzzled for a moment before holding up a flimsy packet. 'Is it jam pot covers you want, lassie?' She put them away when I shook my head.

I could see the danger of being here all day while she held up all her meagre stock. I then saw a well-chewed pencil on the counter and I had a brainwave. Searching in my message bag, I finally found an old paper bag. I wrote the name down and watched as the woman squinted at it.

After a few seconds she ducked under the counter. Moving things around and opening a few drawers, she re-emerged with a pair of tiny round wire-framed spectacles which she carefully tucked behind her ears and adjusted them on the bridge of her thin, bony nose. She scrutinised the name 'Mrs Davidson. Mrs Davidson.' She drew a grimy hand over her mouth. 'Is that the woman with the nine kids that lives in James Street?' she pondered for a moment while I almost fainted. Hattie hadn't mentioned children. The woman was talking again, 'No, no, that's Mrs Richardson. No, lass, I don't know anybody called Davidson.'

Disappointment was written all over my face. Seeing this, she rubbed her chin thoughtfully. 'Try the grocer's shop along the road – the one next to the second-hand shop.'

The woman in the grocer's shop was totally different from the other one – not so nice and certainly not deaf. I got the impression she would hear a scandalous whisper from a distance of five hundred yards. When I entered, she gave me a sharp look before resuming her task of placing a dozen or so tins of pilchards in a pleasing looking pyramid.

I asked her about Marlene. She sniffed the air as she pondered on my question. When she spoke, her voice was as clipped and sharp as her facial features. 'I don't discuss my customers or where they stay with any strangers,' she said, turning her back on me and dismissing both me and my quest.

I was desperate. I didn't have all day to look for Dad as the weekly washing still had to be tackled at the wash-house. 'It's not really Mrs Davidson I'm looking for,' I said, annoyed that I was being forced into discussing our family problems with this martinet. 'It's her lodger I'm looking for. He's my dad but my granny has lost his landlady's address.'

The woman turned. Her lip curled as if to say, 'Pull the other one' but she grudgingly took her attention away from the pilchards. She walked over to me. 'Her lodger, eh? Is that what you call him?' She looked me up and down, her sharp eyes noting my appearance. 'So he's your dad? Well, well.'

I decided to make a show of throwing myself on her mercy, a quality I doubted she owned. 'Aye, he's my dad. He comes every Sunday to see us at my granny's house and yesterday, after he left, my wee sister became ill and now I have to tell him quickly. If you know where he is, missus, tell me because it's urgent.'

She stepped back smartish – she was taking no chances with something that might be infectious. 'Mrs Davidson stays in Powrie Place. I don't know the number of her close but I'm sure somebody will tell you.'

With an exaggerated show of thanks, I bolted through the door but, to my dismay, Powrie Place was similar to the Hilltown and the Overgate – an absolute warren of tenements, closes and stairs. After a few fruitless encounters with dead ends in this maze of humanity, I finally found an old man who not only knew Mrs Davidson but seemed to be fully informed on her entire life's history.

'That'll be Marlene you're looking for. She lives on the top stair,' he said pointing a thin, yellow nicotine-stained finger upwards, as if pointing to heaven. 'Aye she's had a hard life has Marlene. No luck with men if you know what I mean. Men seem to die on her. Poor lass. But this latest one seems healthy enough. Mind you, her last three were healthy enough at some stage before they popped their clogs.'

I realised he was describing Dad and I tried to escape before I heard something I didn't want to hear but the old chap was still talking. 'I'm not sure about this latest flame of hers, though. I think she's more interested in him than he is with her but maybe that's the attraction.' He chuckled loudly before almost collapsing with a coughing fit.

I didn't want to leave him alone while he was choking and gasping for air but he assured me in between wheezy gasps that he was fine. 'I get these attacks from time to time but they don't last long.'

Marlene's close was like a long dark tunnel. There was a dank, musty odour that spoke of too many visitations from the cat and dog populations. This animal mustiness also mingled with numerous human smells – the pungent aroma of fried onions taking top billing.

I climbed the stair and was surprised to come out on to a stone plettie which was high enough to catch the sun, a luxury that was denied to the lower dwellings. This little corner was already bathed in warm sunshine and Marlene was taking advantage of it. She sat beneath her window in an old fireside chair which was so threadbare that the pattern had long since vanished. Minus her make-up and with her thin legs all brown scorch-marked from sitting too close to the fire, she looked old – much older than Dad. She turned suddenly at the sound of my footsteps and a thin white, scrawny hand shot up to her mouth.

Not wanting to alarm her, I held up my hand. 'Mrs Davidson, I'm sorry to bother you but I really need to see my dad. Is he here?'

She nodded wordlessly and inclined her head towards the window behind her.

I skirted round her and knocked on the door which lay beside her left arm. There was no answer so I knocked again.

Now slightly recovered from her surprise at seeing me, she said, 'Just go in. He's probably sleeping in the chair.'

I stepped inside and another surprise awaited

me. Hattie had told us that Marlene was sluttish as a housewife but I now saw this wasn't true. Although sparsely furnished, the room was spotlessly clean. Dad was indeed asleep on a large Rexene-covered armchair. He had been listening to the wireless and the clipped cultured voice of the announcer droned on unheard.

'Dad,' I called. There was no answer and I soon realised why when I saw the two empty beer bottles lying at his feet. I marched over and gave him a hard shake. He opened his eyes and gave me a puzzled look until he focused on me. He suddenly sat upright but was still puzzled-looking, no doubt wondering how I had managed to find him.

'Ann, what's the matter? Is something wrong?' His voice shook slightly but I was in no mood to pander to him.

'Dad, I want you to come to the Overgate with me. We have things to sort out.' I knew I sounded angry but I couldn't help myself.

Although I hadn't heard her, Marlene had entered the room and she was standing behind me. Dad gave her a warning look and made a slight movement with his hand. She tactfully left the room and resumed her seat in the sunshine.

'We can discuss things here, Ann. What do you want?'

I decided to ignore the preliminaries and go straight for the jugular. 'Hattie tells me you're to be evicted from the house. Is that true?'

To my surprise he didn't bat an eyelid.

'She also says you haven't paid your rent for weeks.'

He nodded. 'That's right – I haven't paid the rent for two months now and I don't care about it. It's a right unhappy place and I never want to set foot in it again.'

Tears ran down my cheeks and his voice softened. 'Don't take it to heart, Ann. You've got your granny's house to stay in and well...' He stopped and gazed around the small clean room. 'Well, I've got here.'

'So you're getting married to Mrs Davidson?'

For a brief moment the old sparkle appeared in his tired eyes and he laughed softly. 'Oh, no, not me. Not that Marlene's not good to me because she's kind and she looks after me. She's a good-hearted lass but being married to her is another thing. Oh, no, Ann, marriage is the last thing on my mind.'

I was confused and I said so.

He said, 'This arrangement suits us both. I'm the lodger with my own room.' He pointed to a door at the far wall. 'No Marlene and I are just good friends and a damn good landlady she is and she looks after me so well.'

'But Hattie said you wanted money to pay the rent.'

'Aye that's right but I needed the money to pay the rent here. I can't expect Marlene to keep me for nothing.'

I knew there was nothing else to say to him except to make the arrangements to empty our old house. After all, the factor would want to get a new tenant in as soon as possible.

'Dad, I have to go and do the washing this afternoon but we'll meet later at the house and get it all sorted out. Now remember and be there.'

I stepped out into the sunlight. Planning to say a few words to Marlene to thank her for looking after Dad but, to my consternation, I found that she was crying. Huge teardrops ran down her pale face – tears which she tried to brush away when she saw me.

Suddenly a blast of music and the announcer's voice from the wireless came from the window which I saw was open and I realised then that she had overheard our conversation – every word of Dad's intentions. Feeling so sorry for her, I mumbled a few words of thanks and made my escape down the stairs. Before I reached the bottom, I stopped as something was puzzling me.

Why had I not heard the wireless on my arrival? Then it dawned on me. Marlene, curious to hear everything, must have opened the window quietly from outside. Poor Marlene – in her case, it was true about eavesdroppers not hearing anything good.

As I passed the grocer's shop, I noted with amusement that the sharp-faced woman was now assembling a similar pyramid of pilchards in the window. It was obviously going to be a pilchard week in Ann Street.

Back at the Overgate, I told Granny all the news while we loaded the big bath of dirty washing on to the folding pram. This was such a blessing to us instead of the cumbersome high pram which had been the washing transport for ages. That pram had been given away to another family who lived in the Westport. Granny laughed at the time and said it was getting nearer to Hattie with every move.

Granny put her coat on. Heatwave or not, she never went anywhere without her coat. 'I'll just come with you and give you a wee hand with the washing. Your grandad can keep an eye on Lily.'

'No, Granny,' I was being quite firm, 'I'll manage all right on my own. You've enough to cope with all week as it is – both you and Grandad. Now you have a rest.'

She tried to protest but I was adamant. She said, 'Remember you have to meet your dad later on and I just hope he's there – the devil that he is. Sometimes I could cheerfully wring his neck.'

They were my feelings exactly. Although angry with him when we were apart, the minute I saw him I couldn't help but pity him and, like lots of other people, I always gave in to his charm. But not this time, I promised myself, as I struggled uphill with my heavy load.

A fleeting feeling of annoyance crossed my mind when I saw how busy it was. Mondays were always the busiest day at the wash-house and today, with the lovely weather, women wanted to take advantage of the outside drying facilities. Washing lines were full of sheets and towels flapping in the gentle breeze. It was a perfect combination of sunshine and wind and, at times like this, it was easy to believe in a heaven.

The heat was intense inside my tiny cubicle but I had no option but to get on with the task ahead. Granny helped out by doing small washes every night, drying the things on her kitchen pulley. Big items like the sheets needed to be boiled and the

249

metal boiler stood beside the sinks. Before long, sweat was running down my face in long rivulets, soaking the neck of my thin blouse.

Granny owned a thick apron made from jute hessian which she had used for many years. I was now the owner of this bulky garment which almost reached my ankles but it was perfect for keeping me dry – or reasonably dry at least.

Scores of voices echoed overhead and it was a comforting hum. Now and then, someone would screech loudly before breaking out in a loud laugh. Once more I marvelled at the cheeriness of the women and they enjoyed their gossip in spite of the backbreaking work.

'My man was a painter in the shipyard before they closed it,' shouted one anonymous voice, not caring if a dozen people heard her. 'Then, when it opened again last September, he made straight for the yard and do you know how many men were ahead of him in the queue?'

Someone shouted they didn't know.

'Well, there was two hundred ahead of him and another few hundred behind him It's a bloody disgrace this country has no work for our men.' She sounded tired and disgruntled and who could blame her?

'Did he get a job?' shouted another anonymous voice.

'Did he hell. There was folk there saying they were painters and they didn't know one end of a paintbrush from the other, Anyway they only took on a handful of men.'

I thought of Rita and Nellie. Their men were also chasing every job but they were competing with two or three hundred men for each vacancy. I wondered what chance Dad would have and was immediately depressed by the answer.

I dried my hands on the rough apron. It was in a different bracket from Maddie's home-sewn garments but it was more practical and I was grateful for that.

I let the conversations float over my head as I scrubbed the dirty clothes and then suddenly I heard the name Marlene.

'I hear she's hoping to get married again. Is that true?'

A burst of laughter was followed by another voice. 'How many men has she had?'

The voices drifted away. I rushed out of my cubicle but the aisle was merely populated with tired women pulling their baths of wet washing to the extractors. The trouble with this building was the construction. The chattering women could well be at the faraway end, such was the way the sound carried.

I was becoming obsessed by Marlene. It didn't have to be Dad's friend they were discussing – there must be a thousand or more women in the city called Marlene, I thought.

I was still troubled when I arrived home. Granny hung the washing on the pulley and it seemed such a shame to bypass the warm sunshine outside but this house didn't have a drying green. Some lucky households had the luxury of an outside line that stretched from their window to a communal greenie pole that was situated in the backyard and always looked as if it was bending in the wind.

I thought wistfully of the green meadows I had left behind at the wash-house but with so many women vying for space, drying a washing there always added time to a busy day. And it was time I didn't have – not if I had to meet Dad.

It was five o'clock when I reached the Hilltown. Rita and Nellie were standing at the entrance to the close, enjoying the sunshine and having a good gossip. They were so drawn, thin and tired looking that I was shocked by their appearance. Even Rita who, last year, had had the added advantage of her plumpness now looked malnourished and, as for Nellie, well, she was just gaunt.

Rita patted the bulge and muttered gloomily, 'Just another month to go then goodness only knows what we'll do.'

I mentioned Dad's coming eviction but to my surprise they sympathised with him. 'Well, Ann, he's never going to be happy in that house so maybe it's for the best that he's giving it up,' said Rita while Nellie nodded in agreement.

Then to my immense relief, I saw him heading towards us. All day, I'd had the dreaded notion that this was another venture he would duck out of but we all made our way upstairs while the two women tactfully retired to their own abodes.

We made our way down the dark lobby. Inside, the house was just as I had left it on my last visit. Debris from Dad's few visits was evident and the same air of neglect and abandonment hung in the airless room. I could have cried but that wouldn't have helped matters, I thought. Instead, we decided what to do about the contents. We drew up a plan that anything small and portable was to be kept.

'Do you think Granny has use for some of these ornaments, Ann?' he said, in a calm flat voice that annoyed me. 'Or maybe Hattie will like these knick-knacks?' When I glared at him, he mumbled, 'She can look after them till you get a place of your own when you're older.'

'Hattie's not getting Mum's knick-knacks as you call them, Dad. I'll take them to Granny.' I removed the few treasured ornaments from the mantelpiece. They had been Mum's pride and joy, all these little decorations.

I glanced around, looking for a discarded newspaper to wrap them in. We used to put papers under the chair cushion so I lifted it up and found an old yellowed newspaper there. But, when I lifted it up, I stopped dead. Underneath was a small half-knitted matinee jacket with a ball of wool pushed firmly through the two knitting needles.

Dad's gaze landed on it when I cried out. Suddenly we both burst into a flood of tears. As we held each other, a year's grief spilled out like a well overflowing and the tears streamed down our faces.

I tried to take a breath but my throat felt constricted and a pain shot across my ribs as a result of the racking sobs that arose from somewhere deep inside my body.

Rita appeared in the doorway, looking apprehensive. 'I couldn't help overhearing the crying. Look, Johnny and Ann, let Nellie and me clear the house out for you.'

Dad wiped tears from his eyes and his voice

was rough with emotion. It was no longer the calm flat tones that had irritated me earlier. 'No thanks, Rita. You see this is something we have to do but if we need any help we'll give you a shout.'

Rita's eyes landed on the small garment. She went white. 'Oh no, we must have missed it when we cleaned up afterwards. I'm so sorry that it's brought you all this grief.'

She looked miserable but Dad stepped over to her and placed his arm around her shoulder. 'No, Rita, we're glad we found it. It's something belonging to her mum that Ann can keep – a memento of happier times that she can treasure all her life.'

I hadn't viewed it like that and my earlier mortification turned now to tender memories of Mum sitting in that chair, her hands forever busy. It was such a happy memory and so strong in my mind that I almost felt her presence in the room along with us – almost as if she was watching over us. With this comforting feeling in my mind, I carefully wrapped the scrap of knitting in a clean pillowcase and placed it in my bag along with the paper-wrapped ornaments.

Dad reappeared after seeing Rita to her door but his face was still streaked with tears. He glanced around the room as if seeing it for the first time. 'We came to live here, your mum and me, just after we got married. You were born in this room, Ann, and the only help your poor mum had was from Granny and Bunty Grey, the midwife. I was fighting in the war, wasn't I? Fighting in the Great War that they said was the war to end all wars. I was at the battle of Neuve

Chapelle when half of the 4th Battalion Black Watch were killed.' His face clouded over. 'After that battle, there wasn't one house in Dundee that didn't get bad news about a loved one. That's what they say.'

He turned towards the small window, still talking, but it seemed as if he was speaking to himself. 'But I survived somehow and we had such a happy life here in spite of having no work. When I think of all the politicians, I could cheerfully choke the lot of them. Maybe they thought we would all be killed in the war and that would have suited them, no doubt – a lot less people to cater for.'

This was the first time I had heard this story and a wave of realisation swept over me and I suddenly knew how he felt. All the frustration and grief was enough to throw even the strongest man.

'Mum wouldn't want you to live like this, Dad – all this drinking and neglecting yourself. She would want you to be the person she loved and knew.'

He placed his hand on my shoulder. 'I'm trying but it's very hard without her.'

'Mum would want you to be strong for Lily's sake.'

He sighed. 'It'll just take time, Ann. Your granny is right when she says that it's in the lap of the gods when you recover from grief.'

'Has John Pringle no word about a job yet?' Although I asked the question, I knew what the answer would be.

'No but, when that old employee leaves, then

the job is seemingly mine.' His voice matched the despair on his face.

'I was hearing the other day that the waiting list for jobs at the Transport Department, two thousand names, have been taken off the list because the ex-employees of the Broughty Ferry tramway company have now got first call on any vacancies. What a pity the Ferry trams were taken over by Dundee Corporation.'

I sympathised with him and wished I could wave a magic wand over all the unemployment in the city. 'Has the means test man been back here? I met him once in Rita's house.'

'Don't mention that,' he said. 'I've always got to hide when he comes to see Marlene. She's an out-of-work jute weaver but, if they knew she had a lodger, her dole would be cut off.'

I almost let the cat out of the bag by looking surprised. I said, 'Oh, she works, does she?' I didn't mention that Bella and Hattie were under the misapprehension that Marlene lived well on the insurance profits from three dead husbands.

Dad looked equally surprised, no doubt by the tone of my voice. 'Well, she used to – in the days when the jute mills were busy. Still, she has a few bob tucked under her bed has our Marlene.' He laughed and winked at me.

I mentally awarded Bella and Co. ten out often for perception.

'I'll make a cup of tea, Ann,' said Dad, fishing in his pockets for some loose change. 'Nip down to the baker and get two hot pies. We'll have our last meal in this house.' He grew sad again and his eyes misted over.

The baker's shop had a small oven in the back store so the pies were piping hot as I carried them carefully up the stairs. Dad had made a pot of strong black tea – none of your weak Russian tea here, I thought – and we sat and discussed the best way to deal with the furniture. Most of it was large and I knew there was no room at the Overgate for anything. As for Hattie, well, I couldn't see her welcoming any of our slightly tatty items in her house.

We agreed to offer it to Rita and Nellie and if they didn't want it then perhaps the second-hand shop across the road would buy it. Rita looked relieved to see our happier faces but she sadly had to decline our offer. Nellie was the same. They just didn't have the room in their cramped little houses. They did however offer the services of their husbands to help carry the heavier items downstairs.

'Just give us a shout, Johnny, and the men will help you carry them to the shop,' said Rita, as we finished the last scraps of our pies and drank the dregs from the old teapot.

Dad dismantled the bed using a special key that loosened the screws in the two metal bars that held the wooden ends together. We then gingerly lifted the spring base from the metal supports and placed it on its side, where it lay in all its dust-ingrained glory.

I went in search of a duster but Dad said, 'Just leave it. It'll soon get dustier lying about the shop.'

I didn't like the shop owner to think we were a slovenly family but further thoughts on this subject were dispelled by the arrival of the man. He was a tiny thin man and almost bald with a face like an undertaker – very serious looking as if viewing a body instead of old furniture. He had small round spectacles perched on his nose and exceptionally large hands which showed deep blue raised veins.

He viewed the furniture with a calculating and cynical eye. He peered into the sideboard drawers and cupboards before finally doing a disappearing act behind the wooden press. Sharp tapping noises emerged from this direction and Dad gave me a quizzical look which almost made me burst out laughing. The man popped back in view. 'It's in quite good condition although a bit old-fashioned, if you don't mind me saying so, but it's not bad. No, not bad at all.'

'What will you give us for the furniture?' asked Dad, trying hard not to sound too eager.

The man hummed and hawed for a bit before disappearing behind the press again. He then peered into the drawers for a second view. 'It's like this – with most folk out of work, I'm lucky if I can sell anything. I've had to slash my prices dramatically this year.' He scratched his bald head and looked at the ceiling. 'Well, then, let me see. I can let you have five shillings for the bed but I'll need the bedclothes as well.'

He stopped when I gasped. I had been hoping to take all the bedclothes with me to the Overgate.

The little man looked at us, his shrewd eyes summing up the situation. 'I'm sorry, lassie, but it's almost impossible to sell a bed without its

258

covers. Some sheets and blankets come as a wee bit extra and it makes all the difference between a sale or not. Aye, it's hard times we're living in and no doubt about it.'

Dad said nothing but I saw the silent appeal in his eyes. I shrugged my shoulders. To a casual onlooker, I probably looked quite unruffled but, inside, I was fuming. This little pile of bedclothes would have been a boon – perhaps making my weekly trip to the wash-house a fortnightly one. Also, with a couple of pairs of extra sheets and some towels in her cupboard, Granny would have had a small surplus instead of the bare minimum.

We turned our attention to the rest of the items. 'The press is a bit bashed looking so I can only offer three shillings for that but the sideboard is not too bad. It's been well looked after.'

He could say that, I thought bitterly. Mum had spent ages every week polishing it with her rag and small tin of Mansion polish. It had been her pride and joy and now it was being appraised with an eye for resale. I wondered if everything in life came down to the simple arithmetic of pounds, shillings and pence – the common denominator for the working classes without the work.

The man was still talking, still running his eye over it. For a minute, he looked surprised by the tears in my eyes but sensibly said nothing. 'I'll give you nine and a tanner for it. No, wait a minute – because you didn't want to part with the bedclothes, I'll throw in another half crown. What do you think of that offer?'

Dad looked at me but I said, 'It's up to you, Dad. It's your furniture.'

259

Dad turned to the man who now stood on the sidelines of our small domestic discussion and said, 'Right then, we'll take it.'

The man whipped out a small pencil from a waistcoat pocket and proceeded to write on the palm of his hand. 'Now let's see. That's five shillings for the bed, three shillings for the press and nine shillings and sixpence for the sideboard.' He did a quick calculation.

I reminded him, 'Don't forget the extra half crown.'

He looked up but didn't look directly at me. 'That's five bob, three bob, nine and a tanner plus two and six. That makes a grand total of two pounds.'

Now that the deal was completed, Dad cheered up. 'That's fine then, Mr Bell. You can take the stuff away anytime you like.'

So that was his name – Mr Bell. Although he had traded on the Hilltown for a good few years, I had always known his shop as the 'Rake and Rummage'. This name was due to the large notice in his window which cordially invited the general populace to 'Come in for a closer inspection. No objection to browsers. You are welcome to rake and rummage.' This was all very well but Mrs Bell also worked in the shop. She had the stern disapproving countenance of one who would strongly object to anyone turning the stock upside down. But the notice had been in the window so long that it had turned yellow with age and I doubt if anyone ever read it now.

Mr Bell was speaking again and Dad looked unhappy. 'I'm afraid I never carry money on me,' he said. 'You never know who you're going to bump into these days with so many folk out of work and I wouldn't want to be robbed.'

This statement made Dad even more unhappy. 'I thought we could get everything settled today. There's two men next door ready to help and I know they're planning on going on the Hunger March next week so they might not be available then.'

Mr Bell pondered on this predicament. 'Well, I have my horse and cart downstairs but I've no money on my person or in the house. I don't believe in keeping cash around me in these hard times.'

Because he was in danger of repeating himself over and over again and we didn't need reminding how hard the times were, I butted in, 'Can Mr Bell not take the furniture now, Dad, then you can collect the money at his shop tomorrow.'

Dad looked doubtful. 'I really wanted the money for you and Lily – to take back to Granny.'

I was taken aback but also touched. 'Oh, Dad, what a nice thought! Well, let Mr Bell take everything away now and I'll collect the money next Monday.'

Mr Bell beamed. If he was lucky then maybe the furniture would be sold by then and he wouldn't have to open his cash-box which was hidden in the chimney of his bedroom or wherever it was he kept it. 'That suits me fine, lassie,' he said.

He turned to Dad who nodded reluctantly. 'Well, we'll shift the stuff now and the money will be waiting for you next Monday.'

Apart from Rita, who stood in her doorway,

keeping an eye on her little boy, we all mucked in and helped Mr Bell with the furniture. Getting it all down the narrow stairwell was difficult but, with a bit of manoeuvring from Dad and the two neighbours, everything was soon out on the sun-splashed pavement

The horse, as Mr Bell called it, was no more than a pony, mangy looking but with a sweet placid expression. The pony stood patiently while the first item was loaded on to the flat-based cart. Mr Bell, knowing the capabilities of his little pony, made the suggestion of one item at a time. 'It's a long haul up the Hilltown and I don't want to tax my horse so we'll take the bed first then the press and finally the sideboard.'

At that moment, a noisy band of children went running past, following one of the urchins who was on a rickety wooden scooter. Mr Bell looked shaken as they narrowly missed the furniture.

'I've changed my mind. I'll take the sideboard first then the bed. The press can go last.'

Nellie's man, who was growing more agitated by the minute, growled, 'For heaven's sake, will you make up your mind? We're standing here in this bloody heat and sweating like pigs while you're dithering like a gibbering idiot.'

Dad looked embarrassed but Mr Bell didn't bat an eye. 'Right, then, men, it's the sideboard first.'

I watched as the small pony struggled uphill with its load and I felt sorry for it. Still, within ten minutes, it was back, looking as placid and unworried as before.

When the last load went off, Dad thanked his neighbours. 'I'll have to give you both a couple of shillings for all your help.'

They shook their heads in protest. 'Not at all – if we can't help a neighbour out, who can we help?'

Dad accepted this graciously. 'Right, then, I'll stand you both a pint in the Windmill bar.'

Before they all set off, I cornered Dad. 'I can't accept the money. The furniture belonged to you and Mum.'

He stopped me. 'I don't want to hear another word. It's for you and Lily – especially as you had to part with the bedclothes.'

I knew the money was badly needed. Lily was walking now and she needed a new pair of shoes. Also, Grandad's shoes were in need of repair. He was using a thick piece of cardboard as an insole which was fine in the dry weather but, once the rain came, it would be another story.

As Dad hurried up the hill I called after him, 'Thanks, Dad – we'll use it well.'

I went back into the house. Now devoid of all the furniture, it looked sad and faded, without any character – just a small square room. Mum had been so fond of the wallpaper but the faded scuffed flowers were now an anaemic version of their former glory. I smiled when I saw the bare patch where the press stood. Dad had insisted that it didn't need to be moved so he had papered around it. There were some markings beside this bare patch – just a few pencil lines. I bent down and saw my name and a date beside each line. My parents had recorded my height at various times during my childhood. Suddenly more warm memories came flooding back.

Memories of a warm and loving home – like the smell of soup simmering on the stove and the aroma of wet washing as it dried around the fire.

I picked up the pillowcase with my small pile of treasures and turned to leave. Rita and Nellie stood outside, both looking sad. For a moment, I almost burst into tears but Mum wouldn't have wanted all this sadness so I lifted my chin. 'Cheerio, Rita and Nellie – mind and let us know when the bairn comes.'

Rita smiled. 'Aye, I'll do that, Ann. The bells of the auld steeple will be ringing out the glad tidings when it happens,' she said as she wiped a tear away. 'Cheerio, Ann, and mind and keep well – you and Lily.'

I turned to Nellie. 'Thanks for all your help, You've both been so good to us all. I'll never forget it.'

Nellie dabbed her eyes with a piece of cloth. 'It's for the best, Ann. The man from the means test is always asking questions and he was getting suspicious, wasn't he, Rita?'

Rita nodded. 'That's right. We keep fobbing him off but he is aye prying and nosing around. Sooner or later he would have worked it all out.'

Outside in the street, I met Mr Bell. He was heading across the road to his shop. There was something bothering me. 'Mr Bell, why did you not carry everything over to the shop instead of taking it up the Hill? It would have saved a journey for the wee pony.'

He gave me a suspicious look. 'Oh, I don't keep everything in my shop. I've got a wee shed up the road where I store the bigger items of furniture.'

Rita and Nellie had followed me downstairs and I bade them and the Hilltown a fond farewell. I tried not to think of the little house that had been my home for sixteen years. But, maybe with a bit of luck. Lily and I would return at some future date. I knew Mum would have liked that.

The following Monday morning, I made my way back to Mr Bell's shop. He looked surprised to see me. 'Oh, your dad collected the money last Tuesday morning. Look, here's the receipt.' He thrust a small book under my nose and I saw Dad's signature. 'Mind you, I did think it was strange at the time,' he went on, 'especially as he said you were to get the money. I did hear however through the grapevine that he had to pay his bill at the Windmill bar as he had quite a bit of drink on the slate. Still, I expect he'll give it back to you when he's flush again.' His voice stammered into silence and his fingers gripped the edge of the receipt book. 'I'm really .... really sorry. Aye, really ... sorry.'

I tried to look as dignified as possible. 'Aye, that's all right, Mr Bell. It was his furniture and the money was always his to spend as he thought fit.'

As I walked away with Mr Bell's sympathetic eyes following me, I thought, 'Damn you, Dad. How could you do this to your poor little girl? Poor Lily.'

11

Danny had good news. He burst into the house the following Sunday afternoon, his young face beaming with pride. Instead of being a lowly message boy, he was now a very junior assistant in the shop. 'Actually, I'm not really an assistant yet,' he explained, 'I'm in the back shop, making up all the orders but Mr Burnett the manager says that I can work my way up if I stick in and work hard. Maybe this time next year I'll be serving behind the counter.' His eyes were sparkling and we were all pleased for him, especially Granny and Grandad. 'Oh, I always knew you would go far, Danny,' said Granny. 'Aye, we always knew that.'

I was also pleased for him. It was the first bit of good news in ages. I had spent a depressing week at the Ferry, worried about Dad's drinking and the wasted loss of the hard-earned money from the furniture. I could have spent it so well but it now lay in the pub's cash register.

Hattie was full of pride at her Danny's promotion as she called it. However, she would have preferred it if he had been made an instant manager instead of slowly working his way up the Lipton's ladder. 'Well, even if I say it myself,' she said smugly, 'I've always turned you out well and now it's paying off although it could have been a higher position you were offered, Danny.'

Granny screwed up her face. 'Honestly, Hattie, what a backhanded compliment. Don't give Danny any praise, will you?' She turned to him and said, 'Everyone has to start at the foot of the ladder, son. You'll make it and we're all proud of you.'

Danny turned to me. 'I'm going to Lochee to tell them about my good luck. Would you like to come with me?' He grinned, knowing full well that his mother had made a face behind his back. This was her usual response whenever the Lochee relations were mentioned. 'We'll take Lily with us and go on the tramcar.'

I needed no second invitation and I hurried to get my coat. Hattie glared at me because she hadn't succeeded in prising my treasured coat away from me in spite of a great deal of bribery and wheedling. Now, because she realised it was a lost cause, she merely resorted to scowls and mutterings every time she saw it.

Lily loved the tramcar and we always took her up to the upper deck so she could stand on the wooden seat and look out the window. As we slowly made our way to Lochee, I told Danny about Dad and the now empty house.

As usual he was sympathetic. 'Maddie says that her uncle John is hoping that the old man will retire soon but he's staying on till the last moment. But who can blame him? He'll miss his wage packet every week but, on the other hand, it would be great if your dad got the job.'

'Well, one bit of good news is that it doesn't look like there's to be a wedding with Marlene.' Her pale face loomed large in my mind. 'But I

267

still feel sorry for her.'

Danny laughed. 'Well, Mum doesn't – a painted hussy is the latest description being bandied about.'

'Maybe she is,' I replied truthfully, 'but she's also a very lonely woman. At least that's the impression I got last Monday.'

We then spoke about his promotion. 'They'll all be pleased at Lochee, Danny. What's the position on the job front for them?'

He shook his head. 'No one's got a job yet and, although I try and help out a bit, they're all having a hard time. Do you remember the family that were all ill last New Year's Day? Well they're all dead and what's this country doing about it? Nothing.' He sounded bitter.

I realised we were lucky to have good health which was a blessing, even if we had little or no money.

When we alighted from the tramcar, the street was as busy with children as usual. Their swooping and screaming bodies swirled around us as we made our way to Kit's house. Their thin legs and arms poked out of ragged skirts and trousers and their jumpers were full of holes.

We spotted Kathleen amongst this throng, her red hair shining like a beacon on a dark night. She saw us and came running over, followed by a score of children. 'Danny, Mum says to go to her house as Granny is visiting a sick pal in Louis Square.' She waved a grimy hand before departing with her mob.

We climbed the outside stair and entered the cave-like lobby. Kit had obviously heard our voices because she opened the door before we reached it. She looked more careworn and thinner than I remembered her but her spirit was as strong as ever. There was no sign of George or her sisters.

She looked pleased to see us and immediately put the kettle on. 'Sit down,' she said, pulling the chairs towards the meagre fire that burned fitfully in the grate. There was hardly any heat in the room and a chill swept under the gap in the front door. The sunny weather had disappeared a few days ago to be replaced by grey cloud and drizzle. The dampness seemed to seep into the house and into our bodies but I suppose we were all in the same boat. The walls at the Overgate were also damp on occasions as were those of the Hilltown house.

I sat facing the plaster crucifix on the far wall and I noticed three patches of bright wallpaper that contrasted with the pattern on the rest of the walls and I realised that pictures which had recently hung on the wall were now missing.

Kit saw my gaze and she flushed, her face turning almost as red as her hair. 'I had to pawn the pictures to tide us over this week although what we'll pawn next week is anybody's guess.'

Danny was upset. 'Let me help you out, Kit,' he said, putting his hand in his pocket.

She stopped him. 'No, no, Danny, you're good to your granny and we appreciate that but you can't be expected to subsidise the whole family. George is getting depressed by the small amount he gets from the dole and this means test is biting into everyone's lives.'

She poured out three cups of strong black tea. 'George was saying that it'll take another war to get us all back to work. Then the swines in the government will need men to fight for their country again. Oh, aye, they'll recognise working men again after bloody ignoring them for years. In fact, George was saying that the working classes are an embarrassment to the government and, if we all starve, then that'll suit them fine. They'll have less benefits to pay out for one thing.'

She took Lily on her lap. 'You're getting to be a big, strong lass. Your uncle tells me that you're walking and speaking now.'

On cue, Lily opened her mouth, 'Da-da-da-da-da,' she said. She began squirming on Kit's lap, wanting to be down on the floor and running around.

I mentioned Danny's new job.

Kit looked at her nephew. 'A new job, Danny?'

'That's what I came to tell you and Ma. I've been promoted to the back shop at Lipton's.' He beamed at her and she looked pleased.

'Ma will be so pleased for you and so am I. What a pity the rest of the family are not here to wish you well. George is over at Dad's house, playing cards. It helps to pass the time for them,' she said with a rueful smile. 'Mind you, they gamble with matches because they don't have a penny between them – not a toss. Ma is visiting an old neighbour who is ill and she's making her something to eat.'

But the words were hardly out of her mouth when the door opened and Ma Ryan appeared. She sat down, obviously out of breath. 'I swear the steps get steeper every time I climb them, Kit.' She smiled at us. 'It's good to see you again, Ann – and Lily. Now, Danny – I see him every week and he's really good to his auld granny. Coming to see this auld wife and him so young as well.'

Danny grinned. 'Oh, you're just fishing for compliments, Ma. You're not old.'

She pretended to swipe him with a thin, wrinkled hand. 'You wee besom, you're just kidding me on.' She waited till Kit handed her a cup of tea. 'You've got some good news for me, Danny?'

I glanced at her sharply. 'How could you know that, Ma?'

She just nodded wisely.

Danny told her all his good news and she nodded again. 'I had a feeling this was coming. You'll do well, Danny, but it'll all be in God's own good time.'

I was determined to speak to her alone before we left and I got my chance when Kit and Danny went ahead of me down the stairs with Lily toddling between them.

'Mrs Ryan, do you remember you warned me about a blackbird the last time I saw you? Can you tell me more because you said I was in some kind of danger from it?'

She looked intently into my eyes, placing a wrinkled hand on my arm. 'You're in the vicinity of the bird and the danger is coming. Watch out for it.'

'But, Mrs Ryan, they're are loads of blackbirds in the garden at the Ferry. Will one of them attack me?'

Ma Ryan said, 'I can't tell you the whole scene, lass. It's sometimes just fragments I pick up and other times the scene is so clear but, in your case, all I can say is that you're in some kind of danger from a blackbird. I'm sorry.'

Kit appeared as I was on my way downstairs. I decided to say nothing to her about the prediction. And to be honest I wasn't entirely sure about Ma's so-called second sight.

Perhaps her predictions were true on some occasions but were there others that never came true? Like in my case? Even though I was a bit wary of the blackbirds in the garden, they never bothered me. In fact they usually flew away at the sound of my step and surely viewing them through the window wouldn't place me in any danger. No, I thought, Ma Ryan was just an old woman who had fancies and prided herself on having the gift of prophecy.

As for Danny – if he was pleased at his success then it paled into insignificance against Maddie's pleasure. She would drag me into the shop as soon as I returned to the Overgate on my days off. We laughed so much the first time we saw him. His white apron was so long that it skimmed his ankles and it was so voluminous that it wrapped around his slender body like an enormous sheet.

Maddie voted him the most handsome assistant in the shop, an opinion that could have been contested by most of the male staff but Maddie was adamant. As she was in the habit of visiting the shop every other day, she was fast becoming an expert in the grocery trade.

She bought four slices of black pudding on her

first visit, which her mother refused to eat. After this rejection, she would pop into Granny's house and almost beg for a grocery line. Failing that, she would canvass the entire close and offer to do their shopping but, as nearly everyone in the vicinity was perpetually short of money, this wasn't often successful. As Granny said to her, 'It's not as if you see Danny – he's in the back shop, is he not?'

Maddie agreed. 'Yes but sometimes he comes through into the front to collect the orders and I give him a big smile.'

She confessed as much to me as we sat in her mother's sewing room that winter. With the light fading fast and the small lamps glowing, I loved this little room under the eaves. As she snipped and cut the material, working out the intricacies of the paper pattern, the selvedges and numerous nuances of home-dressmaking, she said, 'I just go and browse around and sometimes I see him and sometimes not. There's this thin girl with a pretty face but screwed up like this...' She made a face like someone sucking lemons. 'And she says, "If you're looking for Danny, well, he's in the back shop and he's busy."' Maddie stopped and scowled. 'I once saw a picture of Miss Muffet eating her curds and whey and she had the same screwed up face when she saw the spider.'

I was suddenly afraid. 'Maddie, I hope he doesn't get into trouble over you always popping in and out.' What if the manager took offence at her odd behaviour, I thought. Would he then be annoyed at Danny?

'Well, just remember that I'm a customer,' she

stressed the words in case I missed the message. 'After all, I'm bringing loads of trade to the shop.'

I laughed. 'Four slices of black pudding is hardly a huge order, Maddie.'

She became defensive. 'Don't forget the groceries I get for your granny. Then there's Alice and Bella and that wizened old woman who lives on the top stair. You know the one – she buys all those fish heads to feed her cats.' She stopped and looked puzzled. 'I've even asked Hattie if I can do her shopping but she thinks I'm crazy.'

I burst out laughing at her expression.

She looked hurt for a moment then started to laugh as well. 'Well, maybe I am crazy but I'll tell you something, Ann, I'll be glad to leave school and get a job like you and Danny.'

I sighed and thought of the Ryan family. They would give anything to be in jobs but in the meantime they lived in desperate circumstances while Maddie was cushioned with wealth and privilege. I told her so.

She looked at me sadly and I knew it wasn't her fault that her parents were well off. Just as my poverty stricken ones – an evicted one as well – weren't my fault.

'I know,' she said, 'that's why I'm going to be a nurse so I can help poor people who are ill. Shall I tell you something, Ann? I think people are more important than money, don't you?'

When I agreed, she cheered up. 'I think I'll put a small notice in the window in that small shop at the foot of your close, offering to do people's shopping for them. What do you think?'

'Well, I think you're daft but, if it pleases you, then where's the harm?'

I left her writing out a postcard for the window, pursing her lips in such concentration that it could well have been the start of some epic novel.

Meanwhile, back at the Overgate, Hattie was still smarting over her in-laws being invited to Lily and Joy's birthday party, even although it was over and done with months ago.

'I was never so embarrassed when that lot arrived from Lochee and started to slander me. And, as for Bella – well, she had almost to be carried home,' she said through gritted teeth, rolling her eyes heavenwards as though seeking divine help.

Granny, who was fast becoming fed up with this regular rehash of the long-past party, was annoyed by this latest tirade. 'Hattie, will you get it through your thick head that the Pringle family know all about you and your relations and they still employ you. If they had wanted only toffs at the party, they wouldn't have invited the entire clan to the bunfight.'

Hattie winced at this turn of phrase used by her mother. Although she was ignorant of the fact, we all knew she was fast becoming more uppity than her employers.

Granny continued, 'We all know Maddie has a lovely home and advantages that thousands will never have but she is also a good friend to Ann and Danny. Have you ever stopped to think that she gets something back from them? And, as for Bella, well, she was tired with the heat and her legs were playing her up. She didn't have too much to drink.'

Hattie nodded glumly but she was desperate to have the final word on the subject. 'I wouldn't have been surprised to see Kit and Lizzie put their tea in their saucer to drink it,' she muttered.

'Heavens, Hattie, this is your dead man's sisters you're miscalling,' said Granny. 'You thought Pat was a lovely chap so his sisters can't be that bad.'

Hattie muttered something under her breath as she left – something we didn't catch. Granny sighed while I got ready for the trip back to work the following morning.

When I went through the door of Whitegate Lodge, I was aware of the strong, acrid smell of wintergreen ointment. Its pungency seemed to seep into every cranny and even the back kitchen wasn't immune from its aroma.

As usual, Miss Hood ignored me completely, merely thrusting a pencilled list at me as she swished past in the narrow lobby. It was my chores for the day. After quickly depositing my small suitcase in my room, I put on my pinny and set about tackling the first job on the list. I had long since learned that this was how the house-keeper wanted the jobs done and, although I was curious about the ever-pervading smell, I knew not to ask.

It wasn't until Jean entered the kitchen that the reason became clear. 'Poor Mrs Barrie is awfully ill with the flu. The doctor is coming in again this morning and she has had a very bad weekend.' She shook her chubby cheeks. 'Poor soul and her at the tender mercies of Miss Hood.'

The words were hardly out of her mouth when

the housekeeper appeared. At first we thought she had maybe overheard this remark but she gave no sign of it. She made a beeline for the noisily boiling kettle. Clutched in her hand was a china cup with a spoonful of blackcurrant jam in its base.

She seemed distracted for, when a few spots of hot water splashed on to her hand, she merely winced slightly before carrying on with making the drink.

Jean piped up, 'Can I do anything to help, Miss Hood? Make a light meal for Mrs Barrie and something to eat for yourself?'

Miss Hood stiffened slightly at these words but, when she answered she was quite pleasant, 'Thank you, Mrs Peters, at the moment, all she wants is this blackcurrant drink but, when she does start to eat, food will have to be light and in small portions.'

She walked away and Jean looked surprised. 'Heavens, the woman's almost human. Mind you, though I say it myself, there has never been any doubt about her devotion to the mistress. Aye, give her her due about that.'

I was beginning to think the same thing and I relaxed. Maybe Miss Hood was over her dislike of me and this thought made me feel happy.

The doctor arrived at ten o'clock. He stood on the doorstep, dressed entirely in black and the bulging bag he carried was made of black leather. His face must have been fuller in his youth because large sections of his skin now hung loosely from his face, giving him the appearance of a sad-looking bloodhound.

I showed him upstairs to Mrs Barrie's bedroom and, as I set off downstairs, I heard a soft footfall in the hall below. It was Miss Hood. I was suddenly wary. Since my near accident when she pushed me, I never liked meeting her on the stairs but she very quietly walked across the hall and slipped into the lounge.

I hesitated at the door. According to my list, this was my next chore. Should I go in, I wondered, or should I go and clean the next room on the list. After a few minutes and because she was such a stickler for keeping the same routine, I tapped on the door. There was no answer so I thought I had been mistaken about which door she had opened. From my high vantage point on the stairs it had looked like the lounge but perhaps she had gone into the dining room instead. I had been so tense at the sight of her that it would have been easy to make a mistake.

I pushed open the door and saw, to my dismay, that she was in the room although she hadn't heard me entering. She was sitting with her back to me on a chair by the window. She had her head in her hands and she was crying – not harshly or loudly but with a soft whimpering sound similar to an injured animal.

Horrified, I hesitated again, unsure of how I should react to this new development. I then realised she would be furious with me for witnessing this uncharacteristic side of her nature so I quickly backed out into the hall, eternally grateful for the thick pile on the carpet. Still unsure how to behave, I decided to gave her another few moments. On the one hand, I didn't want her to think I was shirking my duties but, on the other hand, I didn't know how long she would be in the lounge.

The doctor then appeared at the top of the stairs. 'Is Miss Hood there, Miss?'

With relief flooding over me, I knocked hard on the door, grateful for having a genuine reason to enter.

She answered at once although her voice still trembled with emotion, 'What is it?'

'It's the doctor, Miss Hood. He's asking for you.' I noticed that she had now composed herself and sat as if looking out of the window at the grey seascape. She stood up and smoothed a few wrinkles from her frock before heading up the stairs. She looked dreadful and had visibly aged since the weekend. I heard the soft murmurs as she spoke to the doctor just as I closed the door. The list stated quite clearly, 'Polish furniture in lounge.'

I couldn't understand this new side to the housekeeper but if, as Jean said, she was truly devoted to Mrs Barrie, then this would account for her distress.

I was on my hands and knees, polishing the lower shelves of a small corner cupboard when I spotted a small scrap of cardboard. Turning it over I discovered it was a sepia-toned photograph of a small child about Lily's age. Because the child was dressed in a romper suit, I surmised it was a boy. He had large dark eyes, a mop of dark curls and lovely coffee-coloured skin. At least that was my first impression but I could be wrong, I thought. I could tell the photograph was quite old but there was no clue to the boy's age or where the photo had been taken. Also, how it came to be lying on Mrs Barrie's lounge carpet was another mystery. It was certainly lying near the spot where Miss Hood had been sitting weeping but, apart from that, there was nothing to associate it with her.

Unsure what to do with it, I placed it back where I found it and scuttled to the other side of the room. And, as it turned out, it was not a moment too soon. The door suddenly flew open and the housekeeper almost jumped in, so agitated was she. Her eyes swept over to the window then back to me.

'Have you finished in here?' she snapped, sounding like the old Miss Hood I knew.

I decided to tell a white lie as I was still unsure about the photograph. 'I've just started here Miss Hood and I still have the furniture to polish over by the window.'

She looked so relieved and her old face coloured slightly. 'Just finish off now. Mrs Peters wants you in the kitchen – for a cup of tea and something to eat.' She didn't look at me as she spoke. Her eyes were fixed firmly on the spot where the small piece of cardboard lay.

Meanwhile I almost fell over in shock. I had been at Whitegate Lodge for a long time now and never once had she mentioned stopping work for a cup of tea, let alone something to eat. It was obvious she wanted me out of the lounge and the only reason must be the photo.

Jean was surprised to see me. She was elbow deep in soapy suds in the large sink, washing the huge soup pot in readiness for a new lot to be made. Like Granny, she always made enough for at least a week.

She glanced anxiously at the kitchen clock 'Is it time for our tea break already?' When she saw the time, she shook her head. 'No, it's too early.'

I passed on the housekeeper's message and Jean's eyes widened in amazement. 'Miss Hood said that I was looking for you?' She shook her head again. 'I think the woman's going off her head. It must be because of Mrs Barrie's illness. Maybe Miss Hood thinks her days here are numbered – and ours as well.'

I was suddenly worried. 'Oh, I never thought of it like that. I just thought Mrs Bane had a wee dose of the flu and that she would soon get better.' Although I didn't want to admit it, a cold feeling settled in my stomach and I was worried I would lose my job.

Jean smiled. 'Och, don't worry, Ann. Mrs Barrie has had bouts of illness before and she's always got over it. After all, she has the best of medical help. What that doctor charges would keep a family of four for a month and that's just for his visits. The medicine costs extra.'

Reassured, I said, 'Well, if you don't want me for anything, I'll get back to my work.'

She nodded. 'We'll have our cuppie after I get the soup on.' She returned to the mountain of suds that now threatened to erupt as far as the window.

I returned to the lounge, feeling apprehensive but there was no sign of Miss Hood or the photograph. I had just returned to my polishing position at the window when the door opened and she came in, followed by the doctor. His bloodhound face was serious and Miss Hood's hands were shaking. Her face looked as if it had shrunk several sizes and I suddenly noticed her neck and how thin and wrinkled it was. Then I realised she wasn't wearing one of her usual high-necked blouses nor did she have on one of her many and varied scarves which she usually draped around her throat. Worry and grief had not improved her appearance but the snooty, arrogant look was also missing. In spite of her previous malice towards me, I suddenly felt so sorry for her. She was no longer a dragon but merely an old woman.

She ushered the doctor to one of the comfy chairs. Rubbing her hands together as if cold, she put a match to the fire which was already laid in the grate and soon flames danced up the chimney.

'Sit down, Doctor Little, I'll get the housemaid to bring us some tea.' She turned to me. 'Please bring a tea tray for two in here, Ann.'

I almost fell over in surprise on hearing my name mentioned. In all my time in the house, never once had she referred to me by name. Things were definitely improving but what a pity if it was all to end should Mrs Barrie not recover.

As Jean busied herself with the teapot, I mentioned this change in the housekeeper and she seemed equally nonplussed by it.

'Oh, well, I suppose people do change their habits but it seems so unlikely with Miss Hood. Still we must be grateful for any change in her,' she laughed as she placed a small selection of home-made biscuits on a doily-covered plate. As always, I was unable to understand all the niceties of a well-heeled house. Biscuits were a luxury in our house but, should we manage to buy the occasional half pound of broken biscuits which usually cost a lot less than perfect ones, then they normally stayed in the brown paper bag or in an old bashed tin that Granny had owned for years. I had never even seen a doily till I came to work here.

My mind drifted back from this display of etiquette. 'The doctor's face looked serious, Jean,' I said. 'I do hope it's not bad news.' Cold fear still fluttered around my body – almost as if ice was circulating instead of blood.

Jean shook her head again. 'No, she'll be all right. I've seen her worse than this and she's recovered.'

When I entered the lounge, the doctor was speaking. 'Mrs Barrie is quite a strong lady in spite of her frail appearance. You know that better than anyone, Miss Hood. Still, that being said, the next few days will be crucial. Keep her warm and give her lots of liquids and I'll come back this afternoon.'

As I placed the tray on the low table by the now blazing fire, I couldn't help feeling surprised again by the sound of his voice. Perhaps because he resembled a bloodhound, I had expected him to have a deep growling timbre to his voice but it was quite high pitched and soft. It was also extremely cultured and posh sounding.

Later that morning, all the thoughts of doilies

and doctors' voices were swept from my mind by the sudden realisation that this was bang in the middle of the month. My little arrangement with Mrs Barrie regarding my wages had gone on month after month with no hiccups. She paid me every week and I reimbursed her on pay day at the end of the month. Now, because of her grave illness, she wouldn't be able to see me, let alone pay me. I wondered briefly if the new-look Miss Hood would now be sympathetic to my plight but there was nothing I could do until her day off. Maybe I could approach her just prior to her departure.

I also remembered that I hadn't mentioned the photograph to Jean but, on reflection and without any good reason, I decided to stay silent.

Over the next few days, an uneasy calm settled on the house. Miss Hood rarely put in an appearance except to pick up hot drinks and the tray with small, delicious portions of light food and equally tiny plates of pudding. Without exception, every tray came back with the food uneaten. We were even loath to put the wireless on. Jean liked the Light Programme with its cheery mix of comedy and music. Even Miss Hood's little wireless set, which she kept in her room, was silent.

I began to miss all the homely sounds – even the serious voices that wafted from the housekeeper's room. Being a devotee of the Home Service, Miss Hood liked to listen to some weighty debate or a serious-sounding play. I had become used to hearing snatches from it as I placed the hot-water bottles in both their rooms every night. Now even that small job was taken over by the housekeeper.

As Saturday approached, Mrs Barrie was still quite ill and still confined to her bed. The doctor spent so much time at the house that he almost became part of the household. I was forever taking trays to the lounge.

Every day I rehearsed my speech which I intended to deliver to Miss Hood on her departure. Perhaps, if I caught her at the right time and in the right frame of mind, she would give me my money. I was almost sick with worry, so much so that Jean noticed my agitation. I was reluctant to discuss my finances with her as I knew she would offer to help out and I didn't want that.

Although she hadn't said a lot about it, from small snippets of conversation, I guessed her husband Will was finding it difficult to get work. People who needed small joinery jobs doing were holding off and even the small businesses that were his main source of income were also putting their repairs on hold. In fact, the other day, she had said as much. She sat at the table, her hands encircling a cup of tea. 'You know, Ann, this is a good job and it's the best-paid position I've ever had. Still, we've put some savings aside for a rainy day but I'm hoping the sunny days are still here.'

I almost blurted out my own worries but then decided to say nothing. Perhaps it was the unfamiliar quiet hush, the deathly calm which had descended over us since Mrs Barrie's illness, that made me hold my tongue. After all, we all had worries on our minds.

On Saturday morning, I fully expected Miss Hood to appear in one of her nauseating costumes but to my astonishment she appeared in the kitchen, dressed in an old skirt and an equally ancient-looking cardigan. Her thin legs were stockingless and her feet were thrust into her checked slippers. I had never, in all my time at the house, seen her dressed in such a slapdash manner.

She was carrying her purse and a slip of paper. 'Go down to chemist for me. I won't be taking my days off this week – not while Mrs Barrie is still ill.' She handed over the list and half a crown.

Jean pursed her lips and frowned. 'Ann and I will stay on as well. We will also work our time off...'

Before she could finish, Miss Hood turned sharply and snapped, 'That won't be necessary – I'll look after the mistress.'

As I ran upstairs towards my room, I was filled with dismay, not only at the thought of having the housekeeper's company for the next day and a half but also the apparent return of her snappy and arrogant manner.

Although it was the month of March, spring had failed to arrive and thin flakes of snow drifted down on a bitterly cold east wind. Even the windows shook in its blast. Without thinking, I grabbed my treasured coat and wrapped it around me. It wasn't until the return journey that I realised my foolishness. After months of subterfuge, of dodging past the housekeeper with my bag, I had undone all the good work with a moment's stupidity.

As I approached the house, I wondered if her prying eyes were watching me. I gazed up at the shining windows, certain that no one was standing there but should she notice me, would I see her standing behind the thick curtains? I wondered.

The pavement was slippy and I had to watch my step but, in spite of that, I tried to walk as quickly as I could in order to reach the sanctuary of my room. With my breath escaping in white icy puffs, I ran as hard as I could towards the back door. I was just below Mrs Barrie's window when I caught a small movement of the curtains. I stopped dead, my heart pounding so hard that I was sure it must be heard in the house. But there was no other movement – just a flurry of snowflakes that brushed the glass with a silent kiss. I ran quickly to the door, giving a sigh of relief. I had obviously imagined that small movement. But, if she had seen me, well, I knew I was in for a severe quizzing.

There was no sign of her inside the house. The house was so quiet that the ticking of the grandfather clock in the hall sounded loud. I headed towards my room with my coat before delivering my errand and my heart sank when I realised she was inside Mrs Barrie's bedroom.

I knocked. 'It's me, Miss Hood. I've got your message from the chemist.'

She opened the door and I braced myself for her furious onslaught but she merely held out her hand for the small parcel and the change. Behind her, I saw Mrs Barrie lying propped up on her enormous pillows, her face was white – almost the same colour as the pillowcases. But her eyes were bright and she held up a wizened hand, almost as if she was waving to me and her mouth moved soundlessly.

'Is Mrs Barrie feeling better?' I asked, still peering over Miss Hood's shoulder.

She moved out into the hall, closing the door behind her. 'That is none of your business but, if you must know, yes, she is making a good recovery. In fact, I'm reading to her at the moment.' She sounded smug.

I had noticed the paperback on the eiderdown but, as to the author, I hadn't a clue. I hoped it was one of Mrs Barrie's favourite detectives. I was torn between annoyance at her waspish manner and relief that she hadn't spotted my coat.

I told Jean about my narrow escape. 'Just think what she would have done if she had seen me.'

The cook dismissed my worry. 'Look, Ann, you've had that coat for months now. Miss Hood will never remember every item in Mrs Barrie's wardrobe and you could have bought your coat from McGill's and paid it up weekly. She's not to know that.'

I relaxed. 'Of course, you're right, Jean. I could have owned it for years and even brought it with me when I started here.'

The doctor paid another call just before Jean and I left for our time off. I was on tenterhooks and hanging around the hall, trying to pluck up the courage to ask for my wages.

When the doctor and Miss Hood both descended the staircase, the doctor seemed more cheerful – not boisterously so but a small smile was visible on his fleshy lips.

'Yes, I think we can safely say that our patient is

on the mend. Although it will take her a while to regain her strength, she's over the worst. I'll bring a good tonic for her later today.'

When Miss Hood saw me, she froze slightly, the same old expression on her face. 'Well, what do you want?'

Suddenly my well-rehearsed speech deserted me and I stuttered, 'I've been waiting ... waiting to ... to ... bring in the tea.' I hated myself for stammering but her transformation from a distressed old woman to her usual old dragon personality left me tongue-tied.

'Well, bring it in and just go.' She was so rude and curt that even Doctor Little looked at her with astonishment.

As they moved into the lounge, I considered running upstairs to Mrs Barrie's bedroom but I knew I couldn't disturb her – not now when she was thankfully recovering. No, I thought, I'll just have to tell Granny about the changed situation. There was no doubt she could maybe manage for one week but another week ... well, that was another story.

The house at the Overgate felt cold but I thought it was just the difference from Whitegate Lodge with its cosiness in all the rooms. There was a tiny fire burning in the grate but the coal bucket was empty.

The look of delight on Granny's face was soon replaced by a worried frown when I mentioned my bad news. 'Och, well, Ann, it's not your fault if Mrs Barrie is not well. I just hope she gets better soon – the poor soul.'

'But, Granny, it'll be the same next week as

well. I didn't tell you that I'm on a monthly wage because Mrs Barrie has been so good to me and I didn't want to worry you.' I told her the whole story and she was very angry.

'I've a good mind to go to the Ferry and give that nasty besom a piece of my mind and then make sure she pays you every week. After all, Ann, you work damn hard for that ten shillings.'

I turned pale at the thought and, although Granny was more than a match for Miss Hood, it would most definitely mean the end of my job.

She saw my face and said, 'Don't worry, Ann, I'll not take your housekeeper into the boxing ring and give her ten hard rounds – no, we'll just sit here and call her all the evil names we can think of!'

I had to laugh but then I remembered that I would soon be back in the cosy confines of White-gate Lodge while my grandparents and Lily would have to suffer the consequences of a cold house and no money. After all, there was never enough money for real comfort – just a bare living from hand to mouth and my grandparents deserved better than this. At that moment, I could have cheerfully have gone ten rounds with Miss Hood myself and given her a few home truths as well.

'I'll try and see Mrs Barrie this week, Granny, and ask for my wages.'

Then I looked around the kitchen but there was no sign of Grandad or Lily. 'Has Grandad taken Lily for a walk?'

She shook her head. 'No, he's upstairs having a blether with Pete. Maddie came over and took the bairn to see Joy. She's bringing her back at teatime because she wants to see you.'

'Is Maddie still doing all the messages for the street?'

Granny screwed up her face. 'For heaven's sake, don't mention Lipton's to her. Danny seems to be taking an interest in some lassie that works in the shop. I wouldn't say he's winching – at least not yet.'

I thought about the girl with the sour lemon face. 'Surely he's not serious about her?'

'Well, I don't think he is. They go to the pictures once a week. Her name's Minnie McFarlane and her folks live on the Hawkhill. She was in Danny's class at school and I think they like to talk about their younger days.'

She put another two small lumps of coal on the fire and I was dismayed to see the bunker was almost as empty as the coal bucket.

'Mind you,' said Granny, laughing, 'Hattie's face is tripping her. She always thought Danny would hit it off with Maddie but now he's seeing Minnie. The McFarlanes are just toerags, according to Hattie.'

To be quite honest I was upset too. I also thought Danny and I would be a pair – not in any romantic sense but it was just something I couldn't put into words. Now he was growing up fast and not only leaving me behind but also Maddie – poor Maddie with her shattered dreams.

I heard Lily and Maddie long before they reached the door. Lily's clear childish voice carried up the stair and I smiled when I heard her voice counting each step, not quite accurately,

'One, two, seven, three.'

Maddie looked cheerful enough when she came in. The wind and the exertion of the long walk had given both of them pink cheeks and Maddie's blonde hair was swept up under an enormous knitted tammy.

However, it was a different face I saw when I walked with her to the end of Tay Street and she started to lament about Danny's new friend or old school friend. 'I've stopped going into the shop because that Minnie is always so smug looking,' Maddie said, sounding distressed. 'Danny asked me out to the pictures as well but I don't think I'll go.'

'For goodness' sake, Maddie, don't be so daft. He's obviously not that keen on Minnie if he's asked you out as well.'

She nodded. 'I know I'm being daft but I wonder if he thinks I'm too young for him – just because I'm still at school.'

'I think you're right, Maddie, but you'll never know if you don't take up his offer of an innocent night at the pictures.'

'What about a night out tomorrow with me? We can go to the King's picture house to see that Busby Berkeley musical or maybe go to see Claude Rains in *The Invisible Man*. I think it's on at the Plaza.'

It was an attractive notion but I had no money – not now or in the foreseeable future – but, before I could answer, Maddie said, 'It'll be my treat.'

When I looked at her, she said, 'I know how you feel about people paying for you but I can't go to

292

the pictures on my own as my mother won't allow it. So you see, Ann, you'll be doing me a great favour. Please, please.'

She looked so sad that I relented but only under the promise that the next pictures treat would be mine. Hopefully I would be paid by then.

It dawned bitterly cold the next day and the pavements were white with snow. It had been falling for most of the night. As I made my way to the grocer's shop for a loaf of bread, I had to pass a group of small children who were eagerly throwing snowballs at one another. Sometimes their aim wasn't accurate and the snowball would strike a passerby, much to their disgust and chagrin. 'You wee devils,' shouted one old woman to the children as they made a quick getaway. She wiped the snow from her coat and headed on down the street, still muttering loudly.

To be truthful, most of this activity went over my head because of my money problems. I had put the fire on that morning and Granny had tried to hide the almost empty coal bunker. 'The coalman's late this week so you're not to worry about it. I'll get a bag of coal on tick – after all, I'm a good customer.' She failed to hide the worried expression that flitted across her face and I knew this cold spell was being a big drain on the budget.

It was then that I decided to pawn my coat. It would just be for a couple of weeks until I got paid and then I would redeem it. It broke my heart to part with it, especially in this wintry weather but the money would tide Granny over for a few days at least. Later that afternoon I approached Dickson's pawnshop on the Hilltown. His window was a kaleidoscope of objects, both domestic and valuable. Items that hadn't been redeemed now lay in a jumbled collection behind the glass – all awaiting a sale.

The entrance to the pawnshop office lay up a very narrow close beside the shop. It was dark and dank with water running down the flagstones and the walls. It was the most depressing close I had ever seen. In fact, in a world of depressing places, this one deserved a medal for awfulness. I pushed open the swing door and entered a high-roofed cavern of an office. The counter was divided into sections with thin wooden walls that were obviously designed to offer some degree of privacy – a buffer against the entire clientele knowing their neighbours' business. In that respect, it failed dismally.

The place was busy and I had to wait inside the door until a cubicle became vacant. A poor-looking woman with two small crying children brushed past me. Her face was full of misery and I noticed the small rumpled parcel under her arm. It looked as if the pawnbroker had rejected her meagre wares.

I waited until my turn then took the coat from my bag and placed it on the small counter, smoothing it as I laid it down. A small man with a wizened face picked up the fur-trimmed sleeve and I thought I saw a glimmer of surprise in his eyes. This glint was instantly replaced by a professional manner. 'How much do you want for this?' he asked, peering at me through his half-moon specs.

I hadn't a clue about the going rate but I stammered, 'Seven ... seven and sixpence.'

He shook his head, felt the fur once more and looked at me. 'I can let you have five shillings for it.'

I produced the shoes and bag. 'If I add these can you make it seven and six?'

He pondered for a few moments, taking a step back and giving my beloved belongings a critical look. 'Right, then, I'll make it seven shillings.'

I took the money and ran like a scalded cat from this horrible close, knowing full well I was lucky – not like the poor woman before me.

Granny demanded to know where the money had come from and I told her. 'Oh, no, not your swanky coat.' She was dismayed.

'Don't worry, Granny, it'll just be for two weeks until I get paid then I'll redeem it.' I handed over the seven shillings. 'Will this be enough?'

She nodded. 'It'll buy a bag of coal and the messages and, next week, I can always get a few things on tick.'

I placed the pawn ticket in the vase on the mantelpiece. 'I'll keep the ticket here in case it gets lost.'

Granny looked worried. 'For heaven's sake, don't let Hattie know about that ticket. She's always coveted that coat and she would redeem it and not say a word.'

I assured her it was safe enough. Later that evening, I joined Maddie at the foot of the stairs and we headed happily towards the King's picture house. I was wearing my trench coat and, although she glanced at it, she said nothing. She obviously still had Danny on her mind.

When we reached the King's, a large queue had formed, standing hunched up and miserable on this cold night. The snow had stopped but an icy wind swirled around the feet of the waiting picture-goers. We headed towards the end of the queue and, because I had my head down, I didn't notice Danny and his friend but Maddie did.

'Hullo,' he shouted cheerfully, 'are you coming to see the picture as well?'

Maddie's face turned chalk white. She would have walked on but I stopped.

He turned to the girl at his side. 'This is Minnie,' he said as he introduced us.

She was a small, very thin girl with an elfin look about her. Her very dark hair hung in a straight style and skimmed her shoulders. And she was very pretty.

Perhaps because of her name and her dark hair she reminded me of Minnehaha, the Indian maiden in *Hiawatha*. I instantly rebuked myself for putting a nickname on her because this was a trait I was using a lot and it had to stop – people were not like characters in books.

We chatted for a moment or two – at least I did – and then we made our way down the street and past the snake-like queue of people.

Maddie suddenly turned to me. 'I don't think I want to see this film. Let's go and see *The Invisible Man* at the Plaza.'

Although slightly annoyed that she hadn't asked my opinion, I stayed silent. However she didn't want to be seen by either Danny or Minnie so we made our way along the Seagate and into the High Street before heading up the Hilltown to the Plaza, like two thieves in the night.

12

While Maddie was unhappy at Danny's romance, I was feeling more optimistic. Mrs Barrie was on the mend and, although she was still weak and confined to her bed, the atmosphere in the house changed from the deathly hush to a more normal routine. For a start, the wireless was now switched on every day and, as Jean remarked, 'I never thought I would miss all the cheery banter so much.'

In the middle of the week, one of the jobs, after my cleaning chores were finished, was to take the accumulators to be charged up. In this house of plenty, there was even a special carrier for this task – a strong wicker basket with two compartments that held the accumulators upright – and, although it was quite heavy to carry, it meant they didn't wobble around.

Alfie Drummond owned the shop where the accumulators were taken. It was situated at the far end of Gray Street, tucked in between a cafe that catered for the summer visitors and the chemist. Nondescript in appearance, it was a Mecca for all the wireless owners in the Ferry. Alfie had fought in the Great War and he arrived back in Blighty minus half his leg. Shortly after, with a few pounds from his savings, he opened his small business. Although the world didn't quite beat a path to his door, he still made a reasonable living with his charging services and wireless repairs. His shop always fascinated me, especially the large gramophone which took pride of place on the counter. It sported a large fluted horn and a small plaque stating 'His Master's Voice' and showing a small dog listening to a similar gramophone.

The local myth was that this was a forgotten repair – the owner, having put it in to be repaired, had then somehow forgotten about it. How anyone could overlook such a large piece of musical equipment was beyond my comprehension but perhaps the truth, should it ever become known, was more mundane.

Being an astute businessman, Alfie knew it always drew comments. In fact, one customer was remarking on it as I entered. 'I see you've still got the gramophone, Alfie. Is the owner still saving up for your bill?'

Alfie laughed. He was a large-built, jovial man with the deepest, loudest voice I had ever heard. I often thought he could have used this to great effect in the trenches of France. This deep, booming voice resonating over no-man's-land would soon have sent the German soldiers running away in panic.

'Now, young Ann, how is Mrs Barrie feeling today? Better I hope?' He leaned over the counter and grasped the handle of the heavy basket. He took out the two accumulators and replaced them with two fully charged-up ones. Once again

I was struck by what money could buy – in this case, the luxury of having entertainment every day from the airwaves. The majority of poor people in the crowded streets of Dundee were lucky if they had the price of a wireless or the few pennies it cost for the charging service.

Although the wind was still chilly with a hint of snow on its cutting edge, I was delighted to see clumps of daffodils and crocuses in the gardens. The snowdrops however were fading but they had been a brave show of flowers a few weeks ago. Spring would soon be here and, in a few months' time, Lily would be two years old. I thought she was becoming a wee rascal with her Grandad but Granny kept her on a tight rein.

A piercing blast swept straight from the sea and whipped around my legs. My thin trenchcoat wasn't warm enough against this onslaught and I mentally counted the hours till I could redeem my lovely coat.

With Mrs Barrie now feeling much better, I hoped I would get the chance to speak to her and get my wages. Miss Hood was in the kitchen when I arrived back and, although she still looked dreadful, her tongue was as sharp as ever. She made no sign that she was going to help and it was left to Jean and me to manhandle the heavy objects.

'For goodness' sake, Ann,' Jean wailed, 'it's a wonder you're not bowly-legged carrying this. What a weight!'

'Well, that's what she's here for,' snapped the housekeeper, glaring at me. 'She's here to do all the hard work and leave me to do my job. The one I came for – the job as a companion.'

Her glare was now replaced by a speculative glance at my old coat and I was suddenly grateful I wasn't wearing my good one. In spite of Jean's protestations I just knew Miss Hood would never believe I had bought it from McGill's – or any other department store, for that matter.

As the week wore on, all my earlier optimism evaporated as I realised the housekeeper was still dealing with all of Mrs Barrie's needs. Even when I carried the food tray upstairs, the housekeeper would suddenly materialise from the shadows on the top landing and snatch it from my hands – sometimes with a grunt but mostly in silence. I found this treatment unnerving and I began to be afraid to climb the stairs as I knew a quick, quiet shove from her would send me toppling backwards. Still, I had no option as this job was just one of many for me.

On the Thursday afternoon, she appeared as usual and grabbed the tray from my hands. Perhaps it was the rough way she grabbed it or maybe Jean had overfilled the hot water jug but some hot water splashed on to her wrist. A string of oaths came from her refined mouth and I was shocked. I was used to hearing people cursing and swearing on the streets of Dundee but to hear them being uttered by this genteel spinster took me aback.

I told Jean about the incident and she shook her head. 'I've always known she was no lady – just somebody who managed to work themselves up in the theatre but, with her airs and graces, she thinks she's nobility. Now Mrs Barrie is a lady.

She comes from titled stock. Her mother married a lord and Mrs Barrie herself married into money but she as nice as nine pence and there's nothing stuck up about her. No siree.'

I remembered something. 'She never swore like that yon time when she splashed herself making the blackcurrant drink. Do you mind?'

'Aye, I do but maybe she got a bigger splash of hot water this time or maybe she was distracted by Mrs Barrie's illness last time. We'll never know.'

I nodded gloomily. 'Do you think she'll take her time off this weekend?'

Jean said, 'No, I don't think she will – at least not the way she's speaking at the moment. "I'll be here as long as the mistress needs me,"' said the cook, putting on a posh accent. 'When it comes to speaking in a panloafy voice, well, our Lottie is a past master.' Jean grinned. 'Except when she's cursing like a shipwrecked sailor.'

Although I laughed along with Jean, I was also worried. I knew Granny couldn't possibly cope another week without my wages so I watched Miss Hood's movements like a demented hawk. I thought she might go off to the shops but she didn't budge an inch. Then, at breakfast time on Friday morning, a small miracle happened. Miss Hood wasn't on the landing when I climbed the stairs so I tapped gently on Mrs Barrie's door.

Her voice sounded much stronger. 'Come in, Lottie, I'm awake.'

I couldn't believe my luck as I entered and Mrs Barrie's face broke into a big smile. 'How lovely to see you, Ann. I'm afraid the only people I've seen over these last few weeks are Lottie and Doctor Little. What a pleasure to see a young face at last!'

Suddenly Miss Hood burst in. This barging in was a trait which I was beginning to notice was normal for her. She tumbled in with all the grace of Mr Bell's pony and even that comparison was a huge slur on the pony.

I placed the tray in front of the patient and although the illness had taken its toll on her weight, her eyes were alert and bright with amusement. After all, she could hardly have failed to notice that, as the housekeeper ground to a halt, she almost toppled into the bed beside her.

'I was saying to Ann what a lovely change to see a young face...' She suddenly stopped as she realised her faux pas. 'Not that I don't enjoy looking at you, Lottie, because you've got me through this illness and I don't think anyone else could have done that. Thank you...' Her voice trailed away and she busied herself with the teapot.

Meanwhile, Lottie didn't know where to look. On the one hand, she was full of pride at Mrs Barrie's words of gratitude but, on the other hand, she was wild at me for breaching the cordon. I could only assume she had overslept because her hair was uncombed and her long, sagging knitted cardigan was outside in.

Mrs Barrie was still fiddling with her tray. She didn't lift her eyes as she spoke. 'Now, Lottie, I know you haven't taken your time off during my illness and I'm very grateful for all your kindness in looking after me so I insist you take your time off this week.'

Miss Hood's face drained of the little colour it had. 'No, no, Eva, I enjoy looking after you. I'm your companion after all.'

Mrs Barrie then looked at her with a steady gaze and held up her hand. 'No, Lottie, I insist. You look worn out and I don't want you to fall ill as well, now, do I? What would I do if you caught this awful flu? No, my dear, go and have a restful few days off and I'll see you on Sunday.'

'But this is just Friday, Eva. I'll go tomorrow as usual.' Her voice sounded ragged, no doubt with suppressed rage.

'No,' said Mrs Barrie, 'take an extra day off with my blessing and have a rest. You deserve it.'

Faced with this dismissal, she had no option but to retreat to her room and pack her small overnight case. I took advantage of this lull and made my way quickly downstairs. I knew at that moment she would be like an enraged dragon, breathing and spitting fire – the more so because I had been a witness to the exchange of dialogue.

My weekly letter from Maddie was waiting for me in the kitchen. 'Here's the letter from your pal,' said Jean.

I quickly told her about the conversation upstairs and her mouth opened in surprise but, before she could utter a word, Miss Hood swept through. She was dressed in her bile-green costume and a tight-fitting cloche hat in the same nauseating colour. She looked like an alien from the planet Mars, an effect further heightened by the quickness of her step. She marched out the door at the speed of light and we watched as her retreating figure stomped across the courtyard, scattering a clutch of blackbirds that rose in a noisy, black cloud as she walked past them. The moment her stamping feet and her fury had departed, they flew back to peck once more at the kitchen crumbs.

Jean chuckled. 'Well, well, imagine that – the mistress has sent her packing.' She craned her neck as the housekeeper disappeared down the drive. 'Still I don't think she's too upset about it. She didn't kick the cat from along the road and it almost ran in front of her.'

'Maybe she didn't see it,' I replied. 'After all, she always walks with her nose in the air.' What a calamity that would have been, I thought. This was certainly not her day and tripping over a roaming feline would have ended it on a high note. As usual Maddie's letter was long and gossipy.

What a disaster to see Danny and Miss Muffet together. Still, not to worry as I've decided to give up on men and love and concentrate on my career. I finish my exams soon and I can apply for a nursing course. At the moment I'm helping out in Dad's office, making the tea and posting the letters.

I laughed and Jean looked over my shoulder. 'Good news is it?

'No it's just Maddie – she's always so cheerful,' I said, turning the page over. Maddie had added a postscript.

Good news on the job front. I've just heard that Willie will be leaving this summer and the job will be offered to your dad.

'Oh, it is good news, Jean,' I said, telling her about the job.

'Aye, your star is ascending, Ann,' she replied.

I looked puzzled but she explained. 'It just means that things are beginning to look up for you and your family – you mark my words.'

As I set off upstairs to do my chores, I sincerely hoped so. Mrs Barrie had finished most of her breakfast. 'Oh dear,' she said, her thin shoulders drooping, 'I think I've upset Lottie. She barely said goodbye. But never mind.' She suddenly brightened up. Holding a book in her hand, she announced, 'I've got the latest Agatha Christie novel so maybe you can read to me this afternoon, Ann?'

'I'm really glad you're looking much better Mrs Barrie. Mrs Peters and I were worried about you.' I added hastily, 'Miss Hood was as well.'

I had made up my mind not to mention my wages to her. I didn't want to worry her as she still looked so frail but, at the same time, I was secretly hoping she might mention it herself.

Later that afternoon, after I had read a couple of chapters of her new novel, she lay back on her pillows, 'Can we stop there, Ann? Maybe you can read to me again this evening. I seem to be still so weary.'

I smiled at her as I closed the book. I was on the verge of going through the door when she called me back. 'Ann, please forgive me, I meant to ask you something but my brain seems to be suffering from the same weariness as my body. Did Miss Hood give you your wages last week? I was so worried about your grandmother that I mentioned our little secret arrangement – against my will, I have to say, but there was no other way of doing it.'

'No, Mrs Barrie, she never mentioned it.' A surge of anger swept over me at the thought of the horrid old woman and the memory of Granny's hardship. The thought of the almost-empty coal bunker and the poor paltry fire made my blood boil. I might have seen the point if the money belonged to Miss Hood but it didn't. Why she had to be so penny-pinching with me was a mystery.

'Oh dear, she must have forgotten,' said Mrs Barrie diplomatically. 'Here is two weeks' wages and you must make sure you come to see me every week without fail. Your poor family can't exist on air.'

I was so grateful to her. With her kind, weary eyes on mine, I almost blurted out the story of the pawned coat but I knew Granny would be mortified by such an admission. I could well imagine her face. 'You didn't tell her that, did you? Speak about being black affronted – and her so good to us. I just hope she doesn't think we're a family of scroungers.' So I stayed silent but hugged the money tightly as I ran to my room. Granny would now have enough for the coal and the food for the week. I would also be able to redeem my coat. Also the good news about Dad's job filled me with delight and it seemed as if things were at last looking up for us.

That weekend passed in a pleasant blur. I did all my jobs happily without Miss Hood lurking over my shoulder and I read every day to Mrs Barrie.

Even Jean seemed to be affected by the happier atmosphere and she laughed a lot as she cooked and baked. It all changed when the housekeeper returned. As soon as we saw her scowling face, our spirits sank but not for long because we were getting ready to leave ourselves for our time off.

I wondered if she would maybe mention my wages as instructed by Mrs Barrie but, once again, nothing was said. The old devil, I thought. As Jean and I left the kitchen, I felt sorry for leaving Mrs Barrie to the housekeeper's tender mercies but I was also eager to return to the Overgate with the much-needed cash.

Dad and Hattie were in the house when I arrived and I thought Granny looked really tired as she stood at the cooker, stirring her large pot of soup. Dad was over the moon at the news of his job. 'I start at the beginning of August,' he said, 'but I feel so sorry for our old neighbours on the Hilltown. I was speaking to Joe and he was saying that they have nothing to look forward to – no jobs and no money. It's a bloody disgrace.'

Hattie piped up, 'Well, your good fortune is down to me. I'm a good worker and the Pringle family appreciate it. Your good luck is thanks to that – Ann's too. You've both got your jobs because of my good reputation.' If she wasn't blowing her own trumpet, well, she was just a hair's breadth away from it.

Dad said as much: 'Thank you, Hattie, for reminding us jobless and lower classes to mind our manners and doff our caps.'

I wasn't really listening to them because, according to Granny, they had always fought with each other, right from when they were young children. The reason for my abstraction was the bruise on the side of Dad's face. It had started life as a black eye but it was now at the purple, yellow and maroon stage. He saw me staring at it and he put a hand over it as if to cover it.

Hattie spotted this movement and crowed. 'Got a black eye from Marlene, didn't you know?' She scowled at him.

He retaliated bitterly, 'No, I did not get a black eye from Marlene – at least not intentionally. She threw a vase at me, hoping it would miss but I got a glancing blow from it.'

Hattie screeched. 'A glancing blow my foot. You don't get a bruise like that with a near miss. No, my lad, she meant to hit you and she did.'

Granny turned her attention away from the soup pot. 'I take it that the romance is over?'

Dad laughed. 'Och, there was never any romance. I was just her lodger and her pal in the pub.' He rubbed his face ruefully. 'She was the one that was always yapping on and on about getting married. Well, as soon as I put her right on that question, she tossed me out.' He turned to Hattie. 'I was hoping you could put me up for a week or two – just till I find somewhere else.'

Hattie looked doubtful.

'I promise it'll just be for a couple of weeks. You know Granny doesn't have room for me as well as looking after Ann and Lily,' said Dad, with a beseeching look. 'Then, when I get my job we'll be able to make a few plans, Ann and I. Please Hattie.'

Before she could answer, Granny butted in, 'Or

until you find another woman daft enough to put up with you in return for a bit of charm.'

This charm was wasted on his mother and sister but Hattie was in an awkward position. She didn't really want him to be homeless and Granny certainly didn't have the room for him. He gave her another of his boyish looks – his wide-eyed, pleading expression.

'All right but only for the maximum of two weeks – no more.'

So it was settled. Dad would move in right away and he would make enquiries about new lodgings. Then, when he got his job, we could make plans for a wee house together for the three of us.

We were sitting at the table and I was spooning the soup into Lily's ever-hungry little mouth when Rosie appeared.

'Come in, Rosie,' said Granny.

Rosie looked nonplussed at the entire family sitting at the table. 'Oh, I'm sorry – I didn't know you were here, Johnny, or you either, Hattie. I'm just getting ready to go to the Salvation Army Citadel but Mum wondered if you would look in later, Nan, just to have a wee gossip?'

Granny said she would. I thought Dad would make a snide comment about the Sally Ann as usual but he was full of charm today. 'Heavens, it's good to see you again, Rosie. You're looking really well.'

Poor Rosie blushed a deep crimson and I felt sorry for her. Dad was impossible with women but, to give him his due, I don't think he realised it.

She noticed his bruised face. 'Have you had an

accident, Johnny?'

Before he could reply, Hattie butted in. 'No, Rosie, he got that black eye by walking into a door. Imagine a grown man walking into a door.' She tried to laugh lightly but it didn't quite come off and she sounded more like a strangled chicken.

Rosie, with her innocent plain face, just nodded but she still looked puzzled. 'I'll tell Mum you'll see her later, Nan.'

After she left, Hattie turned to her brother. 'Now I want it understood that, should you meet any of my neighbours, then you'll tell them you walked into a door. You do not say you got that black eye as a result of a vase being thrown at you by Marlene Davidson.'

When Dad laughed, she looked sternly at him. 'I mean it, Johnny. I've got a good reputation in my close and Mrs Davidson is well known – even in the Westport. I don't want people to think that a brother of mine has even known that woman, let alone associated with her.'

Dad looked serious and drew his hand across lips. 'Cross my heart and hope to die, Hattie. Marlene's name will never cross my lips – I promise.'

When she departed, Dad made us all laugh when he stated, 'No wonder Hattie has never found another man – the poor bloke would have to sign ten declarations at least before he even got over her doorstep.'

Grandad chuckled. 'Then he'd have to sign another twenty testimonials to his good character and his finances before he got his feet under her table.'

It was with a happy heart that I made my way to the pawnbroker the following afternoon. It was a dismally grey day with steely clouds that promised more snow. The wind was still as biting as ever and I thought longingly of my cosy coat. Although it was not quite dark, a grey shadowy atmosphere hung over the close, making it look both dangerous and mysterious. I heard the sharp clatter of the pawn office door as it shut behind a client and I saw the woman with her two children from my previous visit. My heart sank as she drew abreast of me but I saw she was minus her parcel and she looked cheerier. The children had even perked up and they weren't crying.

I was on the point of entering when I suddenly drew to a halt. I had forgotten to pick up the ticket from the vase on the mantelpiece. I could have kicked myself for my stupidity. I turned quickly and ran down the hill. I had to hurry in case the office closed early.

When I arrived back at the house, Granny looked surprised. 'Where's your coat, Ann?'

'I forgot to take the ticket with me so I've had to run back for it.' I made my way over to the mantelpiece and I was poking my finger in the vase when Granny spoke.

'The ticket's not there – I thought you took it with you, Ann.' When she saw my puzzlement, she said, 'Maybe it's fallen down to the bottom of the vase so have another look.'

But it wasn't there. We searched the dusty depths of the matching vase on the other side of the mantelpiece but it wasn't there either. We opened every drawer and we even turned some of

311

them upside down on the bed, raking through the odds and ends that were regularly stuffed away out of sight.

After thirty minutes I started to panic. 'It must be somewhere, Granny, because I've never touched it since I put it in the vase. Where else can it be?'

Granny had a brainwave. 'Go back to the shop and tell the man that the ticket is mislaid. He'll remember who you are when you describe the coat and the shoes and bag.'

With that thought in mind, I raced back to the Hilltown and careered up the close which now lay in darkness. My mind was so full of worry over my coat that this darkness failed to deter me. I would gladly have confronted an entire army of ghosties and ghoulies for the sake of my coat.

The office was empty and very dimly lit. The high shelves were shrouded in shadows and the whole place resembled a creepy cavern. A figure suddenly appeared from the gloom and headed my way. To my utter dismay I saw it was a woman and not the wizened old man from my initial visit.

'Are you putting something in or taking it out?' she asked, quite briskly.

I was speechless and unsure what to say. She must have taken this silence as confirmation that I was either daft, dumb or maybe even deaf.

She raised her voice to a higher pitch. 'I said are you...'

I stopped her in mid flow. When she noticed I wasn't deficient in any of the above three categories, the realisation made her look comical and she stood there with her mouth wide open.

'I came in here last Monday but it was an old man who served me,' I told her. My breath escaping in short gasps. 'I pawned a coat, shoes and a bag but the problem is that I've mislaid my ticket. Can I still redeem my things?'

She moved nearer the light and peered at me. I then noticed she was almost as old as the man but not nearly so shrivelled up although her face was wrinkled and her skin looked like old leather. She pointed a finger at a notice on the wall. The gist of it was it was not allowed to redeem any articles without the ticket.

I tried again. 'If I could speak to the man, he'll remember me.' I could hear the desperation in my voice. 'Is he in?'

She shook her head. 'No, he's not.'

She glanced at a clock which was ticking loudly on the far wall. Was that someone's unclaimed item, I wondered bitterly. Would my beloved coat join the hotch-potch in the window should the ticket not show up? I pushed this unhappy thought from my mind.

'The office is closing now,' she said gloomily. 'Come back tomorrow.'

I was almost in tears. 'I'll be at my work tomorrow and all this week and it'll be next Monday when I can come back in.' I made one last effort with the woman. 'If I describe the things, could you maybe look for them?'

'I'm sorry, lassie, but it's not allowed.' She came round my side of the counter and ushered me towards the door and, once outside, I heard it being bolted behind me. It was a loud metallic sound that echoed around the dark close. I was so upset at the loss of my coat and another thing that annoyed me was the fact that the woman hadn't looked in the least a bit sorry. Business was business as far as she was concerned. There was no room for sentimentality in the pawnshop trade.

Granny was annoyed when I relayed the news to her. 'You would think there's not a lot of russet-coloured fur-trimmed coats gallivanting around the Hilltown. Surely she could have looked for you and when your description matched ... well, rules are meant to be broken now and again.'

I was beside myself with worry. 'What if I've lost the ticket? Maybe it's slipped out of my pocket and I'll never see it again.'

Granny scoffed at this suggestion. 'Don't be daft, Ann. It's bound to be in the kitchen in some wee spot.' She stopped, as if remembering something. 'I wonder if your grandad knows anything about it? Maybe he shifted it to a safer place?'

'Where is he? I'll go and ask.'

'He's gone to Easifit for a new pair of boots. The last pair were done. Nip down the road and you'll meet him.'

I knew his boots were beyond repair and I was glad he was getting a replacement. I was passing Jeemy's Emporium when I saw Grandad inside. The shop was piled high with musty smelling second-hand clothing, general bric-a-brac and a mountain of boots and shoes, all in various stages of decay.

When Jeemy saw me coming, he gave me a

toothless grin. 'Here's Ann coming, Neilly.' He had always called Grandad by this nickname, ever since their schooldays.

I saw, with dismay, that Grandad was trying on a pair of old leather boots. He looked guilty. 'Oh, I'm just trying on a pair of these grand boots, Ann. I did try Easifit but they didn't have such a good selection as Jeemy.' He turned to the toothless owner. 'Ann is paying for my boots as she wants her auld grandad to look smart so I want a good pair from you and not any old rubbish.'

Jeemy beamed at me. 'He's come to the right shop because I've got every item under the sun in here.' He backed up this statement with a wide sweep of his arm.

As to his statement, I didn't doubt a word of it but I was worried about Granny's reaction when she heard where Grandad had bought his new boots. Even with the best will in the world, there was no way Grandad could pass off a pair of Jeemy's boots for a pair bought at the Easifit store.

Grandad didn't worry about these little nuances in life. His philosophy was, if the boots fitted, it mattered not a jot where they came from.

Jeemy raked about in the mountain of footwear and emerged with another pair in his hand.

Grandad's eyes lit up and he held them aloft, scrutinising the soles. 'Aye, these are grand. I'll take them.'

I was annoyed. 'Grandad, you'll have to try them on.'

He sat down again on the decrepit-looking

chair which, even under his modest weight, gave a loud creaking groan. It was just as well Bella wasn't sitting on it because I'm sure the chair would have packed up and died. Grandad pulled one boot over his thick, woolly socks. These socks were too big for him but he merely solved this by pulling four inches of sock over his toes and flattening the excess under his instep.

'There now, what did I tell you? They fit like a glove. I can aye tell the size of a boot just by looking at it.' He awarded himself a mental pat on the back for his cleverness.

As we walked home, he promised me he wouldn't mention where he had bought them. How well I recalled Granny's reaction to Lily's pram.

'We'll just say I bought them at Easifit and she'll not know the difference,' he said confidentially.

I decided not to mention the missing ticket until we got home. I was hoping to get the thorny issue of Grandad's boots out of the way first which was just as well because Granny wasn't impressed by his purchase.

'You never bought these auld boots from Easifit. If you did, then I'm Lillian Gish,' she snapped.

Grandad tried to look baffled. 'Not bought out of Easifit? Where do you think Ann would buy them?'

Granny fixed him with a beady eye. 'Well, Ann would maybe buy them from Easifit but, knowing you, it was probably out of Jeemy's Emporium. And they better not have fleas or else they're getting tossed out.'

Grandad ignored these threats and began to polish them with black Cherry Blossom shoe polish, digging the brush into the gooey residue at the side of the tin.

Lily was growing up so fast and she was repeating everything she heard. 'Lily likes Grandad's boots. Granny no like them 'cos they've got fleas but Lily like them.' She crooned the words as she ran around the room, playing with a little paper plane that Grandad had made her.

I was suddenly filled with such a surge of love for my family that this emotion threatened to erupt into a flood of tears or maybe something worse – like a gushing statement. So instead I started to lay the table for our tea.

Granny tackled Grandad about the missing ticket but he was as puzzled as we were. 'You didn't get it caught up in the paper when you made Lily's plane?' she asked but he shook his head.

'I'm sure that ticket wasn't even there when I made the plane. I looked for a bit of string in the vase and I can't remember seeing a pawn ticket,' he said.

In our house, the newspaper was never wasted. Every page was duly cut up into small squares and granny threaded a bit of string through the corners with her huge darning needle. This neat pile then hung from a nail in the outside lavatory. The remaining remnants of paper were then twisted into slender tapers that were used to light the fire and the gas cooker. They resided in an old fancy tin that had formerly held oatcakes and was always within easy reach of the fireplace. After all, matches cost money and granny was a past master at saving her pennies when she could.

I just knew in my heart that the ticket hadn't got caught up in any paper. I must have thrust the ticket into my trench-coat pocket without thinking. I always meant to repair the holes in the pockets but I hadn't got round to it and, as a result, each pocket still sported a large hole.

I knew I had to face the prospect of never seeing my beloved coat again and the thought depressed me. Granny cheered me up a bit when she said. 'Go to the pawnshop next Monday, Ann. The old man is sure to recognise you and he'll take pity on you. I'm sure of that.'

To make matters worse there was no sign of Maddie that weekend. It was clear for all to see that, along with Danny, Minnie and love, she had added the picture house to her things not to do. Still I was grateful that one problem seemed under control – namely, the fact that my father was now under the pristine roof of Hattie's house. Whether it would last long was another question but for the time being I was happy with the situation.

The following Monday found me back again at the narrow close but this time the pawnshop was seething with customers. The queue stretched right down the passageway and almost out on to the Hilltown. They were a motley bunch of tired-looking women, thin-faced men and a gaggle of children who were all in various stages of emotions from running about shouting to whimpering tears and whining incessantly. As a result of this crowd, by the time I reached an empty cubicle, the old man behind the counter looked frazzled. My heart sank when he demanded my ticket.

'I've mislaid my ticket but you'll maybe remember me from two weeks ago. I brought in a coat, shoes and a bag.'

He started to speak while pointing to the notice that gave dire warning to ticketless customers but I stopped his stream of protest. 'Please, I think my ticket is in the house but maybe you can have a look for me and you'll recognise my articles.'

He began to mutter again but to my delight he trotted away towards the stacked shelves at the back of the office. He returned almost immediately but he wasn't carrying my goods.

He gave me a very shrewd glance, opened his ledger and ran a finger down the list of hand-written entries. He looked at me again. He gave another glance at the ledger then came right to me and peered at me closely. He said. 'According to my ledger, you redeemed your articles a week past Thursday.'

I gasped in astonishment. 'I can't have – I'm at work every Thursday.'

'Well, that's not for me to know,' he replied waspishly. 'Your ticket was brought in and we returned your goods. It's as simple as that.'

I was desperate. 'Can you describe the person who redeemed them?'

By now, the queue behind me was growing restless. He glanced over my shoulder. 'Look, lassie, the ticket was handed in and we returned the goods so there's nothing more to say.'

With that final sentence ringing through my

head, I had no option but to return home.

Granny was mortified. 'Somebody did what? Redeemed your coat?'

I mentioned the holes in my pockets and the fear that I had lost the ticket through my own stupidity.

Then the door opened and Dad and Bella appeared, looking for all the world like a double act on the stage. In fact, I half suspected Bella to say something outrageous which to my surprise she did.

'I've just seen Hattie swanking away to work in her new orange coat,' she said.

Granny looked furious while I was merely stunned. Granny snapped, 'What kind of orange coat?'

Bella looked pleased at our reaction. 'Just a normal kind of coat with furry sleeves and collar.'

Dad butted in, 'I'm looking for a house or a couple of rooms to rent, Ann. I don't think I can stay under Kaiser Hattie's roof any longer. I did hear that there might be some houses on the Hilltown available.'

I was stunned – first the coat and now this. He had just given up one house and now he was looking for another one.

He seemed to read my thoughts. 'I know I was stupid about the house but let's go and see Rita, Nellie and Joe – they might have heard about a vacant place.'

I looked at Granny and she was grim-faced. She motioned for me to go with Dad and she turned to Bella. 'You'll have to excuse me but I'm going out so I don't have time to make you a cup of tea and Ann is going with her dad so we'll see you another time, Bella.'

Bella was most put out by this offhand dismissal. Still, she had no option but to shift her large frame from the armchair. She muttered to herself as she left. It sounded like dark threats never to cross this threshold again but Granny wasn't listening.

'You go with your dad, Ann, and I'll make sure Hattie is in this house tonight.'

On that note, Dad lifted Lily from her chair and we hurried out on our journey to the Hilltown. As we walked up the Wellgate steps, Dad apologised for the furniture money. 'It wasn't all spent on beer, Ann, although that's what you might think.' He looked abashed. 'The truth is that Marlene wasn't taking any rent from me. I suppose she thought we were getting married but after your visit, when she realised what my true intentions were ... well, she not only demanded my rent but also the back money.'

I looked at him. 'It doesn't matter, Dad – it was your money.'

'No, I want you to know the truth,' he said. 'I gave Marlene twenty-five shillings and that left me fifteen bob for myself. I thought that was the end of the matter but the rot had set in and we had that big argy-bargy. That's when she stotted me with the vase.'

'You must have led Marlene to believe you wanted to marry her. She wouldn't just assume she had a future with you. You must have mentioned the word marriage.'

'I swear to God I didn't,' he said firmly. Then

321

he hung his head. 'At least not when I was sober but maybe she got the wrong idea after I had a few pints of beer.'

I was sceptical and it showed.

No doubt desperate to change the subject, he grinned and said, 'Oh, I meant to mention it – Rita has had a wee lass.'

Our old neighbours were glad to see us. Joe was standing on the pavement with the usual gang and he immediately pulled out his tin with its numerous cigarette stubs and began to roll a cigarette for Dad.

I took Lily up the dark stairs. Nellie was in Rita's house and I was once again shocked to see how thin Rita was and, come to that, Nellie wasn't far behind her in the weight stakes.

The baby was being fed and she sucked noisily at Rita's breast. Her son Jimmy was sitting on the bed with an ancient-looking comic which he was reading upside down. Still, as Rita explained, it kept him quiet and judging from the conversation, that wasn't very usual.

Lily ran over and clambered on to the bed beside him. He gave her a scornful glance and proceeded to scrutinise his comic. I looked round the dark room. In spite of it being a bright day outside, the gas mantle was lit and it threw its pale light over the small room. After Granny's bright kitchen and the even brighter Whitegate Lodge, this room resembled a dungeon. The baby finished her feed and Rita held her upright to pat her back gently and bring up any wind.

'What's the wee lass called, Rita?' I asked.

'We've called her after me,' she said wearily.

'She's called Margarita.'

I was taken aback by this lovely name. 'What a nice name, Rita. You should have mentioned your name and we would all have called you Margarita.'

'That's what I was afraid of,' she said, laughing. 'When I was a bairn, a lot of folk thought I was Spanish. Now, I ask you, do I look Spanish?'

I had to agree she didn't. 'But you're all keeping fine?'

Nellie nodded but Rita seemed to be too weary even to nod her head. She said, 'We've got our ups and downs – mostly downs as it happens. As for me, well, I have to give the bairn a bottle as well as feeding her myself because my milk is drying up. Seemingly it happens if you're undernourished or just damn worn out. Take your pick of these two explanations, Ann.'

I felt so sorry for them and, although there was no sign of their husbands, it turned out they were still unemployed.

'They go for every job they hear about but there's hundreds chasing each one. The Caledon shipyard is looking for men but it's a hit or a miss if you're hired.'

Because of this, I decided not to mention Dad's job as I didn't want to hurt their feelings. I hoped that Dad had done the same with his pals. Although we were grateful to the Pringle family, I always felt guilty about their help. Instead, I mentioned we were looking for another house. 'I don't know if you've heard but Dad's no longer living at Marlene's house.'

I saw from their amused expressions that they

had heard every nuance of the sordid saga over the smashed vase. Nellie's face brightened and Rita laughed. 'Aye,' said Nellie, 'it was the main gossip on the Hilltown and Ann Street for days on end. Believe me, Ann, it fair cheered up our dismal lives as there's nothing as stimulating as a good-going fight.'

I hadn't realised it had been a fight as such but Rita laughed again. 'Och, don't listen to Nellie. Although they had a good ding-dong, it was hardly a fight – more of a shouting match with Marlene doing most of the shouting.'

Mentally, I could have given Dad a good kick but I put on a brittle smile. 'What a pity we gave up this house but, if you hear of anything, will you let me know?'

Nellie said, 'I did hear through the Hilltown gossip that there is an empty house near the top of the hill – number 226, I think – and the factor has his office in Commercial Street.' She turned to Rita. 'Do you know the factor's name?'

Rita said she didn't.

Never one to give up easily, Nellie made a couple of suggestions. 'You can maybe go to the close and ask some of the tenants who the factor is or else you can go to Commercial Street and just visit all the factors' offices and ask about this house.'

I was on the point of leaving when a loud screech came from the bed. Lily was trying to prise the comic away from Jimmy's grubby fist. He held on to it with a grim look on his face while Lily was equally determined to remove it. I knew it was time to go and I promised to let the

324

two women know the outcome in our search for a house. As I went downstairs, I couldn't help but think how life had moved on. During all the years I had lived in the close, I hadn't noticed the dark and gloomy interior but now I realised just how depressing it was.

On the way back to the Overgate, I mentioned the house at 226 Hilltown to Dad and he promised to visit the factor – after all, he was starting work at the beginning of August and we would be able to pay the rent.

Hattie was waiting for me when we arrived. Granny looked livid and for one heart-stopping moment I thought she was ill but it was anger that suffused her face with a deep red colour.

'Well, explain yourself, Hattie,' said Granny as soon as we walked in.

I noticed my coat, bag and shoes lying on the bed.

Hattie looked quite cool and slightly arrogant – almost as if being found with someone else's clothes was an everyday occurrence for her. She frowned at me. 'I don't see what all the fuss is about. I redeemed your coat out of the goodness of my heart, to save you paying the money out of your wages, and what do I get? Nothing but aggravation from Granny.' She pointed a finger at Granny who almost choked with anger.

'Don't you give me that nonsense, Hattie,' she said. 'Out of the goodness of your heart never entered your head. No, you always wanted and even coveted Ann's coat and you were determined to get your hands on it – one way or another.'

Hattie's coolness evaporated now that she was

faced with her mother's wrath. She turned an appealing face to me. 'Honestly, Ann, I thought you were going to keep the coat pledged for the full six months and I thought to myself, what a waste. Surely it was better being worn and out in the fresh air rather than being stuffed in that awful pawnshop beside lots of grubby things. I was just going to wear it for a couple of weeks then turn up here with it. That way you would have saved yourself seven shillings plus the pawn-broker's interest.'

Granny was still angry. 'Even if you were feeling like Lady Bountiful, Hattie, you could have redeemed it and brought it straight here to Ann. Why all the secrecy? Tell us that?'

As usual Hattie had her answer. 'Oh yes and what would you both have said about that? "No thank you, Hattie. We can manage, Hattie." That's what I would have heard from you both.'

A sudden tiredness swept over me and I wanted this argument to stop. 'All right, Hattie, thank you for redeeming my coat but it's a pity you didn't stop to think how worried I was because I thought I had lost the ticket. But, now that it's back, we'll say no more about it.'

'That's fine, then,' said Granny, going over to the stove to put the kettle on. 'We'll say no more about it and we'll just have to take your word that you were going to return it. I mean, if Bella hadn't spotted you wearing it, then we would never have known where it was.'

Hattie spluttered, 'I might have guessed it was that nosy old besom that started this.'

Meanwhile, throughout all this dialogue

between Hattie and us, Dad had sat quietly at the fire. Hattie suddenly spotted him. 'And another thing, Johnny – how long have I got to put you up?'

It was now his turn to be angry. 'Well, as a matter of fact, Ann and I were looking for a house today and I'll go and see the factor tomorrow so it shouldn't be for much longer.'

It was obviously Hattie's day for upsetting everyone but she was determined not to back down, even when she knew she was in the wrong. 'That's fine, then. After all, the neighbours are beginning to wonder how long you'll be staying.'

We were all speechless but, on that note, she swept out of the kitchen.

Granny shook her head. 'She's feeling guilty – that's why she's acting like a spoilt brat.'

Dad laughed. 'She is a spoilt brat but we all have to be grateful for her influence with the Pringle family. After all, Ann has her job and I'll soon have mine. Those poor pals of mine on the Hilltown have no hope of anything and they're not even getting enough to eat.'

I turned to him. 'It's the same with Rita and Nellie. Rita is so thin, Granny, and she's trying to feed the baby. It breaks your heart to see people having to live like that. This damned government should be put on the same money as the poor population and then they would maybe get jobs organised for the working classes.'

'Hear! Hear!' said Dad. 'So three cheers for the wonderful Hattie.'

We all laughed – even Lily who didn't know what she was laughing at but she wanted to join in.

13

Dad got the key for a house in July. It was on a Monday, a week before Lily's birthday, when he arrived at the Overgate, brandishing a large key. He was holding it aloft like some victorious trophy and his face was flushed with excitement. Granny and I looked at his animated expression with amazement. After years of seeing him being so downhearted and listless, the change was spectacular.

'I've been going round all the factors for weeks now and it's worked,' he boasted. 'It's not the same house Rita and Nellie mentioned but it's in the same close – number 226 Hilltown.'

Granny was so pleased for him. 'Oh, that's great news, Johnny. You must be so happy that everything's working out for you now.'

If Granny was pleased then I was delirious with joy. 'When are we moving in, Dad?'

Dad laughed. 'As soon as possible – living with Hattie these few months has been a real trial, I can tell you. There were times when I would gladly have proposed to Marlene just to escape!'

Granny laughed but her voice held a gentle reproof. 'Now, Johnny, it's not as bad as that. And your sister did put you up when you were homeless.'

Dad didn't seem to be abashed at this reproof and he laughed again. 'I know but it's such a relief to be leaving. Now I know how prisoners feel when they're released from jail.' He continued, 'The rent for the house is six shillings a week and I think I can just manage that until my job starts.'

Mr Pringle had said the job would start in August but so far there had been no more word about Willie retiring. Deep down in my heart, I prayed that nothing would happen to change this plan. I was frightened to count Dad's chickens.

'Let's go and see the house now, Ann.' He looked at granny. 'You come as well, Mum. Are Lily and Dad out somewhere?'

I nodded. 'Aye, they've gone for a walk along the Esplanade.'

Dad nodded. 'Och, well, they can see the house another day.'

We set off in happy spirits and, for the first time since Lily's birth, Dad was full of plans. The house was one stair up and we all thought it was wonderful. It had three rooms and, although they weren't large, they weren't tiny either. They were a bit like Goldilocks's third choice – just right. A lovely small bay window overlooked the street and the Shakespeare bar in particular. At this time of day, the bar was quiet but it would be busy at weekends. Still, I liked the sound of voices and the general hubbub of daily life on the streets.

Although I loved the Ferry, I could never get used to the silence and the sound of the wind and sea. We inspected the flat and the minuscule toilet which was situated on the stair. Another bonus was the postage-stamp-sized drying green that lay to the rear of the building.

'You'll need some Congoleum for the floor and curtains for the two windows. Luckily the wee room at the back has such a tiny window it'll not need much material,' said Granny.

For the first time, Dad looked downcast. 'I should never have sold the furniture.'

Granny, desperate to keep his spirits up, suggested, 'You can always take the wee bed out of Ann's room at the Overgate and maybe Mr Bell will have some bargains in his shop. It'll just be a matter of furnishing it slowly.'

He cheered up. 'Aye, that's true – one step at a time.'

'What about Hattie?' I said. 'Does she not have anything spare we can borrow till we get settled and Dad gets his job?'

Dad looked mortified. 'Over my dead body, Ann. That woman would torment the devil and still come off the winner. She would never let us forget her help.'

Granny chided him again, 'Now, Johnny.'

This time he did look ashamed. 'I know, I know. She does have her good points.' He gave me a quick wink and muttered something under his breath which I didn't catch.

Granny and I then measured the floors and windows before Dad locked up and we all trooped down the hill. Mr Bell's Rake and Rummage shop was packed with furniture but the prices all seemed to be out of our range. Forever the optimist, Granny said, 'Leave it for now, Johnny. Something always turns up.'

As it turned out, the Pringle family was that something. Maddie came round that night and she was as pleased as we were about our house. 'My mother has loads of material in her sewing room that she never uses – maybe we can make curtains from it.' She sounded excited.

I tried to protest but Danny's appearance soon put a stop to our plans. 'Hullo, girls,' he said, 'are you still coming to the pictures with me on Friday, Maddie?' He had a twinkle in his eye when he said it.

Maddie beamed. 'Of course I am. You can pick me up after your work.'

I looked at her, my face a picture of disbelief. Whatever happened, I thought, to her life of celibacy? A life without love and Danny and certainly without pleasures like going to the pictures?

I hadn't seen Danny for over a fortnight so I was obviously out of touch with the news. I gave him my wide-eyed, innocent look – the look he always said was intimidating. I didn't mention Minnie but I was wondering if he was still taking her to the pictures.

No doubt reading my thoughts, he squirmed slightly under my scrutiny. 'I'm taking Maddie to the King's,' he said.

Maddie grabbed the measurements and said cheerio. 'See you on Friday, Danny.' On that cryptic note she was gone.

Danny looked amused. 'Did Maddie not tell you that I'm not seeing Minnie now?'

I shook my head.

He said, 'Minnie was just a school pal and we both felt that way. It was just a friendship for both of us. Anyway, she has her eye on another lad in the shop. When I realised I was never going to see Maddie again, well, I had to tell Minnie.'

'Never see Maddie again?' I was puzzled by this statement.

'Aye, she stopped coming into the shop – completely stopped,' he emphasised the words. 'Then, when I asked her out to the pictures, she refused. After a few weeks, I was missing her so much I decided to tell her that Minnie had a new lad and she seemed pleased by this.'

'Danny, your love life is so complicated,' I said.

He blushed. The sight of his beetroot-red face reminded me of the old Danny I knew. 'I've always been besotted by her,' he confessed, 'ever since I was a laddie but I thought she would want someone more prosperous and in a good job. I never thought I stood a chance and there was also the fact she was still at school. But she's passed her exams and hopes to take up a nursing career soon.'

I knew all this as Maddie had been full of her exam success and I knew she was looking forward to joining the world of work. As Danny rattled on, I was struck again at the stupidity of the male population. Dad couldn't understand Marlene and he understood Rosie even less and Danny didn't think he stood a chance with Maddie – even after all her attempts to attract him, excite him and downright browbeat him. I was glad we both had good news.

Then, without warning, Maddie rushed in. She was clutching a large parcel and her face was red with exertion.

Granny was mystified. 'What have you got it that huge parcel, Maddie?'

Maddie opened it and a small bale of flowery material spilled out on to the kitchen table. 'My mother was going to put this out,' she said, trying to look like she was speaking the truth. 'She says we can make curtains with it.'

I didn't believe her and I said so.

'Honestly, she doesn't want it. Maybe she wasn't going to throw it out but she said she doesn't need it and I've to give it to you, Ann.'

Granny intervened. 'Ann and her dad can't take this Maddie. Your family have been so good to us but we can't keep on being a burden to your mum.' She suddenly stopped and looked at the bulky parcel. 'Don't tell me you carried that heavy parcel all the way from the Perth Road?'

Maddie shook her head. 'No, my father gave me a lift in the car. He's on his way to the office.'

Granny looked at the clock. 'At this time of night?'

Maddie nodded again. 'My mother says she doesn't need this material. It belonged to some old relation who left it and never picked it up again. It was in our attic. Also my father remembered the office floor got recovered a few years ago and some spare linoleum was put away in a stockroom. He thinks there might be enough to cover the floors of your new house.'

We all looked at her – my grandparents, Dad, Danny and me – and the only person oblivious to this grand gesture was Lily who was running around, making the sound of a train. Watching the trains cross the Tay Bridge was her favourite thing on her walks along the Esplanade.

Maddie went on. 'My father will deliver the

linoleum to the house but just if you want it.'

For the first time, Dad spoke up, 'Well, Maddie, it's really good of your parents to help us out again. We'll take them but on one condition – when I start work at your uncle's warehouse, your dad gets him to deduct a few shillings a week to pay for them. We can't accept charity all the time.'

Maddie clapped her hands together. 'Right then, Mr Neill, I'll get him to do that.' She turned to me. 'We can make up the curtains next week-end, Ann, and you can put them up.'

On that note, it was all settled and Granny spoke for us all after Danny and Maddie departed. 'What would we do without the Pringles? You should be thanking your sister for being there, Johnny, so no more miscalling her.'

Dad grinned. 'Aye you're right – another three cheers for Hattie.' But he only said it after Danny had gone, I noticed.

The next few weeks flew by in a flurry of house-hold chores. The curtains looked lovely when hung and the blue linoleum proved to be of a far better quality than we could ever have afforded. The fact that it was all to be paid in instalments meant we could enjoy it with feeling guilty. The rooms had an empty look due to the lack of furniture but we were prepared to furnish them slowly when the money became available.

As it turned out, it was Rosie who came to our aid. She turned up at the flat one Sunday after-noon. Dad looked pleased to see her and this fact delighted me. She seemed flustered to start with. 'Hullo, Johnny. Now I know how you feel about the Salvation Army but I want you to listen to what I have to say.' As this was all said without taking a breath, she stopped to regain her breath. I realised she was nervous. 'We occasionally have to clear out houses if someone leaves them.' I noticed she didn't use the words 'dead people'. 'Well, some furniture has turned up and we were wondering if you would like some of it for the house.' She lapsed into silence and gave Dad a nervous glance, no doubt expecting a withering reply.

To our astonishment, he gave her a big smile, making her face go red with pleasure. 'That's very good of you, Rosie. Of course we'll take some of it. But only what we need and maybe someone else can benefit as well.'

Rosie glowed. 'It's in a shed at the moment but you can look at it any time you want.'

We decided that now was the best time so we made our way to this shed which was situated behind a tall tenement on the Hawkhill. We were expecting the things to be tatty but were pleasantly surprised to see they were in good condition. There was a double bed with a spotless, blue striped mattress, a table and four chairs, a dresser and a sideboard.

Rosie explained, 'This belonged to Mrs Moncur – her husband was in the band before he died a few years ago. She originally came from a small hamlet in Angus and she inherited this furniture from her folks so it's good quality. When I heard about your house, I thought you might be able to use this.' She swept her hand over the shed's contents.

Dad said, 'As I told Maddie, we'll only take it if

335

we can pay for it.'

I was mentally tallying everything up. At this rate we would be paying for things forever. I wished we had some savings put aside but this was out of the question.

Rosie looked disappointed. 'Oh, well, Johnny, you can't have it. Mrs Moncur said in her will that it had to be given to a family with her blessing and that no money was to change hands.'

Dad rubbed his chin thoughtfully. After a few moments, he said, 'Right, we'll take it, Rosie, and thank you very much.'

Rosie's face glowed with pleasure once more and I let out a sigh of relief at such a wonderful windfall. We were truly blessed I thought – especially compared to all our neighbours who had so little. We didn't have a lot either but things kept dropping in our laps – my job, this house and the furnishings and very soon, Dad's job. Oh yes we were truly blessed.

I knew in my heart that things would be hard in the beginning but, as soon as Dad got his job, then things should look up. At the Ferry, Jean must have grown tired of hearing my happy chatter. Still, she never showed it and she was always happy for me. 'I did say your star was rising, Ann.'

I nodded happily. 'You must come and visit us in the new house when we get everything in place, Jean. Dad and Joe laid the linoleum first and I put up the curtains. Maddie did say the material wasn't suitable for heavyweight curtains but they are so fresh and flowery and a lovely sunshiny yellow – just like a garden.'

Jean smiled. 'What about the furniture? Have you got it delivered yet?'

The thought of that brought a smile to my face. Dad had suggested asking Mr Bell if we could maybe rent his little horse and cart but, on second thoughts, had rejected the idea. The late Mrs Moncur's shed lay on a steep part of the Hawkhill and our house was, likewise, on a steep part of the Hilltown. The thought of the poor wee spindly-legged pony pulling a heavy load had filled me with horror. So, instead, we rented the coalman's horse and cart.

The horse was large and furry-legged with a huge halter around its neck. His name was Henry and he was stabled in a small street off the Seagate. He looked so strong that I could well imagine him pulling a troupe of circus elephants. I said as much to Jean. 'The coalman is charging us two shillings for a couple of hours and Dad has enlisted lots of helpers… Well, we've got Dad and Joe and Danny and me but, between the four of us, we'll manage fine.'

The following weekend, we did manage it, albeit with a lot of sweat, muscle and huffing and puffing. Afterwards, the four of us stood in a small knot in the middle of the kitchen and I was so happy I could have cried. The small flat was clean, snug and homely.

Joe spoke for us all when he said, 'I hope you all have years and years of happiness, health and prosperity in your wee house. You certainly deserve it, Johnny and Ann and Lily.'

I repeated this story over the following few days to Maddie and Jean.

One day, over our morning tea, Jean asked, 'Any word of your father's job yet, Ann?'

We were now in the middle of August and Dad was becoming a bit alarmed at not hearing anything. Also, we were becoming more financially stretched by the day. The plan had been to keep Lily with her grandparents all week and Dad and I would have her on my days off. This situation meant that most of my wages went to Granny every week while the remaining tiny sum went towards the rent. Dad paid the balance of rent and also the food and pennies for the gas meter. Later, come winter, we would also need coal for the fire.

I shook my head. 'No, not yet – Maddie's uncle did say it would be in August but here we are in the middle of the month and he's heard nothing.'

As it turned out, at that precise moment, Dad was hearing about his job but the news wasn't what we were expecting. I heard all about it on the Sunday afternoon.

Dad said, 'The old man who's due to retire wants to stay on for a wee while yet. He seemingly needs his wages.' He stopped when he saw my face which was tight with anxiety. 'Now, Ann, don't get all upset because it's not all bad news. John Pringle is a very fair man and, although he wants the job to go to me, he obviously doesn't want to cause trouble for his old employee.' He stopped again to wipe the perspiration from his face. It was one of those warm humid days that often appear in August and it seemed as if thunder wasn't far away.

Dad continued, 'As I was saying, being a fair

man, John Pringle has decided to employ me as well but instead of a full-time job, I'm afraid it'll be part time for the moment.'

'Will we be able to keep the house, Dad?' My voice sounded ragged with worry. The future had looked so bright a few weeks ago and now ... well, I wasn't so sure.

'Of course we will. It'll just mean trimming our costs for the time being. The winter will be the hardest but we'll face that when it comes.' He gave me an enquiring look. 'I don't suppose your employer would maybe give you a raise in wages?'

'Oh, no, Dad. She gives me an extra half crown as it is. I couldn't possibly ask her.'

He held his hand up. 'It was just a suggestion. Anyway, maybe Willie will finish before the winter. After all, he's on part-time wages as well and he doesn't seem very happy with this. Still, it's an awful world when people are chasing others out of their jobs. I feel terrible about this but it's a dog-eat-dog world we live in now.'

I was still worried. 'Dad, you can give me the rent money every week and I'll pay it to the office on the Monday.'

He laughed loudly. 'You don't trust me, do you?'

I shook my head but he laughed even louder. 'Anyway the rent man comes every Friday night for the rent and you're at the Ferry then.'

There was nothing I could do but trust him and, although I had the gut feeling I could, I hoped that temptation didn't appear within two miles of him.

Meanwhile, if I was worried, then Maddie was radiant. She was now going out every week with Danny to the pictures and, although I was pleased for them both, a tiny bit of me longed for the old days when the three of us went everywhere together.

Granny noticed this one night. 'You miss being with Maddie and Danny, don't you, Ann?'

I tried to deny it but she was a wise old woman. 'Never mind, you'll soon have a lad of your own one of these days.'

I doubted that. For one thing, when would I have time to see him, let alone going out gallivanting with him?

Granny was still chatting. 'I see Minnie McFarlane is getting married next month.'

Minnehaha, I thought, good for you.

'Aye,' said Granny, 'she's marrying the under-manager of Lipton's. He's in the branch where Danny works. Danny told me she always liked this chap and, when he showed some interest in her, she was over the moon. At least Minnie's not sly like her mother but you wait and see, Ann. A bairn will be born in about seven months' time and Mrs McFarlane will be telling all and sundry that it's a premature birth.'

'Is she expecting a baby?' I asked, wondering about this great wide world that lay beyond my life of work at the Ferry and at home.

Granny grinned and winked. 'Well, not officially, that is, but you wait and see. The wee bundle will pop out around March next year.'

'Does Danny know about the wedding?'

'Oh, aye, and he says he's very pleased for them

both but I've heard he was glad to escape from her clutches.' She roared with laughter. 'And Hattie is even more delirious with joy that he's seeing more of Maddie.' She became serious. 'Mind you, I don't believe a word of it myself.'

I knew Danny and Minnie had been good friends but I also knew they weren't serious about one another. Minnie had been upfront with Danny about Peter, her intended groom, and Danny had told her about Maddie. But that didn't matter with the gossips – they only wanted to believe in a bit of scandal and chitchat.

On the third of September, Minnie walked down the aisle with her under-manager. He was a thin-faced gangly-looking man, a bit older than Minnie, and he looked decidedly nervous.

She wore a long white frock and carried a small bunch of flowers and she had a happy, satisfied expression on her pretty face.

Some of the neighbours said later that her slight bulge was noticeable and, although the rumour was sweeping the Hawkhill where she lived, her house-proud and sharp-tongued mother was denying it with strongly worded sentences at every turn. That part of the story was related to us by Bella who was enjoying every minute of this matrimonial drama, even going as far as saying the poor groom had tried for an exchange to another branch in Glasgow but had been unsuccessful in his quest to escape from his formidable mother-in-law. Poor Minnie, I thought.

Bella also knew the entire menu of the wedding breakfast. The bride and groom's family and a few friends had gathered in a tiny church hall in

Hunter Street, a street which branched off the Hawkhill. According to Bella, they had a choice of sandwiches and a slice of wedding cake.

'Aye,' said Bella, smacking her lips at being the bearer of all this gossip, 'Mrs McFarlane put on a choice of fish paste and boiled ham sandwiches. There was a one-tiered cake which was supposed to be baked in yon wee home bakery at the foot of the Hawkhill but it was cancelled.'

'Imagine,' said Granny, 'having a cake – it must have cost a wee fortune.'

Bella poured cold water over this suggestion of extravagance. 'No, no, it wasn't a real fruitcake – just a few sultanas in the mixture and it was made by Minnie's auntie Jeannie. Mind you,' said Bella darkly, 'she likes to think she's a good baker but I wouldn't eat anything she baked.'

Leaving the women to their gossiping, I decided to take Lily for a walk. We set off towards Dock Street and my plan was to saunter past the warehouse where Dad worked. He was still part-time but it was better than no job. I wanted Lily to see it and, if I was being truthful with myself, I was also curious.

The doors were wide open when we arrived and the interior was a buzz of activity. It was one of those lovely autumn days when the sun had a shimmering quality in its warmth and it shone brightly on our faces as we peeked inside. Yellow shafts of sunlight slanted downwards from the dusty skylights on the roof, showing up filmy cobwebs that clung like grey lace to the corners of the wooden walls.

Stacked up high against each wall were boxes of

bananas, oranges and apples plus the more mundane selection of vegetables. Some of the fruit boxes displayed labels with exotic sounding names – labels that had been stuck on in far-distant lands. A few men toiled with their loads, their voices echoing in the warehouse and also on the street where the gaffer's voice could be heard as he issued orders.

We spotted Dad. He was pushing a pile of boxes which were leaning precariously against a two-wheeled trolley. A large blue label marked 'Fyffes bananas' could clearly be seen.

As if feeling the intense scrutiny of Lily and me, he turned his head and smiled at us. A small, stout man in a grey overall counted the boxes and made a pencilled note in a ledger. Mean-while, Dad returned for another load and he gave Lily a big wink in the passing but he didn't come to the entrance.

Lily couldn't understand this and she cried, 'Daddy, Daddy!' Her thin, childish voice carried over the noise inside, causing Dad to turn with a worried frown but I made a sign that we were leaving. Lily waggled her chubby fingers at him and we set off for home.

If someone had asked me at that time to describe my happiness at our good fortune, I would have been unable to do so. A warm feeling of well-being wrapped itself around my heart and I felt truly that our lives were going to get better. Dad would soon be on full-time in his job and we would be a happy family again. With this happy frame of mind, I returned to the Ferry, full of plans for the future. Our load would ease and we would all live happily ever after. Our future looked as bright as a shiny red apple on Christmas morning.

Then, on the Thursday morning, Jean had her accident. One minute she was outside in the courtyard feeding the birds with some stale cake crumbs and the next she was lying on the flagstones, crying in agony. I heard her distressed cries through the open kitchen window and I ran out. I tried to lift her on to her feet but she roared with pain. 'I think my leg is broken, Ann. Go fetch Miss Hood or Mrs Barrie.'

I raced back through the kitchen, almost knocking the housekeeper over. She opened her mouth to chastise me but I grabbed her hand. 'It's Mrs Peters.' She didn't seem to understand and I shouted at her. 'It's Mrs Peters. She's broken her leg.' I pushed her through the doorway towards the yard.

When we got there, Mr Potter was there. He had been working in the garden and had been curious about all the kerfuffle as he called it. Mrs Barrie had also heard the noise and she stood at her bedroom window but, because it faced the front of the house, she was unaware of the accident.

She called out, 'Mr Potter, what is it?'

The gardener heard her and he detached himself from our little group and made his way to the front of the house. 'It's the cook, missus. Broken her leg by the look of it.'

This news upset Mrs Barrie. 'Send Miss Hood in to telephone for Doctor Little.' As he retreated back to the courtyard, she called after him, 'Mr

Potter, did you hear what I said?'

Mr Potter muttered to himself as he trotted back, 'I heard you, missus, I'm not deaf.'

I brought a blanket from the linen cupboard and placed it over Jean and I also put a pillow under her head. Her leg lay at an unnatural-looking angle and she was shivering violently. In spite of it being a warm day, the flagstones in the yard were nearly always cold and damp because they lay in deep shadow.

Miss Hood had hurried indoors to telephone the doctor and she was on her way back out when we were joined by Mrs Barrie. She was pale-faced and frail looking as she stood in the courtyard, leaning heavily on her stick.

The housekeeper spoke for us all when she said, 'Eva, I think you should be inside. When the doctor arrives I'll let you know.'

Mrs Barrie was having none of this and her voice, when she answered, was resolute. 'Nonsense, Lottie, I'm fine and I want to speak to Mrs Peters.' She walked slowly towards the prostrate figure on the ground.

I was kneeling at Jean's side and I didn't like the look of her grey, pain-filled face. A film of sweat was now noticeable on her brow and upper lip but, in spite of this perspiration, she was still shivering.

Although in considerable pain, Jean looked embarrassed. 'I forgot about yon cracked flag-stone, Mrs Barrie. Normally when I come out to feed the blackbirds I avoid it but not today.' She sounded rueful and her face contorted with pain.

My mind went numb at the mention of the

345

blackbirds. Was this what Ma Ryan had warned me about? But surely the danger was aimed at me and not poor Jean who didn't even know Danny's grandmother? Then I thought how I often went out to throw the crumbs but I always made a quick dash for the door. Was I meant to be out here today?

Fortunately the doctor arrived at that moment and put these unhappy thoughts out of my mind. His initial diagnosis was swift and it matched Jean's own suspicion. 'Your leg is broken, Mrs Peters.' He looked at Mrs Barrie. 'I'm afraid it's a bad break so I'm going to send Mrs Peters to the casualty department in the infirmary in Dundee. But first of all I'll put your leg in a splint, Mrs Peters.'

I held her hand as he worked on her leg and I was upset when she moaned in pain. Poor Jean – my friend and saviour in this house and now, because of feeding the blackbirds, she was suffering all this pain.

Mrs Barrie asked Miss Hood to phone for a taxi. 'Go to Mr Roberts, Lottie. His limousine is more comfortable and roomier than the one from the other garage.'

Lottie ran inside and I felt sorry for her. She seemed genuinely upset about Jean and she was certainly quick on the uptake regarding the telephone. She also had the proper authoritative voice for dealing with an emergency. 'We need your limousine, Mr Roberts. It's urgent so can you come to Whitegate Lodge at once?'

When he arrived, he viewed the scene with a nonchalant air. According to the Ferry grapevine, nothing ever upset Mr Roberts. The doctor had asked Mr Potter to make a temporary stretcher and, with the doctor and me at one end and the gardener and Mr Roberts at the other end, we managed to transfer Jean to the waiting car. We slid the stretcher along the length of the leather-upholstered back seat.

Mrs Barrie then gave him his instructions. 'Make sure you drive slowly and look out for potholes on the road.' She looked through the open window. 'You'll soon have your leg fixed, Mrs Peters, and Ann will go with you.'

I was surprised but Mr Roberts calmly opened the passenger door for me. If the circumstances hadn't been so tragic, I would have felt like a queen at such grand transport.

Mrs Barrie was speaking again, 'The doctor is going to telephone the infirmary, Ann, and I want you to wait till Mrs Peters has had her treatment before you come back. Mr Roberts will wait for you.' She glanced again at the back seat but the cook was quiet. 'Good, I'm glad she has had something to make her sleep.' Although I hadn't noticed it, the doctor had obviously given her a sedative.

'I can easily get the bus back, Mrs Barrie. There's no need to keep the car waiting,' I said. Although I didn't want to admit it, I felt Jean's treatment would be lengthy and I wanted to stay until she was safely over whatever lay ahead of her. If the car was waiting for me, I would be under pressure to maybe leave earlier. 'Honestly, Mrs Barrie, I don't mind coming back on the bus and that way I can stay as long as it takes to make sure she's comfortable.'

Mrs Barrie looked dubious but she agreed to my request. 'I would feel better if you were there with her, Ann,' she admitted. She turned to Miss Hood. 'Lottie, I've no money on me. Can you please lend me a half crown to give to Ann to see she gets back safely?'

Miss Hood darted back inside and within a moment was back, her purse in her hand. She gave me the coin but her expression was blank and her pale eyes unfathomable.

As the car purred away, I heard Mrs Barrie ask the housekeeper to inform Jean's husband. 'I don't think they have a telephone so can you please go to Long Lane and tell him personally. I would be so grateful, Lottie.'

Lottie's reaction to this request went unheard as the car slipped through the front gates and along the road that skimmed the sea.

Thankfully, Jean slept through the entire journey which didn't take too long. When we reached the infirmary, the casualty department was busy but, because of the serious nature of Jean's injury and the earlier telephone call from Doctor Little, she was whisked away immediately.

I sat down in the busy waiting room as a motley procession of injured people came and went. Most of these casualties were children who had obviously taken a few tumbles. Sitting amongst this childish mob were a few grey-faced and ill-looking adults who waited patiently for their turn in the queue.

I noticed the small boy who sat beside me. His harassed mother obviously knew this department well because I overheard her tell another worried-looking mother that this was her third visit to the hospital in a month. The boy had a gory-looking ring of dried blood around his throat that extended from ear to ear. It looked horrific and his mother was of the same opinion. 'You wee besom,' she said, 'the nurses will think I've tried to throttle you. Playing cowboys and Indians with the greenie washing line. It's a bloody wonder you didn't strangle yourself.'

After about an hour and a half, a young nurse appeared and said, 'Mrs Peters has had her leg set but we're keeping her in the ward overnight. Depending on how she feels tomorrow, she may get home. But she's comfortable at the moment.'

This was what we all expected. If Mrs Barrie hadn't thought it as well, she would have insisted to Mr Roberts that he had to wait but, as it was, he had set off back to the Ferry the moment Jean was transferred to the hospital.

I left through the main door, leaving behind the human cargo of half-strangled little boys and broken legs. Then I suddenly remembered this was the place where Mum had died – in this lovely grey-bricked building with its shining windows and impressive appearance. The memory of that terrible day came flooding back and I had tears in my eyes as I ran down the steep hill to the bus stop. The tears were mostly for my mother but I shed a few for Jean too.

As it turned out, Jean didn't get home the next day. In fact, she was in the ward for over a week before Mr Roberts was despatched again to bring her home. I missed her so much in the house.

Even the kitchen had a forlorn atmosphere and I had no one to chat to. I had become so used to her company, telling her all my hopes and dreams for the future, but I also missed the friendly chitchat of everyday gossip.

Mrs Barrie hired a temporary cook – a brash young woman with a loud voice and extremely poor cooking skills. Even Miss Hood was affected by our loss. She said one day, 'I'll be so glad when Mrs Peters is back. She's such a good cook and a wonderful baker. Not like...' She shuddered and walked away.

One thing I did notice, however, was that this new cook stood no nonsense from the house-keeper and, once again, I was convinced it was me and only me that Miss Hood disliked.

I offered to stay at the house to cover for Jean but Mrs Barrie wouldn't hear of it. 'Not at all, Ann – your family need you more than we do. Lottie and I can live quite easily. The cook, although inadequate, makes reasonably edible food and Lottie can always make us a snack.'

I was packing my suitcase the following morning in preparation for my time off when I noticed my coat wasn't hanging in the wardrobe. For a brief moment, I wondered if I had brought it with me but I knew I had. Granny was always frightened Hattie would secrete it away again so she was most insistent I took it away with me every week. But, because of the mild weather, I hadn't worn it since arriving back at the Ferry a week ago. I was really worried as I searched every corner of my room. I even went through the lobby and bathroom with a fine-tooth comb but it had vanished into thin air.

I scanned my memory, wondering when I had last worn it. Did I wear it to the shops on one of my errands? Had Jean's fall made me forget the last time I had it on? Maybe, I thought, it was in the kitchen, hanging on the coat hooks, but it wasn't. I tried all the kitchen cupboards which I knew was stupid because there was no way I would leave my precious coat in the steamy kitchen but I was clutching at straws. Because of my agitation, I didn't hear Miss Hood enter the kitchen. Although it was officially her time off, since Jean's accident, she had forgone her days off. She stood quietly behind me until I turned and I almost passed out from fright at the sight of her silent figure. I gasped.

She looked at me. 'Have you lost something?'

Although I'd felt sympathy for her on occasions, ever since Jean's accident, her manner had been back to what it had been during my first few weeks in the house. It was as if she knew how much I relied on Jean for my support and, now that my ally and friend was no longer here, I was totally alone and at her mercy again.

I decided to stick up for myself as Jean had suggested to me away back in the beginning. 'I've lost my coat, Miss Hood. I can't find it anywhere.'

She lifted her eyebrows in surprise. 'You've lost your trench coat?'

'No, it's not my trench coat – it's my good coat.'

She shrugged her thin shoulders. 'I've never seen you wearing a good coat.' She emphasised the word 'good'. 'Forgive me for saying this but you've always worn that old trench coat. What good coat is this? Something you've bought for yourself?' By now the eyebrows had almost disappeared into her hairline.

I hated to tell a lie but I nodded.

'Well then,' she said, 'describe it to me and I'll help you look for it.'

Much against my will, I said, 'It's a bonny russet-coloured coat with fur trimmings.' I was beside myself with misery, having to stand here explaining everything but maybe she was just trying to be kind with her offer of help.

She cast her eyes around the kitchen. 'Your coat sounds really grand and expensive. What a lucky girl you are to own such a coat. Now I've always wanted something like that but I couldn't afford it.'

'Pigs might fly,' I thought, remembering Jean telling me Miss Hood was feathering her own nest whilst living here.

She smiled but as usual, the smile failed to reach her eyes.

I made a decision. 'It's all right, Miss Hood, don't bother looking for it. Maybe I've left it at my Granny's house. I'm sure that's where it'll be.' Yet I knew with certainty that it wasn't there but it also wasn't here. The mystery was where was it?

She clasped her hands. 'Are you sure? It won't be a bother to me to help you in your search but let me know when you find it, won't you? It will be interesting to see the odd spot in which you left it.'

On that note, she turned quietly and left the

kitchen while I returned to my room to ponder over the missing coat.

Back home, Granny was as confused as I was. 'I don't think Hattie has anything to do with this, Ann,' she said but she didn't sound too sure.

'No, Granny, I remember putting it my wardrobe. I do it every week. I know I haven't worn it for a wee while because it's been quite mild weather and it's been over a week since I last saw it.'

She had another theory. 'I don't suppose the new cook has pinched it?'

I doubted it. Although she wasn't like Jean, I got on all right with her. I hadn't worn my coat in her company and she didn't live in the house. Like Jean, she came in every day to work and I doubted if she knew the layout of the house. Another thing I was sure of was that she didn't know where my room was.

14

Maddie had started her nursing training and she was full of enthusiasm when I met her on her day off.

'I really enjoy the work, Ann, even although I only get one day off in the month and start at seven in the morning and work right through until early evening.' She rolled her eyes and groaned. 'Getting up at six o'clock in the morning is terrible, especially for a sleepyhead like me. The other morning I gave one old man the bedpan straight from the steriliser and it burned his backside.'

I looked shocked but she laughed. 'Oh, I didn't really burn him – I just gave him a hot bottom.' She mimicked his voice. '"Ye've burned my erse, you silly wee bugger!"'

We both chuckled at this bit of hospital humour. I was also amused by Maddie's interpretation of a long day. I thought it sounded quite normal and I worked hours like that day in and day out. Still there was no stopping her when she was in a chatty mood.

'The patients sometimes bring in their own food. Mostly eggs. The other morning I put one on to boil for a patient and I forgot all about it. It was so hard-boiled that he couldn't eat it with a spoon. "What am I supposed to do with this, nurse? Eat it or play a game of ruddy tennis with it?"'

'What did you say?'

'I said I had got his egg mixed up with someone else's but he shouted out, "No you've not – this egg's still got my bloody name on it!"' She laughed again. 'We have to write the patient's name on their egg before we cook it, just to make sure they get the egg that was brought in for them. I had to end up slicing his egg and putting it on his toast and even then he moaned all through breakfast time.'

'Still, as long as you like the job, Maddie, that's the main thing.' Even as I said this, my mind was back at the Ferry. Life there was growing more unhappy every day and I couldn't see a way out of this terrible situation with Miss Hood. Since

Jean's accident, she had picked on me every day and there was no pleasing her.

Maddie was chatting on about having to scrape the fluff from the legs of the beds in the ward – all forty of them – and how sore her poor knees were.

'We also get semolina for dinner every day. It's either thin and watery or thick and lumpy and the nurses have christened it 365 because it's on the menu every day in the year.' Suddenly she stopped and looked me straight in the eye. 'Ann, will you do me a great favour?'

I was taken aback by this intensity and also a little bit unnerved. She wasn't in the habit of asking anything from me. In fact, it was always me who was beholden to her and her family. 'If I can, Maddie.'

'There's this poor man in the ward who never has a visitor. His family live miles and miles away on a hill farm near Trinafour, wherever that is.' She stopped and gave me another searching look. 'Will you visit him? Just out of the goodness of your heart and it'll be your good deed for the week.'

I was taken aback. 'I can't possibly visit a total stranger, Maddie. What would I say to him? And have you thought that he might not want any visitors?'

She waved these worries away. 'Of course he'll enjoy a visit from you. He works in the library in Albert Square and I've told him how much you like books and he's potty about books as well so you'll get on like a house on fire.'

I shook my head. 'No, Maddie, I can't do it.'

She put on her pleading face. 'Do it for me, Ann. His name is Gregor Borland and he's quite old so you won't have to worry about any romantic intentions.'

Oh thank you very much, Maddie, I thought. 'All right, I'll come but just for the one visit and no more.'

The following Sunday saw me standing in a queue by the side door of the Royal Infirmary. As the long queue moved slowly forwards, I was kicking myself for agreeing to come but Maddie was so persuasive. Also I felt I owed her a favour or four. As I walked along the long corridors and up endless stairs, I wished I was wearing my cashmere coat but it was still missing.

How Hattie had crowed when she heard the story. 'Well, if you had exchanged it with me, it would still be here.'

Still, she had given me one of her cast-offs that she said she'd grown tired of and she told me I was welcome to it. It was an unflattering shade of grey and I felt it didn't suit me but beggars couldn't be choosers.

The smell of floor polish and antiseptic hung in the air of this large building and, once again, I was reminded that my mother had died within these walls. I tried hard to shake off these sad thoughts but I was feeling apprehensive when I reached Maddie's ward. A nurse sat at a small table at the entrance. When I mentioned the man's name, she pointed in the direction of a long row of identical beds that lined the wall. As she turned her head, I noticed that her stiffly starched cap crackled slightly with the movement.

The patient in the first bed was decrepit looking, with a toothless smile and a bald head. 'Mr Borland?' I asked, cursing Maddie for inflicting this on me.

The old man smiled again, showing a row of pink gums. 'No, lass, you've got the wrong man. Try up the ward a bit.'

I suddenly spotted Maddie trying to attract my attention which wasn't an easy feat because she was keeping an eye out for the ward sister. She pointed quickly to a bed before disappearing around a folded screen.

A fresh-faced man was in the bed, sitting upright with his hands on the smooth, wrinkle-free bedcover. He gave me a lovely smile.

'Mr Borland?'

'Call me Greg,' he said, his face screwing up in a large grin. He wore a pair of vivid blue pyjamas and he had the greenest eyes I had ever seen. He had been lying against the pillows and his hair stood up in a thick brown thatch. 'So you are Ann, the girl sent by the fair nurse Pringle?'

I nodded. 'What are you in here for?' I suddenly blushed at my faux pas – maybe it was something unmentionable.

He noticed my distress and laughed. 'Oh, it's nothing infectious. It's my leg. I fell off a horse when I was a lad and I've got this slightly gammy leg and I'm left with a limp. Now and again I get pain in it and I've to spend a couple of days in hospital.'

I was alarmed by his mention of a horse. The image of one of the huge Clydesdale horses appeared in my mind. These strongly built horses were regularly to be seen on the streets of Dundee, pulling carts piled high with bales of jute. They made numerous trips between the mills and the warehouses every day. In fact, Henry, the coalman's horse we had for our flitting, was one of this grand breed of horses.

As if reading my mind, he grinned. 'It was just a pony but I fell off and broke my leg. Sadly it didn't mend properly.'

Another picture flashed into my mind. I thought about Jean and her broken leg. She was recovering slowly and I promised myself I would go and see her some night after my chores were finished.

Greg mentioned his job in the library and I thought how lovely it would be to have such a great job. I said so.

His face lit up. 'I really enjoy it very much and the customers are all friendly. One or two of the staff are a bit snooty and stand-offish but, on the whole, they are very helpful – especially to a country lad like myself.'

I wondered if the library had the equivalent of Miss Hood but decided she was definitely a one-off person. Surely there couldn't be another like her.

We talked about books and more books and we were both surprised when the bell sounded the end of visiting time. I couldn't believe how quickly the time had flown in and I really enjoyed his company As I was leaving, he said, 'I'll be out of here this week. Can we meet up next Sunday afternoon?' I nodded and he smiled. 'Right then, I'll pick you up at your house. Nurse Pringle gave me your address.'

Oh, she did, did she? I thought. Clever Nurse Pringle. But I wasn't annoyed because he was such good company. I mentally thanked her and then realised it had been a day for mental thoughts and images.

I passed her on my way out and she looked at me with a satisfied gleam in her eyes. I couldn't resist it and I murmured in passing, 'Greg isn't old, Maddie. He isn't thirty yet.' But she just winked and scurried past the stern gaze of the ward sister.

I went back to work, full of well-being after my meeting with Greg. For some reason, he filled my thoughts all that week and I could hardly wait for the following Sunday to arrive.

Miss Hood appeared to be even stranger than normal but I put her terrible mood down to the presence of the new cook. Unlike Jean, she wasn't averse to taking a few days off work without warning. On these days, all the cooking fell on the housekeeper's shoulders and I got the brunt of her vile temper. I did offer to help out with the cooking but was brushed off rudely.

Sunday arrived in a blaze of crisply cold but dazzling sunshine. I stood at the end of the close that afternoon, waiting for Greg to arrive. I had almost called the whole thing off because of Lily. I didn't see a lot of her and I always felt my time off should be spent with her but Rosie had stepped in. 'Just you go away and have a nice afternoon with your young man and I'll look after Lily.'

Dad gave her such a grateful look that I was

beginning to harbour hopes about them. I had noticed that Rosie didn't seem to attend the same number of Salvation Army meetings as she used to. I thought this was a great pity and hoped it hadn't been Dad's atheist views that were the reason for this. But maybe Rosie had her own reasons for this change in her Sundays.

As I stood waiting, I wondered where we would go. Sunday was such a quiet day so I thought we would maybe go for a walk. Then suddenly the quiet air was shattered by a metallic, roaring sound. Chugging up the Hilltown, in a cloud of dense grey smoke, was a motorbike and I was flabbergasted to see Greg was the driver.

I opened my mouth to speak but was immediately drowned out by the noisy revving sounds. He switched the bike off and called out. 'Hop on, Ann. We'll go for a spin.'

I hesitated for a moment then hopped on. We made our way noisily up the Hilltown, our progress witnessed by scores of open-mouthed pedestrians.

'Where are we going?' I shouted in his ear.

'A wee spin in the country. I bought this bike from a pal and you're the first pillion passenger on it.'

I felt honoured and snuggled up against his back. It felt comforting.

We got as far as Tullybaccart Brae when the metallic noise became more rasping. To make matters worse, this grating sound was accompanied by thick black smoke that belched from the exhaust. We ground to a halt.

Greg tinkered around with the bike's innards

before uttering in disgust, 'I think we'll have to leave it here. I'll get the man who sold it to me to come and fix it this week. He's a mechanic.' He took my arm. 'There should be a bus coming this way soon so we'll get back to Dundee.'

The words were no sooner out of his mouth when a single-decker bus trundled into view.

'You can't leave the bike on the road, Greg,' I said.

He thrust a half crown into my hand. 'Quick, get two tickets while I push the bike into that garden over there.' He pointed to a small cottage that was set back from the road. I saw Greg approach an old woman who nodded her head at the intrusion of a bike at the edge of her garden.

It was still a golden day with bright sunshine as the bus made its way through the leafy roads towards the city. Greg told me about himself. His parents lived in the country and his father was a shepherd on a small hill farm near Trinafour. He said it was about twelve miles from Pitlochry.

'I stay in lodgings with an old woman in her house in Victoria Road. As a landlady she's an old dragon but her cooking is wonderful and my stomach won the toss in my search for somewhere to stay.'

As I sat beside him, I felt I had known him forever and I was so happy I could have burst with wonderful emotion. I told him all about Lily and our family circumstances and he looked sad on hearing about Mum's death.

This happy feeling lasted until Wednesday morning. I was singing softly as I tackled my chores at the Ferry. The one blot on my horizon

361

was Miss Hood. Her manner had been becoming even stranger but, on this particular morning, it was bizarre. I had never seen her like this before. She was standing at the pantry window which overlooked the back garden. She was watching Mr Potter but there was a terrible gloating expression on her thin face. As far as I could see, there was no reason for her strange demeanour because the gardener was merely burning a huge pile of leaves and garden debris. Miss Hood rubbed her wrinkled hands together as if in glee before hurrying away with a queer little chuckle.

Mrs Barrie was sitting in her chair by the window. She looked so frail that I almost put my arms around her. She smiled brightly when I entered. 'It's so lovely to hear you sing, Ann. What a delight it is to have your young face around the house.'

I moved over to make the bed.

'Will you open the window and let in some of this lovely autumn air?' she said.

When I did as she'd asked, a thick belch of smoke, not unlike the cloud from Greg's bike, wafted in. Mrs Barrie coughed in the acrid atmosphere. 'Where is that smoke coming from?'

Voices from the front of the house also wafted up. They sounded annoyed. Outside, a young couple with a baby in pram had walked into the smoky cloud as the stiff breeze carried it towards the sea. It was quite thick and grey with small fragments of material mixed through it.

Mrs Barrie coughed again. 'What on earth is Mr Potter burning, Ann?' Then, as I closed the window again, she said, 'Please go down and tell him to put out this bonfire.'

I ran into the garden but I couldn't see the gardener at first. So thick was the smoke. Then I saw him, making his way through the acrid stench of burning fog. I made my way towards his ghostly figure. I then noticed Miss Hood had returned to the pantry window and she had such a strange look on her face, it made a shiver run down my spine. I really wished Jean was back in her kitchen but she was still in her 'stookie plaster' as she called her plaster cast.

'Mr Potter,' I called out but there was no answer. I could hear the loud complaints from another couple of irate walkers who were moaning about the choking smog. The breeze had now lifted this column of smoke over the roof of the house where it swept over the passing pedestrians.

I shouted again, 'Mr Potter, Mrs Barrie says can you please put your bonfire out? It's causing too much smoke.'

He came into view like some spirit arising from the mists of eternity. His watery eyes surveyed me for a brief moment. 'I'm just doing my job, missus. Yon housekeeper tells me to burn this rubbish and that's what I'm doing.'

The smoke was burning the back of my throat and I put my hand over my mouth. 'Well, Mrs Barrie wants it put out, Mr Potter – please.'

He mumbled something under his breath but he did place a thick blanket over the flames and then he beat this with a huge spade. This made the smoke worse but it subsided after a few moments.

As he strolled away, he muttered loudly, 'That's the worst of working in a house full of women –

they dinnae ken what they want.'

I decided to stay for a few minutes just to make sure the fire was indeed out. Mr Potter had removed the blanket and I beat the smouldering pile with the spade. I was puzzled. This fire seemed to be too large for a mere pile of leaves and twigs and garden rubbish. With the edge of the spade I moved the smoking twigs to one side. Under the embers was a thick, paper-wrapped parcel. With curiosity getting the better of me, I poked at the partially charred paper which burst open. Inside was a garment which was all black and sooty but, when I prodded it with the spade, a piece of fur flew into the air along with a spiral of smoke. I suddenly recognised it but, the last time I had seen it, it hadn't been black and charred but a lovely russet colour. Then I saw Miss Hood's gaze. She smirked at me through the window then laughed out loud.

Without stopping to think, I picked the parcel up with the spade. Stamping on it to make sure there were no more pockets of fire within its folds. Then I went inside. She was still in the pantry when I marched in and confronted her. The anger inside me was now on the brink of a gigantic eruption. I was furious but I was a bit surprised when I heard myself speak for my voice, although quiet, was controlled. 'I found my coat, Miss Hood.'

She clapped her hands together as if applauding my words. 'Well, good for you, madam. I thought it might disappear forever but that idiot Potter can't be trusted to do anything properly.'

I was shocked. 'Was Mr Potter in on this?' I

couldn't believe it.

She chuckled. It was a deep, fearsome sound. 'Him, him,' she snorted. 'That fool can't even burn a pile of leaves. Now it looks like he can't burn "my lovely coat".' Her voice changed as she tried to mimic my voice. 'I told him to use paraffin but not him. The stupid old fool should have been sacked years ago.'

Looking back years later, I realised it was her attempt at mimicry that was the final straw – that and her horrible gloating expression. I could no longer control my anger and I said, 'I think you are the most loathsome person I have ever met.'

She opened her mouth in surprise but I silenced any statement from her. 'Not only are you loathsome but you're miserable as well. You even resented me having breakfast on my first morning and you've taken great delight in making me suffer at every turn. If it hadn't been for Mrs Barrie's and Jean's kindness to me then this would have been the worst job ever.'

Her eyes glittered with a strange malevolent look. Her voice was now a barely concealed snarl. 'I never wanted you in this house, reading aloud for Eva and trying to worm your way into her affections but you won't succeed, madam – not if I can help it.'

'You horrible old woman,' I shouted, annoyed that my composure had vanished. But I wasn't going to let her get away with another word even if it meant my job was over. She could sack me later but not before a few home truths were aimed in her direction. 'You even kept my wages from me, you rotten old besom. You, who has never had any poverty in your life – not like my poor granny and little sister.'

She rubbed her hands together and smirked. To say she was acting strangely was an understatement. In fact, I thought she was going off her head.

'My granny is a hundred times better a woman than you'll ever be. She is always kind, even to total strangers – makes them tea and gives them a bite to eat even if it means going without herself while you're a wicked, selfish woman. I did everything you asked me to do. Every bit of work without a grumble but did it please you? No, it didn't.'

'I've always considered you to be a common work-shy piece of trash,' she shouted.

'Oh, you did, did you? And what about yourself? What work did you ever do around here? Tell me, Miss Hood, just in case I missed it.'

By now, my anger was evaporating and I walked towards the hall but not before delivering my parting shot. 'No, the only work you ever did was to knock me off the stairs and jump out of hidey-holes and accuse me of pinching Mrs Barrie's books when I had permission to read them. But do you know the worst thing you've done? No? Well, I'll tell you. It was burning my coat and the sad thing is I don't know why you did it. Surely you didn't begrudge me a nice coat. Mrs Barrie must have been good to you over all these years.'

Suddenly and without warning, she sprang at me. 'Begrudge you a coat. If I had my way you would no longer be here. I didn't shove you hard enough on the stairs. I see that now but I'll not fail the next time. No, indeed.'

She walked over to the hall table and picked up one of the heavy candlesticks. She was speaking to herself while inspecting it. I thought she was looking to see if I had dusted it properly but she carried it over to where I was standing with my back to the stairs. As she raised it, I was suddenly aware how deranged she was. It was as if a mist was lifted from my eyes and all her strange habits fell into place. I couldn't believe my eyes as she pranced towards me and I was transfixed to the spot. Her thin colourless mouth was crooning a tuneless melody. I didn't feel afraid but I was perplexed. Surely she didn't intend to hit me with the candlestick – not in broad daylight and in Mrs Barrie's front hall?

'Miss Hood, give me that candlestick.' I held out my hand and looked her straight in the eye. I was now convinced she was ill and I wished I hadn't tackled her – even though she deserved it. She was still an old woman and I was brought up always to respect my elders.

Without warning she brought it down with a loud crash. It missed my head by half an inch and smashed into the banister, splintering the wood with its force. She raised it again. 'I won't miss this time,' she crooned.

'Put it down,' a firm voice called from over my shoulder. 'Put it down, Lottie.' It was Mrs Barrie.

The housekeeper's eyes cleared slightly. 'I'm just chastising this little madam. She can't do her work so she deserves a beating.' She cradled the candlestick in her hand.

I heard the clock chime twelve and I realised in

dismay that this confrontation had lasted a good half hour. I was also sorry that my raised voice must have disturbed Mrs Barrie. She looked like a frail, pale-skinned porcelain doll as she stood at the top of the stairs, her blue-veined hands clutching the wooden banister. I rushed upwards to help her descend the stairs but Miss Hood barred my way, raising the candlestick as if to strike again.

Mrs Barrie shouted at her and I was taken aback by the anger in her normally quiet voice. 'I've told you to put that down, Lottie. Come up to my room.'

'It wasn't me who started this, Eva. It was this miserable little twerp, accusing me of stealing and burning a nonexistent coat – the little liar. Now, if she had mentioned the coat you gave her, then I wouldn't have minded but she had to sneak about like a thief in the night.' Miss Hood was defiant. She was so sure Mrs Barrie would believe her and, at that moment, I was of the same opinion.

Miss Hood was so beside herself with anger and bitterness that she hadn't noticed her mistake. With one breath, she called the coat nonexistent and, with the next breath, she admitted its existence.

Mrs Barrie held out her hand and took the candlestick. She placed it on the stairs. 'Come up to my room, Lottie.' She made her way back up the stairs with the now sullen housekeeper in tow. When she reached the top landing, Mrs Barrie stopped and looked down at me. 'It's all right, Ann, don't worry – I overheard everything.'

I tried to explain but she held up her hand and

368

went into her room. I thought about finishing my chores but the voices from the bedroom kept me glued to the staircase. I thought the bedroom door must be open because Mrs Barrie's voice carried right down into the hall and I heard her say, 'I gave you a good position here, Lottie. You had the best of everything and a good salary but that wasn't enough, was it? You've driven a lot of good staff away from this house over the years – don't think I haven't noticed. Mrs Peters is still here because she isn't afraid of you and now it's young Ann's turn. Just because she isn't afraid of you either, you have made her life here so miserable. She's a motherless girl with a young sister to support. How could you do this, Lottie?'

Lottie's answer was inaudible. I was also quite surprised by Mrs Barrie's assumption that I was unafraid of the housekeeper because, on the contrary, up until today when I had the courage to face her, I was constantly afraid of her.

Suddenly Miss Hood gave a piercing scream and I jumped up in alarm. Then I heard Mrs Barrie shout at her, 'For heaven's sake, go to your room and calm down.'

I heard a door slam then total silence. I don't know how long I sat on the stairs. I was thinking how happy I had been a few short hours ago. There was no sign of the cook and it looked like she was having another impromptu day off. I wondered about making some lunch for us all but I didn't want to incur the housekeeper's wrath should she appear downstairs and see I had taken over her domain.

It was Mrs Barrie's bell that broke the silence in

the house. Then it rang again but this time it seemed more strident but maybe I was imagining it. I waited for Miss Hood to come out of her room because she never let a summons from her mistress to go unheeded but the bell rang again. Its sharp peals drifted down the stairs, shattering the tomb-like silence. I ran quickly up stairs and knocked loudly on Miss Hood's door.

'Miss Hood, Miss Hood, are you in there? Mrs Barrie is ringing her bell.' I knocked again but it was as if the house was deserted except for the bell.

Emboldened by worry, I turned the doorknob, something I would never have done before. 'Miss Hood,' I called.

I thought the room was empty because it was in total darkness. The thick curtains were pulled across the window, giving the room a kaleidoscope of dark shadows. I marched over and yanked the curtains apart. Miss Hood was sitting on her bed, still crooning strangely. She had a small pair of scissors in her hand and she was cutting something up into tiny fragments.

I went over and shook her. 'Miss Hood, Mrs Barrie is ringing her bell – she wants you.'

The housekeeper looked at me but went on cutting the small square. I recognised the photograph of the small coloured child. I started to speak again but she stopped me. The crooning was now replaced by a firm tone. 'I no longer work here so go and answer the bell yourself. That's what you wanted, wasn't it?'

'Oh, no, Miss Hood, I just wanted to be happy in my job but maybe we'll get on better after this.'

I hoped so.

The bell rang again but she ignored it, turning her attention once more to the shredded photograph. In a panic, I ran to Mrs Barrie's room and saw to my horror that she was lying on the floor. For one terrible minute I thought the housekeeper had hit her but she whispered, 'Get the doctor, Ann. I've got these awful pains again.'

I ran back to Miss Hood. 'Quickly, send for the doctor. It's Mrs Barrie and I think it's her heart.'

This made her leap to her feet and she loped out of the room. She tried to lift Mrs Barrie into a chair but the old lady groaned weakly. 'Get the doctor, Lottie. It's my heart trouble again.'

Lottie smiled. 'Of course it's not your heart trouble, Eva. It'll just be a touch of indigestion. Now let's get you into a chair.'

I ran over. 'Leave her alone. Tell me the doctor's number – quickly.'

Lottie started her crooning again and I watched as the colour drained from Mrs Barrie's face. I went over to the bureau to look for the number. I knew his name and where he lived but as to his telephone number ... well, that was a mystery.

I silently cursed Miss Hood for keeping all these things a secret. Everything of importance in this house was now locked away in her addled brain. I tried hard not to panic, striving to think what Granny would do in this situation. The answer was Mrs Barrie. I knelt down beside her. 'Can you hear me, Mrs Barrie? Where do you keep the doctor's number?'

Her eyes fluttered open and she weakly pointed in the direction of the bedside cabinet. Meanwhile, Miss Hood sat in a chair and gazed into space. I ignored her as I rummaged in the drawer, giving a silent prayer when I found the slim book. I ran down the stairs two at a time and reached the telephone in the hall. Thankfully, I had used it a couple of times when Jean had needed some supplies from the shops.

I got the doctor's wife. 'It's Mrs Barrie from Whitegate Lodge,' I cried, 'I think it's her heart.'

The woman sounded shocked and I heard her call her husband who took the phone from her. 'Is that you, Miss Hood?'

'No, it's Ann Neill, the housemaid – Miss Hood's not well either. Please come quickly.'

He was inside the house within five minutes. I led him to the bedroom and helped him lift Mrs Barrie on to the bed. She looked so white that I thought she was dead but the doctor felt a slight pulse.

Miss Hood sat in her chair, ignoring us both. Apart from one queer glance in her direction, the doctor gave all his attention to the desperately ill woman. Thankfully he didn't ask questions as he ministered to his patient but I felt so guilty. If I hadn't tackled Miss Hood, then this wouldn't have happened.

The doctor left the room and made a sign for me to follow. 'I'm going to put Mrs Barrie into hospital. I suspect a massive heart attack and she will need all the specialist care of a hospital.' He didn't mention the housekeeper and I was at a loss to explain her condition.

The doctor was on the telephone when Mrs Barrie called out. I went over and held her hand.

'What is it?' I asked gently.

She gazed at me with her lovely, tired-looking eyes and whispered, 'Where is the doctor, Ann?'

I went into the hall to call him and he hurried up to her room. 'I'm going to put you in hospital, Mrs Barrie,' he explained but she shook her head.

'No, it's better I stay here.'

He tried to talk her out of this but her mind was made up. She called me over again. 'Go and make us all a cup of tea, Ann – I want to talk to the doctor and Lottie.'

I held her hand for a minute then left her. As I pottered around the deserted kitchen, placing things on the tea tray, I felt tears sting my eyes. 'Please, please God,' I prayed, 'please let Mrs Barrie get well again.'

Sadly my prayers weren't answered and, as I was taking the tea tray into the bedroom, the solemn-faced doctor was placing the sheet over her head.

'No, no,' I cried out, 'not Mrs Barrie.'

He was sympathetic. 'This could have happened at any time because her heart was weak and has been for years.'

'But it was my fault, doctor,' I cried out in anguish.

'No, it wasn't anyone's fault. Mrs Barrie told me the whole story and, believe me, this is the way she always wanted to die – quickly.' He picked up his bag, went over to Miss Hood and put a comforting arm around her shoulder.

Later, Mr Pringle arrived in his car, followed soon after by the undertaker. He was a small officious man with a dark, sombre suit and a deferential manner – a bit like Uriah Heep, I thought.

He was soon closeted with Maddie's dad in Mrs Barrie's bedroom.

I sat in the kitchen, ill with worry. I hoped Miss Hood was in her own room but, now she was under the care of the doctor, I knew she was in good hands.

The undertaker, Mr Chapman, crept quietly about the house. Later on I came face to face with him on the stairs and he blinked nervously at me, his two hands clasped under his nose. He stepped smartly to one side to let me pass, his back almost brushing the wallpaper. This action was unnecessary since the staircase was wide enough to accommodate a bus.

The rest of the day passed in a blur. I remember Mr Potter coming back into the house, carefully wiping his feet before going into the lounge. He was wearing a pair of clean shoes but I thought he must have forgotten he wasn't wearing his usual mud-caked boots, hence the wiping of his feet. It's strange, I thought, how grief affects people. Here I was, broken-hearted over Mrs Barrie's death, and I was noticing stupid things like Mr Potter's shoes and Mr Chapman's hands. It was the same after Mum's death when I recalled the salty tears.

Mr Potter hadn't closed the lounge door properly. I could hear the low murmured voices of the two men. Mr Pringle was questioning the gardener and I was dismayed to hear the words 'fire' and 'burning parcel'. Although it was too late, I now realised I should have kept my mouth shut. It was ironic that after being as quiet as a mouse for most of my life, I should now emerge from my shell of timidity and cause all this needless grief. A few minutes later, Mr Pringle emerged from the lounge with Mr Potter and they both went in search of the undertaker. They both then stood at the door and said their goodbyes to Mr Pringle.

Maddie's dad then turned to me, his face full of sympathy. 'You had better pack your belongings, Ann,' he said sadly.

I did as I was told, gazing in sadness at my lovely room in the tower. How happy I had been here, even with the animosity of Miss Hood. I was aware Mr Pringle was waiting in the hall so I knew I couldn't linger. When I emerged from the back stairs, he was ready to leave. He looked so careworn and I realised that money didn't protect one from sorrow.

'I'll take you home, Ann. There's nothing left to do here. Eva ... Mrs Barrie has been taken to the funeral home so I have to lock up the house.'

I was taken aback. There was no mention of the housekeeper. 'What about Miss Hood? I'm really worried about her.'

He put on his gloves. 'Miss Hood is fine, Ann. She has also left and is in good hands. Before we leave the Ferry we must go and see Mrs Peters as she won't know about Mrs Barrie's death.'

Oh, Jean! I had forgotten about her in my own grief. Poor Jean. Like me, she would be broken-hearted but it was best that Mr Pringle should be the one to break the bad news. He was a sympathetic man but he wouldn't break down in tears. I felt my own tears weren't very far away but I wanted to keep some dignity in front of Maddie's father.

Before entering the car, I looked long and hard at Whitegate Lodge, making sure all its details were in my mind's eye. I had a terrible feeling that I would never see it again. And I was right – I never went back.

15

Mrs Barrie's funeral was a very sad occasion. This sadness lay in my heart like a heavy weight. The little church in the Ferry was packed with mourners and I felt the dark cloud of collective grief hang in the air. It was so tangible, I felt I could grasp it in my hand.

Some people sat with their heads bowed and others were talking in soft whispers. It was a struggle not to cry and I was grateful that Dad and Grandad had come with me – dear Grandad who sat so solemnly in his best but slightly threadbare jacket. Their heads were both bare.

Greg had wanted to come but, at the last moment, he couldn't get away. However, I was glad in a perverse sort of way because I wanted to say farewell to Mrs Barrie on my own and not be distracted by his presence.

Jean arrived with her husband and she hobbled over to where we were sitting. We made room for them in the pew and Jean sighed deeply as she sat down. We exchanged a quick look and she squeezed my arm but we didn't speak. I felt, if I opened my mouth, a torrent of tears would erupt and I wouldn't be able to stop them.

Maddie sat with her parents in the front pew, along with some distant cousins of Mrs Barrie. This tight knot of elderly ladies were all dressed from head to toe in black but they had reached the age when death didn't seem to be the tragedy that was felt by someone younger.

Mrs Barrie had been such a lovely popular woman and most of the community were present in the church – shopkeepers, business folk and neighbours alike. However there was one person missing and this puzzled me. Where was Miss Hood? My eyes roamed around the church but I couldn't see her. Perhaps, I thought, she was sitting behind one of the stone pillars.

The minister appeared and I forgot about Miss Hood as I let the man's solemn words wash over me – words that were accompanied by the heady scents from the myriad wreaths that sat on the coffin and spilled down on to the altar steps. The wreaths were made from autumn flowers – large-headed chrysanthemums in deep shades of yellow, bronze, red and russet, russet like my coat. I swallowed hard and pushed the dreadful memory out of my mind – at least for the moment.

Outside, in the charming little graveyard, a coolish autumn breeze swirled around our legs. As the coffin was laid in the ground, I could no longer hold back my tears and I felt their warmth as they streaked down my face. I had cried a lot since that terrible day but Granny had tried to make me understand that the problem had been Miss Hood's, not mine.

'She made your life a misery, Ann, and all you

did was finally stick up for yourself. You'll soon see that for yourself. Mrs Barrie was a wonderful woman and you'll always have your lovely memories of her. Just think of all the nice things she did for you and vice versa. After all, she did enjoy you reading her stories, didn't she?'

Granny was right. As I stood beside Jean, Dad and Grandad on the damp turf of the cemetery, I knew I would never be able to read a detective novel again without thinking of our wonderful times in the cosy morning room or on the sun-dappled grass in the garden.

I looked up and saw the Pringles moving towards the minister. Maddie came over. She looked cold and miserable and her hands were thrust deep into her coat pockets. Like Greg, Danny had also been unable to get away from work to come to the funeral and that possibly explained Maddie's miserable expression. That and the fact that she had been deeply attached to Mrs Barrie, her godmother.

Still, she cheered up a bit when she reached me and she tucked her arm through mine as we walked towards the gates.

'Maddie, do you know what's happened to Miss Hood?' I asked but she shook her head.

'I don't know, Ann. I did hear she wasn't well and is maybe in hospital but she isn't in the Royal Infirmary. Maybe she's in some private hospital.'

'You heard about what happened? The day Mrs Bathe died?'

She nodded miserably then said, 'I know Dad wants to speak to you, Ann, to explain every-thing, but what a terrible time you must have had at Whitegate Lodge.'

I thought she was on the verge of tears. I could feel the cold seeping through my shoes and I also tried hard not to burst into tears. 'It was fine until Jean broke her leg,' I said truthfully. 'At least it was bearable but, when Jean left, it got worse and worse and, of course, my coat didn't help. Miss Hood took such a spite at my having it. Poor Mrs Barrie...' Tears threatened to erupt again and I wiped my eyes with the sleeve of my grey coat – Hattie's coat.

I saw Jean's motherly figure coming towards us. She had overheard our conversation. 'Aye, if I hadn't broke this ruddy leg, then I wouldn't have let Miss Hood bully you, Ann, but you've got to understand that Mrs Barrie had a dicky heart and she could have dropped dead at any time. And all these bouts of flu didn't help but she always said she wanted to die quickly...'

I saw Jean was crying as well. I looked around for Dad and Grandad but they were with Maddie's father. Jean moved ahead but Maddie held me back. She obviously wanted to tell me something that she didn't want the mourners to overhear. 'Do you remember the photograph, Ann? The one of the small child?'

I nodded.

'Well I overheard my mother and Eva discuss Miss Hood a few weeks ago. It seems Miss Hood got involved with some actor when she worked in the theatre in London. She was a wardrobe mistress to Eva in those days. Well this actor came from the West Indies to play the part of Othello and to cut a long story short, she fell in love with

379

him and she had a child. She thought they would get married but instead he took the little boy and disappeared back to Jamaica. The child was only about two at the time and Eva did all she could to help.'

I was shocked. 'What a terrible thing to happen to her.' I tried to imagine how I would feel if someone went off with Lily. I would be devastated. 'Did she ever find her child?'

Maddie shook her head. 'No. Eva even hired a private investigator but they had vanished. The investigator traced them to Jamaica but, by then, they had left and gone off to America and the trail went cold after that.'

'She was cutting up the photograph on the day Mrs Barrie died. Why do you think she did that, Maddie?'

Maddie didn't have the answer. 'I'm just a student nurse in the men's surgical ward so I wouldn't know anything about mental health.'

Suddenly Jean was back at my side. 'Ann, I've been told by yon man over there that we have to be at his office in Commercial Street next Wednesday.' She pointed to a serious-looking elderly man who stood beside Mr Pringle, Dad and Grandad. 'He's a solicitor.'

'We've to go to a solicitor's office?' I was perplexed.

'Aye, next Wednesday at ten o'clock.'

Maddie said, 'Yes, that's one of my father's partners – Mr Chambers.'

I looked at Maddie but she shrugged. 'I don't know anything,' she said.

Back at the Overgate, Granny was as puzzled as

I was. Hattie, however, was agog with excitement. 'You must be getting a wee memento, Ann,' she chirped. 'Maybe it's another coat.'

I was suddenly very angry. 'Don't mention that again, Hattie. That coat was the cause of all this tragedy, I'm sure about that.'

Greg didn't share this view but he knew all about my terrible nightmares – night terrors of heavy candlesticks and a ravaged-looking Miss Hood.

It was the day after the funeral when he mentioned the visit to his parents' house. 'We can take Lily with us and go by bus. She will enjoy the change and maybe Rosie will have your handsome father all to herself for a couple of days.'

How perceptive he was. It was true Dad was looking a lot cheerier these days and, although he still had his pint of beer on a Saturday, he seemed to want to stay in the house with us – and Rosie, of course, who was a regular visitor to the Hilltown. Yes, I thought, things were definitely looking up in that direction. As it turned out, the weekend was just the tonic I needed.

The sun shone steadily and although the autumn air was crisp, the countryside was ablaze with multicoloured trees and fresh smokeless air. Lily was fascinated by the new scenery and she loved every minute of the visit, as I did.

Mr and Mrs Borland lived a few miles from Trinafour. The house, built of grey stone, was situated by the side of a grass-covered hill and right beside a clear running stream. It was enchanting, especially to my city eyes.

Mr Borland was a shepherd and, every morning, he set off early with his two dogs, Jassy and Jed. Lily went with him that first morning, just as far as the first sheep pen on the hill, but she arrived back in high spirits, her small face pink with pleasure and sunshine.

Later I helped Greg's mum make a gigantic high tea of bacon and eggs, home-made bread and scones and pancakes, all washed down with strong sweet tea. As I stood in the warm, homely kitchen, my memories of Miss Hood slowly receded in my mind. Afterwards we all sat around a big roaring fire, listening to the trees swaying in the wind and hearing stories of lost sheep and wild winters – the daily job of a shepherd in fact.

'You must call me Barbara or Babs and Dad's name is Dave,' said Greg's mum. It was obvious she was proud of her son because she never stopped singing his praises – much to his embarrassment.

'We were both so proud when he went away to the university in Glasgow,' she said.

Dave nodded and I thought Greg blushed slightly. 'Oh, stop it, Mum. Ann doesn't want to hear about me. Heavens, it'll be the family album soon.'

The words were no sooner out of his mouth than his mother scurried away into a wooden cupboard.

I hadn't known about the university and I was pleased to hear about his achievements. 'What did you study at Glasgow?' I asked.

He grinned in his lopsided manner. 'What else? English Literature.'

'Oh, how wonderful,' I gasped. Still, I wasn't

382

surprised because Maddie had said he was a bookworm.

Babs appeared from the depths of the cupboard with a small leather-bound book. It was full of small sepia-toned and black-and-white photos of the family, all taken over a period of about twenty years.

There was Greg as a child and as a schoolboy and a studio portrait taken after his graduation – a serious-looking young man with a scroll in his hand.

He laughed out loud. 'So now you know my case history, Miss Neill. Do you still want to know me?'

Lily clapped her hands. 'Yes, yes, Greg. I want to come back and see the lambs. Dave said I could.'

Babs gathered her up on to her lap and gave her a cuddle.

'Of course you must come back – anytime you both want to.' She smiled at me over Lily's head and I was filled with emotion at this cosy domestic scene. I couldn't help but wonder if it would have been the same for us had Mum lived. But she hadn't so there was no use in thinking about it.

Dave was speaking as he filled his pipe with tobacco from a well-worn pouch. 'I hope you don't mind, Ann, but Greg has told us about the awful situation at your work.'

Greg threw him a warning look but the man was just trying to be sympathetic. Suddenly the spectre of Miss Hood returned to my mind. Dave was still talking but I wasn't listening. Then the words Salvation Army stood out and I looked at him.

'Does the Salvation Army come here?' I said, quite mystified.

Greg laughed. 'Good Lord, no. It's just that my cousin is a major in the Salvation Army in Dundee. We both went to Glasgow University and he's now an accountant with a firm in Dundee. He loves the Army, just like Rosie.'

'Well, Rosie doesn't seem to attend so much these days.' I didn't mention that this could be Dad's doing. Suddenly a memory emerged from the deep recesses of my mind – a memory from a few years ago. The memory was of Balgay cemetery under rain-filled skies and the young Salvation Army major who so movingly performed the service. The one I thought had been press-ganged by Rosie.

'A Major Borland conducted my mum's service,' I said. 'Would that be your cousin?'

Greg nodded. 'Certainly looks like it. I met up with him after the service and I remember him saying it was heartbreaking – two children left motherless. Was that you and Lily? To think I could have met you then.' He smiled at me.

'What a small world, Ann,' said Babs. 'But no more talk of sad things. Get the board games out, Dave, and we'll take Lily on at Snakes and Ladders and Ludo.'

Lily's laughter was a joy to my ears as Greg and I sat quietly talking by the fire. Tomorrow it would be time to go home to Dundee but for now, it was pleasant to sit and dream in the semi-darkness that lay beyond the golden circle of the oil lamp.

Then on Wednesday, sharp at ten o'clock, I met Jean outside the solicitor's office. A brass plaque at the end of the close stated that Jackson, Chambers & Pringle was to be found on the first floor. We gingerly ascended the stone stairs with their fancy wrought-iron banisters and finally arrived at a door with a frosted glass panel which had the firm's name embellished on it in gold letters. This was where Maddie's father worked.

Inside, a well-groomed young woman arose from behind an imposing desk. A typist sat at another desk but she didn't look up when we entered. We were ushered into a small book-lined inner sanctum, the shelves of which were overflowing with thick binders and even thicker law books. A man sat in the chair by the window. To our surprise, it was Mr Potter. Jean still had her plaster on and she hobbled over to him. He turned his watery eyes to us and muttered, 'A bad business this, missus. Aye a right bad business.'

I stood stock-still, shock washing over me. But he muttered again, 'I'm not meaning you, lass. No, it wasn't your fault. It was that evil besom of a housekeeper.'

Before I could answer, a middle-aged man, with a wrinkled scraggy-looking neck and a thin emaciated body that seemed to be dwarfed by his sober dark suit, entered and introduced himself. 'I'm Mr Jackson, solicitor for the late Mrs Barrie's estate.'

We followed him into his office, a larger room with a window overlooking the street. It was a haven of silence except for the muffled voices rising up from the street.

Mr Jackson said, 'We have handled Mrs Barrie's affairs ever since her arrival at Broughty Ferry – not so much me as my late father. He knew Mrs Barrie well and he conducted most of her business affairs but now the estate is in my hands.' As if running out of words, he sat down and began to polish his spectacles. 'Please sit down, ladies and Mr Potter.'

He coughed and I tried hard not to smile because it sounded just as I had always imagined a solicitor would cough – discreetly and delicately. He began to read from a document which he held in his surprisingly muscular hands. His voice was formal, almost as if he were reading some official document. 'It is my duty to inform you that, under the terms of the last will and testament of the late Eva Caroline Barrie, the sum of one year's wages is to be paid to Mr Archibald Potter, Mrs Jean Peters and Miss Ann Neill.'

Jean gasped while I felt faint. 'That was very good of Mrs Barrie to think of us,' she said, her eyes bright with unshed tears.

We wondered if we should rise but the solicitor waggled his hand. 'There is more,' he said in his stuffy formal tone. 'To Mr Archibald Potter I leave the sum of six hundred pounds and all the garden tools and any plants he wishes to take in full appreciation of all his hard work and dedication. To Mrs Jean Peters I leave the sum of six hundred pounds plus the choice of anything from the house, also in appreciation of her hard work and dedication.'

I felt so pleased for them. This windfall would

be such a blessing for them. Then, to my utter surprise, he looked at me. 'To Miss Ann Neill in loving appreciation of all her kindness in bringing alive my favourite reading material, I leave the sum of six hundred pounds plus all the books in the house – the leather-bound books and the novels – in the fond hope that she will remember an old lady.'

For a moment, I thought I was going to burst into tears and I tried hard to remain composed.

Jean, however, was unable to contain herself. She wiped her brow with large handkerchief. 'Mr Jackson, may I say that Mrs Barrie was the nicest woman I've ever met and it was a pleasure to work for her. Bless her,' said Jean while I nodded dumbly. 'She was always kind to Ann and me and we'll never forget her.'

There was no way I would ever forget her and, now she had left me this wonderful legacy, never, as long as I lived, would I forget her.

As usual, Mr Potter was as calm as ever. 'Aye, she was a real nice woman, was the missus. It was a pleasure to do her garden. She never interfered – not like some I could mention,' he said darkly.

His words brought back the memory of Miss Hood. 'Mr Jackson, is Miss Hood in a hospital?' I asked.

He gave me a questioning look over the top of his spectacles. 'Mr Pringle wants to see you all after this meeting.'

We were then ushered from his office to another identical one which also faced the street. This was Maddie's dad's domain. He made us all welcome and ordered tea to be brought in.

When we were sitting with our cups and saucers, I said, 'Mr Pringle, is Miss Hood in the Royal Infirmary?'

'No, she isn't,' he said.

I cheered up. 'Oh, I'm so glad she's better. I've been really worried about her since that day at the Ferry. Is she living in her cottage in Monifieth? Or at Whitegate Lodge?'

Jean and Mr Potter looked as mystified as I was.

Mr Pringle looked at me sadly. 'Miss Hood was admitted to a mental asylum on the night of Mrs Barrie's death. She's in Westlea and has been there ever since. I doubt if she'll ever get out again.'

This statement hit me like a sledgehammer. 'Oh, surely she'll get home sometime?' Then I thought, what did I know about mental illness? Surely it was hard not to have any hope of release ever. My voice sounded choked. 'But she'll be cured ... I mean someday?'

He shook his head sadly. 'No, Ann, she won't.'

I was upset. 'This was all my doing, Mr Pringle. If I hadn't confronted her about my coat, then this could all have been avoided.'

He shook his head. 'That is the reason I've brought you all here. To explain what's behind Miss Hood's condition. Years ago Miss Hood had a broken love affair. She had an illegitimate child, a boy, and the child was taken away from her by the father. Eva, Mrs Barrie, tried all she could to help at the time but, over the years, Eva lost touch with her. Then, out of the blue, a letter arrived explaining how Miss Hood had tried to kill herself. And that was when Eva brought her to the Ferry in order to look after her because it was clear, even then, that she was mentally ill. Eva thought she could look after her and she would be safe while under her roof.'

He stopped to let us digest this terrible news. 'Everything went well to start with even although Miss Hood got rid of a lot of staff in the beginning. Then you started work, Mrs Peters, and she knew she couldn't bully you or Mr Potter. My wife and I are kicking ourselves for introducing Ann into this situation but we thought Miss Hood had settled down. Mrs Barrie however was growing increasingly worried about you, Ann. She wrote a letter to me a week before she died and she wanted my help in getting Miss Hood to retire. She would have a good pension and she already owned her own cottage. Miss Hood went berserk at this news and Eva was on the point of telling Ann to leave – for your own safety, my dear.'

'Why did you not tell me or Jean about this, Mr Pringle? We could have made allowances for her and I would have understood her malice towards me.'

He shook his head. 'Eva wanted to protect her and we think Miss Hood was beyond any help by this time.'

Jean and I looked at one another. This was how the lovely Mrs Barrie would act – to protect her housekeeper.

When we were outside, I said to Jean and Mr Potter, 'Even although I didn't cause her mental condition, that fight must have put her over the edge, Jean. That's why she's now in a mental hospital.'

Jean was annoyed but firm. 'Now don't you be daft, Ann. We've all been blessed by our wonderful bequests from a lovely lady so just you enjoy the money and the books and not give yon housekeeper another thought.' She turned to the gardener. 'What do you say, Mr Potter?'

'Aye, she's right. Yon besom was a horrible woman. She might have been deferential to the missus but she was an evil, wilful woman to everybody else.'

Although this advice was good, trying to put the terrible guilt from my mind wasn't easy. I was over the moon about my legacy and the lovely books but I still felt it was partially my fault the housekeeper was in the hospital – no matter what anyone said.

That evening, in the midst of my confusion, Maddie and Danny turned up at the house. Danny was teasing me. 'I see you're a rich heiress now, Ann. Maybe I should be getting married to you instead of waiting till Maddie finishes her training for our wedding.'

I was happy for both of them but couldn't help but feel how our paths had diverged. 'Oh, that's good news.'

Maddie made a face. 'But until that blissful time I'll have to endure the infirmary's semolina pudding. The good old 365.'

I knew I should be feeling happy. With my money, I was going to ensure my family would be as comfy as possible – especially after the hardships we had endured. Dad had settled into a relationship with Rosie, Lily was growing up fast and, now that I was no longer at work, the added burden of my sister was lifted from my grandparents. Then there was Maddie and Danny with their forthcoming engagement. And last, but not least, was Greg – dear Greg. I should have been overwhelmed with happiness but the spectre of Miss Hood kept appearing in my mind.

The nightmares were getting worse as I relived that terrible day over and over again. One night, while strolling home from the pictures, I turned to Greg. 'I'm going to see Miss Hood – just to satisfy myself that she doesn't hold me responsible for her situation.'

He didn't look happy about this. 'I don't think that would be a good idea, Ann.'

'I have to go, Greg – even although I'm afraid of what I'll hear,' I said to him. 'I keep thinking about it and I can't go on like this, with all these nightmares and guilty feelings.'

He gave me a stern look. 'Well, you can go on one condition – that I come with you.'

'I can't drag you into this nightmare, Greg – it's my problem.'

He gave me another stern look and I realised how nice it was to be able to lean on him. 'All right, I'd be grateful for the lift as I don't know if any buses or trams go to this hospital.' I knew I had to keep calling it a hospital because my mind couldn't cope with the term 'asylum'.

We went to Westlea the following Sunday. Apart from Mr Pringle, who made the appointment for me to see her, I told no one. It was a grey dismal day with the hint of rain in the low mist that clung to the houses and hedgerows. In a perverse way, I was glad of this gloomy weather because it matched my feelings.

Greg arrived on the motorbike, assuring me it was now fully repaired and roadworthy. To my surprise, we buzzed along the narrow country roads at a speed I found breathtaking and also exhilarating. There was the occasional puff of black smoke from the exhaust but, on this dismal day, the smoke merely disappeared into the landscape with hardly a trace – except perhaps for the slight smell of acrid vapour that seemed to linger in the air as we sped along. Then, before I was truly prepared for it, the gates of Westlea loomed out of the drizzle.

Greg parked the bike just inside the high wall and we walked up the wide gravel drive. We couldn't help but notice how the grounds of the hospital almost merged with the imposing but grim-looking grey stone building. The windows looked bare and lifeless, giving the building a strange featureless quality, and I was dismayed to see some of the windows were barred. It looked more like a prison than a hospital but I had to remind myself that I knew almost nothing about mental illnesses.

Even the name filled me with dread because it was something I hadn't come across in my life. Oh, I knew the Hilltown and Overgate had their fair share of eccentric people but being sent out here was another matter – a life sentence if Mr Pringle was to be believed.

We approached the entrance with trepidation. The large hall had a geometric tiled floor in three bright colours and it seemed a cheery start to the place but, once through the inner glass door, all the initial colour was obliterated. The corridor was painted in a sludgy grey colour while the polished floor was covered in nondescript plain linoleum. It was a grey corridor in a grey building in an equally grey world.

I was grateful for Mr Pringle's help in arranging this meeting. Although I was doing this much against his wishes, he understood I had to make this journey.

I put my hand on Greg's arm. 'I have to go on my own, Greg. This is something that has to be done alone.' He looked annoyed but I went on. 'You do understand, don't you?'

He nodded and smiled – a smile that lit up that depressing place like a hundred candles. 'I'll wait beside the bike for you.'

A middle-aged nurse with a stocky figure and a jolly face took me along endless corridors. She opened each door with a key that hung from a huge bunch on her belt. She hardly spoke except to ask me to wait while she opened yet another door. Her voice, in contrast to her plump face and sturdy looking arms, was delicately soft and pleasing and it made me think that perhaps the place wasn't as bad as it looked. Maybe I was seeing it on a bad day. Maybe, with the sun shining through the windows, it was a happy place of peace and meditation.

Miss Hood was in a small room at the end of a corridor. She was dressed in a simple black frock that looked much too large for her shrivelled body. She was sitting in a chair in the corner, rocking back and forth with her body. She looked terrible. I walked over to her but there was no recognition on her haggard face. Even her eyes looked blank and vacant. 'Miss Hood, do you remember me?'

She didn't look at me but she shouted, 'Who are you?'

'I worked at Whitegate Lodge with you,' I explained slowly, as if speaking to a child. 'Don't you remember? With Mrs Barrie?'

I thought I saw tears in her eyes but I wasn't sure. Then she suddenly looked at me and I recoiled from the look of intense hatred on her face.

'Go away. I don't like you,' she snapped. She sounded like she did in her heyday at the house.

The nurse had remained silent but she now went over to the corner and put her hand out to stop the rocking movement. To my surprise, Miss Hood slapped her hand hard and the nurse moved back to the door.

I tried once more. 'Do you mind the day Mrs Barrie died, Miss Hood? We had a fight. Do you mind that?'

But there was no more reaction from her. Miss Hood rocked silently in her chair and looked at the floor. The nurse motioned that I should leave.

'You'll not get anything out of her. Her mind's completely gone.'

I explained how I thought I had triggered this off but the nurse laughed harshly. 'For heaven's sake, lassie, you didn't cause this. This patient's been like this for years. If it hadn't been for her employer sheltering her under her protection, then she would have been in here long ago.'

I knew in my heart that this was the way Mrs Barrie would act. She was a lovely, kind-hearted woman and a charitable one at that, keeping this mentally ill woman in her house all these years.

'Mr Pringle says she'll never get better,' I said and the nurse confirmed this.

'She's grown more ill over the years and, because of her problems, she has also grown more bitter. It's very sad.'

Poor Miss Hood – what a cruel world it could be. Maybe, if she hadn't met her Othello or had her illegitimate child taken away from her, then her life would have been happier. Then I remembered Granny – she had nothing to face adversity with but her strong character and good humour. Still, maybe Miss Hood wasn't blessed with these sterling qualities. We would never know.

As I turned to thank the nurse, a stream of oaths came from the room. Once again, I was shocked but the nurse took it in her stride as she hurried me away. As we retreated down the corridor, I could hear Miss Hood snarling after me, 'Young madam, young madam...' over and over again.

The nurse said, 'You were very lucky she didn't harm you in that house as you seem to have become the focus of her hate. I believe Mrs Barrie had arranged with Mr Pringle to get you away that very week, she was so worried about the danger you were in.'

When we reached the staircase, the nurse said goodbye and hurried off in a different direction. An elderly woman was mopping the stairs, her large mop swishing over the lino and slapping against the banisters. As I approached, she gave me a knowing look so I stopped. 'I'm sorry for walking over your clean floor,' I said, thinking she was annoyed at me.

She waved my protest aside. 'Oh, there will be plenty of folk walking over it. We do get visitors in here.' She must have read my thoughts. 'Oh, aye, some of the patients get visitors but some folk don't.' She cocked her sideways. 'You were visiting Miss Hood were you not?'

I looked at her in surprise. How could the cleaner possibly know who I had visited?

She tapped the side of her nose. 'Aye, it's a great thing, my mop bucket. I have to go into places that would normally be out of bounds. I was mopping the corridor just along from Miss Hood's room when I heard you.'

I tried to side-step the woman, desperate to be out of this dreadful place.

The cleaner, however, was in a chatty mood. 'Did you notice she was dressed entirely in black?'

I nodded. I hadn't made anything of it, thinking it was the regulation uniform.

'Well, that's the reason us cleaners call her the auld crow. She's like a black hoodie crow and that's her nickname in here – "black hoodie crow".' The small woman gazed at me, satisfaction written all over her face at her descriptive narrative.

It was then that a huge weight was lifted from my shoulders and a veil stripped from my eyes. A blackbird – of course. Even before I set foot in Whitegate Lodge, Ma Ryan had warned me about being in danger from a blackbird but it was a black bird she'd meant, not a blackbird, and there was surely no bird blacker that a crow. For the first time in weeks, ever since that terrible day at Whitegate Lodge, I felt free.

I now knew with clarity that Miss Hood's illness had nothing to do with me. Her troubles had all happened a long, long time ago – before I was even born – and this canker had eaten away the mind of the housekeeper. It had festered away day in and day out, year after year. Unfortunately, the jealous rage she'd directed towards me had been the final straw for her but it wasn't my fault. Everyone had told me this but I had been too blind to see. But now I was free.

Greg was waiting for me, a worried looking frown on his face. I ran over. 'It's all over, Greg – no more guilt about Miss Hood.'

He grinned and put a comforting arm around my shoulders. 'That's good news, Ann. Now just enjoy yourself. You've got your nest egg, Lily is growing up, Danny and Maddie are getting engaged and Rosie is hoping she'll finally hook your father.'

I raised my face to his. 'You've forgotten someone.'

He looked perplexed.

'You forgot us!' I laughed, looking at his lovely cheery face. 'And to think Maddie had to push me into thinking you were lonely at that first meeting.'

He put on a mock miserable face. 'Oh, I was, I was.'

I thought of my family and especially my grandparents. Never again would they want for anything – I would see to that. As for Greg and me ... well, time would no doubt tell.

He grinned at me. 'Your chariot awaits you, young damsel.'

On the far horizon, a chink appeared in the layer of grey clouds and a thin shaft of sunlight pierced the gloom.

Greg noticed it. 'Maybe it's going to be a good day after all.'

When I nodded happily, he took my hand. 'Hop on the bike, Ann, and we'll go home.'

The publishers hope that this book has given you enjoyable reading. Large Print Books are especially designed to be as easy to see and hold as possible. If you wish a complete list of our books please ask at your local library or write directly to:

Magna Large Print Books
Magna House, Long Preston,
Skipton, North Yorkshire.
BD23 4ND

This Large Print Book for the partially sighted, who cannot read normal print, is published under the auspices of

THE ULVERSCROFT FOUNDATION